Praise and Accolades for
The Jericho River

WINNER, Next Generation Indie Book Awards for Sci-Fi/Fantasy
WINNER, London Book Festival for Best Young Adult Work
BRONZE MEDALIST, Readers' Favorite Book Reviews & Award Contest
FINALIST, Foreword Reviews Book of the Year Awards
HONORABLE MENTION, New York Book Festival

The Jericho River is a delightful, mystical romp through World
History. Beginning with ancient Sumer and progressing rapidly
to modern times, it is a useful gateway book which will appeal
to younger readers and should encourage them to look deeper
into the past and ultimately to assume the challenges of more
traditional sources. The regular inclusions of excerpts from the
lectures of William Gallo add to this appeal and are stimulat-
ing and thought-provoking. Through historical fiction, David
[Tollen] has provided a valuable tool for teachers and students in
their continuing quest to study the past.
— Philip Bigler, 1998 National Teacher of the Year

This epic follows young Jason Gallo on a quest to rescue his historian father—and the journey leads him through chronological
epochs of Western history … The genesis of myths, legends, and
cultural relics flow through this adventure that is as educational as
it is entertaining! Highly recommended.
— Midwest Book Review

The cast of characters in *The Jericho River* is huge, the canvas
of history is enormous and the tale telling is ambitious. Many
young people and adults would gain a great deal from reading
Jericho River. The lecture notes interspersed throughout the text
are very enjoyable and hold many nuggets of really entertaining
and thought-provoking facts and opinions…. It all seems to hang
together and the wide range of ideas seem to sit happily side by
side in this erudite and entertaining work.
— Graham Peacock, M.Ed, Principal Lecturer in Education,
Sheffield Hallam University; author of *The Oxford Primary
Science Dictionary, Primary Science: Teaching Theory and
Practice*, and other works

Wow. Just, wow.
— Amazon Top 500 Reviewer, 5-star review

I was learning new information and being thoroughly entertained with the action all at the same time. ... The historical situations were so engaging and action-packed, I would have enjoyed even more of this book; it was very well written and enjoyable.
— ZoeDessoye1, teen blogger at LitPick.com

The Jericho River is a carefully researched and very accurate journey through Western Civilization that will appeal not only to the teenage audience but to adults as well. You can trust the accuracy of detail and depth of interpretation, and at the same time you learn history in an exciting manner and with an entertaining read.
—Robert J. Littman, M.Litt., Ph.D., Professor of Classics, University of Hawaii; author of *The Greek Experiment: Imperialism and Social Conflict: 800–400 B.C., A Concise History of the Jewish People*, and other works

In my opinion, David [Tollen] is a pioneer ... who has found a way to ... teach us by supplanting and supporting historical education with entertainment.... This book smashes the molds of cookie cutter education, then uses the fragments remaining to create a mosaic of myth and magic that follows the fabric of time. I hope to soon see this book as required reading material in literature and/or history classes....
—*The Northern Star*

It's a grand adventure! The action never stops. What a fabulous vehicle for the memes of history.... *The Jericho River* provides a genuine service and benefit—in a package that is wholly entertaining....
—A. A. Attanasio, Nebula-nominated author of *The Radix Tetrad* novels

The creation of strange creatures and mythical environments is extremely creative and portrays a talented David Tollen with an imagination worthy of the silver screen. The book is also fast-paced and action-packed from start to finish ... [A] must read for history buffs everywhere who will receive great joy in coming across contextual adventures they'll surely be familiar with.
— C.J. Leger

This is a clever, well-written first book that's hard to put down. Jason's journey down the Jericho River is a story about growing up, understanding life and death and finding a sense of wonder for the mystery of human life. It has something for everyone — interesting historical notes about western history and religion, a narrative that probes the meaning of personal maturity and change, and one hero's unexpected discovery of the power of older myths, traditions and symbols that modernity had abandoned. The Jericho River is an exciting retelling of the history of western civilization, one that makes us question how that history unfolded and wonder what might have been.

— Christopher White, Ph.D., Associate Professor of Religion in America, Vassar College; author of *Unsettled Minds: Psychology and the American Search for Spiritual Assurance*

This was an amazing book that ... makes history come alive and jump out.... So hold on to your hat and be ready for a fun ride as this book will take you on an adventure that you will not forget!
—*Dad of Divas Reviews*

In *The Jericho River*, a relatively short novel, David [Tollen] manages to chart the course of human history—and with countless refreshing takes on it. It is historically illuminating to be sure, for young and old alike, but it is first and foremost a wonderful story about a boy and his relationship to his father, told with plenty of adventure, magic, and humor.
—Larry Townsend, author of *Secrets of the Wholly Grill*

The Jericho River is a fast moving quest romance that follows its young hero down the river of time from early Mesopotamia to the present day. Lots of action and lots of history are cleverly woven together in a light-hearted narrative that ultimately insists on the values of magic and wonder as opposed to the mere calculus of utilitarian science.
—Mark Rose, Ph.D., Emeritus Professor of English, U.C. Santa Barbara; author of *Alien Encounters: Anatomy of Science Fiction*, and other books; editor of *The Norton Shakespeare Workshop*; former Director of the University of California Humanities Research Institute

Against his will Jason Gallo is thrust into the land of Fiore on a quest to find his missing father. Jason follows a rollercoaster ride of an adventure through a number of ancient civilizations, including Ancient Sumer, Egypt, Greece, and even ... Medieval Europe. He meets up with mythical creatures, barbarians, and an Egyptian priestess. Jason learns about courage, betrayal, love and friendship, but most importantly, he begins healing the resentment he has towards his father and discovers he may have more in common with his father than he thought.... [Tollen] weaves historical information into this fast paced adventure, making learning about history fun for any reader. As an educator, I recommend *The Jericho River* for anyone looking to enhance an ancient civilization curriculum.

—Pamela Pizzimenti, teacher and author of *The River Whispers*

Please visit www.DavidTollen.com
for art, ideas, and other resources
about history and about this book.

THE JERICHO RIVER

David W. Tollen

Winifred Press

ISBN: 978-0-9854517-4-5 (softcover)
ISBN: 978-0-9854517-5-2 (ebook)
Library of Congress Control Number: 2017914577

11 10 9 8 7 6 5 4 3

3rd Edition (3.02)
The first edition of this book was published under the pen name *David Carthage*. The first edition also included the word *"Magical"* before *"Novel"* in the subtitle, while some versions of the second edition had no subtitle.

Published by Winifred Press, Mill Valley, California
www.WinifredPress.com
www.DavidTollen.com

Printed and bound in the United States of America

Book Design by Lorie DeWorken, www.MindtheMargins.com and Jill Ronsley, www.SunEditWrite.com
Cover art by Andrei Bat, Romania. Cover maps by David W. Tollen. Certain cover elements courtesy of Pixabay.com.

The author drew the three maps in the interior. The underlying shorelines come from maps provided by d-maps.com, as do the rivers in the Fertile Crescent and Mediterranean maps, at the following URLs: (1) Fertile Crescent: http://d-maps.com/carte.php?lib=alexander_empire_map&num_car=1965&lang=en; (2) Mediterranean: http://d-maps.com/carte.php?lib=wide_mediterranean_sea_map&num_car=3137&lang=en; and (3) Europe: http://d-maps.com/carte.php?lib=europe_map&num_car=2225&lang=en. The compass roses come from fuzzimo.com, though each has been modified from the fuzzimo original. Kimmia Forouzesh, Maia Kobabe, and Jill Ronsley provided technical assistance with the maps' computer-generated elements.

For James and Zack

Acknowledgements

Thank you to my wife, Wendy, who made all of this possible.

Thank you also to my sister, Laura Tollen, my unpaid editor. And thank you to Augusto Andres, A. A. Attanasio, Bruce Belton, Monica Christie, Rudy Edwards, Jeff Follett, Kim Greenwood, Jerry Gross (book doctor/editor extraordinaire), Robert Horowitz, Harry I. Johnson, Tom Kennedy, Laura Onopchenko, Suzanna Sahakian, Ellen Tollen (my mom), Larry Townsend, and Neil Vanderplas. Finally, thank you to my Kickstarter patrons, Mani Adeli, Mike Anguera, Simone Anguera, Sandra Connolly, Kathy O'Sullivan, Betty Strathman Pagett (my mother-in-law), Marc and Caroline Schuyler, and Bob Skubic—and to my prime patron, John M. Keagy.

Table of Contents

Author's Note

THIS IS THE STORY of Jason Gallo's adventures along the Jericho River. I offer it for your enjoyment but also because it provides a surprising opportunity to learn history. Strange as it may sound, Jason's journey took him through the cornerstone realms of the ancient Middle East and Western Civilization—in chronological order. So in a sense, his tale gives us the entire five thousand year history. And instead of a chopped-up account, Jason's adventures show us the timeline, from first to last. We need that to understand the past.

Also, many of us find it easier to remember personal stories, like novels, than long lists of battles, plagues, and dates. Jason's otherworld journey turns history into an adventure novel—except that it's entirely true, of course.

Finally, Jason's adventure pairs historic societies with images many of us already know, like centaurs, cherubs, knights, tall ships, and pyramids. Putting already-familiar images into the right societies, in the right order, makes history easier to remember.

I hope you enjoy, and learn.

Prologue

The Eggs, the Doctor, and the Desert

JERICHO, LADIES AND GENTLEMEN. What's important about this little town near Jerusalem? The Bible made it famous. In the Book of Joshua, the Israelites kindly immortalize Jericho by completely destroying it. I'm sure you've heard the old spiritual song. You know, "Joshua fought the battle of Jericho, and the walls came tumbling down." But Joshua's story—true or not—only goes back to around 1400 BC. That makes biblical Jericho one of the most recent settlements at the site. What really grabs me about this place is its incredible age. Stone Age farmers built permanent houses there at the very dawn of agriculture, around 9600 BC. It's been called the world's first town. And even then Jericho was already ancient. The site began thousands of years before, as a cabin camp for hunter-gatherers.

~ William Gallo, Recorded Lectures, History 56: The Ancient Middle East (Fall Semester 2009).

ooooo

Dream vistas marched across Jason's sleeping mind. He saw towering castles, wild-eyed swordsmen, wide rivers, and eagles with the heads of men. He saw candlelight dancing behind cathedral windows, where stained glass angels and fairies came to life and did battle. He watched hunters prowl a starlit forest, armed with muskets and dressed in powdered wigs and lace. Finally, he saw the moon, swollen out of all proportion. It rose over a ruined temple where an impatient girl waited for him, her lioness eyes scanning the desert.

Rock music shattered the dream, and Jason jolted and fumbled for his clock radio, finally managing to smack the snooze button. He lay back in bed. Usually he'd sleep another half hour or more, hitting snooze every nine minutes, then break into a panicked rush to wash and dress for school. But he was restless, so he got up.

Sunlight streamed in between partly drawn curtains, revealing books and posters and piles of laundry, some clean and some dirty. Jason was rifling through a clean pile when a movement beyond the window caught his eye. A slim woman stood at the end of the driveway. She had long hair and wore an ankle-length trench coat. She was staring right at his window. He yanked the curtains closed. What was she, some kind of Peeping Tina? He wasn't dressed yet. Jason parted the curtains again, just enough to peer through. The woman was smiling. Then something moved near her hip. He blinked several times. Was that a snake peeking out of her coat pocket?

"Jason!" called a high voice.

"What?" he snapped, turning from the window.

The bedroom door creaked open and his little sister, Athena, stepped in. "Um, Dad's not up yet."

"Thanks for the news flash. Now go away." He turned back to the gap in the curtains. The woman still stood by the driveway, watching and smiling.

"I've been up forever," whined Athena. "I want some eggs. Can you please make me eggs, Jason?"

"No. Go bother Dad. He's the idiot who brought you into this world."

"I did. He wouldn't wake up. And I'm starved. I hate cereal. It gets soggy, and it makes me sick. Please, Jason?"

Athena had an eight-year-old's knack for drama. Jason, at sixteen, found her performances both amusing and annoying. "Suffering builds character," he said, still watching the intruder. "Ask anyone."

"What are you looking at?" Athena demanded, advancing into the room.

"Nothing." Jason turned to stare at his sister. She had curly, pale-brown hair, like their father's, and dark brown eyes, like Jason's. "Athena, is it possible you're in my room right after I told you to go away?"

"*Pleeease* can you make me eggs, Jason?" She twisted the lace fringe of her purple blouse. "Please, please, please?"

Jason sighed and ran a hand through his short, black hair. "Okay, fine, I'll make you eggs—if you're out of my room in one second."

Athena shot out the door, grinning, and Jason peered through the curtains again. He scanned the driveway and the street beyond. Parked cars lined the curbs, quiet yards fronted one-story houses, and a few lights glowed in kitchen and bedroom windows. But the woman and her snake were gone.

He sighed and returned to the clothes on the floor. Just a nosy neighbor? He wondered why a classy-looking woman would walk around with a scaly reptile in her pocket.

He extracted a relatively clean T-shirt and jeans from the laundry piles and put them on, then headed down the hall. "Dad," he called, rapping on the master bedroom door. "Athena wants eggs." He waited. "Athena wants you to make breakfast!"

He heard nothing, so after a minute he knocked again. "Hey, Dad! Wake up!" Still nothing. "Not that I care, but aren't you going to campus?"

His father didn't answer, so he pressed an ear to the door. He heard a light snore. Finally, he eased the door open and poked his head in. "Dad?" The room was stuffy. In the dimness, Jason could see a blur of hair and one arm protruding from the blankets on the bed.

"Dad?" he called a fourth time. His father snored away. "Hey!" Jason entered the bedroom and flipped on the light. "What's wrong with you?"

William Gallo snored on, oblivious. "Dad!" Jason cried yet again, striding forward to jostle his father's arm. "Wake up!" No response. He shook harder. Still nothing. Jason's blood turned cold. "Are you sick? Wake up!" He rolled his father over and found that he was fully dressed and had an old backpack looped over one arm. Weird, but Jason couldn't stop to wonder. His father had stopped snoring, but his eyes did not open. His face was lined with blanket creases but was otherwise as peaceful as death. "Dad!" Jason yelled. He grabbed both his father's shoulders and shook him. "Wake up! WAKE UP!"

ooooo

The next two weeks were awful.

Jason and Athena eventually returned to school. Friends and classes provided some distraction, but Jason found he couldn't concentrate on homework. That was no great loss, of course. Most nights, he spent hours watching TV or gaming on the good computer in his father's study, particularly after his sister went to bed. He felt like a trespasser in the study, surrounded by his father's books and maps and knick-knacks, and the scattered pages of his notes. Some of the notes featured sketches of long-lost buildings and monuments that his dad's colleagues called "oddly realistic—as if he's been there." These personal touches added to Jason's sense of intrusion, yet he never moved the pages of notes, or disturbed anything else in the office, as if his father might come home any minute and return to work.

Jason had just booted up the good computer late one night when he heard Athena crying. Swearing under his breath, he padded down the hall. He turned on the light in Athena's room but didn't speak. What could he say? He just sat on the bed, and his little sister curled up against him. She cried quietly for a few minutes, and he rubbed her back. Then she wiped her nose on her wrist and leaned back against the peach-colored pillows.

"What will we do if Dad doesn't come home from the hospital soon?" Athena finally said, turning wide eyes onto her brother. "Won't Aunt Rachel have to go back to New Jersey?"

Jason shuffled his feet, both bare but half-swallowed by overlong jeans. "I guess so. She's got her job and everything."

"So then what?" Athena's tear-streaked face was intense.

"Well, then we won't have to listen to her snore anymore." His sister didn't even smile, and Jason sighed. "I dunno. We can't stay with Grandma in the old folks' place. I guess we'd have to go live with Aunt Rachel."

Athena gnawed her lower lip. "I don't want to move. I don't want to leave Jessica and Haley and Alan—and go to a new school."

Jason nodded. He couldn't imagine a new school either. Of course, his high school status was only so-so, and he had no girlfriend. But he knew his way around. And he had his wingmen, Chuck and Nadji. "It would just be temporary." He hoped.

"I don't think Aunt Rachel really likes us," whispered Athena.

Aunt Rachel was actually very nice to them—sugary sweet. But she seemed uncomfortable around young people. There *was* one advantage to her visit, though. Her commands— "Maybe you should do your homework," "Isn't that enough television?"—lacked the crack of authority their father wielded, and Jason found he could just ignore them.

"Maybe we could stay here," Jason said. He'd been considering this possibility. "You could stay with Haley and her mom, and maybe I could stay at Nadji's." He certainly wouldn't want to stay at Chuck's.

Athena's eyes filled with tears again.

"Okay!" he exclaimed. "Forget about that. We'll stay together. I promise, okay?" She snuffled and wiped her eyes. Jason smiled, glad to be so important to someone.

"I miss Mom," she said.

A lump rose in his throat, and he didn't answer.

"Jason," Athena said after a while, "you're smart like Dad."

He forced a laugh. "Yeah, right. It's too bad my teachers don't know."

She still didn't smile. "You know what I mean. Dad always knows how to do things—solving problems and stuff. You're like that, too. Maybe you can do something. Maybe you can figure something out."

Figure something out—like how to snap their father out of a coma? Did she think he was a medical genius? If so, he would've cured mild acne by now. Or was she thinking of their other problem, about what would happen … after … if their dad didn't make it? Jason had no idea what they'd live on without their father's salary, or how they'd pay for the car he wanted, or college. And he doubted any clever solutions would dawn on him, despite Athena's surprising faith.

"Well," he said, "if I can do anything, I will."

"Can we sleep in the hospital tomorrow night—in Dad's room?"

Jason blinked. Conversations with Athena often bounced around. "Sleep there? Why? We can't do anything."

"Maybe he'll know we're there … and try to wake up. And … I just wanna sleep there. The nurse said people sometimes sleep in the extra beds when they've got sick relatives. Please, Jason?"

He sighed. Visitors meant nothing to their father. He lived in his dreams now. But Athena's eyes had filled with tears once again.

"There's only one extra bed," he finally said. "I hope you'll be comfortable on the floor." Athena grinned.

ooooo

Jason and Athena spent most of their hospital evening talking and watching TV, each of them occasionally glancing at the patient, as if their voices might rouse him. Athena finally closed her eyes around 10:00, but Jason stayed up another hour. He was about to turn out the lights when his father began to mumble.

Jason rose from his cot for a look. Sensors had been stuck to his father's temples and to one finger. Stubble hardened the lines of his face. He lay motionless, except for the slow rise and fall of his chest. He'd slept that way for more than two weeks. No amount of shaking or yelling could rouse him. It seemed nothing could.

"My own angel?" mumbled the patient.

Jason shook his head. His father had done this once or twice a day since the coma began. Usually his sleep talk was unintelligible, or he'd murmur strange words like "secunda." But once in a while he'd say something clear, and sometimes he strung together nearly complete sentences. A few days ago, he'd said, "Got all the way up to Sumer ... visited Nagiru in First Lagash ... near the high temple."

Jason wondered what dreams were running through his father's head. It sounded like history and mythology—his usual obsessions.

"The problem," the neurologist had told Jason, "is that your father's dream never ends. We're supposed to cycle in and out of dreams every half hour or so, and our brain's meant to get a break in between. But your father never gets a break, even for a second, according to our instruments." The result would be brain damage if the coma continued, and eventually death.

Jason stared down at his father, feeling numb and thinking of their last fight. He'd been provoked, but still. He wondered if an apology now would help. Would it penetrate his father's coma? But all that came out was, "Do you have any idea what a pain in the ass you are?"

His father lay silent, apparently done sleep-talking. Eventually, Jason turned out the light and slipped into his cot.

That night, Jason dreamed of a hospital conference room full of doctors in white coats. They were arguing, and they kept asking Jason for his opinion. He felt he should know the answer, but he couldn't remember, so he kept quiet.

One of the doctors was not arguing or even talking. She simply stared at Jason, her green eyes intense. "This is useless," she finally said. "Come on."

The other doctors fell silent as Jason rose and followed her into the corridor.

"I'm Doctor Valencia," she said as they walked. "I'm here to give you my diagnosis, and my help."

Doctor Valencia had long brown hair, lightly streaked with gray. She was tall and slim, and she looked about his father's age or a bit younger.

"Your father's trapped in another world. That's why he's comatose, and that's why it looks as if he's dreaming. He *is* dreaming, in a way. He's dream voyaging. That's how you visit the other world: with your mind."

"Oh," said Jason. "That makes sense." He wondered if he might be dreaming himself.

"You've got to enter the other world and rescue your father, Jason. It's dangerous, but that's the only way to get him back— the only way he'll wake up here, in this world."

"Sure. No problem."

"And you've got to do it now. I've never heard of anyone dream voyaging for more than a day. It taxes the brain. Your father's been in more than two weeks. If this goes on much longer, it'll kill him."

The hospital corridor had grown into a labyrinth: a maze of nurse's stations, operating rooms, lounges, and patient bedrooms. Doctor Valencia led Jason up and down stairways, through wide double doors, and around preposterously sharp corners.

"First, you've got to *find* your father. The best clues come from sleep-talk. Has he spoken in his sleep? Has he said anything about where he is, or where he's been?"

"Actually, yeah," Jason answered, feeling loopy. "He mentioned a place, Sumer. That's a country from history, right? He said he went to visit someone named ..." He stretched his memory. "Named Nagiru ... near the high temple in First something ... First Lagash."

"So I suspected." She flashed him a grin. "How shall I explain this? The other world ... The other world is a map of history, in a sense. It shares places and cultures with our world's past. Did your father mention any other places from history, any other names?"

Jason shook his head, distracted. Suddenly, Doctor Valencia seemed familiar.

"Well then, I'll send you there, to First Lagash. When you get there, find this Nagiru. With any luck, he can direct you to your father."

"Were you outside our house that morning?"

"Pay attention, Jason. Once you find your father, you've got to get him out of the other world. Normally, a dream voyage ends when the voyager wakes up. It's simple. An alarm clock goes off back here in our world, or someone shakes the dream voyager. For some reason, that's not happening with your father. I have no idea why. It's your job to find out, and wake him."

"Okay."

"Two other warnings." Her green eyes scanned his face, her expression grim. "You've got to take the other world seriously, Jason. Don't assume you're safe because your body remains here, asleep in our world. If you're killed in the other world, your brain will shut down here, and you'll die."

"I'll die. Got it."

"Also, you've got to understand about time. Time flows faster in the other world. You'll be asleep here in the hospital for one night—until someone wakes you, actually—but to your mind, it may seem like months. It may *be* months in the other world, or even longer."

"Even longer. Check! No problem."

"Of course, it won't take long at all if you find your father quickly, and bring him home. As soon as he wakes up here in the hospital, I'm sure he'll wake you. Or the nurses will come running, and they'll wake you. Either way, your father's your fastest route home."

She stopped before a familiar-looking door and led him through—into the darkness of his father's hospital room. Jason was surprised to see his own body asleep on the cot. His father snored away nearby, and Athena lay curled up on her bed, too, breathing evenly.

"You're not appropriately dressed, though, are you?" said Doctor Valencia.

Jason tore his eyes from his other body, the sleeping one, and looked down. He'd been walking around the hospital labyrinth in a T-shirt, boxers, and socks.

"What's in that bag?" she asked, pointing at the backpack by the foot of his cot.

"Just a couple changes of clothes."

"Excellent. Pick it up and strap it over your chest. And put on those pants and shoes, too."

Jason reached for the bag and the jeans and sneakers he'd left on the floor, but Doctor Valencia stopped him.

"No. Really reach, with *that* body."

He turned to the slumbering form on the cot—and reached. Jason watched as his body sat up, eyes still closed, slipped on the jeans and shoes, and strapped the backpack on the wrong way, over the chest. As the sleeping Jason returned to the cot, the dreaming Jason realized that he, too, wore the jeans and sneakers now, and the backwards backpack.

"Good," said Doctor Valencia. "Whatever you're holding appears with you in the other world, and you'll need the clothes. I only wish I could give you some supplies, but there's nothing useful in this room."

She led him to the corner and stood before a door Jason hadn't noticed before. A small sign read, "Ether Room—Authorized Personnel Only."

Doctor Valencia put a warm hand on Jason's arm. "I hope your father's still with this Nagiru, in Sumer. If not ..." Her eyes fell to the floor. "Well, you may have a difficult task if not. History is very long, and prehistory even longer.* So the other world is a big place."

---

* History is a drop in humanity's bucket of time. The period we usually call "history" takes up the last five thousand years. By its start—the start of writing and civilization—many people had already been living in farming societies for six thousand years. And before that we'd been hunter-gatherers for two hundred thousand years. When history began, we already had a long history.
~ William Gallo, *The Historical Factoids Pocket Guide* (Chicago, 2009), 5.

She held his eyes a moment, then turned and swung the door open. Jason gasped. Beyond, stars twinkled in an endless cosmos, as if the door opened onto outer space.

"Is this really a dream?" he cried, his heart hammering.

"It was." Her hand rose to his back, and she pushed him through.

"I don't want to do this!" Jason screamed as he fell into the sky.

The last thing he heard, before oblivion swept in, was Doctor Valencia calling, "Good luck, Jason!"

ooooo

Jason awoke. Slowly he sat up and opened his eyes, blinking furiously into the light of a golden-white sun.

He saw no sign of the hospital room or his father or sister. In fact, he saw nothing familiar except his backpack, still backwards, over his chest. Jason sat on hard ground in a barren valley, surrounded by sandy yellow hills shot through with streaks of rust orange. The sky was cloudless, and the place was hot as an oven. No wind stirred the dry air.

"Doctor Valencia?" he called, looking around. He rose to his feet, dropping the bag. "Doctor Valencia?" he yelled again, in the general direction of the sky. "I don't want to do this! Please! I wanna go home!" He scanned the blue emptiness above, praying the mysterious doctor would appear there, apologize, and send him back. "I never said I'd come here! I don't know what to do! I wanna go home!"

Jason fell silent, his heart beating hard. He doubted Doctor Valencia could hear him, and he wasn't certain she'd help if she could. He gulped and looked around, wishing Chuck and Nadji were there. Of course, his friends would be scared out of their minds, too, and expecting Jason to figure out what to do. But at least he'd have company.

The sound of falling pebbles drew his gaze to the hills above him. Four figures had crested the ridge. They moved down into the valley, running—charging him. "It's okay," he whispered. "I'll just—"

He jumped as something long and thin careened into the earth with a *thwack!* a yard in front of his feet. An arrow quivered in the hardpan.

"Boy!" called a voice. "Do not move!" Two of the hurrying figures held bows, one with an arrow cocked and pointing at him, the other restringing as he ran.

Jason stood wide-eyed as the running figures surrounded him—dark, bearded men in billowing, off-white robes.

"You!" cried one of the men, the burliest of the four and the tallest—standing more than half-a-head taller than Jason. He brandished a nasty-looking curved knife. "You come from beyond, yes? Say who you are!"

At least the cutthroat spoke English, though Jason couldn't imagine how.

"I'm Ja-Jason Gallo," he stammered. He convulsed slightly, imagining an arrow fired from behind, into the small of his back. "I didn't mean to do anything wrong. I'm …" What should he say? "I'm looking for my father, Professor William Gallo. Do you know him?"

A grin spread over the leader's swarthy face, and the others laughed. Jason forced a smile, too, hoping this was a good sign.

"No, little man," said the leader. "We don't know him, but we know someone else—someone who's looking for *you*. The Rector wants you. You'll come with us."

"Um, I think there's been some kind of mistake," Jason said humbly. "I didn't even really want to come—" A blow to his inner leg cut him off. He fell to one knee, and before he could move, the leader leapt forward and slammed a fist into his belly. The air shot out of his lungs with an *oof!* and he fell sprawling beside his backpack.

"Seize his arms!" cried the leader. "Seize his wrists!"

Then all of them were on him, one jumping on top and the others restraining his arms and legs. As he struggled for breath, he caught a whiff of the bodies beneath the robes. They stank.

"Ho there!" said a new voice. "What is happening here? Who are you men?"

Jason's assailants froze, but only the leader let go of him. With amazing speed, the man fitted an arrow to one of the discarded bows and pointed it up at the hill. Heaving and whimpering, Jason looked where the arrow pointed. What he saw shocked him more than the blow to his belly.

Trotting down the hill was a creature on four legs. At first, Jason thought it was a giant tawny cat. But it had the head of a man.

Jason's assailants grew tense, but they did not let him go.

"Ho there!" said the creature again, halting near the leader, who had lowered his bow but kept it strung. "Who are you barbarians? From what tribe? And what have you done here?"

The creature had the body of a small lion. Its human head was dark-skinned and perfectly bald. A fluffy, black beard flowed down onto its feline chest. Jason blinked and blinked, as if the thing might take some more reasonable, acceptable shape if he just cleared his vision. It looked like a sphinx from one of his father's myths.

"Who we are is none of your concern, lumin," the lead man snarled. "Go away."

The lion-man surveyed the scene. Its eyes gleamed like a cat's reflecting headlights at night, though the sun could not have been brighter. "I ask you again," he said, "who are you? And why have you assaulted this foreign lord?"

"And I tell you again, lumin," the leader answered, "that's none of your concern. We know you won't hurt us, so go back to your city and leave us alone."

The creature sat down like an attentive house pet. Then it spoke slowly, its voice rich and masculine. "I am Zidu, warden of the high temple of First Lagash. You stand on land sacred to the gods of Sumer, and I am the eyes and ears of Sumer, land of the black-headed people, place of the civilized lords. I tell you to stand away from this young lord, unless you mean to offend mighty Sumer."

Jason's attackers snarled, and their leader cursed under his breath. No one moved, except that after a moment, the hands holding Jason slackened. Dizzy with fear, he sat up, wincing at the pain in his belly. Could he get away? Moving slowly, afraid he'd be struck at any moment, he reached for his backpack and stood. The men growled and exchanged furious glances. The bizarre lion-man's gleaming eyes held Jason as he approached. He wondered which was more dangerous, his attackers or the impossible creature who'd stopped them with words.

The men began to whisper.

"Young lord," said the creature, "will you follow me?" It turned slowly and began to climb back up the way it had come. Jason followed, slinging his backpack over his shoulders, hoping it would stop an arrow.

The crumbling, yellow-red rocks and sand made for difficult footing, even with his sneaker-treads. Soon he was sweating, and his belly ached. He and the creature climbed up and over the ridge. Beyond, a plain stretched toward the horizon. *Great*, thought Jason, it's a desert. The plain faded into a heat haze in all directions but one. That way, many miles in the distance, the countryside turned greenish-brown.

Jason glanced back into the valley once before the ridge blocked his view. The four men were huddled together, talking and gesturing. Just before Jason turned away, the leader looked up and caught his eye. Even from this distance, Jason could see the malice on his bearded face.

"Young lord," said the creature as they descended toward the desert.

Jason jumped. He'd almost forgotten the thing could talk.

"I am afraid we face some difficulty."

Jason stared at the bald, bearded human head with its gleaming eyes.

"Those barbarians will not be intimidated for long, and, truly, my threat was just words. I can do little to protect you so far from my city. I think our best escape is across the desert, but that way is not safe at this time of day, or this time of year. And, the only people on this side are more barbarians, and I do no think we can count on their help. Do you have water in your bag?"

"No, j-j-just clothes." Jason couldn't believe he was talking to a man with the body of a lion, or a lion with the head of a man. One of his father's annoying admonitions ran through his brain: *There are more things in heaven and earth, Jason, than are dreamt of in your textbooks.*

The creature paused, apparently listening. "They come! We have no choice. Run!"

It turned and scrambled down the slope, and Jason followed. Soon they reached the edge of the desert and ran out onto the plain. It was an endless expanse of hard, dry, tawny-white earth, covered by a thin layer of sand and dotted here and there with parched shrubs. *At least it's flat*, thought Jason, hurrying to keep up. But the level terrain gave little comfort after a few seconds' running. Jason had never imagined a place so hot. His jeans felt like sheaves of insulation, smothering his running legs. Soon his body was slick with sweat, and his head spun.

He glanced back and saw the four barbarians cresting the ridge behind him. That was all he needed. Despite the heat, he quickened his pace, and he and his guide rushed far out into the desert.

Finally, Jason staggered to a halt. "Have to get my jeans off," he gasped.

"You are very red, young lord," said the creature, looking alarmed.

Jason pulled off his belt and jeans, too miserable to care about modesty. Sweat streamed down his body. He moved to tear off his T-shirt, but the creature spoke up again: "No, no, young lord. I think that would not be wise. You need some protection here, for the desert sun is cruel, and your skin is pale. And if you have some covering for your head, I think you must wear it."

A wave of nausea washed over Jason, and he realized the creature was right. Even his scalp was blazing, as if the sun had super-heated his black hair. He inhaled to keep from retching, then dug in his bag for another T-shirt. This he draped over his head. The cloth brushed the back of his neck, and he winced. He was already sunburned.

Jason guessed he cut quite a figure: a sweating kid in boxer shorts with a T-shirt over his head. He was glad no one from his high school could see. But the creature nodded.

"Good. You need rest, young lord, but I fear we cannot wait. I do not see those barbarians in the haze of heat behind us, but whether they still follow or not, we face a deadlier enemy. The desert will kill you if we do not escape it quickly. Two hours will bring us to greener lands alongside the Jericho River and soon after to my city, where you will have shade and rest and water. Can you continue?"

"Yes," Jason croaked. The dizziness had passed, but the mention of water filled him with longing. "Let's go."

The creature spoke as they walked: "We have not been introduced, young lord. I am Zidu, and I am honored to meet you."

"Jason Gallo." Speaking required real effort, but it kept his mind off the heat and the nausea. "Thank you for the help."

"Good service rewards the giver, Lord Jessun-gallu. It is fortunate I was nearby. I visit the thin place only rarely, to meditate and listen to the tides of the other world. I had just crossed the desert when I saw the light. I guessed some shaman made a work of great power, but I saw no other lumin. Do you have no lumin? Do you travel alone?"

"Yes. Alone." Jason had almost stopped sweating, but his skin felt hotter than the blinding desert and his head ached.

"Then what made the light?"

He shook his head. "I didn't see a light." He couldn't manage more conversation. It took all his energy to keep walking. He longed for water. But the desert stretched out in all directions, a world of pale sand and rocks under a brilliant blue sky—and nothing else.

"Odd." Zidu shrugged his lion shoulders. "Did you know those barbarians? Did you have dealings with them?"

Jason shook his head again.

"Then I suspect the same light drew them to the valley. Tribesmen of the desert, they probably recognized you as a wealthy lord and hoped for a ransom. It is a shame, so close to First Lagash. But the priests of the wetlands cannot patrol the wide desert. Here, lawlessness reigns, even at the very edge of Sumer. Let us hope our pursuers do not catch us before we reach safety."

They walked in silence, occasionally glancing behind them. Soon the world began to spin for Jason, not enough to throw him off balance, but it frightened him. Once, he'd almost fainted after soccer practice on a hot day. This was much worse. He looked at his arms. They were sunburned, and he guessed his legs were, too.

"Why have you come to this land, Lord Jessun-gallu?" asked Zidu.

Forced, Jason almost said, *by a nightmare witch doctor.* But he wasn't ready for that conversation. "Looking for someone," he croaked. "M-maybe you know him." Hope gave him a rush of energy. "Looking for my father ... named Professor William Gallo. He was visiting someone named ..." Jason struggled to remember his lead, his one clue. "Named Nagiru. Lives in First Lagash."

Zidu turned to face him, his eyes gleaming but his face long. "Ah, then, young lord, I am sorry. I do not know this Professir-wilmun-gallu. Nor have I ever heard such a name. But Nagiru is a man I have met: a merchant. I regret to tell you his ghost fled some months ago. He is dead. I hope you have not lost one dear to you."

Dead? Jason stumbled and fell to his knees. The impossibly distant horizon teetered.

"Young lord!" cried Zidu, bounding toward him.

If Nagiru was dead, Jason had no leads, nowhere to look. His father could be anywhere in this world. Jason was trapped here, and the whole journey had just become pointless.

He swayed, overwhelmed by nausea and the heat of his smoldering skin. He'd be dead soon himself, and as Zidu's face swam above him, he thought that might not be so bad. *I wonder if it's cool when you die, and if they give you any water.* Then he fell into a pool of quiet darkness.

PART ONE

ANCIENT PASSAGE

1

A King in Sumer

DURING THE CENTURIES LEADING up to 3000 BC, farmers in southern Iraq discovered the joys of agri-business: of large-scale, cooperative irrigation and farming. Food production shot up, and the key villages grew into towns, some of which ballooned into the largest settlements the world had ever seen. In other words, these primitive Mesopotamian farmers built cities—several with thirty or forty thousand people. They called their country Sumer. It was the world's first civilization, though not the only one to develop independently. It's also the primary great-grandma society for both Western and Middle Eastern Civilizations.

The Sumerians invented the plow and yoked it to oxen. At last, livestock started pulling their weight around the farm. They also created the first real writing system, while in their spare time they invented the game of checkers. What else? They pioneered law courts, jails, and bureaucracy, which was probably already a bad word. And they built the world's first monumental buildings: mud-brick temples where the gods could rest when they visited the cities.

We can thank Sumer's urban elites for most of those advances. As in all agricultural societies, most people remained peasant farmers: somewhat downtrodden, despite playing the central role in making civilization possible.

~ William Gallo, Lectures, History 56.

ooooo

Jason died and was buried.

Or so he thought. But then strong hands lifted him and poured water into his mouth. He saw distorted faces and felt nauseating motion. He saw palm trees and green fields and strange creatures with shimmering eyes, and a town of mud and clay beside a great river. He tossed and moaned and retched, and his skin burned.

And then he was still.

"Where am I?" he asked. He opened his eyes. He lay on the floor of a plain room with mud-colored walls. Sunlight streamed in through a low doorway. It was warm, but not so hot as the scorching desert. A bald, bearded man with dark, glinting eyes hovered over him. But he wasn't a man. He had the body of a lion. Weird.

"You are in the houses of the high temple," said Zidu quietly, "and you are safe, for now."

Jason sat up slowly. His head swam. "What happened? How did I get here?"

"The sun was too much for you. You fainted on the desert, so I dug a hole and buried you, and covered you with your clothes." Zidu nodded at Jason's backpack, which lay on the floor nearby. "Thank the gods those barbarians did not find you before I could return. It was a risk I had to take. I ran ahead and brought help, and had you taken here. You have been the guest of Abgallu, senior priest of the temple."

Jason looked around, blinking. The room's walls weren't just mud-colored, they actually appeared to be made of mud— of dried mud bricks. And the floor was packed earth. *This is a temple?* He saw no furniture, but several mats lay rolled up by the wall, alongside a red and yellow jug and thirty or forty piles of rectangular clay tablets, each about the size of a wallet.

He reached up to rub his eyes and winced. His arms were definitely sunburned. So were his neck and face. A wave of exhaustion broke over him. "How long have I been here?"

"Not long. It is the morning after the day I found you. The medicine priest said you should rest through another day at least, and drink plenty of water. Then you will be well enough."

"That sounds right." Jason sank back down and found he'd been sleeping on a straw mat in the middle of the floor. "I ... I hope I won't be in anyone's way." Didn't these people have beds?

"You will not." Zidu smiled. "The temple has many rooms, and no one has used this one for years, except to store records."

Records? He glanced around and realized the clay tablets were covered with chicken-scratch marks, like ancient writing. *Oh, God, they don't even have paper.* How primitive were these people?*

But he was too tired to worry for long. Soon, his eyelids were fluttering.

That afternoon, Jason dreamed of a dark hospital room with two beds and a cot. On one bed lay a sleeping man: his father, wired with sensors. On the other was Athena, also asleep. And on the cot lay Jason's own sleeping body. A back-pack was strapped to his chest. None of the sleepers moved. Nothing happened. Jason floated above them for what seemed a long time.

ooooo

"So, Lord Jessun-gallu," said Abgallu, half smiling at Jason, "where do you come from?"

The light from the high, narrow windows had almost faded, but clay bowls of burning liquid—oil lamps—cast a cheery glow over the bare dining room. Like most chambers in the mud-brick complex, the room was furnished with reed floor mats and little else. Jason had seen nothing made of metal and little wood or stone—and of course, no TVs, refrigerators, or

---

* So up on the screen, we've got Sumerian cuneiform from a baked clay tablet. It reads, "The chief of the cattle market of Abbasagga delivers eleven oxen, five sheep, three lambs, ten rams, and two kids to Intaea, on the thirteenth of the month *ezen-an-na*, sixth year of *Bur-Sin*." Pretty gripping stuff, huh? That's what you get in a lot of these tablets—business records.

~ William Gallo, Lectures, History 56.

even toilets. He wondered how he'd survive. But the food was okay. Jason, Zidu, and Abgallu had sat down to a meal of flat bread, baked fish, and grapes.

"Um, I'm from pretty far away." He shifted on his mat, feeling painfully aware of his sunburn.

"Zidu thinks you come from beyond Fore," said Abgallu, "from the other world. Is that so?"

Abgallu seemed perfectly human, unlike Zidu. He was a handsome man of twenty-five or thirty, with copper-colored skin, wiry black hair, and a short beard. Like the other men of the busy temple complex—also apparently human—he wore only a cloth skirt. His torso was lean but well-muscled.

Jason stuffed a piece of bread into his mouth, buying time. Doctor Valencia hadn't said what he should tell the people he met here. He'd been forthright with the desert barbarians, and they'd attacked him.

"Um," he said after making a show of swallowing the bread. "I ... I do come from another world." He scanned their faces, looking for signs of danger or doubt.

"Our guest is still recovering," said Zidu. "Perhaps it is too early for questions."

Abgallu cocked an eyebrow at the lion-man. "Just making conversation. You of all people should appreciate the opportunity, Zidu: the chance to talk with someone from the other word." He turned back to Jason. "Are you too tired to tell us about your world, Lord Jessun-gallu? For instance, do your people scratch a living in the wild, or have the gods given you a city of mud brick like ours, and taught you to farm wheat and barley?"

"Uh, well, I'm from a city."

"So I suspected, from your fine clothes." Abgallu nodded. "And how is your city managed? Zidu and I share a keen interest in management."

"Abgallu," Zidu chided, "do not involve him."

"No, it's okay," said Jason, relieved to avoid discussing his origins in more detail. "What do you mean 'managed'?"

"Well, what priest commands when you make war? Do you have a war-leader?"

"I guess we have a war-leader. He's called the president."

"Ah, good." Abgallu's deep-set eyes regarded Jason from beneath thick, dark eyebrows. "And does this president truly command, as An commands the stars—as Enki rules the lesser gods of crafts and earth? Or does he bow to a gaggle of old men, forever arguing and worrying?"

"An unfair question," said Zidu.

"The president definitely commands," said Jason. "He's commander-in-chief, and there aren't any old men above him." He wondered, though, if Congress counted as *a gaggle of old men, forever arguing and worrying*.

Abgallu nodded heartily, grinning at Zidu. "Surely the gods have blessed your city with wisdom, Lord Jessun-gallu." He leaned forward. "And when it comes time for a new president, how is he chosen? Does the old commander choose someone worthy and strong—a younger kinsman, perhaps?"

"Nope." Jason was proud that he knew the answers. "No way. The new president gets elected. We have an election every four years."

Zidu laughed, while Abgallu bared his teeth, looking back and forth between Jason and the lion-man. "I suppose such a thing works in a primitive town," he finally said. "But we have larger problems in this great city."

Jason could only stare, wondering what he'd done wrong. After a moment, Abgallu rose. "Well, I've stayed too long. I'm glad to see you're recovering, Lord Jessun-gallu. The temple is pleased to welcome you—for a few days more, until your full strength is back. Then I'll be honored to see you off and wish you well."

Jason's stomach tightened. Where would he go?

"Zidu will see to you until then. Gods protect you." With that, the priest bowed and left.

The lion-man shook his bald head, no longer laughing. "I am sorry for Abgallu's manners. This is an uneasy time for him. His father is very ill."

"I know how he feels. Uh, listen, I've gotta figure out what to do. Do you … Do you by any chance know how people … get *back* to my world?"

Zidu's eyebrows rose over glimmering eyes. "No. I could not guess—at that, or at how you came here in the first place. Do you not know?"

"Sure; it's no big deal." He *did* know, if Doctor Valencia could be trusted, but he didn't like her answer. "Um, well I've got to find my father. Do you have any idea …?"

"I have asked the priests and scribes of the temple," said Zidu. The clay oil lamps cast shadows across his face. "I am sorry to say: none has heard of your father—or of any foreigner who came to see Nagiru."

Jason slumped. Now what? If he couldn't find his father, how would he get home? He rubbed his forehead, trying to remember manhunt episodes from TV detective shows. "Well what about Nagiru's family?" he finally asked. "Maybe they'd know something."

"An excellent idea," said Zidu brightly. "I think Nagiru's wife still lives. The house is not far from here."

"Okay." Jason nodded. "I might as well go ask her. It's not like I've got a busy schedule or anything." He glanced shyly at Zidu. "Is there any chance you could …? Would you mind …?"

"I will take you, Lord Jessun-gallu," said the lion-man. "We will go first thing tomorrow."

Jason breathed a shuddering sigh. "Thank you. And thanks for the place to stay and for—you know—helping me out when I was sick. I really appreciate it."

The meal was over, and the world beyond the high, glassless windows was fully dark. "Can I ask just one more question?" said Jason. Zidu nodded eagerly. "Why does everyone here call me Lord?"

"Why, for simple courtesy," the lion-man exclaimed. "Are you not a great priest or a landlord?"

Jason sat back. What? "No. I'm just a regular guy."

Zidu laughed and rested a paw on Jason's leg. "Your spirit is far humbler than your costume. You have on the finest cloth I have ever seen."

Of course. Jason had put on canvas shorts from his backpack, and a clean T-shirt. His factory-made outfit was smoother, finer, and better fitting than anything he'd seen here in Sumer. "Oh, yeah, my clothes. But I'm not really exactly a lord. You can just call me Jason."

After a stop in a smelly outhouse, Jason washed his hands and face from a clay jug of water. He'd brought no bathroom kit: no hairbrush, toothbrush, acne gel, nothing. He wondered what kind of girls he'd meet here, and how he'd look—or smell—after a few days.

"Hmmm," said Zidu as they entered Jason's room. The mud-brick chamber was hot and stuffy. "Let me show you a better place to sleep."

Jason picked up some mats and blankets, and Zidu led him through a packed-earth courtyard to a corner staircase. They climbed up and found a wooden porch partly covering the reed and mud rooftops. It offered a sweeping view. A few buildings away, the river sparkled in the moonlight. The city's huts and houses crowded the bank and ran far inland, too, lit here and there by orange lamp-flames. A dark structure rose nearby into the blue-blackness—far taller and more massive than the humble dwellings around it. It was a wide platform with a square building on top, like a two-level step-pyramid.

"That is the high temple itself," said Zidu, "the heart of First Lagash."

Above the black hulk of the temple, a billion points of silver light dusted the heavens. But these stars were strange. They glimmered and rippled, as if they shone through a pool of still, dark water.

"On hot nights, this is where I sleep," said Zidu, yawning and stretching out on a mat.

"Yeah," said Jason, staring at the strange stars as he lay down. He could already feel himself fading. "Zidu," he asked once he was comfortable on his mat. "What's with the stars? How come the sky looks like … water?"

"It is water, of course," said the lion-man in his low voice. "The freshwater sea surrounds the universe—above the heavens and beneath the earth. You must know that."

"I dunno ... I guess I've heard something like it, some-where." But as he drifted off, he couldn't think where.[†]

ooooo

The next day, Jason and Zidu headed for Nagiru's house. The town was a maze of winding alleys between primitive, mud-brick buildings, mostly one story. The buildings' walls were generally bare, though some sported colorful geomet-ric designs. The companions made their way among droves of laughing, squabbling people. They also shared the street with sheep, goats, and donkeys hurrying before stick-wielding herdsmen, as well as mangy dogs. The reek of manure blended with the odor of hot, close-packed people. Occasionally, Jason had to grit his teeth to keep from retching.

His eyebrows rose as they turned a corner and confronted a winged woman strolling down the street on scaly bird-feet. She had shimmering eyes, like Zidu's. He'd seen two other glowing-eyed creatures on the streets: a red gazelle and a bull with a beard—both *talking* to companions as they passed. Most of the Sumerians paid little attention to these "lumins," as he'd heard them called. But some smiled and touched Zidu and the others as they went by.

"So what was that all about last night?" asked Jason as they edged around a crowd of shrieking boys. "Why did Abgallu want to talk about war and management and all that?"

Zidu sighed. "Abgallu's father is the ensi of First Lagash."

---

† In the Bible, in the beginning, "the Spirit of God moved upon the face of the waters.... And God said, Let there be a firmament in the midst of the waters, and let it divide the waters from the waters. And God made the firmament, and divided the waters which were under the firmament from the waters which were above the firmament.... And God called the firmament Heaven." Genesis 1:2, 1:6–1:8. It was actually the Sumerians who first recorded this vision of the world, not the Bible. The Sumerians believed an endless sea surrounds the uni-verse, above the heavens and below the earth.

~ William Gallo, *Palace of the Sphinx: The Rise of Ethical Monotheism in the Ancient Near East* (New York, 2001), 29.

He glanced up at Jason. "Ensi is like your president, I suppose—high priest and war-leader. Abgallu's father wants his son to follow him—he wants Abgallu to be the next ensi. But the chief anointer and the other senior priests will not have it, and without their support, the assembly will not choose Abgallu. So he feels bitter and frustrated, as you saw." Zidu shook his bald head. "All the more so because the soldiers love Abgallu, and he takes that as a sign of the gods' favor and their will that he should rule."

"Oh. So it sounds like you guys argue about this a lot."

"Abgallu is my shaman," said the lion-man. "But the wars have changed him, and now it seems we argue more than we share. For me, this is hard almost past bearing. We lumins live to serve, of course, but I am nearly useless to Abgallu now, because we agree so little. And the other priests mistrust me because I am Abgallu's lumin. So I am lost."

Zidu's voice had become thick, and Jason bit his lip. "I'm sorry," he said. "Sorry to … hear that."

"I am sorry, too," said Zidu. He looked up. "Ah, here we are: the house of Nagiru."

Nagiru's house was large by Sumerian standards. It had two stories and a real wooden door. Zidu had no knuckles, so Jason knocked.

A short, middle-aged woman opened the door. She wore the female outfit Jason had seen on the streets: a simple ankle-length dress, hung over one shoulder.

"Good morning, honorable woman," said the lion-man. "I am Zidu, warden of the high temple, and this young foreigner is Lord Jessun-gallu—or rather, he is Jason. We offer our sincerest apologies for troubling you. We seek the widow of the merchant Nagiru."

The woman put a hand over a hairy mole on her chin. "I'm Nagiru's widow," she said, her eyes darting back and forth. "My sons are away. Why do you want me?"

"Um, hi, ma'am," said Jason, shifting uncomfortably as his T-shirt rubbed against his sunburned neck. "I'm looking for my father, and I think he visited your husband—your late husband. So, if you wouldn't mind … I'm hoping to find out where he is—my dad. His name's William Gallo."

She squinted up at Jason, and her compressed lips spread into a smile. "Yes," she breathed. "William Gallo, I remember him."

Jason's heart leapt.

"He visited long ago—more than a dozen years."

Now, his heart sank.

"He met my husband on the river, and he stayed with us for many days." Her grin broadened. "He was quite a charmer, William Gallo."

Jason stared at the woman. His father had only been comatose two weeks. Could that translate into twelve years in the world of Fore? Doctor Valencia had said time here flowed faster, but … "Was it really twelve years ago?"

"I think so. I remember it was just before the terrible flood of Enlil."

"The flood was thirteen years ago," said Zidu softly.

"Do you have any idea where he might be now?" Jason croaked.

"No. It was so long ago."

"Good lady," said Zidu, "is there anyone else in your household who spoke with William Gallo? Would anyone else know where he went?"

"Only my husband, who's gone. My younger sons were children then, and my eldest died half-a-dozen years ago. We have a slave," she said, straightening proudly, "but she is new and would not know."

Jason stared at the woman. "What was my father doing here?"

Nagiru's widow shook her head. "He walked about and looked at the city, but that's all I know."

"Um, do you know where he came from—where he was before he came here?"

Her eyes scanned the sky. "Yes," she eventually answered. "He came to us from the barbarians—from Sheikh Zimri, down the river. He was staying with them when he met my husband. That's a famous barbarian, Sheikh Zimri. Not too hard to find, if you want."

Now the widow took a step back into the shadows. "I don't remember anything else. Is that all, good masters? May I leave you?"

Zidu looked pityingly at Jason, who nodded. "Yeah, thanks," he whispered as she closed the door.

"Now what?" Jason moaned as they trudged down a twisting street. "Am I supposed to go see some barbarian my dad *might* have visited thirteen years ago?"

"If I were you," said Zidu, "I would not."

ooooo

"Don't put much hope in help from barbarians," said Abgallu. "They're thieves and beggars, most of them. They don't even make good slaves."

Jason and Zidu sat on floor mats, sipping thick, soupy beer by the light of the clay oil lamps. Abgallu had just joined them, though he did not drink. The priest seemed tense, and he was armed. A long dagger hung from a rope around his waist, sheathed in leather. It was the most metal Jason had seen in First Lagash.

"Do you think this Sheikh Zimri might have anything to do with those other barbarians," Jason asked, "the guys who attacked me in the desert?" His whole body was tense.

"Probably not," said Abgallu. "The barbarians are countless, and if two even know each other, they're more likely enemies than conspirators. Those men probably hoped for a quick ransom, and most likely their plan reached no further than the four of them."

Jason sighed, relieved.

"But I still wouldn't look for help from barbarians. It's true they're ferocious fighters." Abgallu fingered a white scar on his left forearm. "But most can hardly think for themselves. I doubt a barbarian could even remember a man who visited a dozen years ago."

Jason rubbed his chin. Abgallu's view on barbarians seemed ... racist. He reminded Jason of white settlers in movies about the Old West, talking about Native Americans. "Are they really that bad?"

"They are … not always to be trusted," said Zidu.

Jason glanced at the lion-man. More racism?

"I think a visit to Sheikh Zimri could be dangerous," Zidu continued. "Also, getting to the sheikh is no simple task. His territory lies a week down the Jericho River, and the journey would take much longer on foot. Perhaps we could find some merchant boat to drop you there on its way downstream, but how would you find Zimri's camp, and how would you get back? And all this might be for nothing. Even if Sheikh Zimri remembers your father after all these years, he may have no more to offer than Nagiru's widow."

"Well, what else am I supposed to do?"

"Perhaps we can offer another way forward." Zidu faced Abgallu. "It would require your help, Abgallu, your willingness to grant our guest an unusual honor."

The priest's eyes narrowed. "Don't you think I have enough to do right now?"

"This would take your mind off your troubles. The gods most often grant us peace when we look beyond our own concerns."

Abgallu rolled his eyes.

"Besides, you would only need to ask the chief anointer. Then you could return to your own affairs."

"That's all very well," said Abgallu, tugging on a pendant hanging from his neck, an engraved stone cylinder. "But I'm used to a large bribe for such services."

"You will soon be the richest man in the city," pressed the lion-man. "And I ask this as a favor, for me."

Jason looked back and forth between the two Sumerians. "What?" he finally demanded. "What are you talking about?"

"All right," Abgallu said. He faced Jason. "We mean the rite of finding, Jason. I would be pleased to provide it for you, if that old lizard agrees—the chief anointer. Do you know the rite from your world?"

"Uh, no."

"It is a ritual of the temple," said Zidu. "The chief anointer and the other priests will call on Holy Ningal, goddess of dreams and insight. They will ask the goddess for vision. With her power and guidance, we will reach across the world of Fore and search for your father."

Jason exhaled, exasperated. "Look, guys, I appreciate it, but I don't think voodoo's gonna help here. I need something real. I need …" He stopped as shocked expressions spread across his hosts' faces.

"I don't know this word *voodoo*," said Abgallu, "but this *is* real. This is shaman power and a rite of Sumer, mother of civilization."

"Truly, Jason," said Zidu hastily, "I think you misunderstand. Abgallu offers you a likely solution. We might find your father, if the goddess favors us. And this is a great honor, and usually an expensive one."

"Oh." Jason winced, eyeing Abgallu's dagger. "I'm sorry. Really. I didn't mean anything. I'm always shooting off my mouth. I'd be really honored to have a … rite of finding. Really. Thank you. Thank you very much."

"No thanks are necessary," said Abgallu, his dark eyes narrow. "I'm not doing it for you." He turned to Zidu. "But after this, I am done with this matter. Jason will leave the complex—the next day. This is the high temple of First Lagash, Zidu, not a manger for your pets."

It wasn't until late that night, as Jason lay awake on his mat, that he wondered if the superstitious rite could actually work.

He wondered, too, if he'd ever learn to keep his mouth shut. He'd obviously offended Abgallu. Where would he sleep when the ferocious priest kicked him out of the temple, and what would he eat? Could he get some kind of job? He suspected the Sumerians could always use an extra slave.

When Jason finally fell asleep, he dreamed again of the hospital room, with its sleeping father, daughter, and son.

ooooo

The external stairs were covered in some kind of rocky mortar. It felt rough against Jason's bare knees. He'd been told to kneel on the final step leading up to the temple's high, massive platform. In front of him, a lone building squatted at the center of the flattop, beneath endless stars and a thick crescent moon. It was smaller than some of the houses Jason had seen, though more colorful, with painted columns and geometric mosaics. The Sumerians called it "the sanctuary," and most of the ceremony had taken place in front of it, before a blue stone altar. Jason had watched for almost a half hour—eventually growing bored—as the chief anointer and three other priests chanted and sang.

The chanting began again, and now two servants carried a goat to the altar and laid it on the blue stone. The animal struggled, but its feet were tied together, and the men held it down. Jason stared—no longer bored—as the chief anointer approached, holding a curved dagger. Jason knew what would happen, but he couldn't look away. The knife flashed, and the goat jerked and kicked, but just for a moment. Jason gagged as blood flowed from the animal's throat into a wide stone bowl held by one of the priests.

"O Holy Ningal," the chief anointer intoned to the sky, his voice loud despite his age and frail frame, "we offer you this sacrifice, and we pray that you will look upon us with favor."

The servants swept the goat's carcass away, and now a priestess with waist-length brown hair walked out from behind the altar. She was a young woman, draped head-to-toe in a white cloak. She'd played only a small role so far, burning incense and singing, but now she took center stage. She stood facing the altar and sang in a high, sweet soprano:

> O Ningal, lovely daughter of Enki,
> O Ningal, Ningikuga's child,
> O Ningal, wife of Nanna, the moon,
> O goddess of dreams and insight,
> Guide me again this night.
> Lift me over city and river.
> Lift me over field and desert
> Into the plains of the sky,
> Where the sun and the stars dance.
> Carry me where dreams glide like unseen birds.

O mother of Inanna and Utu,
Dream with me, you who weep for mankind,
Helpless before the wrath of the gods.
This I pray, O goddess Ningal,
O wife of Nanna, the moon.

As the priestess finished her prayer, she swept off her white
cloak and spread it over the altar in a single fluid motion. Jason
drew in a quick breath. She now wore nothing at all.

He certainly wasn't bored now. He watched as the slightly
plump young priestess walked around the altar, chanting. Four
lumins stood in a row in front of the sanctuary. They had not
moved since the start of the ceremony, and Jason had come to
think of them as scenery. But now the priestess glided along
the row, touching each creature. The first had a man's body
with a bull's legs, tail, and horns. The second and third had
animal shapes: a winged dog and a small giraffe-like creature covered in red scales. Zidu was the fourth. As the nude
priestess touched each lumin, its glowing eyes shone brighter.
Jason's own eyes widened. What had caused that?

The four lumins began to hum, adding their voices to the
priests' deep chanting as the priestess returned to the altar and
sat on top, on her outspread white cloak—now red-spotted
from the goat's blood left on the altar. The chief anointer and
the other three priests knelt before her. "O Holy Ningal," the
priestess cried, "come take me up on wings of sleep!"

Her words hung on the night air, and the lumins' eyes
blazed. Then Jason gasped. The stars were moving! Hundreds
of stars, thousands, descended from the heavens into the night
air. Soon they surrounded the temple, floating around the
sanctuary and the altar and the people there.

Afraid it wasn't allowed but unable to resist, Jason reached
for a star. The night air rippled before his hand, and the tiny,
glimmering mote drifted out of reach. The air had turned liquid. He looked around. Everything he saw, even the sparkling
river and the dark city below the temple, wavered and swam.
It was as if he were looking through clean, clear water, full of

stars like glimmering bubbles.

He shook his head, blinking. Had they put drugs in his dinner? He looked up at the priestess and the four humming lumins. He sensed some connection between them, as if they were touching.

"Jason Gallo!" the priestess called out. He cringed, sure he was in trouble for trying to grab the star. "Come forward and kneel before the altar." His heart hammering, he rose and walked onto the high terrace, passing between floating stars and kneeling priests. A few feet before the altar, he knelt again and looked up at the enthroned priestess, trying not to stare, though with little success. He'd never seen a nude woman up close, except in his dreams.

"Supplicant before the high temple and before the goddess Ningal," she said, "you seek one who is lost to you. I will search for him, and the goddess will guide my sight."

Jason had almost forgotten the reason for the ceremony. Maybe it really *could* work.

"Give me the one who is lost. Tell me who it is you seek, and how I will know his aura."

Jason blinked. Zidu hadn't warned him about this part. "He's my father, and his name's Professor William Peter Gallo." He glanced at Zidu, hoping for guidance, but the glowing-eyed lumins stood still as statues. "He's got light brown hair, kind of curly, and he's a couple inches taller than me. Uh, he's not really fat or thin or anything—or maybe just a little thin." Jason looked at the priestess. This sort of description didn't seem to fit the setting. "He's a professor of history, with a PhD, and he studies mythology—and that's almost all he ever talks about. Um ... you want his driver's license number?" He bit his lip. This wasn't a good time for wisecracks.

"That is not sufficient," said the priestess, her voice stern.

"But how—"

"It is not for me to tell you how. I do not know your land or your people. I do not know what moves your spirits, what shapes your auras. You must tell me, or the rite is at an end."

Okay then, he almost said, *thanks for playing!* This was

their game, and they hadn't bothered to tell him the rules. But unless Jason was hallucinating—dreaming up floating stars and watery air—the priestess's magic was at least partly real. If there was even a chance she could find his father, he had to try.

"Okay," he said, "lemme think."

Jason tried to concentrate on the problem at hand, and not on the priestess' moonlit body. Should he talk about his father's interests and hobbies? He'd already mentioned the only one: his work. What about his taste in clothes or food, his favorite TV shows, his parents, his friends, his car?

Jason was nearly ready to give up when a memory struck. His father had once told him that ancient religions, and some modern ones, defined people through totems. "Everyone has his own spirit guide," his father had said, "like a mythic animal. Or he's got a saint's day or a guardian angel. Or some myth—maybe the story of his particular hero or minor god. It's special for him or his family." Could this totem idea answer the priestess's question? But what was his father's god or myth ... or hero?

"It's Jason!" he shouted, looking up at the priestess. "That's his favorite hero, from his work!"

Her face was impassive.

"He was this legendary hero, and he had this ship called the *Argo*. And all these other heroes—called the Argonauts—went to help him steal this Golden Fleece: you know, like a sheep's skin made of gold." Jason hadn't thought of the Golden Fleece myth in years. As a little boy, he'd loved hearing stories about his heroic Greek namesake, and his father had told them over and over. "So they had all these adventures, and they scared off these harpies who were ruining this blind old guy's food. And one of the heroes had a boxing match with this king and killed him—and Jason had to drive this bull that breathed fire." His words tumbled over one another. "And then this hot sorceress called Medea helped Jason steal the Golden Fleece, and he married her, but she turned bad in the end. They actually made a cool movie about it, like in the fifties, with old-fashioned special effects." He bit his lip.

Obviously, that wouldn't help the priestess. "Anyway, my dad wrote his PhD thesis about Jason and the Argonauts. That's why he named me Jason—after his favorite hero."

"Very well, supplicant," said the priestess, a small smile playing across her lips. "I will search for your father, follower of Jason and the Argonauts, and if the goddess gives you her blessing, you will know where he can be found."

The lumins' humming swelled. The enthroned priestess closed her eyes, and the stars around her swirled, like the spiral arms of a galaxy. No one moved or made a sound for several minutes as the stars made their stately dance around the altar.

The priestess's eyes opened. "Jason Gallo!" The stars slowed. "I see for you with Ningal's eyes. Your father, William Gallo, is beyond my sight, but I caught the echo of his aura. I touched the mind of one who saw him when he last traveled through this part of the world of Fore. Go down to the land of Egypt, to the Middle Kingdom, and seek out Senusret. He can tell you of your father."

Who? Where? But before Jason could ask questions, a scream pierced the night, and then another. The priestess froze, and she looked less than certain for the first time. Jason heard the priests whispering behind him. Several more screams followed, along with the sound of shouting. Now even the stately lumins behind the altar shifted and looked around. And as they did, the trance on the temple flattop broke. The floating stars rose back to the heavens, and the liquid drained from the air, like water spilling from an overturned glass.

The priestess leapt down from the altar. "Fire!" she yelled, covering what she could of her nakedness with her arms and hands. Suddenly she was a frightened young woman, rather than a goddess. "They're attacking the temple!"

Jason turned, and so did the priests behind him, and they all ran to the edge of the temple flattop. Smoke rose into the night air from the complex below. He saw running men carrying torches, clubs, and spears. A gang of them threw a white-robed priest to the ground in a courtyard. Jason gaped as weapons rose and fell over the victim.

"Come!" the chief anointer barked. "We must get off the temple. There's no escape from here."

Zidu was at Jason's side, as the whole company ran down the mortar steps. As they reached the courtyard at the bottom, a swarm of men sprinted in from between the mud-brick buildings. The invaders wore no armor or uniforms—only the usual skirts and tunics—but they carried clubs and spears, and Jason was sure they were soldiers. At their head was Abgallu, one hand grasping his dagger, the other a short sword. His white skirt was spattered with blood.

The chief anointer had stopped at the center of the courtyard, and Jason stood frozen, too, along with the other priests, servants, and lumins. Only Abgallu seemed able to move. He strode up to the chief anointer. The old man was taller, but he looked lean and frail compared with the dark warrior-priest.

"My father has gone, old man," said Abgallu, "and I will be ensi. As for you, now you follow my father."

"As will you someday," said the chief anointer, his voice steady. "And I'll wager you go the same way as I."

Abgallu nodded, his smile grim.

At Jason's side, Zidu cried, "No, Abgallu!"

But it was too late. Abgallu's arm swept forward and his dagger flashed in the moonlight. For a moment, the two priests, young and old, faced each other, surrounded by gaping men. Then the chief anointer's knees buckled, and he crumpled. His head hit the dirt with crack and his lifeless eyes stared up at the countless watery stars.

Jason looked up from the bleeding gash in the old man's throat, and his eyes met Abgallu's. The soldiers raised their weapons.[‡]

ooooo

---

‡ In the early centuries, priests apparently governed the city-states, led by a high priest who served as something like a mayor. It looks like an assembly or council chose him. But, as war became more common, the mayor evolved into a commander-in-chief, succeeded by his brother or son instead of an elected replacement. The Sumerians had invented the king.

~ William Gallo, Lectures, History 56.

Far away, the Rector for Enforcement stood before a barred window, his hands clasped behind his back. "You're sure, Mr. Shaw?" he asked, still scanning the black waters of the canal beneath the window.

"Yes, Rector. At least, the cultivars are sure. Jason Gallo entered our world some time during the past few days, far upriver. As expected, the cultivars can't say exactly where."

The Rector turned. Candlelight glinted off polished wooden surfaces and brass fittings. Dark portraits glared down into the chamber. Shaw looked nervous, but Crocker wore his usual self-assured smile. "You're ready for him, then, Mr. Crocker, you and your band of cutthroats and vagabonds?"

"We're watching every known thin spot, Rector, all the way upstream into Old Mesopotamia—even beyond the salt fields,§ all the way to the heart of Sumer. We'll catch him."

---

§ Sumer disappeared from the face of the Earth and mankind forgot about it—even its name—until a couple of centuries ago. That's because salt destroyed the rich, swampy farmland that had made Sumer possible. You see, irrigation leaves salt behind—particularly in dry countries without much rain to wash it away. Over time, salt poisons the soil. Farmers can preserve and revitalize their land by giving the soil breaks and limiting production. But the Sumerians chuffed it, as my son, Jason, likes to say. They didn't do anything to preserve their soil. So Sumerian irrigation—slowly, gradually—turned fertile farmland into the barren salt marshes and desert of today's southern Iraq.

~ William Gallo, Lectures, History 56.

2

Nomad Barbarians

THEY LIVED OFF OF goats, sheep, cattle, donkeys, or horses, depending on the location. They had to keep fresh grass under their grazers' hungry mouths, so they kept moving and often lived in tents. Protecting a herd from predators and rival tribes was bloody work. So they needed to be combat-ready at all times, and that led to warrior cultures....

The nomads had a keen interest in civilization's treasures. Sometimes that interest led to raids on caravans or outlying settlements. Sometimes it led to invasions, in which entire barbarian nations overran the frontiers, raping and pillaging. The nomads had the advantage of a warlike, mobile society, while the civilized lands had more men. When the balance tipped in the nomads' favor, barbarians like Attila the Hun and Genghis Khan shook the world, and empires fell.

~ William Gallo, *Palace of the Sphinx*, 77.

ooooo

"My friend!" Zidu yelled, disrupting Jason's trance of fear. "Come with me! Run!"

The lumin turned quickly, and Jason followed. A spear-wielding man leapt in front of them as the courtyard dissolved into chaos.

"Back away!" Zidu ordered. "This foreign boy is not your prey."

The soldier hesitated, glancing back and forth between Jason and Zidu, and they sprinted past him. They ran into a low-roofed building and then out the other side.

"The temple is on the river," said Zidu, glancing back at Jason. "We will get you out that way."

"Wait!" Jason cried as they plunged into another building. It was the house where he'd slept and eaten for the past few days. "I've gotta get my bag!" He tore across the courtyard and into his own mud-brick chamber, where he grabbed his backpack.

"It's all I have from home," Jason explained when he returned and saw Zidu's exasperated face.

Shouts and smoke accompanied them as they plunged through two more courtyards. But they saw no soldiers—only priests and servants, some frightened, some merely puzzled.

"Run or hide!" Zidu called repeatedly. "Abgallu is taking the temple! The soldiers are killing people!" Some did run, but many appeared not to understand, or to believe.

At last, Jason and Zidu emerged by the riverbank. A wide dirt path separated the water and the temple complex.

"Those are the temple's ships," said Zidu.

He darted across the path to a cluster of small boats tethered to a low, wooden dock running alongside the river. The dock was deserted, though Jason saw movement and lamplight in the distance, upstream and downstream. He realized most of the ships were sailboats, each with a single mast rising into the moonlight.

"We cannot bother with a sail for now," Zidu continued. "We must simply get you downstream, and oars will serve at first, as will the current. It may be wrong to take the temple's boats, but I think the city's new master owes me this favor. Perhaps someday you will return the boat, after your voyage to Egypt."

"Egypt?" Jason exclaimed. "What, you mean to find that guy the priestess mentioned? But ... but I don't even know where I'm going. How am I supposed to find him? She didn't even give me an address!"

"She said go to the Middle Kingdom," Zidu replied. "It lies four weeks down the Jericho River, perhaps less."

Jason stared. Four *weeks*? Shouts echoed from the buildings nearby, and he guessed the fighting had nearly reached the riverbank.

"There is no more time!" cried the lion-man. "I cannot protect you if the soldiers have the bloodlust. You must simply sail down to the Middle Kingdom and ask the Egyptians for this Senusret."

Jason felt nauseous. "Zidu," he implored, "come with me!" The lion-man's eyebrows rose over his shimmering eyes. "You said you're lost here, because you're not getting along with Abgallu. That's just gonna get worse now."

"Abgallu and I are finished."

"See, there you go! And you said lumins need to be needed all the time, right?" More screams issued from the complex, and Jason edged toward the boats, his heart pounding. "If there's anyone who needs your help, it's me. I don't even know where Egypt is, or what a rite of finding is, or how to sail, or anything!"

Zidu was quiet, and Jason held his breath. "Truly, I have no place here now," said the lion-man, his face suddenly contorted with grief. "I would not know whom to serve." He looked up at Jason. "And you do need a guide and helper, perhaps more than anyone I have ever known." Jason grinned, despite his terror.

At that moment, a screaming priest burst from the complex, pursued by two armed men. Zidu and Jason turned and ran for the boats.

ooooo

Jason sat at the edge of the little boat's deck, thinking of home. Two days before the coma, he'd gone over to Chuck's house after school, to play *Renegade Rat* on the Jacksons' widescreen TV. Chuck's gameplay was usually erratic, but that day he'd been on fire.

"You're goin' *down!*" he screamed, clutching his joystick and half jumping off the couch as his rat leapt over a canal of steaming sewage.

"Ah, the sweet sound of fear," Jason replied. He kept his eyes on the screen, where a hydra-gator had cornered his own rat, outside the Lower Sewer Citadel. "Your flimsy lead will soon be ancient history."

"Hey, Jason," Nadji called from the easy chair, where he was working his way through a pile of fruit. "Are you coming to the expo this summer or not?"

"Probably," said Jason, concentrating on the hydra-gator. "I haven't asked my dad yet."

"You've chuffed it!" Chuck shouted, twisting in place. "Can't stop me now!"

"Watch and learn."

Jason was the de facto leader of this group of three, though little status came with the title. "It's kinda like being the toughest kid in the chess club," he'd once explained to his dad, "or the best rapper in Montana." Chuck Jackson was short, wiry, and much too jumpy, and Nadji Mansour was tall, skinny, and spacey. Neither was particularly cool.

"Dung-muncher!" Jason yelled as his laser missed the hydra-gator's chest and struck yet another snapping head.

The head exploded, and two new ones grew in its place. Now he was up to eleven heads, and his rat was in serious trouble. Worse, Chuck's rat had already reached the switching yard. There, lightning-fast subway trains hissed in and out of tunnel openings, flashing blinding blue headlights. As Jason struggled with the hydra-gator, Chuck crossed the yard, leaping over deadly third rails and dodging trains and sewer predators. Finally, his rat reached the glistening, multi-colored pile of garbage at the far end. Seated on top was the Potentate of the Fifth Level: a sexy, six-armed, green she-rat, with a diamond engagement ring for a crown. As Chuck's rat knelt to receive a plenary indulgence, a voice broke the players' concentration.

"You know, you've entered your father's world there, Jason."

Jason glanced up to find Chuck's father standing in the doorway, dangling a pair of keys. He was a big man with a wide belly and a thick, reddish beard, and he liked to be called Big Paul.

"Whaddya mean?" Jason asked, turning back to the screen.

"I mean all that stuff: all those modern monsters in your game there, and the voodoo goddesses and urban castles. That's what your dad writes about." Big Paul laughed, and Jason felt his stomach knot. Big Paul was a professor at the university, in the history department, like Jason's dad. "He actually teaches that stuff to our students," Big Paul continued. "And he calls it history!"

"So what?" Chuck demanded. His shoulders had risen to a hunch.

"So nothing!" Big Paul laughed, walking around the couch, his sandals slapping the floor. "It's just nice to see Jason following in his old man's footsteps. These Gallo boys are experts at demons and dragons and monster hunts. Maybe that's why he always beats you, huh Chuckie?"

Jason glanced at Chuck, who stared at the screen, his jaw clenched. At that moment, the hydra-gator's two newest heads lunged, and each caught a different part of Jason's rat. Within seconds, he'd been torn apart, sending blood dripping down the right half of the screen.

"Anyway," Big Paul concluded, opening the garage door, "I'm going out. Tell Mom I'll be home by 6:30."

Silence fell over the den.

Finally, Nadji spoke up. "Jason doesn't always win." He smiled in his distracted way. "Look, Chuck, he just lost his last rat. You won!"

ooooo

Jason sighed and picked up his makeshift toothbrush—the frayed end of a reed. He scrubbed vigorously at his teeth, then leaned over the side of the little ship's deck and rinsed his mouth with river water.

"Ugh," he said, looking back at Zidu. "Tastes like mud."

He wondered how Chuck or Nadji would handle brushing teeth with a reed. Chuck probably wouldn't bother. But Jason was getting used to doing without modern comforts. His toilet was the great outdoors, his sink and tub were the river, and his bed was a thin reed mat, laid out on the deck or on the soft earth of the left bank. Without a mirror, he had little idea of the acne situation, but he knew he'd traded his sunburn for a deep tan.

The boat was built of light wooden planks and had a tiny storage hold but no cabin. A single mast rose from the deck, supporting a dun-colored, square sail. They'd capsized three times during their first two days, as Jason had learned to sail. Zidu knew the basics, since he'd traveled on the temple's ships many times, but he had no fingers to work the ropes. So most of the physical effort fell to Jason. Now, after more than a week, Jason considered himself an expert. He wished Athena could see him.

They'd named the boat the *Dead Valencia*, which filled Jason with vicious glee. Zidu hadn't understood at first, but after a few days, Jason had told the lion-man about Doctor Valencia and his strange entry into the world of Fore. The story baffled Zidu, though he'd eventually offered a thoughtful suggestion: "Perhaps the whole experience was a dream, including this Doctor Valencia."

That idea troubled Jason, but how could it be true? After all, here he was in the world of Fore, just as she'd promised. And Doctor Valencia seemed real in his memory, more real than anything else in the hospital dream. Of course, in a sense he was dreaming even now—dream voyaging—so perhaps he shouldn't trust his senses. Perhaps the entire world of Fore was a dream, and Zidu, Abgallu, Doctor Valencia, and the rest were characters made up in his overstressed brain. But Jason didn't think so. He'd never experienced a dream so vivid, so realistic, or so persistent. Plus, he suspected Doctor Valencia was the woman with the snake: the woman he'd seen outside his bedroom window. He'd been wide-awake then.

Whenever he thought about the line between dreaming and dream voyaging, Jason's head hurt. And the confusion grew as he pondered his other mysteries. What was Fore? Another planet? An alternate reality? And why did everyone speak English? The questions were endless. In a sense, though, the answers didn't matter, at least for now. Doctor Valencia had said his father was his fastest route home, and Jason had no reason to doubt that. He had to find his father, not answer Alice-in-Wonderland riddles.

Progress on finding his father, however, was slow. "I hope we'll hit a Sumerian airport soon," he muttered as he settled down to watch the water.

The shore lands had been lush and swampy for most of the journey, home to irrigated fields, tiny villages, and an occasional mud-brick city like First Lagash. But as that morning wore on, the scenery changed. The river meandered into a region of dry grasslands and sandy desert, with no sign of human habitation.

"I believe we have reached Sheikh Zimri's territory," said Zidu around midday. "Are you sure you wish to take this risk? I still think we should sail past this land and on to Egypt, to find this Senusret."

Adrenaline turned Jason's stomach. "No, I'm still sure."

Zidu had insisted the Jericho River flowed from Sumer to Egypt, and then on to many other lands. Apparently, Fore's geography did not match the real world's, despite the historical place names and peoples—unless Jason had totally misunderstood the maps he'd studied in school, which he considered possible but unlikely. In any case, Zidu had said Sheikh Zimri's tribe lived between Sumer and Egypt.

"We're here now," Jason continued. "Like I said yesterday, if we don't find anything in Egypt, we'd just have to come back." That seemed a likely outcome. Jason trusted the Sumerian priestess about as much as he'd trust a TV psychic. She could have made up the name Senusret, or hallucinated.

They scanned the left bank for signs of human life. Finally, late in the afternoon, they spotted the remains of a campfire and pulled ashore.

"Two or three days gone," said Zidu, pawing the ashes. "That is a good sign."

They decided to stay for the night and search the area. So as Zidu padded off to relieve himself, Jason strolled inland. He crossed between two low hills separating the river from a yellow, grassy plain that stretched to the horizon. He saw no sign of barbarians, but forty or fifty goats grazed nearby. Jason crouched in the grass, wondering if he and Zidu could hunt down a wild goat, and if Zidu would know how to cook it. Jason was heartily sick of the *Dead Valencia*'s menu: fish caught in the ship's nets and stale bread "bought" with fish.

"You there!" a deep voice bellowed. "What are you doing by my herd? Show yourself! Show yourself, or by Amurru, I'll drench the earth with your blood!"

Jason stood slowly. An enormous, brown-bearded man stood on the hillside above him. He had coppery skin and wore a belted tunic.

"Hi!" Jason gulped as he saw the barbarian's bulging muscles. "I wasn't doing anything! I didn't even notice your goats! I just dropped my watch, and I was looking for it." He took a step back as the huge man advanced down the hill. "I found it, so I'll just leave you alone now. Sorry to bother you. I'll just go now."

"Stay right there!" the barbarian shouted.

Jason stood still, shaking and wondering where Zidu had gone. Soon he and the barbarian faced each other among the rocks and bushes at the foot of the hill. The man stood a foot taller than Jason and looked like he could lift a donkey over his head. He had a hooked nose and carried a massive wooden club, and he wore both a bow and a short sword strapped over his back.

"Ha!" the barbarian finally cried, lowering his club. "You don't look dangerous. A prince, I guess, of the farming people. I'm sorry I was so discourteous. You can't be too careful when you guard wealth such as this." He gestured to the herd of goats. "I am Rim-Hadad, son of Nablanum." He touched his heart and bowed. "I wish you good health."

"Jason, son of William." Jason bowed back, relieved Rim-Hadad wasn't going to drench the earth with his blood. "Uh, good health to you, too."

The barbarian invited him to sit by the hillside and talk. "Herding is lonely work," he explained. "I'd be glad of some company."

Zidu soon joined them. The barbarian reverently touched the lion-man's flank. "The lumins of Sumer are welcome in my land," he said, offering them milk from a skin pouch. Then he asked what had brought them to his country.

"Actually," said Jason, "we're looking for a bar—for someone. Do you know—by any chance—do you know Sheikh Zimri?"

"Zimri!" Rim-Hadad exclaimed. "Of course I do! He's my cousin, on both sides! And he's my master, I'm sorry to say.

"Truth to tell," he pointed to the goats, "this is his herd, not mine. Why do you want him?"

"I'm looking for my father," Jason exclaimed. "I think he visited Sheikh Zimri, like a long time ago, maybe thirteen years. His name's William Gallo. Do you … do you know him? He would've been dressed kind of like me."

Rim-Hadad examined Jason's white T-shirt. "No," he said. "I've never seen such strange finery. And I doubt such a person ever visited our camp, or I'd remember."

Zidu sighed, and Jason slumped. "I'm sorry," the barbarian continued. "But Zimri may remember something."

Before Jason could ask where the sheikh might be found, Rim-Hadad flashed a toothy grin and grasped his shoulder, hard. "Father and son!" he said, "Is that not the greatest bond in a man's life? My own father was a lion of a man, and I loved him like the desert loves the sun. Even in his last years, he could eat an entire lamb at one sitting, drink ten measures of beer, then take a slave girl to his tent, and still rise at dawn, as fresh and strong as the youngest warrior." Rim-Hadad laughed, and Jason wondered if slave girl had any choice in the matter. "Ha! I once saw him kill three men single-handed, with this very club. He

was a great man. He would never have let my viper of a brother
ruin us, if he had not grown so witless at the end."

Jason and Zidu glanced at each other.

"Ruin you, honorable sir?" said Zidu.

"Yes!" cried Rim-Hadad. "Since you insist on knowing, I'll
tell you." He swept his arm out to point at the grazing goats,
taking in also the dry grasslands and the desert beyond. "I
should be tending my own herd on these pastures, not the
goats of another man. My brother Samanu, the fool, killed the
son of a sheikh. Zimri could not afford a feud, so he gave all
my father's herd to pay the blood debt. My poor old father was
so grieved it killed him. Now my fool brother and I labor for
Zimri like slaves, with hardly a kid to call our own." He shook
his head. "Have you ever heard a greater injustice?"

The two shook their heads, and Jason tried to look indignant.
"Ha! You are good friends!" Rim-Hadad proclaimed, smacking
Jason's shoulder so hard he almost fell over. "Why don't you stay
with me tonight? You both look hungry for some fresh meat, and
I mean to slaughter a kid. And in the morning, I'll take you to
Zimri's camp. It's less than a day away. Stay with me tonight, and
you'll eat better than the greatest princes of the farming people!"

Jason looked at Zidu, wondering if Sumerian prejudices
against barbarians still nagged at the lion-man.* Zidu nodded
slowly. "We'd love to stay," said Jason. "Thank you."

ooooo

---

* There's a cuneiform passage that pretty well sums up the Sumerians' feelings
about the Amorite barbarians: "Their hands are destructive and their features are
those of monkeys. They never stop roaming about, they are an abomination to
the gods' dwellings. Their ideas are confused; they cause only disturbance. He
is clothed in sack-leather, lives in a tent, exposed to wind and rain, and cannot
properly recite prayers. He digs up truffles in the foothills, does not know how
to bend the knee, and eats raw flesh."

Ironically, those same monkey-faced raw meat eaters conquered Sumer and
much of Mesopotamia around 2000 BC. They adopted civilized ways, founded
Babylon, and became the torch-bearers of Sumerian culture.

~ William Gallo, Lectures, History 56.

A second barbarian joined them that night: a young man about Jason's age, with a sullen face and very little to say.

"This is the son of my worthless brother," said Rim-Hadad. "He should have caught you stalking our goats long before I did, Jason Gallo, but he was off in the bushes, doing whatever it is boys do in bushes."

Rim-Hadad was an excellent cook. The four enjoyed a dinner of savory goat's meat, seasoned with wild herbs. After dinner, they sat around the fire, and the big barbarian entertained them with a story.

He told a grisly tale about a young man who'd sworn an oath on his father's soul and then broken it. "Then the demons came," Rim-Hadad whispered, shivering, "and devoured the innocent father's soul in its hideous maw of gnashing teeth." His voice swelled. "And such is the fate of any father whose sons do not honor him."

This came with a glare at the young barbarian, who'd gone pale at the mention of demons. Jason guessed Rim-Hadad's absent brother was the real target of his ire.

After the tale, Jason got up to relieve himself. The swollen moon hung low over the grasslands. He hunted for a secluded spot, picking his way between dozing goats. Finally, he chose the far side of a low hill. But just as he was about to unbutton his shorts, he realized he was not alone. Two dark figures moved across the stars. Before Jason could speak, they were next to him. Each grabbed an arm and held him tight.

Jason's stomach clenched as a familiar, low voice spoke into his left ear. "Don't make a sound or move a muscle." It was the barbarian leader from the desert outside First Lagash. Jason knew the other man, too—another of the barbarians who'd attacked him that day.

Something cold pressed against his neck. He flinched, sure it was a knife. He saw now that the second barbarian held another knife to his belly.

"I told you once," the leader murmured, "you belong to the Rector, and I'm sure he has something painful planned for you. But by Amurru and Dagon,[†] I'll do worse if you disobey me again."

○○○○○

The grass rustled as Jason walked between the two barbarians. Why had he come here, into this nest of barbarians, ignoring Zidu's warnings? And who was this "Rector"? Jason remembered the name. "The Rector wants you," the barbarian leader had said on Jason's first day in the world of Fore. What did that mean?

Low hills and rocks cast moon shadows across the grasslands. Jason stumbled over stones and shrubs as the two men marched him toward the river. Before long, the barbarians stopped to listen. Soon they continued but then stopped again. Jason heard nothing and saw nothing, but his captors were clearly troubled.

"Who can it be?" the second man whispered.

The leader glared into the darkness. "It doesn't matter. We can't have anyone following us. You ambush him here." His eyes narrowed. "If he's one of ours, beat him for surprising us. If not, kill him." He turned to snarl at Jason. "And that's what'll happen to you, too, if you give me any trouble."

They marched under the moon, leaving the second barbarian behind. Near silence fell over the grasslands again. Jason's captor had drawn a short sword from beneath his robe, replacing his curved knife. He walked directly behind Jason, occasionally prodding him with the weapon. The barbarian did not make a sound, and Jason guessed he was listening.

---

† Dagon, Martu, and Amurru were gods of the Semitic tribes. By "Semites," we mean the people who speak Semitic languages. The group includes languages such as Akkadian, Amorite, Punic (Carthaginian), and Aramaic (the language of Jesus Christ), not to mention modern Hebrew and Arabic. The Semitic language group wasn't named until the late 1700s, when European scholars started to classify languages. They imagined Semites descend from Noah's son Shem, who was called Sem in Greek.

~ William Gallo, *Palace of the Sphinx*, 75–76.

Jason still heard nothing but his own feet and his pounding heartbeat.

A cry rolled over the plain from behind them. Another followed. Soon Jason heard the sounds of a struggle. Then the silence returned.

"Stop," the barbarian ordered in a low voice. Jason froze. He stood looking at the river to his right, sparkling in the moonlight. Soon a rustle and a gust of air told him his captor had moved. Fear almost paralyzed Jason, but he couldn't keep from turning to look behind him. The big man squatted over a clump of weeds with his back turned, several feet away. He was peering into the darkness.

What Jason did next scared him more than anything else. He turned and ran. He careened across the moonlit grasses, hurtling over dry bushes and rocks. He heard the barbarian leader's bellow and then the big man's footfalls, no longer silent, fast and close behind. A hand clamped on his shoulder, and he shrieked and tried to jump aside. A foot struck his leg from behind, and suddenly Jason's ankles were caught between his pursuer's running feet. He tumbled, and his ribs and chin slammed against the hard earth.

The barbarian roared, and Jason saw that his foe had fallen, too. Was it too late to surrender and apologize? Would the man kill him? The barbarian had dropped his sword, and he was fumbling for it in the dry grass. His eyes were glazed with rage, and he no longer looked eager to take prisoners.

"Help!" Jason screamed. "HELP!"

3

Death in Egypt

As I was saying, Egypt was a river valley society, like Sumer, but it wasn't a bunch of city-states and shifting kingdoms. By 3000 BC, it was a nation—history's first. The Nile Valley's two-dimensional geography made that pretty much inevitable. You've got barren deserts to the east and west, so the only convenient travel is north and south on the river. That means a single king could control the whole country through a few riverbank outposts. The king owned all the land, and he could focus almost all the spare labor on a single project, like building a giant pyramid. Most cultural and scientific growth happened in the royal court, particularly in the early days. The court was Washington DC, Hollywood, Broadway, Vatican City, the Silicon Valley, and MIT, all in one.

The Nile's floods were predictable, the soil was rich, the king kept order, and the deserts kept pushy foreigners away—most of the time. So life was good. Why change anything? The result: a conservative, cheerful, incredibly long-lasting society. The kingdom of Egypt and its fundamental culture lasted for thirty centuries. And *what* a culture! The Egyptians built a society with such unique pizzazz that now, five thousand years later, any one of you can instantly recognize an Egyptian royal headdress or coffin.

~ William Gallo, Lectures, History 56.

ooooo

The sword blow dug into the earth an inch from Jason's leg. He rolled aside, away from the barbarian. Somehow he managed to hurl himself up and forward, stumbling into a sprint across the moonlit plain. The wind whistled in his ears, though not loud enough to drown another cry of rage from behind.

He seemed to be sprinting forever—until his legs burned and he thought his heart would burst. Then one foot caught a rock and he tumbled down a low hill. Bruised and dizzy, he rolled onto his back and looked around. Where was the barbarian? Jason squatted, trying to quiet his panting so he could listen to the night.

"Jason Gallo!" called a voice from over the hill. "My friend, are you there? Are you hurt?" It was Rim-Hadad.

"Over here!" Jason cried, rising to his feet. Soon Rim-Hadad crested the hill, running and carrying his club.

"They kidnapped me!" Jason blurted. "They tried to take me away. Then there was a fight, and I ran!"

Rim-Hadad approached slowly and put a hand on Jason's shoulder. "I know. But they no longer follow you." He hefted the massive club, his face fierce. "No one harms the guest of Rim-Hadad, son of Nablanum." Then he shook Jason's shoulder. "Calm yourself, my friend."

Jason realized he was shaking. Embarrassed, he drew a deep breath and then another. He looked over the moonlit grasslands, then back up at Rim-Hadad. "They might have friends. They said something about 'one of ours' following us."

"Then we must get you far from here."

They jogged back. Halfway to camp, Jason tripped over a dark bundle and fell on something warm and wet. "Oh, God!" he cried, rolling aside and gagging. It was the second barbarian, his right eye staring up at the stars. The left side of his skull had been crushed, exposing his brain.

Rim-Hadad hauled Jason to his feet. "This one I killed easily," he said, "but his fellow fought like a rhino, and I only wounded him. Come."

Soon they approached the camp, and Jason saw what looked like two hazy stars twinkling in the grass. They resolved into Zidu's eyes. "Boy, am I glad to see you!" Jason gasped. "We've gotta leave right away!"

"But why, my friend?" Zidu asked. "What has happened?"

"You were right! I was an idiot. We shouldn't have come here. It's those guys from the desert—the barbarians." Jason's voice shook. "They're here. They tried to kidnap me again. I don't want to wait around and give them another chance. You were right!"

"But what about Sheikh Zimri?"

"I think you should not visit him," said Rim-Hadad. "I'm sure those men came from the southern tribe, friends to my people. Zimri would give you to them if they ask, or maybe sell you."

"Okay, that's that," Jason exclaimed. "We'll go to Egypt and find my dad there, and forget about Zimri."

"To Egypt," the barbarian echoed in a whisper. He looked back and forth between Jason and Zidu.

"I hope you will not be offended, Rim-Hadad," said Zidu, his forehead creasing beneath the dark dome of his head. "You have been a worthy host."

"I am not offended, lumin of Sumer. It is partly my fault, because I didn't warn you that strangers skulked about. I worried only for my goats, not my guests."

Rim-Hadad looked at the ground. Then he turned to Jason. "Take me with you, my friend."

Jason looked up, surprised. Rim-Hadad met his eyes, his face still. "I have nothing here. My nephew can watch the herd. The sheikh owns it. I only work for him. I should have been a great patriarch, if my fool brother hadn't lost our inheritance. I want to travel downriver and win my fortune—to Egypt, or wherever the river takes me.

"I'll help you find your father and seek my own path at the same time. Then someday I'll come back here with enough gold for my own herds and many wives, or even set myself up as a lord in Sumer." He held Jason in a wide-eyed gaze. It was strange to see a man with such broad shoulders pleading. "The river is dangerous. You could use a fighting man. You've seen that tonight. Will you let me come?"

Jason looked at Zidu, who nodded and smiled. "Can you leave right away?" Jason asked.

Rim-Hadad grinned. "I need only a moment to gather my weapons and my other tunic."

ooooo

They did not really discuss the evening's events until the next morning, after a night of drifting down the Jericho River, ever alert for rocks and rapids hidden by the darkness. Finally, the sun rose, casting long shadows across the plains by the shore. Jason raised the *Dead Valencia*'s sail, and the three sat down to talk.

"All I can tell you," said Rim-Hadad, "is that strangers have skulked around our territory for three days. At first, I thought they were goat thieves. Ha! They'd have paid in blood if they'd stolen from the son of Nablanum." He flexed his muscles. "But they paid no attention to the herds. It seemed they were watching the river."

"They must have had a boat in First Lagash," said Zidu. "They must have come ahead of us."

Rim-Hadad shifted on the hard planks of the deck. "If I planned an ambush, I'd do it in a land like this, near my own people—not in Sumer, where soldiers swarm like flies."

"And we walked right into their backyard," said Jason. "I'm an idiot, Zidu. I'm sorry I didn't listen to you."

"There is no need to apologize."

"But wait a second," Jason said. "How could they possibly know we'd come here?"

"That is one mystery," said Zidu, shaking his bald head. "And this Rector is another. Who can he be?" He stared at the river. "'Rector' is not a Sumerian or Akkadian name, or title," he finally said, sitting back on his lion haunches. "Nor is it Amorite, nor from any barbarian nation I know." Rim-Hadad nodded.

"I guess I've heard it before," said Jason. "At least it sounds familiar, from my world. But I don't know what it is."

"Do you have enemies in your world, Jason?" Rim-Hadad asked. They'd told the barbarian that Jason came from another world. "Does your family fight the blood feud?"

"No. I mean, I guess there's people I've pissed off once in a while, you know, saying the wrong thing." Obnoxious sarcasm was rarely the right thing. "But I don't think I've got any real enemies. And almost no one at home knows I'm here." No one but Doctor Valencia—whoever or whatever she was.

They pondered in silence, which was broken only by morning birdsong and the sound of waves splashing the hull.

"If the Rector's barbarians chased me all the way from Sumer," Jason finally said, "how do we know they won't keep on chasing me, wherever I go?"

ooooo

They saw no signs of human life on the right bank, except an occasional village. But as the days marched on, substantial towns returned to the left bank. They occupied a narrow strip of green-brown cultivated land separating the river from the desert.

One morning, Jason sat by the bow, lost in thought. Fore's mud-brick settlements weren't the first cities he'd seen by the edge of the desert. The summer *after*—after a drunk driver had taken his mother's life—Jason and his father and sister had taken a road trip across the American Southwest. They'd seen the Grand Canyon, Anasazi cliff dwellings, artists' colonies, the Hoover Dam, coyotes, and Indian reservations. But the best was the metropolis on the desert: Las Vegas.

Late one afternoon, Jason's father woke him from a front-seat snooze. Jason blinked and found the car had stopped at a deserted turnout. Beyond the windshield, a rocky slope rolled down to the plain, and an impossible city shone beneath the orange of a Nevada sunset.

"Let her sleep," said his father, cocking his head at Athena, who still snoozed in the back seat. "Let's have a look." They got out into the cool air, stretching their stiff joints.

Even from this distance, Jason could see the startling green of trees on city blocks in the middle of the desert, as well as the colored lights. Then his father handed him a little telescope and directed his gaze to the palaces of the Strip.

"Cool," Jason whispered as he caught sight of the great black pyramid, its tip aglow with electric light. The Luxor Hotel and Casino looked futuristic and ancient at the same time.

Jason's father put an arm around his shoulders. "You know," he said, "commercialism has made this world a dry and lonely place." Smile lines radiated from his gray eyes. "But once in a while, we make something cool. I don't care what it costs, we're staying there." Jason grinned. He knew his dad meant the pyramid.

He felt a pang of guilt as he relived the memory.

"Gods of rock and sand!" Rim-Hadad interrupted Jason's reverie. He pointed to the left bank. Beyond the strip of cultivated land, a pyramid rose over the desert. It was a mountain of smooth, white stone, culminating in a cap of sunlit gold. Its four-sided base covered acres, and its shadow stretched far along the riverside.

"Wondrous," Zidu said in a hushed voice. "It makes the temples of Sumer look like anthills. But look there!"

Jason and Rim-Hadad gasped as a titanic beast emerged from behind the pyramid. The creature had a lion's tawny body, the length of a football field, and a human head—or perhaps a giant's head. Its dark eyes shimmered, and it wore a King Tut headdress. Palm trees at the edge of the desert shook as its feet struck the ground.

"Remind me never to steal anything from a pyramid," Jason whispered. Rim-Hadad nodded vigorously.

"The Great Sphinx." Zidu sighed. "It is wondrous to see one so large and yet so like me. We must have reached the Old Kingdom of Egypt."*

---

* "Old Kingdom," "Middle Kingdom," and "New Kingdom" aren't countries. They're periods of Egyptian history, named by modern historians. The Old Kingdom ran from the 2600s BC to the 2100s, and it was the most creative period, when they laid down the basics of Egyptian culture. Two thousand years later, the Egyptians were still going back to Old Kingdom art and architecture and religion for inspiration.

All the big pyramids come from the Old Kingdom. The largest is the Great Pyramid of Giza, which has more than two million stone blocks averaging over two tons each. Many fit together so well that, to this day, you can't slide a knife-blade between them. Unfortunately, the pyramids weren't too effective as security systems for the kings' tombs. A big pyramid was like a gargantuan neon sign that said, "Attention treasure thieves! Gold and silver here!"

~ William Gallo, Lectures, History 56.

ooooo

The band of farmland grew broader as a wide, dark ribbon separated the river's blue from the desert's dusty yellow. Tiny huts stood among the irrigation canals there, and occasionally the *Dead Valencia* passed bustling cities, as well as great stone temples fronted by painted statues. The companions saw many lumins, too, though none quite so striking as the Great Sphinx. These included a falcon with a ram's head, a woman with wide cow's horns, and a talking hippo. All had a distinctively Egyptian style, very different from the creatures Jason had seen in Sumer. He guessed lumins matched the look of their country. He wondered if Fore included a modern, twenty-first century country. What kind of lumins would live there?

For several days, the travelers marveled at temples and palaces from the *Dead Valencia's* deck. Then for two days, they sailed past a borderland—a poorer country with fewer monuments. But finally the sun rose over an Egypt that was prosperous once again. The cities spread out across the left bank in even greater splendor.

"This must be the Middle Kingdom," said Jason, and Zidu agreed. So they stopped at a town crowded with mud-brick blockhouses and dark, friendly people, to ask where they might find Senusret.

A man selling good luck charms knew the name at once. "Yes, of course," said the merchant, who went clean-shaven and wore only a white linen skirt. "His temple lies just past Niwt-Wase. It's only a day's journey downstream. Go and ask. You will find him. Now, will you buy a lovely amulet?"

Jason almost hugged the merchant. Whatever had happened that night on the Sumerian temple platform, the priestess hadn't hallucinated. Senusret was real. He might know—*had* to know—where in this bizarre world Jason's father had gone.

ooooo

Late the next morning, Jason and Zidu stood before what the locals had called "Senusret's temple." They'd left Rim-Hadad to watch the *Dead Valencia*, then hiked more than two miles inland.

The temple was a collection of courtyards and columned buildings in front of a small, white pyramid. Most of the local traffic came in and out of a gate in a low wall, so Jason and Zidu chose that entrance. They found themselves in a long courtyard, lined with trees. People talked, laughed, and hurried back and forth, carrying food and baskets of goods. Some passed in and out of narrow openings in the mud-brick wall to their left. But the more formal-looking entrance was straight ahead, where a stone ramp led up to a large building.

Not knowing what else to do, Jason and Zidu walked up the ramp. Two spear-wielding guards in white skirts stood on the platform at the top. Behind them, a row of massive columns supported a stone roof. The columns were painted with colorful hieroglyphic writing, like holy graffiti.[†]

"Excuse me," said Jason to one of the guards. "I'm here to see Senusret. I was told this is his temple. Is he here?"

Dark eyebrows rose over eyes rimmed with black liner. "The Great Senusret?" the guard said. "You've come to see the Great Senusret?"

"Uh, yes. I ... My father's a friend of his."

The guard and his companion exchanged glances.

"Wait here," the first man said. Then he disappeared

---

† Hieroglyphic writing relied heavily on pictures, like ancient comic books. Up on the screen, we've got hieroglyphs from a cup found in King Tut's tomb. They read, "May he live, Horus, strong bull fair of births, the two goddesses, beautiful of ordinances, quelling the two lands, Horus of gold, wearing the diadems and propitiating the gods, the king of Upper and Lower Egypt, lord of the two lands, Neb Kheperu Re, granted life."

Hieroglyphs could read from left to right, right to left, or top to bottom. So how do you know where to start? It's easy. Look at the birds' beaks. They always point toward the beginning of the sentence.

~ William Gallo, Lectures, History 56.

between the columns and into the shadowy hall behind them. Soon he returned and stiffly proclaimed that someone would be with them shortly.

They waited ten or fifteen minutes, sitting at the edge of the stone ramp. Then a young woman in a white, sleeveless dress walked out of the columned hall. "Who asked for the Great Senusret?" she demanded.

Jason raised his hand meekly as he and Zidu rose to their feet. "I did."

The woman appraised them critically. She looked about Jason's age, really more girl than woman. She was slim, with long, black hair and wide brown eyes, rimmed in thick eyeliner. A turquoise beetle amulet hung from a cord around her neck.

"I am Tia, priestess of the temple," said the girl evenly. As she approached, Jason caught a faint scent, like cinnamon. "What is your name, please, and what's your business with the Great Senusret?"

"I'm Jason Gallo, and this is Zidu. We're looking for my father, Professor William Gallo. I think Senusret—the Great Senusret—might know where he is. I'd like to see him and ask."

Tia's expression grew disdainful. "You want to see the Great Senusret ... about finding a lost family member?" Her brow crinkled. "Do you have a scroll of credentials?"

"Well, no." Jason looked at Zidu, who shrugged.

"Well, I can't just let you *in*," she exclaimed. "Do you have any idea what you're asking? I'm sure you're some kind of tribal prince in your own country, but this is Egypt, the heart of the world. You can't just ask to see someone like the Great Senusret. And I can't interrupt him for every foreigner who comes looking for his father."

"But we don't need a lot of time! I just need to ask him—"

The priestess interrupted. "I'm sorry, there are a lot of very important people who want to see the Great Senusret and don't get to."

Jason had not come all this way to be turned back by a stuck-up, snotty girl, even if she did smell good. "Look, I'm *Lord* Jason Gallo, ruler of ... uh ... the humongous province of Oregon ... in the mighty kingdom of America. I'm here to see the Great Senusret on a quest of cosmic importance to all the people of Oregon. Are you going to tell him that the son of Lord William Gallo wants to see him or not?"

The guards shuffled their feet and glanced at Jason's T-shirt and shorts. But Tia did not seem impressed. She tapped a bare foot on the flagstones and regarded him through narrowed eyes.

"Very well," she finally said. "If it will set you on your way any sooner, I'll tell the Great Senusret your name and your request. Wait here, I may be a while."

"I thought you weren't a lord," Zidu whispered once she'd gone.

"I'll tell her I'm king of England if she gets any snottier."

"King of where?"

They waited for over an hour on the hot platform. Finally Tia returned, with a look of irritation on her face. "The Great Senusret will see you," she snapped. "Follow me." She turned on her heel in a swirl of black hair and stormed into the columned hall.

"I guess the Great Senusret wasn't that busy after all," Jason said to Zidu in a stage whisper.

The towering hall behind the guards was lined with thick pillars painted in bright colors. Illustrations of reeds and flowers decorated the columns, along with hieroglyphs. Even the stone ceiling had been painted. It was blue and dotted with stars and suns. At the far end stood an engraved door covered in shining bronze. Tia opened it, taking a burning torch from one of the four guards posted around the doorway.

Passing through was like stepping into a dark otherworld. Beyond the bronze door was a narrow tunnel of stone. Jason realized they must be inside the little pyramid, or beneath it. Tia led them down stairs and around sharp turns, veering into one narrow side-passage and then skipping another. Jason guessed the odds of ever getting back without a guide were one in fifty. The air grew cold, and only the wavering flame of Tia's torch lit their way.

Finally, after several minutes, a yellow glow appeared at the end of the tunnel. This gave little comfort because it came with an awful odor. The hall smelled of chemicals and rot, and it reminded Jason of the funeral home where they'd taken his mother. He bit his lip.

The light came from a small chamber full of handsome furniture and works of art, including painted statues and figurines of shining metals. Hieroglyphs and color illustrations decorated the stone walls. At the far end, a lean man in white sat in a high-backed chair, and an elderly woman stood next to him. The man wore a tall Egyptian crown, like a bowling pin in a red basket. His skin was pea-soup green. Jason's stomach turned as he realized the man wasn't exactly *dressed* in white. Rather, he was wrapped in white strips, from neck to wrist to toe, like a mummy. His eyes gleamed with lumin fire.

"O great and eternal Osiris Senusret!" said Tia, falling to her knees before the mummy, "Ruler in life over all the Middle Kingdom, beloved son of Osiris, and regent, in his name, over the dead, I present to you Lord Jason Gallo, ruler of Oregon, and his lumin companion, Zidu." Tia touched her forehead to the floor and then stood aside, leaving Jason facing Senusret.

"Greetings, Lord Jason and lumin Zidu," said the mummy. Jason cringed as he executed an awkward bow, wondering if he'd heard a hint of sarcasm around the word Lord. "You are both welcome in the tomb of Senusret." The dead king's voice was deep and even. "I knew your father long ago, Jason Gallo: an affable and interesting man. I granted him several interviews. I am sorry to hear he is lost, and I hope no harm has come to him."

"Thank you ... Your Majesty." Jason choked back a wave of disappointment. Obviously Senusret did not know where his father was. "I came because I'm trying to find my father. There was this priestess, in Sumer, and she said you'd know where he is. At least, she said I should come ask you." He caught a sympathetic nod from the white-haired woman next to Senusret. "My dad and I, we're not from your world, Fore. We're from another world, and that's where he's supposed to be. But he's somewhere here, and he may be in trouble. And you're the only lead I have. Do you have *any* idea where he might be?" He blinked away tears of frustration.

"Come closer, Jason Gallo," said Senusret.

Jason approached, hoping the dead king wouldn't touch him but also filled with morbid curiosity. Was he really talking to a corpse? Senusret sat stiff and still, arms crossed over his mummy-wrapped chest. He held a golden crook in one green hand, and in the other some kind of wand, with short rods dangling from its top, like tiny nunchucks. A rope-like, black beard hung from the center of his chin, and he looked neither young nor old.

"Yes, I can see the resemblance," he said. Gleaming eyes rimmed in black liner gazed at Jason. "It is not strong, but I think it runs deep." The dead king nodded, still stiff. "I know of your Sumerian priestess. I sensed her mind and her goddess weeks ago, and I felt that she searched for your father. But I do not know where he is. It is nearly thirteen years since William Gallo visited me, and I never learned where he went after."

Jason stared at the white wrappings covering Senusret's feet, biting his lip. "Well, um, do you ... do you know where he came *from*—where he was before he came here?"

The dead king turned to the old woman. "Nebetit, you spoke with William Gallo many times. From what land did he come to us?"

"He came from Crete, oh great and eternal king," said the old woman. "He brought tokens of introduction from the king there, from the palace of Red Knossos."

The dead king nodded, and Jason sighed. The Egyptians' information was thirteen years old—at least, thirteen Fore years.

"Do you know—Your Majesty—do you know how long it takes to get to this Crete place?"

"Perhaps two weeks by sail, down the Jericho River, and much longer by land."

Jason glanced at Zidu, who nodded, looking uncomfortable. A trip to Crete would waste time if it was a dead end, but what else did they have?

He turned back to find the smallest of smiles on Senusret's lips. He gulped as it occurred to him that visitors didn't usually

ask the dead king for travel tips, or even glance away during
an interview.

"Uh, thank you very much for seeing us, Your Majesty. I'm
sorry if I did anything wrong."

"I wish I could counsel you more," said Senusret. "But
whatever you choose to do, I see that you need rest and comfort before you set out again. You and your companion will be
guests of my temple." This was not so much an invitation as
a command. "Perhaps some guidance will come with prayer.
My master, the great god Osiris, protects lost fathers and their
sons. After all, he was killed but then redeemed by his son,
mighty Horus. As Osiris was redeemed by Horus, may your
father be redeemed, Jason Gallo, and returned to you."[‡]

ooooo

The priestess Nebetit was called the high chantress, and
she seemed to be in charge. She assigned Tia to look after the
travelers, to the young priestess's obvious dismay. "Foreigners
and barbarians," she muttered, "just what I need."

Rim-Hadad, for his part, was very impressed with Tia.
"Quite a little lioness, isn't she?" he kept saying.

They stayed in a complex of mud-brick villas just outside
the temple. Nebetit and the other senior priests and priestesses lived there, as did Tia.

---

‡ As a young god, Osiris marries his sister, Isis, and rules Egypt. His evil
brother, Set, wants the throne and kills Osiris. Isis, however, resurrects her
husband and lies with him, becoming pregnant. Soon Set discovers the resurrection, and he kills Osiris again. This time, he chops the body into little pieces.
But even this seemingly foolproof strategy fails. Perhaps Set should have killed
Isis, because she collects the pieces—except the genitals, which have been eaten
by fish—reassembles them, and wraps them in linen, making Osiris the first
mummy. Even worse for Set, Isis gives birth to Osiris's son, the hawk-headed
god Horus. Horus grows up and fights his evil uncle. Neither wins, but Horus
does manage to crush Set's genitals. Eventually, the council of gods decides
that Horus is Osiris's rightful heir, not Set. So Horus becomes king of the living,
while mummified Osiris rules as king of the dead.
  ~ William Gallo, *Palace of the Sphinx*, 59.

"Tia is the orphan daughter of our departed second prophet," Nebetit explained to Jason, "She lives with us, and we have raised her as a dedicated priestess and our own daughter. She is a dear child, though not always an easy one." Jason agreed with that last part.

After weeks in the world of Fore, the complex felt like a luxury hotel. Each traveler had a whitewashed room and a bed made of reeds and wood. Best of all, the villas had *bathrooms*. Jason's toilet was just a box with a hole in it, but pipes beneath carried the waste away, which was all that mattered. He also had a bronze hand mirror, and though his black hair was a rat's nest, he was delighted to see that sun and fresh air had driven the acne from his face.

The day after they arrived, Jason went to ask Nebetit about his father's visit. He and Zidu found the high chantress sitting by a small stone pond in her private garden. Birds chattered from the trees, and a very large cat stalked the undergrowth.§

"Your father came here to study," Nebetit recalled. "He wanted to learn about lumins, of all things. He spent his time talking with them, especially the dead master, the Great Senusret. And he watched as the lumins lent power to the priests, to cure the sick and bring forth healthy crops. He asked many questions, in the manner of one who's never seen the rites." She looked over the surface of the pond and shook her head. "He said people in your world have forgotten lumins. I could not imagine such a thing."

Unfortunately, Nebetit did not know why Jason's father had been studying lumins.

"I don't think he learned what he'd hoped to," she said. "I think he found his time in Crete more helpful. The Minos

---

§ Around 8500 BC, wild felines started living near Stone Age villages, because the farmers' grain attracted rodents. We don't really know when cats switched from semi-tame neighbors to domestic pets, bred by humans. The earliest records of breeding come from Egypt around 1500 BC, so it's possible the Egyptians led the way. In any case, today's domestic cats are smaller, calmer, and wimpier than their main wild ancestor, *Felis silvestris libyca*. Cat-breeders apparently chose the runts of the litter over and over. That's why the average modern cat can kill a mouse but not a rat, though both make easy prey for *Felis silvestris libyca*.

~ William Gallo, *Historical Factoids*, 13.

kings were great lovers of lore in their day, so perhaps your father found some treasure house of knowledge there."

The Minos kings? Jason knew the name King Minos.

Nebetit could shed no light on Jason's other mystery either. "I have never heard of this Rector," she said. "And I cannot guess why anyone would want to harm you. I will pray for you—and for your father." She cast Jason a sympathetic look. "You must love him and miss him terribly."

"Yeah, I must."

"I liked your father very much. Such an unusual scholar … I convinced him to tell me some of his ideas. He had strange beliefs. Many must be wrong, but I enjoyed hearing them."

"Strange beliefs?" Like, *all work and no play makes Will a fun guy*? "What kind?"

"It was so long ago, I'm afraid I remember very little." She looked up at Jason. "I do remember one though, because I found it so lovely. He said that our world is made up of dreams—dreams from *your* world."

"What?"

She nodded vigorously, setting her bronze earrings jingling. "I know, it's odd. But that's what he said. He said your people's dreams never fade, so when someone in your world awakens, his dream remains on the ether. For countless years, your people's dreams have collected and formed themselves into a world—the world of Fore. Your father said our world is literally made of dreams—of all your people's dreams." Her brow crinkled. "I can't remember what role he said the gods play, but I thought it a beautiful story. A world made of dreams!"

"Fascinating," said Zidu.

ooooo

Later that day, Tia came to fetch Jason. "The dead master has summoned you. You're to come to the tomb, immediately."

Tia was all dressed up. A white linen dress hugged her slender figure, and she wore a beaded headband over her shining black hair, as well as bronze bracelets on bare upper arms and wrists. Jason had to admit she looked very pretty.

"Is something going on?" he asked as he followed her through the temple's great hall. Priests and servants were rushing around there.

"A high counselor has come from the dead master's grandson." Tia looked back at Jason. "That's the king—the *living* one—in case you didn't know. We're just getting ready for the visit. The king wants the Great Senusret's advice, and the Great Senusret wanted to see you before he gets too busy."

Jason grew uneasy as he followed Tia into the pyramid's stone tunnels, this time without Zidu's reassuring company. The stale whiff of embalming chemicals soon masked the cinnamon scent of the young priestess's perfume. He thought again of his mother and the funeral home.

All remained quiet in Senusret's underground apartment. Nebetit stood by the throne, and a young scribe knelt nearby. "Welcome, Jason Gallo," said Senusret as Jason bowed. "I hope you have found your stay at my temple restful."

"Yes, I have, Your Majesty. Thank you."

The dead king sat crowned and stiff as usual, but he'd laid his crook and wand aside. Both green hands were cupped around a ceramic jar with a stopper shaped like a dog's head.

"I called you here to share some surprising news," he said. "I have spent much of today in meditation." He held up the jar. "Often I meditate on this. It is my stomach, which was removed during my mummification."¶ Jason managed not to gag. "Some days, when I hold this in my hands and quiet my mind, I hear the winds of the ether. Today was such a day,

---

¶ Egyptian mummification started with removal of the stomach, intestines, lungs, and liver. These were preserved in special containers, called canopic jars, and entombed with the mummy. Next came the brain, taken out through the nostrils with metal hooks. The process must have torn the brain apart, but it wasn't considered important. The heart stayed in the body; the Egyptians considered it the home of the mind. Next, the embalmers treated the body with salt and chemicals and dried it. Then, the empty cavities were filled with linen. Finally, the body was wrapped in linen and laid in a coffin. The process took seventy days.

~ William Gallo, *Historical Factoids*, 18.

and today I heard a voice on the wind." His glowing eyes were bright in the lamp-lit tomb. "Today a great mind reached out from far away, Jason Gallo—looking for you. I have promised to send you down the river, to meet this mighty shaman."

4

Chariots and Ruins

WE DON'T KNOW WHAT the ancient Cretans called themselves, but we call them "Minoans," from the Greek myth about Crete's King Minos.

Fertile Crescent civilization was spreading out from the river valleys in those days, and it reached Crete around 2000 BC. The island's rulers probably got rich as merchants, sailing the Mediterranean. They didn't have any real cities, but they did build these sprawling complexes of stone—pseudo-cities, really—which became the centers of Cretan civilization: palaces or temples or maybe both. Unlike most Bronze Agers, the Minoans didn't put up a lot of fortifications. They didn't even have walls around their complexes. The sea was probably their security system, along with their navies. Nice, but it didn't last.

We call Europe's southeastern corner "Greece" because Indo-European nomads invaded it some time after 2000 BC, and they spoke Greek. They eventually settled down, but they kept a lot of barbarian traditions, especially their love of a good war. Around 1450, Greek pirates hit Crete like a storm. In the long run, the Greek conquest left nothing behind but ruined palaces and legends of King Minos.

~ William Gallo, Recorded Lectures, History 113: Comparative Decline (Spring Semester 2002).

ooooo

"This shaman is a very old woman and very strong," said Senusret. "Strong enough to cast her mind across countless miles, looking for you."

"But what did she say?" Jason demanded. "Who is she?" He sensed he should not be interrogating a king, dead or alive.

"She is a great lady of an empire called Rome, far down the river, and she is a high priestess of Isis. She lives in the province of Tarraco-Hispania, in the capital." He shook his head. "I heard no name across the ether, but I did see her in my mind's eye. She has white hair and a thousand wrinkles on her face—the lines of wisdom. That will not help you, of course, but I can tell you enough to find her. Go down the river to this place, this Tarraco-Hispania. It is perhaps two months' journey. Go and find the high priestess of Isis, in the capital. She will know you."

Tarraco-Hispania? "But, um, Your Majesty, I was going to Crete. That seemed like ... like the best place to look."

"No. A journey to Crete can serve no purpose now. This high priestess would not have summoned you if your father remained on Crete. You must look to her for guidance. Any travel involves danger, so you should avoid detours."

Jason gnawed his lip as Senusret continued. "I learned something more in my trance, both from this great priestess and from even more distant minds—minds I could hardly touch." The dead king's green lips bent into a frown. "A great wrong has been done downriver, a wrong I cannot understand or even name. People there are suffering, and they are waiting. They wait for help from upriver. Perhaps, Jason, your quest serves a larger purpose than you know."

ooooo

Late that night, after the commotion surrounding the high counselor's visit had died down, Nebetit summoned Jason to her sitting room. Tia arrived just as he did, still dressed in her VIP-finery. "Ah, you two," said Nebetit. "Please sit."

Frogs croaked in the garden outside as they sat on floor mats near the high chantress's chair.

"Jason," said Nebetit, her voice hoarse, "I have spoken with the dead master about his instructions to you, and he wants me to help. The temple will give you food and supplies for your journey, and silver to spend."

"Thanks!" Jason exclaimed. "That'd be great."

"And I'll give some additional aid," Nebetit continued. "The Great Senusret promised this high priestess of Isis that he would send you to her." She turned to Tia. "Tia, you will be the agent of that promise. I want you to go with Jason and see that he reaches our sister down the river."

"Me?" cried Tia. "I don't want to go with him. Why me?"

Nebetit's faced had turned as hard as stone. "Because you are a priestess of the temple, and your high chantress tells you so."

Tia shrank into her mat. "Yes, High Chantress."

The old woman reached for her hands. "You are a dear child, and you know I love you," Nebetit said. "I want you to go for your own sake, too. The dead master says this high priestess is strong in the ways of the gods. I think you will learn from her. And you and I both know that some time away can only aid your career in the temple." She stroked Tia's face. "Your temper has offended some important people, and I will not always be here to watch out for you. With time away, you will grow and others will forget."

Tia looked down, and black hair draped her face, so Jason couldn't see her expression. For a split second, he'd been pleased she was going to join the quest—until she'd opened her mouth: *I don't want to go with him.* In any case, he was going to Crete, not the Roman Empire, though he couldn't tell the Egyptians that.

He cleared his throat. "High Chantress, I'd just *love* to have Tia come. But we've already had some problems with barbarians, and we might run into more, uh, unfriendlies. Maybe this isn't such a great idea."

"No," the priestess drawled, "I think this is indeed a great idea. You will need allies, perhaps more than you realize. And I predict Tia will be the most ferocious ally you could have. And

I think you will find her a persuasive and persistent advocate."
A wry grin creased Nebetit's lined face. "I sense you don't trust
the Great Senusret's message, and you aren't sure whether to
keep his promise to this priestess of Rome. I send Tia for my
own reasons as much as for yours."

ooooo

The hot sun and the *Dead Valencia*'s gentle rocking had
lulled Jason into daydreams.

A few months before the coma, he'd stopped by the university to meet his father after school. He'd walked in on a history
department beer and pretzels party. Before he could signal his
dad and make a quick getaway, someone had called out, "I
know who *you* are!" A woman in her twenties was smiling at
him. She had long, feathery blonde hair and wore a low-cut
blouse and snug jeans that showed off her figure. "You're Jason
Gallo," she said. "I've seen your picture in your dad's office, but
you're much better looking in person."

Jason flushed as she continued. "I'm Candace Fleming, one
of the peons here. In other words, I'm a grad student. Anyway,
everyone calls me Candi. It's a terrible name for a historian,
don't you think, Jason? It sounds like a weathergirl, or a porn
star." She flashed a brilliant smile and twirled a tassel from her
belt around one little finger. "*You've* got an excellent name, full
of myth. And your sister! You two are lucky."

Jason had never liked his name, but he was delighted Candi
did. He was even more delighted that she stayed by his side,
babbling on as they nibbled pretzels and the party swirled
around them. She seemed to know all about his father's work.

"I love the controversy," she enthused, "and your father's
focus on spiritual icons—and the way he thumbs his nose at
old conventions. Has he told you about the new book?"

Jason shook his head, which was spinning from trying to
keep up with Candi.

"Oh, Jason, it'll be the best one yet. It does much more than teach about ancient religions. It's actually going to show how mythology still shapes our thinking today—even in a world full of science and cynicism. It'll tell all of us where to find myth and magic in our daily lives."

"Huh!" said Jason, finally getting a word in. "Sounds like a self-help book for wannabe psychics."

Candi laughed, putting a warm hand on his arm, and Jason flushed again, excited to have scored a point. Soon his father joined them, grinning. He always seemed happy to see his son at work.

As the three talked, Jason noticed that Candi's eyes now focused mostly on his father. And several times she reached out to touch his arm, and her hand lingered longer than it had on Jason's. He grew tense and quiet. Didn't Candi know his dad was old, and that his wife had died only two years before?

"Jason!" said a sharp voice, dislodging him from the memory. "We're drifting toward the shore again. Aren't you paying attention?"

Jason looked up to find Tia staring down at him, hands on hips. He sighed and got up to correct their course.

He'd told himself he'd enjoy having someone his own age on the *Dead Valencia*. He didn't. Tia criticized everything from Jason's sailing to the lack of privacy, even after they'd crafted the cloth tent for her use at night. And though she bore the loss of Egyptian luxuries surprisingly well, her temper was getting shorter every day. She was particularly unhappy about Jason's plan to stop in Crete.

"Isn't that exactly what you did before?" she'd exclaimed. "Didn't you have perfectly reliable magical advice from that Sumerian priestess, telling you to come see the Great Senusret? And you ignored it and went off to visit barbarians." At this point, she'd cast a narrow-eyed glance at Rim-Hadad. "And you almost got killed. Well now you're doing the same thing again. You've got an Egyptian *king* telling you not to bother with Crete—to go see this high priestess of Isis, in the empire of Rome. And you're ignoring him. Don't you ever learn from your mistakes?"

Geography, however, was on Jason's side. Crete lay downriver along their route to the Roman Empire, so his plan to stop there wouldn't involve much of a detour. But that hadn't satisfied Tia. "You said your barbarian stop was *on the way*, too," she'd argued.

Jason's usually sharp tongue was no match for Tia's temper. Yet he was sure of his choice. No one was warning him about dangerous barbarians this time, so he wasn't going to be sidetracked by mystical dreams about an old lady witch doctor. This *shaman power*—this magic—did seem to work, but he couldn't guess how much was real and how much was superstition. He didn't plan to spend months on a wild goose chase.

ooooo

Early one morning, nearly two weeks after they'd left the Middle Kingdom, a ridge of rocky, yellow land, festooned with cliffs, rose beyond the prow. The island separated the Jericho River into two wide, blue-green channels.

"That must be Crete," said Jason.

Red Knossos, Crete's principal settlement, lay along the right-hand channel, so they bore to starboard.

"Ha!" said Rim-Hadad later that morning. He pointed to the yellow countryside along the right bank, where a rocky fortress perched between a village and a forest. For the first time, they were seeing real construction on the right bank. "I'll wager a fierce tribe lives there."

But the view that afternoon impressed him even more. A chariot rumbled down a dusty road by the shore. Zidu, Tia, and Rim-Hadad stared wide-eyed at the bronze-armored charioteer and his driver, and at their horses.

"What a marvel!" enthused the barbarian. "Think of the speed! Think of the power you'd have on the battlefield, pulled by such beasts!"

Jason realized he couldn't remember seeing horses in Fore until now.*

The companions met a fisherman on the river later that day and asked for directions to Red Knossos. They reached it the next morning. They hid the *Dead Valencia* in a thicket near a stream and then hiked into the interior, crossing through quiet woods and over yellow fields. They saw a settlement in the distance but then found a road leading inland.

"This looks like a king's road," said Zidu, impressed.

Many of the paving stones had cracked, but the thoroughfare cut a straight, wide path across the plain. The road was nearly silent, except for the smacking of Tia's and Rim-Hadad's sandals and the tread of Jason's sneakers. Soon they found themselves between rows of square, stone houses, marching in line down each side of the road. The houses were deserted, and many had crumbled to heaps of rock and wood. Those that still stood were impressive and must have once been handsome. But now shadows lurked beyond wooden window and doorframes and in bare rooms.

"I wonder why they're abandoned," Jason said, his voice low.

Soon, a stone monument rose into view atop a yellow hill, like a giant **U** or a pair of bull's horns pointing into the sky. In the morning sun, the monument cast long shadows on an enormous assembly of buildings covering the hilltop.

"That must be the palace," said Jason.

"There's something wrong with that place," Tia whispered. The hill was perfectly still. They saw no people or animals

---

* The steppe barbarians rode bareback, but people in the Fertile Crescent didn't ride horses much during the Bronze Age, and they certainly didn't ride into battle. If you're going to fight from horseback without falling off and getting killed, you need a really stable saddle, which wasn't invented until after 1000 BC. The light chariot came along first, and it became the ultimate weapon of the late Bronze Age. As for horses themselves, they weren't even particularly popular as beasts of burden until chariot-fighting came along. Donkeys are sturdier, and originally they weren't much smaller. Wild horses are pony-sized, and bigger ones evolved over time through breeding, once enough people realized their value.

~ William Gallo, e-mail to Candace Fleming, "RE: Horse Research" (December 3, 2010).

around the buildings, and they heard nothing.

A rumble drew their gaze to the plain beside the hill. Three chariots were racing toward them, behind galloping horses. The sun reflected off helmets and blades. The charioteers had arrows notched on bowstrings.

"What do we do?" cried Jason.

"Run!" Rim-Hadad bellowed. "We can't fight those things!"

They turned and sprinted down the road. Jason yelped as an arrow clattered against the paving stones at his feet. More fell around them as they reached the slope beneath the looming palace. As they pelted uphill, the rumbling wheels grew louder. Jason glanced back. The chariots had veered onto the road behind them. Thundering hooves, cruel blades, and fierce men in bronze flew toward the travelers before clouds of dust. Tia, running behind Jason, looked back and shrieked. How could they outrun horses?

Jason's legs burned as he poured all his strength into running. An arrow whizzed past his ear, and more fell at the runners' feet. But then he realized he'd reached the top of the hill. Gasping, he leapt off the road, amazed that he'd beaten the chariots to the palace. He hurtled over a low, crumbling wall, just behind Zidu. Tia and Rim-Hadad scrambled over seconds later, and they all looked down at the chariots.

The horses had stopped halfway up the hill. The road's last leg was smooth and straight—perfect for chariots—but the riders did not drive another foot toward the stone horns looming over the palace. They stood in their chariots shouting and shaking their bows. The horses stamped and whinnied.

"Thank the gods, they stopped!" cried Tia.

"Yes," said Zidu. "But how will we ever leave this place with enemies in the countryside, waiting to strike?" He turned to face the complex behind them and looked over the silent domain of pillars, balconies, and dark windows. "And what stopped them from coming here? What could frighten such warriors?"

ooooo

Shadows and near silence greeted the travelers in the palace of Red Knossos. The complex had once been beautiful. But it appeared a fire years before had reduced it to a bare labyrinth of cream-colored stone and dark red pillars. Debris cluttered many of the floors, including broken pottery and tablets covered in strange writing.[†] The four explored eerie corridors, arcades, and empty rooms, looking almost reluctantly for signs of life. They saw several wide stairways leading to higher levels—possibly even to a third story—but they stuck to the ground floor. Many of the walls had fallen, and some entire wings were more rubble than structure, so they didn't risk climbing to floors that might collapse.

Some of the murals had escaped fire damage. Sunlight filtered through windows and open arcades, as well as broken walls and ceilings, so the companions had no trouble viewing the artwork.

"Beautiful," Tia said softly.

Jason agreed. Lovely spiral and flower patterns surrounded illustrations of fish, animals, and people. One striking mural showed an acrobat somersaulting over the back of a charging bull. And another image appeared again and again: an axe with two blades. "I wonder if that's what they use on visitors," he whispered.

After creeping about the ruins for almost an hour, they stumbled into a courtyard longer than a football field. Many of the surrounding buildings had crumbled, but several structures stood tall, topped with rows of white stone horns. They stood, wondering which building to search.

"Do you hear that?" Tia hissed suddenly.

They froze. Somewhere in the palace, heavy feet thudded against hard floors. Jason held his breath as he scanned the

---

† No one has fully deciphered "Linear A," the Minoans' writing system. The following is Linear A script found on a gold pin:

𐘁 𐘂 𐙃 𐙄 · 𐘃 𐘥 𐙅 𐙆 𐙇 𐙈 𐙉 𐙊 𐙋 𐙌 𐙍 𐙎 𐙏 𐙐

~ William Gallo, "A Comparative Analysis of Bronze Age Funerary Inscriptions from the Eastern Mediterranean," 21 *Northern Archive* 289, 291 (2002).

courtyard. Nothing moved. "Hello?" he finally called, speaking above a whisper for the first time since they'd arrived. Tia glared at him. "Is anyone there?"

"Look!" Rim-Hadad whispered.

A shadow moved across a second-floor window on the other side of the courtyard.

"Maybe whoever it is doesn't want to be bothered," Tia whispered back.

"I don't care," said Jason. "We came all this way. The least they can do is talk to us, just for a minute. I only want to ask if they've seen my father." He drew a deep breath. "Let's go up there."

Rim-Hadad threw his shoulders back and brandished his club. "I'll go first!"

A wide, white staircase climbed up from the courtyard. They followed it to the second level and crept down a dim hall. The floor seemed steady enough. Jason's heart hammered as they hunted quietly through rooms of all sizes. Some were dark and full of shadows, some lit by bright sun from windows or gaps in walls and ceilings. Broken pots and worn furniture littered the floors.

Just after they'd turned into a wide, bare hallway lined with windows, they heard movement again. Creaks and bangs and stomps echoed through the palace, but at first they seemed to come from all directions. Soon, though, the companions realized the noise came from behind them, from the room they'd just left. The four huddled near the center of the hall as a shadow moved across the doorway.

Even Rim-Hadad's eyes widened as someone, some *thing*, entered. It was an enormous, nearly naked man, taller than Rim-Hadad, with the black head of a bull, as well as a bull's tail. Thick, sharp horns rose toward the ceiling over gleaming lumin eyes. Those eyes blazed as they fell on the four trespassers. With an earth-shaking roar, the beast lowered its head and charged.

"Blood of the gods!" Rim-Hadad bellowed. He sprinted to meet the monster, swinging his club. The club came down on the beast's head and bounced out of the barbarian's hand.

Not even dazed, the monster roared, "Barbarian!" and backhanded Rim-Hadad so hard he flew across the room. He landed in a heap by the windows and lay still.

"Wait! Wait!" Zidu shouted, leaping on feline feet toward the other lumin. The monster jumped over him and bore down on Tia and Jason. They scrambled, but too slowly. The creature's fist caught Jason in the belly with the force of an earthquake, sending him tumbling over the floor. His head hit the far wall with a crack.

Dazed, Jason tried to get his bearings as he heard Tia scream. "King Minos," he gasped, blinking and shaking his head. A memory flooded his dizzied brain. Nebetit had mentioned "the Minos kings," and Jason had known the name. He remembered sitting on his father's lap, listening to the story of King Minos and the monster he kept in a labyrinth. The monster had the body of a man and the head of a bull.

"King Minos ... King Minos ..." He was still trying to clear his head. Was this King Minos's monster?

"The Minos king?" bellowed a subterranean voice.

Jason's vision finally cleared, and he saw the bull-man standing like a tower of beefy muscle. One hand held Zidu by the throat, high above the floor. The lion-man squirmed like a kitten in its mother's mouth. Tia cowered at the monster's feet.

"Who calls on the Minos king?" The voice shook like a volcano's warning as the monster turned toward Jason. "Who dares?"

Jason gulped. What had he done?

"I dare!" Tia cried, rising to her feet and stepping back. "I am Egyptian. My people and the Minos kings were always friends." She held up the turquoise beetle amulet hanging from her neck. "You see? Egyptian! You owe me more courtesy than this!"

Jason's head swam as the monster's tiny, gleaming eyes peered down at Tia's amulet. "Yes! You *are* Egyptian!" it rumbled, amazed.

The hand around Zidu's neck loosened, and the lion-man fell to the floor. Zidu drew a gasping breath. "She's Egyptian," he rasped. "And none of us is your enemy, as I would have told you if you'd stopped to hear the words of a fellow lumin!"

"Egyptian!" the beast exclaimed again. "No Egyptian has set foot in this place for over a century, since the days of the Minos kings." It stepped back, straightening its only article of clothing, a ragged loincloth. Then, to Jason's surprise, it bowed. "You at least are welcome, lady of Egypt. I am the Minotaur, Minos's bull, and I'm sorry for the fright I gave you."

Jason sighed and fingered his scalp. He wasn't bleeding, but he could feel a lump forming. He looked up to see Rim-Hadad rising behind the Minotaur, and he hoped the big barbarian wouldn't start the fight again.

Tia noticed, too. She raised her chin proudly, though she was still shaking. "Thank you for your welcome," she said, "even if it was a bit rough. These people came with me, and they're friends of Egypt. We were all sent by an Egyptian monarch, Senusret, king of the dead." She strode pointedly over to Jason and helped him to his feet. "So I'd appreciate it if you could be gentler with my companions and welcome them, too."

The Minotaur snorted. "I don't remember Egyptians ever traveling with barbarians." He glanced back at Rim-Hadad. "But if these are your companions, I'll do them no harm, so long as they don't overstay their welcome. Now I guess there's some reason you've violated my privacy and invaded the sacred House of the Labrys. Come with me, and you can tell me what it is!"

He stormed out of the room. Shaken but afraid to disobey, the travelers followed. The Minotaur led them back down the white steps to a handsome room separated from the grand courtyard by dark red pillars. Images of griffins decorated red walls, and a white stone chair stood at one end.

"Sit down," the Minotaur commanded, "but not in that chair. That was the priestess' seat."

There were stone benches against the walls, but these were cluttered with pots and cups and other odds and ends, including several human skulls. Jason wondered if they belonged to travelers who hadn't been graced with an Egyptian companion.

Lacking a better place, the four sat on the stone floor. "Red Knossos didn't always greet travelers this way," the Minotaur rumbled, as he, too, sat cross-legged on the floor. "These are bad times, thanks to the Greeks."

"The Greeks?" asked Tia, brushing dark hair behind her ears. "Are they the horrible warriors with the chariots?"

"Yes. Some call them Achaeans or Hellenes or Mycenaeans, but they're all Greeks to me. They're little better than barbarians, like him." He thrust his bristly, bovine chin at Rim-Hadad. The big man's dark eyes narrowed. "They came here a century ago and destroyed the beautiful palaces, and they killed the last Minos king. It was a black day."

"How awful!" cried Tia. Jason guessed she liked the Minotaur and her special, Egyptian treatment.

"But this palace wasn't destroyed a century ago," said Zidu. "The fire damage looks more recent."

"This is the House of the Labrys," said the Minotaur. "It's always been the first house of Crete, so the Greeks left it standing, to rule from here. But then the fools burned it down years ago, in one of their constant wars. Crete is a shadow of its former self, and all the towns and villages have shrunk, thanks to the Greeks."

"Barbarians!" Tia spat. "I'm sure these Greeks will never amount to anything."

Rim-Hadad rolled his eyes.

"But, sir," said Zidu, "I don't understand. If your own people were conquered a century ago, why are you still here?"

"This is my place!" the Minotaur roared. The four shifted and looked around for the exits. "I stay because I belong here," he continued. "I am Minos's bull." His voice softened. "And I hoped to do some good. I hoped I could convince the Greeks to treat the Minoan people gently. So I spent a long century with people who did not love me—who only kept me as a symbol of the old power."

"That must have been hard," said Zidu. "I have lived with people who did not truly want me, and it was very hard. I feel for you."

"Thank you," the Minotaur rumbled.

"But you are still here," Zidu persisted. "Even the Greeks

are gone from this palace now. You are alone—a lumin without humans."

"Yes, all alone …" The Minotaur's voice trailed off. Then he growled. "I told you, the House of the Labrys is my place. I have been here centuries, since before the great volcano,[‡] since before the Greeks darkened our shores. Besides, no humans need me now. Even the Minoans have forgotten Minos's bull." He snorted, sending a sea spray shooting from his black nostrils. "Only the stones of holy Red Knossos remember me. I stay for them, and I protect this place from trespassers." His gleaming eyes narrowed. "If I didn't cherish the memory of Egyptian visitors to the Minos kings, you'd have died like the rest. So what are you doing here? Why have you violated my privacy?"

Zidu closed his eyes.

The others turned to Jason, who gulped as he glanced at the Minotaur's titanic muscles and sharp horns. "Well, it's because of me, but I didn't mean any disrespect. We came because I'm looking for someone … someone who stayed here for a while, maybe thirteen years ago.

"He wasn't a Greek," Jason added hastily. "He came from very far away. And he was probably dressed kind of like me."

The Minotaur peered at Jason's shorts and T-shirt. "Can you mean Professor Gallo?"

"Yes! You know him? I can't believe it! I'm his son, and he's lost somewhere, and I'm trying to find him. Do you know where he is?"

"No," said the Minotaur. "I haven't heard of him in years, since before this house burned. But I'd like to." He seemed to cheer up, though Jason doubted a bull could smile. "You're his son, eh? Well, then you're welcome, too. Professor Gallo was a ray of

---

‡ During the early 1600s BC, one of the strongest volcanic eruptions in history struck the island of Thera, just north of Crete. It destroyed much of the island, sending the sea rushing in and wiping out the Minoan towns there. Thera's destruction may explain the Greek legend of Atlantis, the ancient island nation drowned by the gods. The resulting tidal wave and fallout may also have weakened the Minoans on Crete, opening the island up to Greek invasion.

~ William Gallo, *The Trouble with Saints and Satyrs: The Role of Myth in the Development of Western Civilization* (New York, 2004), 11.

sunshine in a forest of barbarians. We spoke many times. In fact, I was the chief reason he came to the House of the Labrys."

ooooo

Jason and the Minotaur talked into the afternoon. Zidu listened, while Tia and Rim-Hadad napped.

"You can rest in safety here," said the Minotaur. "The Greeks must be prowling the outer grounds, waiting for you, but neither Greeks nor pirates will enter holy Red Knossos. They all fear Minos's bull." Jason's father had made two visits to Red Knossos thirteen or fourteen years before. He'd stayed several weeks each time, and between visits, he'd traveled to Sumer and back, via Egypt.

"The Greek lords treated him with respect," said the Minotaur. "They liked him, and they could see he was a great man, from his fine clothes. He told them he was a scholar, but of course they'd never heard that word."

"What was he doing here?"

"Studying lumins. He traveled all over Crete, asking us questions. There were many Greek lumins here in Red Knossos, but he spoke with me more than any of them. I was his favorite." The Minotaur raised his chin proudly. "That's why he came back after his trip upriver. He wanted to ask me more questions."

"Did he say why he was studying lumins?"

"I don't remember." The Minotaur scratched between his horns. "It was very odd. I'd never heard of anyone with that kind of interest in lumins before. He asked all about my past and how my life changed when the Greeks came—and how I felt surrounded by foreigners. He was a strange man, I suppose, but I was glad he'd come. No one had paid me much attention since the days of the Minos kings." He peered at Jason. "You know, you remind me of him."

Best of all, the Minotaur knew where Jason's father had gone after Crete. "He went far down the river, to a country he'd visited before. It was called Traco-hispaco, or something like that."

"Tarraco-Hispania?" Jason inquired. "The province of Tarraco-Hispania, in the Roman Empire?"

"Yes!" cried the Minotaur. "That was it."

Jason looked at Zidu.

"Well," said the lion-man, "Tia will be pleased. Now we will certainly keep Senusret's promise to the Roman priestess."

ooooo

That evening, Jason and Zidu stood on a half-fallen wall at the edge of the complex. Clouds on the horizon burned pink and orange as the sun sank into the west. Nearby, the river's right-hand channel wound its way between yellow hills, then joined the left channel at the tip of the island. From there, the blue waterway meandered into the distance and disappeared over the horizon. Jason wondered when he'd realized the Jericho River was a timeline.

"Why do you think your father studied lumins?" Zidu asked after a while. A light wind ruffled his black beard. "And why our friend the Minotaur? Why him more than the Greek lumins, or Senusret, or the other lumins of Egypt?"

"Who knows?" Jason growled. "He's always off on some stupid research project. All he ever thinks about is his work."

They stared at the town below the palace, toy-like in the distance. "You know," said Zidu quietly, "the Minotaur is mad."

"What?" Jason turned to face his friend. The great stone horns loomed behind the lion-man, gray against the darkening sky. "He's crazy?"

"He should have left here long ago, after the Greeks killed the Minos king and his court. Or he should have died. We lumins exist to share life with humans, and to help them. Imagine, the Minotaur lived a century with those Greek lords, who had their own lumins and did not love him. It would push any of us toward madness. But what he's done now hurts him far more." Zidu's face was long. "He has lived for years in this maze, with *no* humans. I think that is why he finally lost his mind. That is why he has become a killer. Lumins do not usually fight humans. We are not very vulnerable to your weapons, so it would be disastrous if we did. And if we ever do fight—for instance against other lumins—we fight for our own people, our own humans. The Minotaur kills for memories. That is madness. Years of solitude, after a century of neglect, have driven him mad."

"Well, it's lucky he's so gentle and easy-going," Jason said, and Zidu laughed. "So we've got barbarians waiting to kill us outside, and the Hamburger Strangler in here." He sighed. "Can we help him?"

"I do not think so. A Minoan lumin might help, at least more than we could. We lumins reach each others' minds most easily when we share the same language of spirit and culture." He turned to the west, where a royal blue had pushed the sunset's orange to the edge of the sky. "But even if another Minoan lumin could be found, I do not think it would matter. The Minotaur wants no help."§

ooooo

They camped in the deserted palace. As they ate that night, they questioned the Minotaur about the charioteers.

"It's no surprise they charged you," he answered with a rumbling chuckle. "Trojan pirates have been raiding lately, so the Greeks tend to kill strangers. The Trojans kidnap women

§ You all probably remember the Greek Minotaur myth. King Minos kept a bull-headed man in a maze under his palace. He made the Athenians send fourteen young people to Crete every year, as food for the monster. Eventually, the hero Theseus volunteered to go, and he killed the Minotaur. The story comes to us from centuries after Minoan times, but it may be based on truth. Some historians think the Minoans staged bull-jumping rituals, where acrobats dodged charging bulls. When Crete was the big bully on the block, the Minoans may have imported Greek teens for the bullring. As for the maze, the complex at Knossos was quite a sprawling, confusing place from the barely civilized Greeks' point of view. In fact, we get the word "labyrinth" from the Minoans' House of the Labrys, the two-headed axe.

~ William Gallo, Recorded Lectures, History 78: Roots of Western Civilization (Fall Semester 2006).

and children and young men—and worse, they steal the gold. But at least someone's giving the Greeks back the misery they've brought on others." He shook his head, tracing arcs in the air with his horns. "When the Minos kings ruled, they kept the river clear of pirates."

Jason prodded. "You said the Greeks would hunt us." He avoided Tia's glare. No doubt she wished to point out that if he'd skipped Crete as he'd been told, they wouldn't be surrounded by barbarians now. "Do you think we can get past them at night?"

"That's the best time to try." The bull-man's voice was faint, and he stared at the ground.

"Minotaur," said Jason, "why don't you come with us?" Tia and Rim-Hadad looked startled, but Zidu smiled sadly. "You don't really have anything left here," continued Jason, "and we could use your help." The Minotaur might be a loose cannon, but with barbarians waiting for them, that was better than no cannon.

"No," said the Minotaur gruffly. He flapped his ears, dislodging a fly. "Thank you, but no. I told you, I belong in the House of the Labrys. Here I'll stay until I fade away." His voice softened again. "I don't think it will be long now."

They made plans to sneak out of Red Knossos after dark the next day. Jason only hoped the Greeks hadn't found the *Dead Valencia*, and wouldn't for another day.

ooooo

The next night, they climbed down the hill, feet quiet and hearts beating rapidly. They avoided the road, picking their way in darkness over rocks and small cliffs. Soon they reached the stone houses at the town's edge and circled them, heading for the river.

As they made their way through a clearing between orchards, they heard a scream and froze. Fires flared, and more screams followed, along with the sound of running feet. Three wild-eyed women burst through the trees, crying and panting. One careened into Tia and fell to the leaf-strewn soil, taking Tia with her.

"Trojans! Pirates!" the woman shrieked as she jumped back to her feet. "Run!"

Then leather-clad men swirled into the clearing, and the world dissolved into chaos. Jason yanked Tia to her feet and turned to run. But a sword butt slammed into his belly, sending him tumbling. Grasping hands came out of nowhere, but Jason rolled out of reach, heaving from the blow. A sandy-haired man in leather lunged at him, but Jason brought both feet up in a vicious kick—acting without thinking—and caught the pirate in the belly.

Jason scrambled to his feet, his heart galloping, his eyes darting around the clearing, desperate for a way out. He couldn't find his friends amid the torches and the running, fighting men, but he heard Rim-Hadad call, "Jason!" Then he saw Tia screaming and punching nearby. Before he could move, someone hit him from behind and he fell, slamming his chin on the ground. His head whirled, and someone pulled his hands behind him. In a moment, his arms were tied.

"Here's a handsome pair!" snarled a cruel voice. Jason's head began to clear, and he saw that he'd been thrown next to Tia and several townspeople, all bound with ropes. Now a gap-toothed, ugly mouth swam into view an inch from his face.

"Behave yourself!" the Trojan pirate barked, choking Jason with hideous breath. "I hate to scar a healthy slave, but I will if I have to."¶

¶ During the 1870s, a treasure hunter dug up a Bronze Age city on the north-west coast of what is now Turkey. The ruins matched features of Homer's Troy mentioned in the *Iliad*. So there's a good chance Homer told some real history....

The Trojans were probably vassals of the Hittite kingdom. It's a good bet they had cultural ties to the Greeks, too. They apparently spoke an Indo-European language called Luwian. Someone destroyed their city around 1250 BC. It's not far-fetched to blame Greek pirate-princes like Homer's Agamemnon, Achilles, and Odysseus. But the Trojans may have been pirates themselves. Who wasn't? In Greek myth, a Trojan prince seduces Helen, queen of Sparta, and spirits her away to Troy, setting the stage for the Trojan War. The Helen of Troy story might recall Trojan pirates kidnapping Greek women.

~ William Gallo, Lectures, History 78.

5

Slaves in Babylon

By 1750 BC, SUMERIAN-STYLE kingdoms dotted the Fertile Crescent. Most were puny, but King Hammurabi of Babylon had conquered most of Mesopotamia and built a river valley dominion that rivaled Egypt. Hammurabi and a lot of the other rulers were Amorites, descended from the desert barbarians who'd invaded centuries before. Like most retired barbarians, the Amorites faced an awful irony: now *they* were the civilized lords with fat treasure-hoards and vulnerable cities to protect.

Starting in the 1700s BC, a new wave of invasions and wars rolled over the Fertile Crescent. The dust finally started to settle in the late 1500s, over a changed map. The little states had been swallowed up by the four big kingdoms of the late Bronze Age: Egypt, the Hittites in Asia Minor, the Assyrians in northern Mesopotamia, and the Kassites in Babylon, in central and southern Mesopotamia. The new regimes looked like European medieval kingdoms, ruled by feudal lords, but with charioteers providing the muscle instead of knights.

With touchy, violent chariot warriors running the country, life had to be tough for peasants, and for slaves.

~ William Gallo, Lectures, History 56.

ooooo

The Trojan ships looked like aircraft carriers after the *Dead Valencia*. Long hulls curved high above the night-black river. Rows of oars and benches lined the decks, running fore and aft from each ship's single mast. Jason and Tia were pushed and bullied to the rear of one of these ships, along with a group of twenty or so Minoans. The pirates forced them to sit among the bags of supplies and booty there, and threatened dire consequences if they moved.

The Trojans worked like lightning. Oarlocks creaked, ropes stretched, and orders flew across the deck as the ship maneuvered into the current. Within ten minutes, the pirates had raised the sail. It blocked out a square, starless patch against the blue-black sky. Soon the dark shoreline of Red Knossos fell away behind them. Zidu and Rim-Hadad and the *Dead Valencia* were gone. Jason didn't know if his friends had been captured or killed or if he'd ever see them again.

More than ever, he wished he could wake up back home and leave this world—this nightmare. But even if he could, he realized he wouldn't. He wouldn't leave Tia alone.

Two Trojans were making their way down the deck, holding smoky torches and looking over the captives. One was the gap-toothed man who'd captured Jason. He wore stained leather chest armor with a dirty tunic beneath. His patchy, brown beard was dirty, too, and he stank. Gap-Tooth looked with particular interest at Jason, inspecting his clothes and especially his sneakers. Then his eyes fell on Tia. Many of the captives were women and children, but Tia stood out because of her white Egyptian dress—and because she was pretty.

With a smirk, the pirate grabbed Tia and dragged her from the other captives. He threw the shrieking girl to the deck between bags and baskets of supplies. She tried to twist away, but her hands were tied behind her back. Grinning viciously, Gap-Tooth fell to his knees, seized her shoulders, and pushed her down.

Blood roared in Jason's head. With a snarl, he rolled onto his back, slammed his knees to his chest, and pulled his bound wrists under his feet, out from behind him. Then he leapt up, careened across the deck, and hurtled into Gap-Tooth and Tia. He wrapped his rope around the pirate's neck and pulled with all his might. He and Gap-Tooth rolled across the hard planks.

A swarm of leather-armored Trojans jumped on Jason, punching him mercilessly. Soon, three were sitting on him, holding him beaten and motionless.

"What's going on?" a voice boomed. A dark man stood with his hands on his hips, looking down at the scene by the stern. He wore a bronze breastplate, engraved with the head of a horse. A red jewel glinted in the torchlight from his left ear.

"Just checking the stock, my lord," gasped Gap-Tooth, who squatted nearby, holding his throat. His voice was ragged. "Then this one went crazy!" He kicked Jason on the hip.

Jason winced but couldn't move under the three pirates. He looked up at the shipmaster. The man's deep-set eyes scanned him, then turned to Tia, who sat on the deck, held still by another pirate. Her face was streaked with tears and running eyeliner.

"Please!" she screeched. "I'm a virgin! I'm worth a lot more if I stay that way. I'll be worth a fortune! *Please!*"

The shipmaster squatted on muscular thighs next to Tia, gazing impassively at the shaking girl. "She's right," the pirate leader finally said, rising and running thick fingers through his short beard. "She'll bring a hefty price in Dur-Babylon if she's untouched. Well then, no one touches her—is that clear?" His dark gaze circled the Trojans. "As for this," he pointed at Jason, "bind his ankles and arms. We'll slit his throat if he tries that again." He peered at Jason once more, especially at his clothes. "But don't bruise him too much more if he behaves. He looks exotic. Might be valuable."

They tied his ankles and pinioned his arms against his sides, then dumped him onto the deck next to Tia.

"Thank you," she whispered, teary-eyed. Jason ached so much he could barely nod.

ooooo

The captives shivered on the deck as the ship rocked and the night wind whistled through the rigging. Then the sun rose and glared down from a hard sky, baking and burning them. Jason heard the pirates' talk and singing and laughter as they alternately rowed and sailed before the wind. They didn't feed the captives and gave them only one ladle of water each. Jason couldn't move beneath his ropes, so his muscles stiffened and cramped. And the bruises from the pirates' blows burned and swelled.

He spent the day nearly motionless in his cocoon of biting ropes, with nothing to occupy his mind but pain and his thoughts. He'd attacked an armed man with his bare hands. Jason had never guessed he could do that. Anger sometimes drove normal caution straight out of his head. *That's what happened with Dad*, he realized—with very different results, though equally painful in their own way.

His mind wandered back to the night before the coma. Jason had stopped by his father's study to ask if he could take a road trip that summer with Chuck and Nadji, to a gaming expo. "Uh," his father began. But his eyes remained glued to the computer screen, and after a moment, he seemed to forget about his son. Lately, he'd been more obsessed with work than usual, writing a new book, *Modern Magic: The Role of Myth in the Age of Isolation and Disenchantment*. More mythology and superstition, of course.

"Sorry," his father finally said, tearing his attention from the screen. "What was that?" Jason repeated his request, and his father shook his head. "That doesn't work, Jason. I'm sorry. I'll be away that week myself, on my research trip, and Grandma's going to be here the whole month. I need you here to help her."

"But why?" Jason demanded. "Grandma doesn't need anyone here. I mean, she's not going to keel over or anything, and this is just a few days."

"Your concern for your grandmother warms my heart." Jason's father ran a hand through brownish hair, streaked with gray, and glanced up at the wall, which was hung with maps he'd drawn in the styles of historic cartographers. "Look, Grandma can't drive anymore. I need you to take her to the store and take Athena around and all that. You'll like that, doing all that driving."

"Yeah, chauffeur for an old lady and a little girl—sounds pretty wild."

"Well, I can't leave Grandma with just Athena." His father sighed and straightened the button-down hanging loose over his lean frame. "She needs help."

"Okay, but why can't you do it? You just planned the research thing. Can't you go another week—*any* other week? You've got the whole summer. I just need these two days!"

"I know, but if I reschedule, it's inconvenient for a lot of people."

"But if you don't, it's inconvenient for me! I'm bored out of my mind here. I don't ever get to go anywhere!"

"Right, Jason, you're a prisoner here." His father sighed again. "I'm sorry about this. If it were just me, I would reschedule. But I can't start rearranging everyone else's summer. It's not fair."

"Is Candi going?" Jason's face felt hot. "Is *that* whose plans you can't rearrange?"

"Don't start that crap again!" His father's gray eyes flashed. "Look, I'm sorry, I really am. But you've got to understand, I need you here that week. You're sixteen now. With Mom gone, you have to shoulder some of these responsibilities."

"Yeah, Mom's gone—makes everything easy for *you*! You can work all the time and do whatever you want, and you don't pay attention to anyone but yourself. You're probably glad she's dead!"

William Gallo's face froze, and Jason cringed. Slowly, his father's mouth opened, and his nostrils flared. "Get out of my study," he growled. "We'll discuss this later."

Jason looked back once on his way out. As his father turned to face the screen, a tear glistened in his eye—something Jason had seen only once before.

ooooo

The ropes kept Jason from lying comfortably, but he finally dozed off the second night, leaning on a sack of apples. He dreamed of the hospital room, as usual. He floated above the dark, clean beds, watching his father's and sister's sleeping bodies and his own. The room looked so comfortable and safe—so modern. He wanted to scream for help. But in the hospital dream, he could make no sound.

As he rose toward consciousness, Jason thought he heard Zidu's voice. Or rather, he thought he *felt* Zidu calling him. Was he hallucinating?

"All right, you!" snapped a cruel voice, jerking him fully conscious. "Up now!"

Jason winced as Gap-Tooth grasped the ropes over his chest and yanked him to his feet. He swayed and almost fell, but Gap-Tooth steadied him. The sun was full up, and it reflected off the ship's wooden surfaces and off the great square sail, stinging Jason's eyes. "We've got to clean you up, you and your pretty clothes." He cut Jason's ropes with a short knife. Then, before Jason's head had cleared, the knife was at his throat. "Now you stretch your muscles and wipe yourself off, so you look saleable," Gap-Tooth growled. "And if you try anything like that stunt before, I'll cut you good. Understand?"

Jason stared hazily at the raw rope-burn on Gap-Tooth's sweaty neck, amazed that he'd done that himself. "Okay," he rasped. He cautiously stretched his arms. They hurt, but he felt a little better almost at once.

The Trojan grinned, displaying blackened gums. "There, then," he said. "You're not such a bad little rascal. You keep behaving yourself and I'm sure you'll get a good master." He tousled Jason's hair. "No hard feelings, eh?"

"Yeah, no hard feelings," Jason muttered. "And if some Greeks ever offer you a wooden horse, I hope you'll take it." Gap-Tooth looked puzzled but then shrugged and went off to rouse more captives.

The ship was no longer moving. The pirates had tied up to a narrow dock, one of several running alongside the left bank. Many boats bobbed nearby, making a small forest of naked masts. Beyond them stood a great city. A heavy brick wall rose alongside the river, topped with rows of rectangular battlements. It stretched away into the distance up and down the waterside, reinforced every few hundred yards by a square tower. Though the city walls stood tall, some of the buildings beyond were even taller. Jason saw castle-like temples and palaces: mesas of thick pillars, walls topped by battlements, and more wide towers. Many of the buildings had been painted yellow or red or, most often, blue. They were squat and heavy, but illustrations of animals on the brick surfaces gave them life. Gardens of palms and flowering bushes sprouted on terraces and rooftops, alongside handsome sculptures. And several massive step-pyramids rose six or more levels into the sky.

"Ziggurats," he whispered. They looked like the temples he'd seen in Sumer, though these were taller and more elaborate.*

"Lower the gangplank!"

Jason turned and saw the Trojans extending a thick board down to the dock. The pirate shipmaster jumped down to greet a woman standing there, surrounded by four burly men. Soon he was helping her on to the ship. She had a round face and a round body beneath a one-shouldered dress. The shipmaster led her past the rows of benches, where the pirates lounged.

"You know I only bring you the best, Lady Shamhat," he was saying as they approached the slaves huddled by the stern. "You there, look alive!" He barked at Gap-Tooth and the other pirates guarding the captives. "Get those slaves into line."

---

* These latter-day step-pyramids—ziggurats—stood much taller than their Sumerian grandparents, though they weren't any competition for the Great Pyramids in Egypt. Babylonian ziggurats may have inspired the Bible's Tower of Babel story. In Genesis, the world's people all speak a single language. Working together, they build a tower reaching into the heavens. God, however, doesn't like the competition, so he scatters humanity and blocks further species-wide cooperation by giving us many languages.

~ William Gallo, Lectures, History 56.

The pirates forced Jason, Tia, and the other captives into a row, and the woman began to inspect them. "Minoans, eh?" she said as she squinted skeptically at a boy of no more than nine.

"I think some are Greek, too," said the shipmaster heartily, "and there are a couple of surprises—you'll see. Anyway, they're all healthy. My men know how to run the herd and corral the best stock."

"Mmm," said the woman, without turning from the slaves. "They look a little mangy to me." She grabbed the jaw of the shaking woman next to the boy and forced her mouth open. "Awful teeth on this one. I don't want her." She continued down the line, occasionally prodding or poking the terrified captives. Then her dark, thin eyebrows rose as she reached Tia. "Ah, lovely. Egyptian, yes? Where did you get an Egyptian?"

The shipmaster shrugged and grinned. "She was there, in Crete, waiting for us. The gods must have smiled on me. And she's a virgin, too. She'll cost you, if you want her."

"Mmm." The round woman looked doubtful. She grabbed Tia's jaw and forced her mouth open. Jason hoped the fiery Egyptian wouldn't bite the woman's finger off. "Teeth are good, and her breath's fresh," said the woman. She looked Tia over once more. Then she turned to Jason. "And what have we here?" She pulled at the fabric of his white T-shirt, rubbing it between her fingers.

"He was with her," the shipmaster answered. "Egyptian, too, probably. He's healthy, and he's very exotic."

"Doesn't look that healthy to me," the woman mumbled. "Looks pretty bruised. And I've never seen clothes like these on an Egyptian." She squatted and stared at Jason's sneakers. "I've never seen shoes like these anywhere." She stood and squinted up at him. Thick lashes surrounded her dark eyes, and powdery makeup covered much of her face. She smelled of heavy perfume. "Where are you from, slave?"

"Egypt," he said, thinking fast. "And our family's really rich. If you let us go, my grandfather will give a great reward, like millions of dollars—I mean, silver pieces." He gulped and tried to keep his hands from shaking. "But you don't want to make him mad. I'm sure he's already sent some, uh, you know, warriors … out looking for us."

"Well, he's a liar," the woman said. "That doesn't help his value. But those clothes are interesting, and maybe we can sell him as an exotic if we leave them on him. He'd be a lot easier to sell if you hadn't beaten him up so much. I'll think about it." She continued down the line without another word to Jason.

After reviewing the captives, the slave-trader and the ship-master retired to the other end of the deck, where they sat on stools near the high prow. Soon they were debating vigorously. Finally, they reached some kind of agreement, and the pirate leader returned to the slaves. He pointed at Jason, Tia, three of the women, and two of the men. Gap-Tooth and the other Trojans shoved the seven along the deck.

"Good luck to you, rascal," the ugly pirate barked as he pushed Jason down the gangplank.

"Listen to me very carefully," said the woman as they assembled on the dock. "You now belong to the House of Shamhat the Kassite. I am Shamhat, and I have very little patience. You will do exactly as my handlers tell you, or you will be severely beaten." Shamhat's four brawny companions loomed over the slaves. They wore ankle-length robes and carried short clubs. "However, if you behave well, you will be well-treated and well-fed," She looked each in the eye. "You'll be sold at market in three days. I sell slaves to some of the best people in Dur-Babylon, so if you stand up straight, you'll likely end up in the house of a priest or a great Kassite lord." She drew her round body up proudly. "I've even sold to the king's buyer." Now her face turned stern. "But behave or not, I *will* sell you—and mangy-looking, slouching, moping slaves will end up in the mines or worse. Now follow along, and don't step out of line." She waddled down the dock.

The party joined the throng on the dusty road between the walls and the river. Most of the locals surrounding them had dark skin and dressed in brightly colored robes and mantles. Many of the men wore long beards and turbans.

As they waded through the river of carts, chariots, donkeys, goats, horses, and pedestrians, a surprising sight distracted Jason from his fear. A familiar-looking lumin walked alongside a man in a conical white hat. The creature had a lion's body and a human head, like Zidu. He had similar features, too, and a thick beard. The two might have been brothers, except eagle wings sprouted from this lumin's shoulders, and he had a full head of black hair.

Jason realized the winged lion-man wasn't the only familiar lumin on the road. All the gleaming-eyed beings looked like the creatures he'd seen in Sumer. So far, he'd found unique lumins in each country. He wondered why these Babylonian lumins looked Sumerian.

Shamhat led the party through a great gate in the wall, between massive blue towers. The city on the other side smelled of garbage. It was a sprawl of narrow alleys and windowless, mud-brick houses, covered with plaster and, in many cases, colorful paint. Finally, after an interminable trudge, Shamhat pushed open a door in one of these plastered walls and led the party inside.

The house was a series of mud-brick rooms, piled two stories high, surrounding a packed-earth courtyard. Shamhat disappeared up a staircase in the courtyard as soon as they arrived, and the handlers led Jason and the others to a dim, unfurnished room on the ground floor. Five men and women already sat against the walls there, looking dejected. Each wore a ragged tunic or loincloth.

"Listen to me," thundered one of the handlers as the new captives filed in. "This is the house of Shamhat, and this is where you'll be staying until you're sold. Food's twice a day, and you've already missed this morning's. You eat at first light and nightfall, and you go to the latrine then and mid-day, so don't ask for any other privileges." He glared around the room and smacked his club against one palm. "Sit quietly, wait for your sale, and don't cause any trouble, or you'll eat nothing, and you'll be very sorry."

With that, the handlers left. Jason heard something heavy bang against the thick door and guessed it was bolted. He noticed that wooden bars reinforced the mud-brick walls. Tia sat down against a wall and started to cry, and Jason sat next to her.

"This is all your fault!" she hissed. "If we hadn't stopped in Crete, we wouldn't be here! Now I'm going to be a slave for the rest of my life!" She buried her face in her hands.

ooooo

Jason wasn't sure how long he'd stared into space before he noticed someone sitting next to him. It was a lean man with a glum face and a bristly, short beard. He was one of the slaves who'd been there when they arrived.

"Hello," the man said when Jason looked his way.

"Hi."

"I'm Tidal." The man spoke very quietly. "I beg forgiveness if I've disturbed you."

"I forgive you. I wasn't doing anything anyway."

Tidal stared at the floor between his knobby, bare feet. "Were you taken in a war?" he asked.

"Well, sort of. We were captured by Trojan pirates. But we weren't at war." Jason's throat thickened. "We were just minding our own business."

"I'm sorry," said Tidal. "That happens to a lot of people. I ... I hope you won't be too sad."

"Were you taken in a war?"

Tidal looked up timidly. "No. My family have been slaves for three generations."

"So how come you're here?"

He looked down again. "My master ... some of his fields are turning to salt, so he couldn't afford as many slaves.† And ... he

---

† The Babylonians knew about Sumer's downfall, of course, but they may not have realized that salt from irrigation had ruined their southern neighbor. Whatever they knew or suspected, they irrigated to their hearts' content, salting the fields, just like the Sumerians. The results weren't quite as awful, thanks to a hardier environment, and thanks to the fact that irrigation started a lot later in upstream Mesopotamia. But irrigation and salt damaged Babylonian soil, too, and the Iraqis live with the consequences to this day.

~ William Gallo, Lectures, History 56.

said he was tired of me moping around the house all the time."

"Oh. Why were you moping?"

Tidal blushed as he noticed Tia listening. "I had two children, a boy and a girl. They'd be just about your age, you two, if they're alive. My master sold them a few years ago, and that's when I grew sad. He said I just shouldn't think about it, and I tried, but I couldn't help it."

"Son of a bitch," Jason muttered.

"No, no, his mother was a great lady. And he's a good man. He tried to find me a home, but no one would buy. I'm the best weaver he ever had, but I'm not so young anymore. So he sold me to Lady Shamhat. He said she could sell concubines to a eunuch."

"Well, I'm sorry about your children."

"They look like you two, a bit. I'm sure they got good masters."

"Do you know who's likely to buy us?" Tia asked. Her voice was steady now that she'd stopped crying.

"No," said Tidal meekly. "You can never know. But I hope you get good masters too. I'm sure I will."

He grasped a figurine hanging from a cord around the waist of his simple tunic. "Holy Ningal will protect me, blessed be her name." He held up the figurine. It was a dried clay sculpture of a woman.

Ningal? Jason knew that name, from the rite of finding at the temple in Sumer. "Goddess of dreams and insight," he said, "guide me again this night."

Tidal's face broke into a smile. "Yes! You love the gentle goddess, too?"

"Well, I know about her. But isn't she Sumerian? How come you worship her here?"

"Well," said Tidal thoughtfully, "I suppose you could call all the gods Sumerian. Most have old Sumerian names that only very wise men know." He smiled tentatively. "Everything ancient and true comes from Sumer."

"Everything ancient and true comes from Egypt," Tia corrected. The little man looked hurt and confused.

"Tidal," Jason whispered after a while, "do slaves ever escape from Du—uh ... Dur-Babylon?"

"Oh, no," he whispered back. "Don't try that." His hands shook, and he wrapped them around the Ningal amulet. "The punishments are terrible."

"But then slaves *do* get away sometimes," Tia said in a low voice, "or they wouldn't need those punishments, right?"

Tidal looked like he'd cry. "Please," he said, "you don't want to do that. I'd hate to see anything happen to you. They torture runaways. And no one will help you. The law—Hammurabi's Code,‡ you know—it's a death sentence for anyone who helps a runaway. It's not worth the risk."

ooooo

Jason didn't know what it was the handlers fed them that evening. Only one word came to mind: *slop*. But at least there was plenty. Jason and Tia hadn't eaten since they left the House of the Labrys, so they slurped the stuff down.

That night, Jason dreamed of the hospital room, as usual. The sight of his sister upset him. His rescue mission had so far failed, and even if he somehow escaped, he'd lost his boat, not to mention Zidu. If he couldn't bring his father home, Athena would be an orphan.

As he rose toward consciousness, he once again imagined Zidu nearby, looking for him. The hallucination was stronger this time. Zidu seemed to be calling, but Jason didn't know how to answer. "I'm right here," he said. "How do I reach you?"

He opened his eyes. Morning sunlight slanted into the bare room from the wood-barred window high in the wall. Motes

---

‡ Babylon's King Hammurabi wrote Mesopotamia's great law code. Hammurabi's Code was liberal in a lot of ways, protecting women and children and encouraging mercy. But punishments were harsh. Death penalty offenses included breaking and entering, receiving stolen temple goods, making false accusations, helping a runaway slave, medical malpractice—if the patient died—and looting. Does it sound like Texas? The most chilling parts of the code ordered the execution of children for their parents' crimes. So for example, if a man killed a pregnant freewoman, his daughter would be put to death.

~ William Gallo, Lectures, History 56.

of dust twinkled in the shafts of light. Most of the slaves were asleep on the floor, and the room buzzed with their snores.

But Tia was awake. She lay next to Jason, her head propped on one hand, looking at him. "How do you reach who?" she asked. "Who were you talking to?"

Jason rubbed his eyes. The room smelled of too many people. "Uh, I guess I was dreaming about Zidu."

Tia sat up. "Zidu? Were you trying to reach Zidu?"

"Well, I was asleep."

"No, stupid, you were almost awake. You were in the place between sleep and wakefulness. I can tell. Did you hear Zidu?" Her dark eyes bore into his. Jason realized she must have wiped off her eyeliner. She looked strange and intense without it.

"Was Zidu calling you?"

He reluctantly told her about the hallucinations. "Don't you know what this means?" Tia whispered. "You must have the shaman gift. And Zidu's your lumin!"

"What?"

"How can anyone possibly be so ignorant? The shaman gift. If you're born with the gift, you can share shaman power with a lumin. That's what your Sumerian priestess did in her rite of finding. She used the power of her lumins to search for your father. She has the shaman gift."

"Well, what makes you think I have it?"

"If you're hearing Zidu's call, you must have it. Only a shaman can hear with his mind. And it makes sense. A shaman can draw power from any willing lumin, but it works best if the two have a shaman bond. You and the lumin have to be close—the closer the better. You're very close to Zidu. Anyone can see that. He must be your lumin. He's trying to find you."

He stared at her. Weird as it sounded, her theory made sense. He'd dreamed of nothing but the hospital room since reaching Fore. Why would he start dreaming of Zidu now? "Actually," he whispered, "now that you mention it ... I guess, sometimes on the *Dead Valencia*, when Zidu was helping me with the ship or the net ... it was like sometimes we didn't really have to talk. Like we just knew ..."

"Yes!" Tia hissed. "That's the shaman bond. You must have been sharing mind-to-mind. You are a shaman. You can get us out of here!"

"But how? I don't know how to do anything. Don't you have to get trained for something like that? And anyway, Zidu's not here. I thought a shaman had to be with his lumin to use shaman power."

"It does take training," she answered, "but all you have to learn for now is the reaching trance. That's one of the first things shamans learn. It's easy." Tia straightened her soiled, white dress, her eyes bright. "And you're right about being together for most rites, but not this one. Usually you can touch your lumin's mind and he can touch yours, even if you're separated. That must be what Zidu's trying to do. You've got to try, too." Her whisper grew urgent. "Maybe Zidu can rescue us. All you have to do is call him. I can teach you the ritual and the reaching trance."

The other slaves were starting to stir, so they kept their conversation to a whisper.

"We don't even know if Zidu's safe, or what happened to Rim-Hadad," Jason complained. "It's ten-to-one odds they want us to rescue *them*. And anyway, I don't know how to do any of this. Can't you do it? Do you have the shaman gift?"

"Yes," Tia whispered, "but the best I could do now is call for help across the ether. Only lumins nearby would hear. And no Babylonian lumin's going to help us. But you and Zidu have the shaman bond, so you could reach him hundreds of miles away if you had to. You don't have to be close in space if you're close in spirit." She grasped his wrist. "It could work, and it's got to be you, Jason. I can teach you."

He shifted uncomfortably. This shaman power sounded so idiotic, so superstitious—like the kind of voodoo his father would write about, to the endless amusement of his critics in the history department.

"Jason," Tia said, tightening her grip. "You got me into this with your stupid trip to Crete. You *have* to do this, and you have to do it *today*. We're going to be sold in two days. We'll probably be separated, so even if Zidu finds you, he'll never find me. I don't have a shaman bond with Zidu." Her eyes filled with tears. "You saw what almost happened to me on the pirate ship. That's what'll happen, soon. That's what happens to slave girls. You *have* to get us out of this!"

"Okay," Jason exclaimed. "I'll do anything you say. I won't let that happen to you."

ooooo

They sat talking in a corner, away from the other slaves.

"Calling with the mind is like the rite of finding you saw in Sumer,"Tia explained, "but much simpler and easier, since you're not searching the whole world." The shaman had to fall into a "reaching trance." It resembled the edge of sleep, so it wasn't surprising Jason had sensed Zidu's call just before he awoke. From there, the shaman would simply call with his mind, like thinking as loud as possible. "Your thoughts go out into the ether," Tia continued. "If your lumin's alert, he'll sense them."

"So how do I get into the trance?"

"Shamans usually start with lots of prayers in a temple. That's the proper way. But we don't have a temple, and we can't perform any of the rituals here. But it can still work without all that, just not as well. The most important thing is a holy amulet. You've got to meditate on an amulet. Then the amulet's god brings you the reaching trance."

"Well we don't have an amulet." Jason doubted the handlers would let him pop down to the amulet store. "Hey, what about your—" He stopped, realizing that Tia's neck was bare. Her blue beetle amulet was gone.

"It broke off in the fight on Crete. My father gave me that scarab beetle." She wiped tears from her eyes and looked away.

They sat in silence. The answer struck each of them at the same moment: "Tidal!"

"His amulet's perfect," said Tia. "You already know this goddess Ningal, and Zidu must know her, too, if she's really Sumerian. I'm sure she'll help us."

But Tidal started shaking at the very thought of mischief. "Please don't do this, children," he whispered. "It's not worth the risk. I'm sure you'll get good masters."

"It's worth the risk to *us*," said Jason. "Besides, we're not talking about escaping. We're just going to let our friends know where we are."

They convinced him in the end, or maybe it was the memory of his children that convinced him. He made them promise not to tell anyone about his help, even if they were caught.

"Tidal," Jason said once he'd handed over the amulet, "I don't know if our friends are anywhere near Dur-Babylon. And I don't know if they'll be able to help us. But if they do, we'll owe you. Do you wanna come with us?"

Tidal shook his head, his eyes wide. "I would never do that." He shrugged miserably. "I just want to find a good master while I'm still young enough—someone who'll feed me when I'm too old to weave."

"Yeah, I understand about all that, but no one has the right to own another person."

"What are you talking about?" Tia asked. "There's nothing wrong with owning a slave."

He turned to face her. "You think all this is just fine, the way we were captured and forced to come here?"

"It's not fine for *us*," she said. "But *some* people have to be slaves."

Jason stared. "You're a great humanitarian. You know that, don't you?"

"Without slaves, how would all the work get done?" Tidal asked meekly.

"Oh, I don't know," Jason exclaimed. "Maybe people would just get *paid*. Where I come from, there aren't any slaves. All the work gets done, and everyone knows slavery's wrong." Tidal and Tia just stared. "But we can't argue now. I just hope you'll change your mind, Tidal. You don't deserve this."

ooooo

They waited for nightfall, afraid the handlers might enter during daylight, or one of the other slaves might report them. Once the room was dark and rumbled with snores, Jason and Tia snuck off to the corner. They sat cross-legged, facing each other.

"Now hold the amulet up and touch it to your forehead and then your lips," Tia whispered, "to show reverence for the goddess." *Whatever*, thought Jason, but he did as she asked. He could hardly see the Ningal figurine in the dark, but it felt reassuringly solid. "Now fold your hands in your lap," she continued, "and hold the amulet in your fingertips. Like this." She rearranged his fingers around the clay figurine. "All right, now close your eyes and breathe very slowly. Just don't pay attention to anything but the amulet—the feel of the clay on your fingers. Think about nothing but that as you breathe. When the goddess gives you the reaching trance and your mind starts to see the ether, you'll know."

Jason breathed in and out, picturing the amulet between his fingers and trying hard to think of nothing else. But his mind kept wandering—sometimes to the most trivial things, like the homework waiting for him back home, or whether Chuck and Nadji were gaming and might start beating him. "It's not working," he finally said. "I keep getting distracted. I can't do this."

"Yes, you can," Tia replied. "You've just got to relax. Don't think about whether it's working. When you notice your mind wandering, just correct yourself. Don't get mad. Just go back to thinking of nothing except the amulet. You can't rush this kind of thing, and we have all night. When you're calm enough, the goddess will come."

Jason's mind wandered again and again. He remembered teaching his grandmother to send text messages and learning ping-pong from his father. He thought of Athena's brown eyes and Doctor Valencia's green ones. He thought of girls he should have asked out back in the real world, and he wondered what his father would say if he brought Zidu home and asked, "Can I keep him?" Whenever he realized he'd drifted off, he corrected himself, bringing his thoughts back to the hard clay between his fingers.

And then it began. In his mind's eye, dim and vague, he saw an endless pool of still, black water. Stars twinkled on the surface, though the blackness above was empty. Jason looked over the surface and knew Zidu was there, looking across the same endless pool. He felt the lion-man's mind, trying to communicate, but he could not understand. So he simply spoke his own message, with the voice of his mind. He told Zidu that he and Tia were prisoners in the house of Shamhat, in Dur-Babylon, and that they would be sold as slaves in two days. And he told his friend what he'd learned: that the Babylonians revered Sumerian ways, and that the city was home to Sumerian gods and temples. Jason didn't know how, but he hoped Zidu could use that information.

Jason couldn't be certain Zidu understood. Nor was he sure of his friend's response or whether the lion-man was even safe.

ooooo

"Ah, great lord, you have excellent taste," said the chief handler. "This slave is a weaver of fantastic skill and long experience. For his last master, he wove wonders you would not believe, cloth anyone would be proud to wear before the altar of any temple. And he's fond of children. He'd make a wonderful servant for the young. And he's docile as a lamb and eats like a bird. This will no doubt shock you, but Lady Shamhat asks only a paltry twenty-two shekels for this hidden gem."

Most of the slaves sat on the ground at the back of Shamhat's red and black tent. But Tidal stood on a wooden pedestal at the center. A customer examined him critically there. Tidal's potential master wore colorful robes, decorated with tassels and beads. His long, dark hair and beard were plaited, and he wore earrings, bracelets, and makeup. Jason guessed the man was a priest. He carried a short, wooden staff and wore a tall, conical hat, instead of the usual turban. Tidal had said the house of a rich priest could be a good place for a slave, so Jason half hoped the man would make the purchase. But how could he want one human being to *buy* another?

Shamhat's roomy tent had opened for business almost an hour before. Already one slave had sold—one of the women from Crete.

"I'll give you fourteen for him," the colorful priest said. Shamhat sat by a low table nearby, counting her shekels and keeping an eye on the slaves.

"Fourteen, sir. You wound me," the chief handler complained. "This skilled craftsman is not worth a measure less than twenty, or I'm no judge of slaves."

"He's gloomy and past his prime," said the priest. "I'll give you seventeen, and that's all."

The chief handler swooned. But then he cast a sidelong glance at Shamhat, who nodded grimly. "You rob us, sir," he said, "but seventeen it will be."

And it was done. The priest gave Shamhat a pile of small silver bars, and the two pressed their seals into wet clay tablets. Jason guessed they were bills of sale. He hoped Shamhat had paid more than seventeen shekels for Tidal, but he doubted it. The slave-trader seemed a shrewd businesswoman.

Tidal stared across the tent at Jason and Tia. Jason held the man's sad eyes and shot him an encouraging smile. The newly purchased slave nodded solemnly, grasping the Ningal amulet at his waist. A knot rose in Jason's throat as Tidal followed his new master out of the tent, like an obedient dog. He disappeared into the noisy crowd of the bazaar and was gone. Jason hoped the poor man would see his children again.

As Tidal left to start his new life, a customer who'd visited that morning returned. He'd taken an interest in Tia, but to Jason's relief, he'd left without asking her price. Now Jason's stomach clenched as the man strode purposefully up to the chief handler.

"That one," he said, pointing at Tia. "I'm interested in that one."

Tia looked at Jason imploringly as the handlers hauled her up from her place among the slaves. They forced her to stand, shaking, on the pedestal before the buyer.

"Ah, sir," began the chief handler, "you could not have made a better choice. This lovely lotus blossom was plucked from the very gardens of Egypt. As you can see, she is smooth as milk and educated in the ways of her homeland. She is not more than sixteen and as pure and untouched as the waters of paradise. On both these points, you have Shamhat's guarantee."

The buyer's hair and beard were light for a Babylonian's, but otherwise he looked like a typical rich man of the city. He wore colorful robes and a yellow and black sash that matched his turban. "How much?" he asked eagerly, fingering the fringe of the sash.

"How much, sir? How can we put a price on such loveliness? It breaks Shamhat's heart to do it, but we live in a world of commerce." The chief handler sighed heavily. "Shamhat asks fifty shekels, a tremendous bargain, but even she can be moved by beauty."

The buyer jolted in exaggerated shock. "Fifty shekels! You must be joking. I could buy four girls for that."

"Not four girls from the house of Shamhat, dear sir. And not four Egyptian girls of such quality, or even two. This is a rare find indeed."

Jason wrung his hands.

"I'll grant you she's unusual," said the man in the yellow and black sash. "But fifty's madness. I'll give you twenty-five for her."

The two began to haggle. The handler praised Tia's merits to the sky, and the buyer downplayed them, calling her, "nothing I haven't seen before." Finally, their prices drew close together.

"Thirty-five shekels," said the buyer, clearly exasperated. "You won't get a better price than that. That's my final offer."

The offer hung on the air as the chief handler turned to Shamhat. The slave-trader looked up from her shekels. Her face was grim as she stared across the tent. Slowly and almost imperceptibly, she nodded.

"Done!" cried the chief handler.

6

Hebrew Tales

DURING THE CENTURY-PLUS AFTER 1250 BC, we get another wave of wars and invasions. The great chariot kingdoms came crashing down, and the territory of Fertile Crescent civilization itself shrank, with frontier areas like Greece lost to barbarism.

The invaders who caused all the fuss included iron-wielding barbarians. So what we're looking at here is a major turning point: the end of the Bronze Age and the start of the Iron Age....

Smaller, more egalitarian states replaced the chariot kingdoms. Two of these little Iron Age realms sprang from a new group of barbarians—recently civilized, more or less: the Israelites. According to the Hebrew Bible, the Israelites gradually conquered Canaan. By the 900s, their King David ruled most of the country. We don't know how much of the biblical story is true, but we do know that by the 800s, a dynasty claiming descent from David ruled the little kingdom of Judah in southern Canaan, and another set of Israelite kings ruled Israel, in the north.

~ William Gallo, Lectures, History 56.

ooooo

The chief handler's cry—*Done!*—still echoed in Jason's ears as a new voice rang from the tent's entrance. "Just a moment!" boomed a tall man hurrying past the red and black door-flap. He hastily replaced a conical hat that had fallen as he'd entered. It was another priest, and beside him trotted a bald, bearded lion-man. Jason's breath caught in his throat. The lumin was Zidu. He looked back at the tall priest kicking up dirt as he stomped across the tent. He almost cheered. It was Rim-Hadad.

The big barbarian looked the part, though he kept switching his wooden staff from hand to hand, so he could adjust his robes or catch his conical hat. The hat was too small and fell off almost as soon as he replaced it.

"Just a moment," Rim-Hadad repeated, sweeping up to the chief handler in a blur of colorful robes. "I've been looking for a girl from Egypt." Jason winced. It sounded very convenient and wasn't too well delivered. "I'm not too late, am I?"

"Yes, you are," cried the light-haired customer with the yellow and black sash. "We just agreed, so you can—"

"The last offer was thirty-five," Shamhat interrupted, rising from her chair. "In the house of Shamhat, no sale is final until the contract's been pressed. Can you do better than thirty-five?"

"Thirty-five!" cried Rim-Hadad. "For a treasure like this?" He looked appreciatively at Tia. Her white dress was now clean, and Shamhat had put some rouge on her cheeks. "I am simply astounded! Of course I can do better!"

Jason winced again and looked at Zidu, who stood by Rim-Hadad's feet. He wished the lion-man could do the talking.

"I'll propose you this," the barbarian declaimed, strolling across the tent as the first buyer fumed. Rim-Hadad casually perused the slaves huddled by the back, seeming to take only a passing interest in Jason. Then he wheeled, swirling his robes around his legs and dislodging his tall hat once again. "I'll propose you this," he repeated, deftly catching the hat. "I need a boy as well, preferably one as unusual as the girl. I want that ugly one back there: the one with the odd clothes. I'll give you seventy shekels for the pair of them."

Jason stifled a gasp. Where had Zidu and Rim-Hadad gotten seventy bars of silver? The man in the yellow and black sash looked just as stunned.

"Seventy for her and *that*?" he said, his blue eyes sweeping over Jason. "You must be mad! Without those clothes, he's hardly worth twenty." He turned to Shamhat at her table. "Lady Shamhat, we had a deal."

"In the house of Shamhat, no sale is final until the contract's been pressed," the slave trader repeated. "Seventy shekels for the pair is acceptable, unless you can beat it, honorable sir."

The man looked at Shamhat. "Well, I could do a little better, but not that much. And I don't even want the boy." He turned to Rim-Hadad. "My friend, if this is how you buy slaves, I hope you're very rich."

"Slave, up here!" Shamhat barked before Rim-Hadad could answer. One of the handlers pushed Jason over to the pedestal, next to Tia.

"Wonderful," Rim-Hadad boomed, pulling his beard. "An excellent pair. I believe I'll train them as poets, or maybe as dog-handlers for my estates." He approached Shamhat's table. "Now, Lady Shamhat, I'll be buying on the credit of the temple of Ea. You know where to apply for cash payment, don't you?"

Shamhat's round face froze beneath its layer of makeup. "Credit? I don't often sell on credit. And with the greatest respect to your office, honorable sir, I don't even know you."

"*What?*" Rim-Hadad thundered. "You doubt the word of a priest of the temple of Ea?" He cast a shocked look at Zidu, who appeared deeply offended. The barbarian paced the tent. "Why, this is sacrilege! I cannot believe my ears! In the name of mighty Enlil and Ninlil, I should curse the house of Shamhat!" As his pacing accelerated, his hands flew wildly through the air. "In the name of Inanna, goddess of war, on her mighty lion steed, in the name of Nanna and his winged bull and his beard of lapis lazuli, in the name of Enki, god of my temple, and his consort Ningikuga, in the name of … uh … In the name of all those kinds of names, my holy wrath knows no bounds!"

Shamhat and the chief handler stared incredulous as the apparently mad priest paced and called on deities. "Lady," the chief handler hissed, "I think those are *Sumerian* names. He's calling the gods by their ancient names—and look at his lumin! Don't let him curse us!"

"*Honorable* priest," cried Shamhat, spreading her arms. Rim-Hadad wheeled to face her, dislodging his hat once again and catching it in midair. "Honorable priest," she repeated, "I humbly apologize. A temporary madness overtook me. Of course the credit of the temple of Ea is good in the house of Shamhat. Please calm yourself, good sir.

"*Well*," said Rim-Hadad, "since you put it so courteously, I forgive you." He beamed at the slave dealer. "And I apologize for losing my temper. We men of the gods are easily carried away by the divine passions of those we serve." He straightened his robes, sashes, and hat. "Now, let's seal this bargain."

ooooo

They hardly said a word before they'd made their way out of the bazaar, through the city streets, and out the tunnel-like gate. Jason jumped for joy when he saw the *Dead Valencia* among the ships bobbing next to the docks. Quick and quiet, the four untied the boat, rowed into the current, and raised the sail.

As the sail caught a light breeze, Jason tied off the main line and threw himself at Rim-Hadad and Zidu. The four hugged and laughed and smiled until their cheeks ached.

"How did you do that?" cried Jason. "Tell us everything!"

"Well," said Rim-Hadad, crossing massive arms over his chest and grinning, "it was no easy task, I'll tell you that. We lost sight of you in the battle on Crete. I struggled against a flood of pirates but could not reach you."

"Our friend fought very bravely," said Zidu. "He killed two pirates with his club."

"Good!" snarled Tia.

"So much for the mighty Trojans," Rim-Hadad continued, beaming.* "After that, they gave up on me, and, of course, they left Zidu alone, since their weapons could do little against him."

"After the raid," said the lion-man, "the Minoans told us the pirates often take captives to Dur-Babylon, for the slave markets. We knew only that, so we decided to go there."

"But before we left, we did make an important discovery," said Rim-Hadad with a mischievous grin. He reached into his sash and withdrew a turquoise scarab beetle on a broken cord. "Ha! What do you think of that?"

"My amulet!" enthused Tia. She scrambled across the deck and threw her arms around the big barbarian. Rim-Hadad grinned from ear to ear.

"Go on," demanded Jason, suddenly cold, despite the hot sun.

"It was that first night when I began to call you, Jason," said Zidu. "I'd sensed your shaman gift, and I knew you and I shared the bond." He looked apologetic. "I would have mentioned it earlier, but you seem uncomfortable with shaman power. I decided to let you come to it in your own time."

"And come to it you did, by Amurru!" cried Rim-Hadad. He smacked Jason hard on the shoulder. "Ha! I'm proud of you."

The two were near Dur-Babylon when Zidu sensed Jason's mind, calling through the ether. They'd reached the city the next day and quickly formulated a plan. That night, Rim-Hadad had tackled a drunken priest coming out of a brothel and stolen his clothes. "You mugged a priest?" Jason exclaimed.

---

* The city of Troy was another casualty of these wars at the end of the Bronze Age. Apparently, the Greeks destroyed it during the 1200s....

For centuries, the Greeks told tall tales about the Trojan War. Homer finally wove these stories into two of the greatest epic poems of all time. If you read the *Iliad* and the *Odyssey*, you'll notice the Greeks don't pat themselves on the back too much for beating the Trojans. In fact, the poems' greatest heroes suffer more *after* the war than during. Maybe that's because the Greeks' own Mycenaean civilization collapsed within a century of Troy's fall, during the same round of invasions and wars.

~ William Gallo, Lectures, History 56.

"Your message about Dur-Babylon's reverence for Sumer gave us the plan," Zidu explained. "As soon as I saw the local lumins, I knew you were right. They speak nearly the same language of spirit as I." His voice had fallen, and he appeared subdued. Jason wondered why. "So I taught Rim-Hadad the Sumerian gods' names. We had to convince people he was a priest from a rich temple."

"But what about the priest?" Tia asked. "What did you do with him?"

A cloud passed over Zidu's face, and Rim-Hadad fumbled with his sash. "Well," the barbarian said, "we had to slit his throat."

"You mean *you* had to slit his throat!" Zidu countered. "I tried to stop you, and I begged you to leave him tied and gagged in some abandoned place!"

"And have him set the watch on us once he was found?" Rim-Hadad barked. "We'd never have rescued Jason and Tia."

"We don't know that!" said Zidu. "It was cold-blooded murder." The lumin's face was drawn with grief.

"By Amurru, you farming people are such hypocrites!" the barbarian growled. "You'll proudly go to war, kill ten thousand men, and lay waste to an entire city. But you won't dirty your hands with a little blood for your friends. I have no patience for it."

The boat fell silent, except for the calls of birds from the reeds. Jason turned to Tia, whose brow was furrowed. What could either of them say? Finally, he simply said, "Thank you for rescuing us. Thank you both."

ooooo

Near the end of the second week from Dur-Babylon, the companions stopped in a town to buy supplies. They'd reached a hot, yellow-green, hilly country, dotted with small woodlands. The town, like its neighbors, stood on a hill, surrounded by pretty valleys full of livestock and grape vines. Even the hillsides had been cultivated, carved into step-like terraces and neatly planted with orchards and grain. But the town itself had been swept clean of greenery. Two-story houses of mud brick marched up and down the crooked streets.

They purchased several flatbreads from a chatty baker in ankle-length robes. As they left the baker's shop, Jason overheard a bearded man on the street, whispering to a companion: "Here comes the cherub!" Jason turned to look down the street and squinted into the afternoon sun, which hung low over the town wall.

At first, wide wings were all he could make out. Then the creature stepped out of the sun's golden glare. It was a tall angel with four wings instead of two. One brown-gold pair wrapped around its body like a cloak, and the other sprouted from its shoulders and rose into the air, feathery wingtips angling forward, as if pointing the way. As the creature strode by, Jason realized four faces covered its head, one pointing in each direction: a man, a lion, a bull, and an eagle—each with glimmering eyes. Its legs ended in mighty hooves, each solid as an ox's foot.

"I thought for a second I might know where we are," Jason whispered. He glanced at Zidu, who was watching the strange, regal lumin. "Maybe I still do." The lumin wasn't the flying baby he'd expected, but the townsmen *had* called it a *cherub*. "I'll try to explain back on the boat."[†]

ooooo

They returned to the gate, where a courtyard fronted two squat, square towers. There they found a group of thirty or forty

---

† Cherubs are fearsome creatures. In the Bible, the Lord sends cherubs with flaming swords to protect the Garden of Eden, after he drives Adam and Eve out. Some believe the devil is a cherub, originally called Lucifer, "the shining one," and renamed Satan, "the adversary," after his fall from grace. We don't know exactly how the ancients pictured the cherubs, but the Bible mentions four wings, cow-feet, and four faces. Cherubs didn't become winged babies until recent centuries, when Westerners confused them with cupid-like creatures in Renaissance art, called *putti*.

The ancient Hebrews apparently believed in many sub-divine spirits in addition to cherubs. In English, we generally use "angel" for all these creatures. The word comes from the Greek *angelos*, meaning "messenger."

~ William Gallo, *Palace of the Sphinx*, 135.

people, many of them children. The townsfolk sat on the ground
or leaned against the off-white houses or the rough stones of the
outer wall. A curly-haired man stood at the center of the crowd.
He wore ragged robes and a dirty white skullcap. "And in the
whole world, there was nothing: no plants and no herbs in the
fields. And rain had never fallen from the sky." The man spoke
with dramatic flair, holding the listeners' eager attention. "So the
Lord our God took the dust in his hand and made a man out of
it, and he breathed life into the man through his nostrils."

"Do you mind if we rest a while and listen?" Tia asked Jason.
"I'm tired, and I haven't heard a story-peddler in a long time."

Jason was eager for a little entertainment, too—like TV
without the TV—so the four edged into the crowd. The
townsfolk made room for them, and a man with three pretty
little girls offered to share his family's olives.

The tale continued. The Lord planted the Garden of Eden
and told the man to care for it. And to give the man company,
the Lord created the animals and birds.

"But none of the animals and none of the birds could keep
the man company, or help him, and he was lonely," continued
the story-peddler, his face drawn and sad. "So the Lord our
God threw the man into a deep sleep, and while he slept, the
Lord took a rib from his chest. And the Lord made the rib
into a woman."

"I think I know this story," Zidu whispered to Jason. "But
in the Sumerian version, the rib came from the god Enki. It
was transformed into a goddess, to heal him."‡

---

‡ In the Bible, why does God make the first woman from Adam's rib? The
answer probably lies in Sumer's Garden of Dilmun myth. The god Enki eats eight
forbidden plants, and eight parts of his body start to die. So the mother goddess
Ninhursag creates eight healing spirits. Since one of the sick parts is a rib, one of the
healing spirits is called Nin-ti, meaning "lady of the rib." But in Sumerian, *ti* means
both "rib" and "to give life," so Nin-ti's name also means "lady who gives life." In
Genesis, Eve is the first woman, made from Adam's rib, and her name means "she
who gives life." For the Sumerians, the rib-lady/life-lady name was probably a play
on words. The ancient Hebrews appear to have adapted the Sumerian story, but they
didn't know the long-dead Sumerian language, so they didn't get the pun.

~ William Gallo, *Palace of the Sphinx*, 149.

"I know it, too," Jason replied. "I definitely think I know where we are."

The creation story ended with a joyous Adam thanking the Lord for Eve, the first woman. Once the story-peddler had finished, a little boy leapt up and demanded Noah's Ark, and the crowd agreed. The crafty story-peddler described the animals climbing aboard the great ship in vivid detail. He lingered especially over the lions' fangs and the elephants' thunderous feet, to the children's delight.

"I certainly know this one," Zidu exclaimed. "But in the Sumerian tale, it's King Ziusudra who built the boat and survived the flood. Then he became a god."

"I'm sure that's right," Jason agreed in a low voice, looking around, "but don't say it too loud. I don't think these people would appreciate hearing about King Ziusudra."

As the shadow of the towers stretched across the courtyard, the story-peddler began a third tale. "This will be my last today, good people," he proclaimed, "so please throw a few mites and help fill a poor performer's shrunken belly." He cast a meaningful glance at a basket near his feet.

For his last tale, the story-peddler told of Moses and of his birth, and the way his mother saved him from Pharaoh by floating him down the Nile in a basket.§ Next, he turned to Moses' adult life. He paced the courtyard, vigorously describing the prophet's encounter with the burning bush. Then he told of Moses' return to Egypt and his struggle with Pharaoh. Soon the crowd shivered and murmured, as the storyteller recounted the terrible plagues the Lord sent against the Egyptians. Pharaoh refused to let the children of Israel leave, so Moses called down the last plague, the smiting of the firstborn. But just as the story-peddler started on the death of Pharaoh's own son, Tia

---

§ Moses' story would've sounded weirdly familiar to the Mesopotamians. Do you know Sargon of Akkad? Sargon was a Semitic king who built a Mesopotamian empire in the mid-2300s BC. He claimed he was the son of a noble priestess who floated him down the Euphrates in a basket. Eventually, the story goes, a gardener found him and raised him. Sound familiar?

~ William Gallo, Recorded Lectures, History 138: Historiography of the Bible (Summer Semester 2000).

jumped up. Jason cringed as he saw the fury on her face.

"How *dare* you?" she spat. "That story's a lie! An Egyptian king would never let some barbarian shaman kill his son!" Her dark eyes blazed, and she shook her fist at the startled story-peddler. "Egypt's gods are mightier than any others in the world! No god of slaves could ever defeat them. You're a liar—and so is this *Moses!*"

"Shut *up!*" Jason hissed, grabbing Tia's wrist and trying to pull her down.

Several of the listeners had risen to their feet, and all gaped at Tia.

"Blasphemy!" shouted a short, brawny man with a light beard and a pinched face. "She called Moses a liar!"

"None of your rabble-rousing today, Isaac," cried a young woman.

But an old woman cut her off. "Bare-headed witch!" She thrust a crooked finger at Tia. "And look at their lumin! Assyrian! They're enemies of the Lord!"

"Enemies of the Lord!" cried the first rabble-rouser. "Don't you hear? Are we going to permit blasphemy in the very shadow of our gates?"

Some of the townsfolk looked uncertain, but others were picking up rocks. "I think you'd better leave," said the man next to them, who'd shared his olives. He was gathering up his daughters and their possessions.

"He's right," Rim-Hadad snapped, rising to his feet and yanking Jason up with him. "Let's take a walk."

He shepherded them down a narrow alley. They walked quickly, but the barbarian told them not to run. Rim-Hadad went last, and for a moment his massive frame deterred the mob. But then someone threw a rock, which cracked against a wall near Tia's head. She screamed, and the crowd roared.

"Run!" Rim-Hadad bellowed.

They dashed down alleys, past startled pedestrians and between houses. They had a head start, but that did little good because the race had no finish line. They had to get out of the town, but the only gate they knew lay behind them.

Fortunately, the alleys were short and turned frequently, so the mob rarely saw them. But Jason feared they were running in circles. The dusty alleys and two-story houses all looked alike.

Soon the shouts grew loud behind them. "Blasphemers!"

"Really nice going!" Jason gasped at Tia as they rounded a corner. Tia's eyes were wide, and her hair rose and fell behind her as she ran, like the wings of a raven.

"Here!" came a voice. "Down here!" A man dressed in ragged robes stood at the head of an alley, waving. It was the story-peddler. "Follow me if you want to live!" he cried.

"Do it!" yelled Jason, after a moment of indecision.

The peddler led them down one alley after another. The noise of the mob now came from several directions. Then, as they heard the cries and footfalls in the very street behind them, the story-peddler ducked into another alley. The four followed but skidded to a halt a moment later, confronted by a cracked but imposing wall of mud brick and stone. It was dead end. Had their guide tricked them? Rim-Hadad looked back and raised his club as the shouts grew closer.

The raggedy story-peddler fell to his knees by the wall, dug his fingers into a crack, and heaved. A wide section of wall came away, scraping against the ground. Without a pause, he scrambled on hands and knees into the hole. "In here," he hissed. Zidu hardly had to stoop. The rest crawled and slid, but soon they'd joined the story-peddler in the dark. He plunged his fingers into a handhold gap in the open section of wall and pulled it back into place, blocking all light and sealing them in.

The travelers lay in the dirt and tried to silence their panting. "Down here!" cried a voice from outside. They heard the sound of many rushing feet. "Where are they?" someone shouted. Then the footfalls resumed but faded away almost as quickly.

They lay still, catching their breath. Finally, a spark flared, and then another. The story-peddler's hands appeared, holding a burning rag to the wick of a clay oil lamp. As a dim, orange glow spread from the lamp, Jason saw beams and floorboards above his head. The companions lay in a basement, wide but low, so that only Zidu could stand. Blankets and odds and ends had been stacked against the walls, including chipped pots, clay oil lamps, and two clay tablets covered with blocky letters.¶ The rocky floor had been swept almost clean of gravel.

"The house is abandoned," said the story-peddler, "so this is one of my favorite hiding holes, though I never thought I'd hide blasphemers and enemies of Moses here." He chuckled.

"We're not enemies of Moses," said Jason hastily, glaring at Tia, who was glaring at the story-peddler. "It was just a misunderstanding."

"Well, don't worry about me," the man said. "I revere Moses, too, but unlike Isaac and his ruffians, I'm not too concerned by mere words."

"Anyway, thank you for helping us," said Jason. Zidu and Rim-Hadad thanked him, too. Tia remained silent, arms crossed over her chest.

"But, sir, what happened out there?" Zidu asked. "Why were they so angry?"

The story-peddler slid across the floor to lean against a wall. The dancing lamplight revealed thoughtful hazel eyes. He looked twenty-five or so.

"Well," he said, "these are good people, but they're very loyal to their prophets—at least, the dead ones. Calling holy Moses a liar ... well, that was guaranteed to end badly, especially lately. Some townswomen got caught worshipping Astarte last week, so religious tensions are running pretty high." He looked back and forth at their blank faces. "Uh, Astarte, she's a Canaanite goddess. In any case, after something like that ... well, some

---

¶ The Canaanites developed what is arguably the first alphabet. Twenty or thirty letters replaced the hundreds of symbols found in Mesopotamian cuneiform and Egyptian hieroglyphs. The new system was easier to learn, so it spread rapidly, particularly among merchants. Around 1400 BC, a people called the Phoenicians developed what was probably the most widely used Canaanite alphabet. It had twenty-two letters: 𐤕𐤀𐤁𐤂 𐤃𐤄𐤅𐤆 𐤇𐤈𐤉𐤊 𐤋𐤌𐤍𐤎 𐤏𐤐𐤑𐤒 𐤓𐤔𐤕 The Phoenician alphabet's descendants include both Greek letters— ΑΒΓΔΕΖΗΘΙΚΛΜΝΞΟΠΡΣΤΥΦΧΨΩ—and the Hebrew alphabet— אבגדהוזחטיכךלמםנןסעפףצץקרשת. The former evolved into the letters you're reading now.

~ William Gallo, *Saints & Satyrs*, 17.

people follow rabble-rousers a bit more readily." **

He stroked his short brown beard and appraised them before continuing. "On top of that, you people already had one count against you." The travelers exchanged mystified glances. "You, my friend," he said to Zidu, "have a Mesopotamian look about you, so some people might think you're Assyrian. The Assyrians have been cruel to these people—more than cruel."

Zidu opened his mouth, looking offended, but Jason spoke up first. Something bothered him about the story-peddler. "What do you mean, 'these people'? You talk like you're not one of them. Aren't you?"

The man grinned. "Well, it depends what you mean by 'one of them.' I don't come from this country, but I guess you could call me an Israelite,†† sort of. I'm Jewish." His eyes narrowed, and he nodded. "And if I read the signs right, I have more in common with *you* than with these ancients. I knew the moment I saw you. You're not from this world, are you? You're from the other world. Somewhere there your body lies asleep, while your mind takes a holiday here. The same goes for me. I'm a dream voyager."

** Astarte was a racy goddess of sex, fertility, and war. She was the Canaanite version of the Babylonians' Ishtar, herself based on the Sumerians' Inanna. Apparently, the Greeks adopted Astarte and gave her a name you know: Aphrodite, goddess of sex—called Venus by the Romans....

The ancient Israelites probably didn't doubt the existence of the Baals and Astarte and the other Canaanite gods. They weren't monotheists yet. They just weren't supposed to worship other gods. Israelite religion only allowed the worship of one national deity, whose name they wrote Y-H-V-H. He is a jealous God, after all, according to Exodus. The "one god" rule didn't prevent a little moonlighting. The Bible is peppered with prophets' complaints about Israelites worshipping foreign deities.

~ William Gallo, Lectures, History 138.

†† The Israelites had several tribes, so their nation may actually have several histories—some reflected in the Bible and some not. It's possible that one tribe descended from Abraham and his barbarian herders, another from escaped Egyptian slaves, and another from Canaanite peasants. It's even possible that one of the tribes, Dan, descended from the notorious "Sea Peoples" who invaded the Middle East around the start of the Iron Age. That means they may have been Greek, though there are other possibilities. "Dan" sounds like one of the names Homer used for the Greeks: "Danaans."

~ William Gallo, Lectures, History 138.

7

Persian Stew

THE OLD MEGA-KINGDOMS EVENTUALLY recovered. First the Assyrians in the 700s, then the Egyptians and Babylonians. But by the 600s, even the strongest kingdoms faced two daunting problems. First, the Fertile Crescent wasn't so fertile anymore, thanks to thousands of years of over-farming, over-grazing, and deforestation. Second, the region was short of iron, and iron was power. The result? During the 500s, foreigners conquered the entire Fertile Crescent. Amazing! The powerhouse of civilization, mere provinces in someone else's empire.

The empire in question was built by the Persians, from Iran. During the 540s, their shah Cyrus the Great set out on a career of conquest, powered by cavalry. By 500 BC, Cyrus and his successors had seized the whole Fertile Crescent, and that was just the beginning....

The Persian Empire marks a new stage in the history of the Near East. During the Bronze Age, the great kingdoms had mostly focused on the river valleys. During the Iron Age, the key empires were behemoths, with territories and populations and resources that dwarfed the river valleys' puny offerings. The Persian Empire ultimately stretched from southeastern Europe to western India. It was the largest state the world had ever seen. In fact, its strength and span gave the Near East an unprecedented two centuries of relative peace and prosperity—what we might call the Pax Persiana.

~ William Gallo, Lectures, History 56.

ooooo

The story-peddler's name was Yakov Zaretsky. "I'm studying to become a rabbi back home, in Kiev," he explained.
Tia, Zidu, and Rim-Hadad looked mystified. "But this is sort
of an extra-curricular activity. I came here to learn about my
people's history. I'm using Fore to study the ancient Israelites."

"But how did you get here?" Jason demanded, feeling jit-
tery. "How did you get to the world of Fore?"

Yakov's eyebrows rose. "Same as you: I entered the dream
trance, floated across the ether, and landed in a thin place, not
far from here."

"A trance?" Jason glanced at Zidu. "Well, did ... did Doctor
Valencia ... help you?"

"Who?" Yakov peered at Jason over the oil lamp. "Who's
Doctor Valencia?"

"She's the, uh ... She sent me here."

"Oh." The rabbinical student sat back against the wall.
"Well, she didn't send me. My mother first taught me the
trance." His long face turned quizzical. "What made you think
I learned from the same person as you?"

Jason's hands were shaking. "I didn't *learn* from her. She just
sent me here. I mean, I didn't want to come. She just pushed
me through the door."

"Door? What door? I don't understand. How can you come
here if you don't want to?"

"Hell, I don't know!" Jason cried. "You tell me. I don't—"
He shook his head. "I don't even know what Fore is. Are we ...
are we on another planet or what?"

Yakov stared at Jason. "It sounds like you've got a lot to
learn," he finally said. "I'll tell you what: you give me your
story, and I'll give you mine."

ooooo

Yakov's explanation matched the one Jason's father had
given Nebetit, except that Yakov spoke in terms of *dream
energy*. "The energy from our world's dreams floats on the

ether, and it pretty much never fades. Over thousands of years, the energy from trillions of dreams combined to form a world, the world of Fore. Fore takes its landscape from the images bound up in that dream energy—the images dreamers have sent into the ether since the dawn of humankind."

"I don't understand," said Tia. "You're saying Fore is a dream?"

"No, not exactly. Fore has a life of its own. People and lumins and other forces here move on their own, even though they're made up of dream energy. The world of Fore was formed out of my people's dreams, but it's grown into something much more."

"Absolutely fascinating," said Zidu as Jason and Tia shook their heads. "Jason and I have heard this theory before, and it makes more and more sense."

"It is interesting, isn't it?" Yakov grinned. "The result is that your world makes a wonderful place to study *our* history. Because dream energy lasts so long, dreams from centuries ago still shape Fore today. That allows me to come here and study a pretty good likeness of ancient Canaan."

"But what about the languages?" Jason demanded. "If this is really like ancient Canaan, how come everyone speaks English?"

"We're not speaking English. We're speaking Ukrainian." Yakov chuckled. "At least, to me we are. You see, dreams work on our minds. We hear our native language."

"And can anyone come here?"

"No. Most people glimpse Fore in their sleep and never know it. Only dream voyagers visit the way you and I have. You have to know the trance, and you've got to have the gift of dream voyaging. It runs in families."

Yakov shook his head. "It's so odd telling you this, Jason. I've never met a dream voyager who didn't know at least some of this. And I've definitely never heard of anyone entering Fore who didn't mean to. Is it possible you did mean to come? I mean, obviously you've got the dream voyager's gift. It sounds like your father does, too. Maybe you came here on your own, like every-one else, and hallucinated this mysterious Doctor Valencia."

"I suggested the same thing long ago," said Zidu, "and it still seems the best explanation."

"Doctor Valencia might be a subconscious mechanism," Yakov continued, "for dealing with dream voyaging. Maybe you've got some prejudice that keeps you from recognizing your gift, so you sort of snuck into Fore, behind your own back."

"I don't buy it," Jason grumbled. "I saw Doctor Valencia when I was wide awake, outside my window, with a snake in her pocket. At least, I think it was her. And anyway, she screwed me. I can't believe I did that to myself."

"The *Dead Valencia*," Rim-Hadad exclaimed. "Now I understand the ship's name."

"Well," said Yakov, "I can't explain Doctor Valencia. But maybe I can shed some light on one of your other mysteries. I have an idea how Fore may have trapped your father—why he won't wake up."

Jason leaned forward.

"You've got to understand the nature of dream voyaging and the connection between Fore and our world. Sleep is the portal that connects the two. Obviously, our real body has to sleep for us to appear here in Fore. But what you might not realize is that we also have to sleep *here in Fore* to return to our real body. No matter how loud the alarm rings in our world, you won't hear it until your body here in Fore falls asleep. When you sleep here, you're connected to the other world, and an alarm or another distraction there can wake you up, can bring you back home."

"That must be why I keep dreaming about the other world," said Jason. "I keep seeing my own sleeping body, back in the hospital room. You're saying it's because when I'm asleep here, I'm connected to the other world."

"Truly fascinating," Zidu breathed.

"Exactly," said Yakov. "I dream of my sleeping body back in Kiev every night. Well, if the alarm went off in the waking world during that dream, or someone called my name, I'd hear it and wake up back home. So would you. But what if you never went to sleep here in Fore? Then you'd never be connected to our world. You'd never hear an alarm there or feel anyone shaking you. You'd be stuck here. I suspect that's what's happened to your father."

"But what could keep him from falling asleep?"

"It sounds like torture," said Tia.

"I have no idea," Yakov replied. "But I can't think of any other way to keep a dream voyager here."

Now he leaned forward. "Listen, Jason, there's one other thing you should know about Fore. Did Doctor Valencia explain that you can't come back any time soon—that you can only visit Fore a few times every year—our world's years?"

"I don't remember. I don't think so."

"Well, dream voyaging taxes the brain. You can't do it more than once every few months." Yakov grimaced. "So if you don't find your father this trip, you won't get another chance for quite a while—and it sounds like your father doesn't have long. To make matters worse, there's really no telling when this trip will end. You could wake up at any time. So don't dawdle. You don't want to run out of time before you find your father. Obviously, that's your highest priority."

"Yeah, obviously."

They pondered a while. Finally, Rim-Hadad spoke up again: "This has all been very interesting, but we're still trapped under an old house in a hostile town. How do we get out of here?"

"Oh, that won't be hard," Yakov replied. "I doubt anyone will charge you with blasphemy. If the elders got involved every time someone insulted the Lord, they'd never have any peace. Besides, they don't like rioters and peace-disturbers." He paused and sat still. "I guess the mob's broken up by now. At least, they're nowhere nearby. Let's rest here a little while longer. Then I'll show you to the gate. I know the night officer. He's from one of the northern tribes, so he knows what it's like to be an outsider here in the south.* I'm sure he'll let you out quietly."

---

* The Jews descend from only two of the twelve tribes of Israel: Benjamin and Judah, the southern kingdom's tribes. The northern kingdom had ten tribes, but they disappeared after the 700s, when the Assyrians conquered them. The Assyrians may have exiled them, and that gives rise to the legend that the Ten Lost Tribes of Israel still exist somewhere. Jewish prophecies say they'll return to Israel someday. The Mormons, on the other hand, think various Native Americans descend from one of the ten lost tribes. Other claimed descendants include the Ethiopian Jews, the Afghans, the Kurds, and, believe it or not, the Japanese and the British.
  ~ William Gallo, Lectures, History 138.

○○○○○

The journey resumed. One warm night several days later, Jason lay awake in their campsite, watching the watery stars above and remembering another fight with his father. It had been a weeknight, about a month before the coma, and Jason's father had called to say he'd be working late. Jason had made dinner for himself and Athena. Shortly after the meal, Athena had thrown up.

Jason's father finally came home close to 11:00.

"You're late," said Jason cheerfully, looking up from his laptop.

"Yeah, I'm sorry about that, kiddo. We worked late and then went out for pizza."

"We?"

His father cocked an eyebrow. "I was with Candace Fleming, the graduate student you met."

"Oh." Jason's tone was casual, but his blood had turned cold. "Well, while you were out having a good time, your daughter practically coughed up a lung."

His father's mouth opened.

"Yeah, she barfed all over the place. And then she got a fever. I thought her head was going to explode. But don't worry. I cleaned her up and ran a bath and everything. She's fine."

"But … why the hell didn't you call me?" His father's eyes blazed.

Jason struggled to keep his voice from shaking. "I didn't want to bother you. I knew you were having a good time."

"God damn it, Jason, if you think I'm buying that crap, you're wrong. You know very well I want a phone call if anything serious happens to either of you, day or night. Now where's your sister?"

"In bed," he answered, raising his chin but not daring to argue. His father stormed off, leaving Jason feeling both smug and shaken.

He sighed as he relived the memory.

"There's a lot of mumbling and rolling around tonight."

Jason looked up and found that Tia had poked her head through the flap of her little privacy tent. He couldn't see her well in the darkness, but he could see one eye, twinkling in the starlight. A swirl of raven hair covered the other. "Can't you sleep?" she whispered.

"No," he whispered back. "You?"

"Someone keeps making noise right next to my tent."

Jason chuckled. "Sorry." He lay still, looking up at countless stars. "Tia," he finally said, "your mom died when you were born right?" She nodded. "So did your dad ever... Were there ever, you know, any other women?"

"I guess there were a lot of temple priestesses. But there wasn't anyone else living with us until I was eight. Then my father bought a peasant woman, to keep house and be his mistress."

Jason blinked. It was too dark to see Tia's expression. "Did you mind?"

"I cried for two weeks," she said matter-of-factly. "Then I burned her clothes and her bed."

He stared, open-mouthed. Then he laughed. Soon Tia was laughing, too, and they had to cover their mouths to keep from waking Zidu and Rim-Hadad.

"Did you get in trouble?" Jason asked.

"Yes. My father beat me."

"Oh." Jason's smile dissolved. "Did you love him, your father?"

"Yes, of course." Her whisper was breathless, and Jason hoped he hadn't made her cry. "He used to scare me when he got angry, but usually he was the most wonderful man I ever knew. He used to make me toys and take me to town whenever he went." She shook her head, and he thought she might be smiling. "I knew he loved me more than any of those women—more than anyone."

"When did he die?"

"Two years ago." She didn't seem to be crying.

Jason nodded. "Same as my mom: two years ago—a little more."

"I'm sorry." Jason was startled to feel a warm hand on his wrist.

"Thanks. I'm sorry, too, about your dad." They lay in silence a while, listening to their companions' snores.

"My dad has another woman, too, I think," he finally said. "But I'm not gonna burn her clothes."

ooooo

For a week or so, the companions sailed past Babylonian-style cities, adorned with ziggurats, including a few covered in rooftop gardens.[†] But then the *Dead Valencia* reached a land of horsemen and camel caravans,[‡] and a new style of architecture appeared among the old temples. The columns of the palaces were slender piers of stone, far more elegant than the heavy pillars they'd seen upstream.

"Their gods must hold up the roofs," said Tia. "Those pretty little columns could never do it."

They pulled ashore at a town near one of these palaces. The afternoon had turned cloudy and cool, so after buying supplies, they treated themselves to a hot meal. They sat in a mud-brick inn, eating "Persian Stew," named for the rulers of this land. The chunks of meat and cooked vegetables were

---

† Most of what we know about the Hanging Gardens of Babylon comes from Herodotus. He tells us King Nebuchadnezzar wanted to comfort his wife, who missed her homeland: green, mountainous Iran. So he built her an artificial mountain of terraces, planted so thick with rooftop gardens that greenery hung over the walls. Unfortunately, Herodotus wasn't history's most dedicated fact-checker. It's possible his hanging gardens represent late-Babylonian roof gardens in general, rather than a single building.
~ William Gallo, *Historical Factoids*, 39.

‡ By Persian times, you get most of the animal-powered transportation we have now, including dromedaries—the "one-humped camels"—which the shahs used for cavalry. The Persians rode horses, too—right on the animal's back, instead of in a chariot. In fact, the shahs set up the fastest horse-based courier system the world had ever seen. Does this sound familiar? "Neither snow nor rain nor heat nor gloom of night stays these couriers from the swift completion of their appointed rounds." Yes, it's what they say about American mailmen. But the New York post office copied it from Herodotus, who was writing about this ancient Persian pony express.
~ William Gallo, *Lectures*, History 56.

spicy and savory, and unquestionably the best dish Jason had eaten in Fore. Tia and Zidu enjoyed the stew, too, and Rim-Hadad ate four bowls.

By the time they returned to the *Dead Valencia*, Rim-Hadad was paying a heavy price for his enthusiasm. "Ooh," he moaned, "my belly's on fire. These people are mad to eat such spices." The others smiled. Jason guessed quantity was the culprit, not spices. "I need medicine," Rim-Hadad wailed, lying flat on the deck. "Whenever I overate, my mother would boil witch thistle for me. It's the only thing for a burn on the belly." He looked plaintively at Tia. "Would you get me some? I'm sure they have it in the town."

Tia didn't know the flower, but Zidu did. "I hope we can find it," he said, looking down at the writhing barbarian. "Will you be well here while we go looking?"

"No!" Rim-Hadad groaned. "Jason, you stay with me." He grasped Jason's ankle weakly. "I'd be easy prey for carrion birds all alone."

Jason rolled his eyes. "Yeah, sure. I'll stay and fight off the vultures."

As Tia and Zidu followed the dirt path back to town, Jason made his patient as comfortable as possible. Then he sat by the prow and stared at the shore and the hazy mountains beyond, daydreaming about ziggurats and magical§ rooftop gardens.

Eventually, a shadow fell over him, and he turned to find Rim-Hadad on his feet again. Jason opened his mouth to congratulate the barbarian on a speedy recovery. But in a sudden rush, Rim-Hadad drove his beefy fist down and then up into Jason's jaw, with the force of a donkey's kick. Jason's head snapped back, and the world went dark.

ooooo

---

§ We get our word "magic" from the Persians—from their caste of priests, who were called magi. They had a reputation for mystical wisdom. The three wise men of the New Testament are magi.
   ~ William Gallo, Lectures, History 138.

The Rector for Enforcement stared at a map of the Jericho River. He'd heard no word from Crocker, but communications were slow upriver, so that didn't concern him. And Crocker was resourceful and reliable, while Jason Gallo was just a boy, and probably had no idea of the forces arrayed against him.

Seiki shifted on the Rector's shoulder, then hopped down onto the map. She scrambled across Chaldean Babylonia,¶ on the left bank, and her wrinkled body came to rest above the words "PERSIAN EMPIRE." She leered up at the Rector, her black in black eyes mocking as always. Her grin stretched the corpselike skin across her skull.

"Don't worry," said the Rector. "We'll catch him." He rubbed his chin, staring at the emaciated creature and the map. "In fact, I have a premonition that we already have."

¶ Nebuchadnezzar and the other late Babylonian kings came from a Semitic tribe called the Chaldeans. Eventually, "Chaldean" got connected with the whole Babylonian upper class. These folks inherited Babylonian scholarship and religion, so the Greeks thought of them as magicians and astrologers. That's why "Chaldean" means occultist in modern English.
~ William Gallo, Lectures, History 56.

8

Philosophers of Greece

BY THE 700s BC, civilization had returned to Greece after a long dark age, and the natives were building a unique society called the *polis*. Poleis were independent city-states with citizens, rather than subjects. Instead of reigning kings or priests, they had magistrates, working under written laws. Athens and a few other poleis even featured democracy, though with limited civil rights and no votes for women, immigrants, or slaves. Whatever the form of government, the Greeks loved these little nations, and the polis trumped tribes, clans, and gods as the focus for Greek loyalty. If this all seems only natural, it's because our modern nations look a lot like giant poleis. Two thousand years after the rise of the polis, Western Civilization built a similar system, possibly influenced by ancient Greek ideas and vocabulary. (We get many government-related words from "polis," including "politics," "police," "policy," and "metropolis," along with city names like "Indianapolis" and "Tripoli.")

By the 400s, the Greeks had developed a culture we call "Classical." Classical humanism produced art and literature focusing on people, rather than gods. Classical science searched for universal laws of nature, relying on observation, rather than myth and magic. Together, humanism and science triggered the rise of philosophy....

Classical society was new, but it was built on old foundations, mostly from the Fertile Crescent.

~ William Gallo, *Saints & Satyrs*, 21, 23.

ooooo

Jason blinked and opened his eyes, then turned to face a beautiful sunset. The western sky glowed purple, blue, and pink, as the watery sphere sank into the clouds. He chuckled. The sun looked like a burning coal in a bowl of three-flavored sherbet.

He opened his mouth to wet his dry lips ... and winced. His jaw ached. Why? Then he remembered. Had Rim-Hadad really hit him?

He tried to jump to his feet but found he couldn't move. He was sitting on the deck, against the mast, with blankets cushioning his rear and back. And he was tied up—his hands against his body and his body against the mast. Even his ankles had been tied together. Fear clenched his stomach as he remembered his voyage on the Trojan ship.

"So, you're up," said Rim-Hadad. He came around the mast.

"Wha ... What ...?"

Rim-Hadad looked grim. "I am sorry, my friend. I once told you my brother Samanu was a viper. But it is Rim-Hadad, Nablanum's second son, who has been the snake in your tent. I wish it could be otherwise. You are worth gold to a powerful man downriver. That gold will bring less cheer than I'd hoped, since you've become my friend, but I must have it. The son of a great man like Nablanum should not tend another man's herds."

"The Rector," breathed Jason. "You're working for the Rector."

The barbarian nodded slowly.

"But how? When?"

Rim-Hadad sat down on the deck. "I have worked for the Rector since before we met. The man you saw in Sumer, who led the hunters there, that was my brother Samanu."

"Your brother!" Jason gasped. "But, but, what's going on?"

"I suppose friendship claims some explanation. But I can't tell you much." The barbarian sighed. "Many months before you came to my land, a man called Crocker visited our clan. He was a servant of this Rector, and he sought strong men for a hard job. That job was you. He wanted you caught and

brought downstream, and he promised payment in gold."
Rim-Hadad shook his head. "We'd lost our herds, Samanu
and I, so we were ripe for the task. We brothers were partners
in this."

"But you fought your brother!" cried Jason. "That night
outside your camp, when he tried to kidnap me. And you
killed one of his guys."

"I told you my brother is a greedy fool." Rim-Hadad bared
yellow-white teeth. "He could not share, not now or ever. He
tried to take you in the night, right out from under my nose,
to keep the gold for himself. So I killed his man and wounded
him—and would have killed him, too, if not for the ties of
blood." The barbarian fingered his club. "To take you by force
was madness anyway. It's a long journey, and you were headed
for Crocker of your own choice. My methods are wiser."

Jason's jaw throbbed, but he clenched his teeth anyway.
"But you saved me in Dur-Babylon, and you fought for me,
for all of us, in Crete." The hurt was worse than the fear.

"Just protecting my prize." Rim-Hadad turned away and
stared at the rugged countryside to starboard. Jason realized
with a start that the shore now lay to the right. Apparently
they'd crossed the river. He gulped. The right bank had so far
been wild and dangerous.

"I don't understand," said Jason. "What does this Rector
want from me?"

"The Rector," said the barbarian slowly, "is some sort of
great chieftain. He has business with your father, and I guess
they're enemies, but I don't know why or what business. They
need to catch you, though Crocker would not say what they'll
do with you."

"But how'd they know I'd come to Sumer?"

"They did not know. Crocker simply sent men to watch
each place where you could have entered the world of Fore.
He called them 'thin places,' and that man Yakov mentioned
them, too. I don't understand it, but Crocker said these are
rare places, places where the fabric of the world grows thin.
Ours was in Sumer, near First Lagash, and my brother went

to watch it. The gods favored the sons of Nablanum when you chose that place. But you slipped through Samanu's fingers, the fool.

"I should have gone myself. After that, my brother left men to search for you in First Lagash and returned home, and we watched the river. Crocker guessed you would come downstream if you turned up in Sumer. I suppose the gods gave us another chance when you came ashore in our land, looking for our sheikh."

Rim-Hadad looked away again, and Jason groaned. If only he'd listened to Zidu's warnings and sailed past Sheikh Zimri's territory. "So you brought me here," he said, his voice hoarse. "Is this the Rector's country?"

"No." Rim-Hadad avoided Jason's gaze. "His tribe comes from further downstream. But they have allies here, and this is where Crocker waits for you. In a city called Athenopolis, there is a clan called the Aristotle Academy."

Jason's eyebrows rose. He knew the name *Aristotle*.

"They're philosophers," Rim-Hadad continued, pronouncing the word with difficulty. "That is where we're going: to Athenopolis and the Aristotle Academy, and Crocker."

"You traitor!" Jason spat, jerking against his ropes. "You don't even know anything about this! You don't have any idea what these guys want or what'll happen to me!" His voice shook. "All you care about is the gold. You're such an ignorant, stupid barbarian, you don't even know what a philosopher is!"

Rim-Hadad's face darkened, and Jason feared he'd gone too far. "I'm not so ignorant as you think. I know philosophers hate shaman power—mad though that may sound—and they fight some battle against shamans and lumins."

What?

Rim-Hadad smirked. "So, the stupid barbarian isn't as ignorant as you think."

He stood. "You have no amulet or other holy tool, so there will be no shaman mischief. You won't be calling Zidu—not that he could help you anyway. We'll reach Athenopolis tomorrow, and then you're no longer my burden." Rim-Hadad turned but then said: "You're right though, Jason: I don't know what will happen to you." Now his voice turned quiet and gruff. "But I will ask Crocker and his Academy* to treat you gently, for what it's worth."

ooooo

The *Dead Valencia* drifted on the current most of the night. Jason stared into the blackness, wrestling with fear and hurt and anger. Worse than any of those, though, was the loneliness. He wondered if he'd ever see Zidu and Tia again.

He tried to focus on more practical concerns. He had only one way to call for help: the reaching trance. Rim-Hadad had said this Aristotle Academy was fighting shamans and lumins. Weird. But if Jason could reach some local lumins, maybe they'd consider him an ally. Maybe they'd ... call the police, or the local king ... or do *something*. In Dur-Babylon, Tia had said a shaman could always call lumins nearby, even without a shaman bond.

But Tia had also said a shaman needed a holy amulet. Jason ground his teeth. He had no amulet, so the idea was useless.

He shivered beneath his blanket. It was ironic, really, that he should want an amulet: a piece of superstition. He'd felt silly using Tidal's clay figurine. Tia had said the amulet would call the goddess, but Jason hadn't noticed any goddess helping him.

His heartbeat quickened. What if Tia was wrong? Or what if she was wrong for him? Amulets and gods played a role in Egypt, but to Jason, the shaman gift seemed more like a sixth sense, not a divine mystery. What if he could use the gift his own way: a twenty-first-century way? What if he didn't need an amulet?

It could work. And he had nothing to lose.

---

* In Athens, Plato set up a school of philosophy more than a decade after the 399 execution of Socrates, his teacher. He taught in a grove named for the legendary hero Academus. So the Greeks called the school the Academy, giving us the English word. Aristotle was one of Plato's students at the Academy, though he eventually set up a rival school called the Lyceum.

~ William Gallo, *Historical Factoids*, 50.

As the night wore on and Rim-Hadad manned the tiller, Jason worked to calm his mind, just as Tia had taught him. His turbulent emotions made concentration difficult, and he was uncomfortable. Despite the blankets, his ropes and his awkward position distracted him.

But finally, after hours, he felt the peace of the reaching trance come over him. In his mind's eye, he saw the endless pool of still, black water and the stars twinkling on its surface. It was working. Without an amulet, without any trappings of ancient superstitions, he had entered the trance.

Jason looked over the water and knew Zidu was there, searching for him. He told his friend about Rim-Hadad's treachery and about their journey to Athenopolis. But Zidu's reply gave no comfort. *We have almost nothing of value, and no way to cross the river.*

So Jason turned and called across the endless pool with the voice of his mind. He called for any lumin nearby, any lumin who might help an enemy of the Aristotle Academy—any lumin who might care that a friend of lumins faced danger. He called and called until exhaustion dimmed the picture in his mind.

ooooo

Jason woke to the sound of smacking and slurping. He grunted and looked up, knocking his head against the *Dead Valencia*'s mast. "Uuuuhh," he moaned. He'd slept sitting up, tied to the mast. Sore muscles screamed as he stretched his neck.

Then his eyes snapped open wide as he realized he had company, and that his companion was not Rim-Hadad. Morning sunlight revealed an enormous, dirty bird, like a vulture, sitting on the deck. Its sharp black talons were shoving strips of dried meat into its mouth. But that mouth had no business on a bird. It was a human mouth, with yellow, crooked teeth. The vulture had the head of a hideously ugly woman, with matted straw-colored hair and beady, gleaming eyes.

"Who are you?" Jason gasped.

"Shhh," the bird-woman responded without looking up. "Your big friend will hear. He's over in the trees, doing his business."

Jason looked around. The *Dead Valencia* bobbed next to a bare, rocky outcropping. Acacias and oaks covered the shore, except where the rocks jutted into the river. Jason couldn't see Rim-Hadad.

He turned back to the bird-woman and whispered: "Have you come to help me?"

"No," she whispered back, still eating. "I heard your call, but I don't get involved with strangers. I came to see if you had anything good to eat."

Jason stared. This was his lumin rescue? "But—but did you understand why I called? I'm an enemy of the Aristotle Academy. Aren't you their enemy, too?"

"No." She smacked her lips and sucked on a talon, almost finished with the meat. "I don't care about them one way or the other."

Jason's heart sank. "But I heard there was a fight between the lumins and the Aristotle Academy."

"There is." The bird-woman belched quietly, sending the stench of rotting meat into the air. "Some lumins fight back, along with a lot of humans, shamans and otherwise. But it's nothing to do with me. Harpies don't get involved in politics and great struggles."

"Great. A conscientious objector." Jason looked around, thinking of the harpies in the Golden Fleece and the other Greek myths his father had told.[†] Did the stories mention any way to sweet talk a harpy? His mind was blank. "Look, I don't need you to get involved. Just untie me. I'll take it from there."

---

† Most of the myths we know were told by Iron Age Greeks about their Bronze Age, Mycenaean ancestors. To the latter-day Greeks, the Bronze Age was the time of myths and heroes. And those myths were about all the Iron Agers remembered about the Mycenaeans, thanks to the long, awful dark age separating them in time. In fact, the latter-day Greeks thought cyclops had built the walls lying in ruins at the old Mycenaean palace sites.

~ William Gallo, Lectures, History 78.

The meat was gone, but the harpy didn't look satisfied. "I'm not too good with ropes." She held up a scaly bird foot, flapping her wings for balance. "And like I said, I don't want to get involved."

Jason sighed as the harpy hopped toward the stern, sniffing the deck. "The food's in the hold," he said, "underneath."

"I know," she said. "That's where I got the meat. But all you've got left down there is bread, and I was hoping for more flesh. Is there another hold?"

"No." Jason hoped Rim-Hadad had gone off a good way and had some serious business to do in the woods. "Look, can you just help me a little bit?" He looked around the sunlit deck, trying to think what he could offer. "If you do, I'll personally see to it that you get something out of it—like a big meal. How about that? I'll get you steak and leg-of-lamb and bacon and … whatever. *Please.*"

She hopped close to him. He tried not to cough at her stench—like chicken dung mixed with halitosis.

"You're making that up," she croaked, "but I forgive you because you're a handsome thing." She tilted her head. "I couldn't untie you, but I suppose I could find someone who will, someone who's fighting the Aristotle Academy." Yellow teeth gnawed at her lower lip. "I'll do it on one condition."

"Anything."

"You have to give me a kiss."

"What? A kiss?"

"Yes." One foot suddenly shot into her matted hair and then reemerged, pincer-like talons holding a squirming louse. The harpy popped it into her mouth before Jason could blink. He recoiled as she continued: "And I want a real kiss, not just a peck on the cheek."

Jason gulped. "Now?"

"No time like the present." Before Jason could speak, the harpy had hopped forward and her clammy lips were on his. He spluttered and tried not to retch at the nasty, wet kiss. He half expected the harpy to turn to a princess, or himself to a frog.

"You have a sweet kiss," she said with a yellow, toothy smile when it was over, "like a blooming honey-lotus, as the poet says.[‡] I know where to find the Academy's enemies. I'll tell them."

"P-p-please, tell them we're headed for Athenopolis," he sputtered. "And tell them they've gotta hurry!"

"I will." She winked, and then with a flutter of dirty feathers, she leapt into the air. Jason did not start spitting until she was out of sight.

ooooo

Rim-Hadad did not notice the missing meat. They sailed downstream and spoke very little. Jason stared at the countryside. This was not the wild right bank he'd seen upriver. A real civilization hugged the hills and valleys along the shore. The *Dead Valencia* sailed past three handsome towns, made up of whitewashed houses with red tile roofs. Docks ran alongside the bank, and long sailing vessels plied the river, some with two sails and three rows of oars, one on top of the other. Jason watched the locals, antlike in the distance, as they farmed, hurried along city streets, worked the docks, and in one odd case, cheered and shouted at a footrace run by naked men.[§] He wished he could call for help, but Rim-Hadad never let the boat stray close to the bank.

---

‡ Sappho was one of Greece's greatest lyric poets and also one of its few career women. She came from the isle of Lesbos, and she wrote a bunch of love poems to women, which led to the modern meaning of the word "lesbian."

~ William Gallo, *Historical Factoids*, 49.

§ In Classical athletic contests, men competed *gymnos*, meaning naked, giving us the word "gymnasium." The most famous contests took place at the festival of Zeus, in Olympia. At first, these Olympic Games involved only a single foot race, in a building called the *stadion*, which led to "stadium." But over the years, the Greeks added events such as wrestling and horse racing. Christian authorities outlawed the games in 393 AD, as a pagan rite. (Europeans established the modern Olympics in 1896 AD.)

~ William Gallo, "Indo-European Roots of Classical, Germanic, and Slavic Public Rituals," *Manchester Historical Review*, VI. 487, 504 (2008).

As early afternoon sun baked the deck, the *Dead Valencia* rounded a wooded promontory and drifted into a wide bay. The surrounding valley was green and yellow with cultivation, and dominated by a city far larger than the others. Jason gaped as he took in the view. Impressive walls and monuments rose over countless houses. And atop a hill near the city's center, on a fortress-like platform, an assembly of breathtaking buildings presided over the valley in mathematical splendor. Rows of creamy-white columns supported painted friezes and tiled roofs. The largest structure looked like a colorful version of the Lincoln Memorial in Washington DC.

Rim-Hadad brought the *Dead Valencia* about and made for this metropolis. Busy docks marked much of the urban shore. But the barbarian ignored these and chose a deserted, rickety platform, just beyond the city limits. The elderly dock fronted a marshy shoreline, home to noisy birds but apparently no one else.

Jason bit his lip. Had they already arrived? Would he fall into the Rector's hands before his rescuers found him?

After tying off, Rim-Hadad knelt in front of Jason and suddenly forced a cloth gag into his mouth. Jason squealed, but he couldn't speak.

"I'm sorry," said Rim-Hadad, as he tied the gag behind Jason's head. "The locals will probably think you're a disobedient slave, but I can't take chances—not this close to my fortune. I will not be long."

Jason watched, furious, as Rim-Hadad crossed the wooden dock and then trudged through the marshes. Soon the barbarian reached the city and waded in among the pedestrians.

Left to himself, Jason growled and strained against his ropes, but he was securely tied. He banged his heels on the deck and tried to call for help, but he could do no more than squeal, and there was no one nearby.

Rim-Hadad returned within an hour and sat down on the deck. Then he waited, and Jason could do nothing but wait himself. He fretted and watched the urban crowd in the distance. These Greeks bore little resemblance to the barbarians who'd attacked them in Crete. And they seemed fairer than most of the people he'd seen on the left bank. He saw several heads of blond hair, something that had been rare until now.

As the shadows lengthened, Jason noticed two men headed across the marshes. They wore white tunics, falling almost to their knees. And each wore a colored, sheet-like cloth hanging from shoulder to hip.

Rim-Hadad's sandals smacked the dock as he jumped down to face the men. He towered over them, his thick legs spread apart, as if ready for a fight. "Crocker," he said gruffly, "well met." He touched his chest and bowed.

The leaner man bowed and smiled. Jason watched in terrified fascination. Crocker had straight, dark blond hair, pulled back into a ponytail.

"Well met, Rim-Hadad," he said. "This is Diokles, of the Aristotle Academy. He is our host."

Diokles bowed, his smile confident. He had short, dark hair and a short beard.

Crocker looked across at Jason. "I see you've brought me the Rector's prize."

"He'll be the Rector's prize when I have my gold," Rim-Hadad responded evenly.

"Of course," said Crocker. "But why are you alone? Where is your brother? I hired both of you."

"Ha!" Rim-Hadad barked. "You hired us both because you do not know the sons of Nablanum. You hired a lion and a cobra and asked them to share their prey. Well, the cobra revealed its nature as soon as our quarry came in sight. My brother tried to steal Jason from me, so I was forced to work alone. But as you can see, I fared well enough, by Amurru." A boastful smile spread across his coppery face, a grin Jason had seen many times. "I expect full price. You'll pay me both my brother's share and my own."

"The lion and the cobra," said Diokles with a watery smile.

"That speech should be enshrined in drama."¶

The barbarian looked confused, but Crocker spoke up quickly. "I don't have the gold with me here, obviously. And before I collect it, I must confirm your quarry, Rim-Hadad. May I speak to the prisoner?"

"Of course." Rim-Hadad held out one arm, inviting the two men aboard the *Dead Valencia*. On the deck, the barbarian squatted and removed Jason's gag. Crocker knelt, and he and Jason examined each other. The Rector's henchman had a long, handsome face with a straight nose.

"Seems a likely enough lad," said Diokles, who stood behind Crocker. "A bit old for my taste, but still, perhaps you could loan him to me for an hour or two."

Jason looked at the bearded Greek, confused. He found something disturbing—very disturbing—about Diokles' gentle smile, his half-pursed lips.

Crocker ignored his companion. "Young man, I am Gregory Samuel Woodward Crocker, and I'm very pleased to make your acquaintance. May I ask your name?"

Jason wrenched his gaze from the Greek. "Nice to meet you, too, I guess," he said slowly. "I'm Scooter Smith."

"That's a lie," snapped Rim-Hadad.

Crocker smiled. "Scooter Smith? Interestingly, Mr. Smith, you bear some resemblance to a man I know: one William Peter Gallo. And you fit his son's description perfectly. So perhaps we can be honest with each other, Jason Oliver Gallo. Are you involved?"

Jason blinked. "Involved in what?"

Crocker's hard, blue eyes narrowed. "What are you doing

¶ Classical Greek drama probably grew out of musical performances at religious festivals. In the early days, a soloist and a chorus sang and danced around an altar, on a stage called the *orchestra*, which gives us the modern word. The audience watched from stands on a semicircular hillside, called the watching place or *theatron*: the source of "theater." Legend has it a Greek named Thespis transformed the soloist into a real actor, which gives us "thespian." Greek drama had three key styles: comedy, tragedy, and satyr plays. Satyr plays were short and raunchy, named for the goat-legged satyrs. They give us the word "satire."

~ William Gallo, *Saints & Satyrs*, 44–45.

in Fore, Mr. Gallo?"

"That's enough," Rim-Hadad interrupted. Jason squealed as the barbarian slipped the gag back over his mouth. Involved? What was he talking about?

Crocker looked angry, but Rim-Hadad growled: "You don't get the milk until you buy the goat. You can see that this is your quarry. Ask him all the questions you want once you've paid me."

The two rose and glared at each other. Finally, Crocker put his hands on his hips. "I need until midday tomorrow. Why don't you bring our guest and come stay with us until then?"

"Ha!" Rim-Hadad retorted. "No, thank you. We're very comfortable here, aren't we Jason?"

Jason shot him a glare full of daggers.

"You bring me my gold tomorrow, right here. Then I'll be on my way. This city does not agree with me."

"You should be more trusting, Rim-Hadad," said Crocker. "We're not going to rob you."

"I apologize, but we play a dirty game, kidnapping an innocent boy. Dirty games call for dirty manners."

"Perhaps," said Crocker. He glanced at Diokles, and Jason cringed at the thought of falling into the creepy Greek's hands.

"Well, we've waited a long time for young Jason," said Crocker. "I suppose we can wait another night. Tomorrow, then. Get plenty of rest, Mr. Gallo. I think you will need it."

9

Hellenistic Myths

MACEDON WAS GREECE'S POOR cousin to the north, a land of barbarians who spoke a language a lot like Greek. When the Macedonian upper crust adopted Greek ways, they created a civilized state with Greek-like power, but on a much bigger scale. Macedon's King Phillip II conquered Greece in 338 BC. That probably would've landed him in the conquerors' hall of fame if his son hadn't totally eclipsed him a few years later. Between 334 and 330, Alexander the Great toppled the mightiest state known to the Mediterranean world, the Persian Empire. Then he just kept conquering....

After Alexander died, his empire broke into several kingdoms, ruled by Macedonians and Greeks. One of the largest of these controlled Macedon and a lot of Greece. Another ruled Egypt, which spelled the beginning of the end for Egyptian culture, after three thousand years. And the third mega-kingdom ruled Alexander's Asian territories, including Syria and Mesopotamia. The great kingdoms overshadowed the polis, but Classical culture continued. In fact, the arts and sciences rose to new heights. Alexander's reign marks the start of the Greek-like, or Hellenistic, age.

~ William Gallo, Lectures, History 113.

ooooo

Rim-Hadad slept off and on, but Jason couldn't. The memory of Diokles' soft smile kept intruding on his thoughts. Did the bearded Greek actually want … to molest him? Then there was the equally terrifying thought of dying. Crocker and the Rector could easily kill him. As if that weren't bad enough, Athena would then be alone.

As Jason's tired mind wandered, he found himself reliving Athena's tears of two years before. One Saturday morning, a month after their mother's funeral, the two Gallo children had been watching TV, and Athena had started to wail. Jason had no idea what had set her off, but he found her tears infectious, and soon he was wiping his own eyes.

"Athena!" cried their father, rushing in from the hall, where he'd been about to leave for the university. Jason shivered with relief as his father scooped Athena into his arms. "Honey, it's okay," he said, rocking the sobbing girl on the couch.

For a while, Athena cried, and their father just held her. "Athena," he finally whispered, "I know why you're crying." He kissed her forehead and continued in a steady voice. "Honey, you've got to understand: Mom would want you to be happy. She'd want you to be sad sometimes, a little bit, but mostly she'd want you to be happy. She'd want you to spend time with your friends and your brother and enjoy yourself." He brushed tears from her cheek and looked into her dark eyes. "It's sunny today. Mom would want you to go play in the fresh air. That's what would matter to her more than anything. Can you do that for Mom?"

Athena's breathing had slowed, and she was no longer crying. She looked at her father and nodded. He smiled and kissed her again.

Jason had been sitting on the floor nearby, fighting back his own tears. As his father turned to face him, he rose, expecting a hug and his own speech about what Mom would want.

"Jason, I want you to take care of your sister," he said. "I've got to stop by the office, but I'll be back soon. I want you to take Athena outside." His eyes held Jason's. "I need you to be strong for her until I get home. Okay?"

Jason shrank back, hoping his father couldn't tell that he'd wanted a hug, too. "Okay," he said.

And he *was* strong that day, and many others.

He screwed his eyes shut and knocked his head against the *Dead Valencia*'s mast. If he didn't return home, safe and sound, who would be strong for Athena?

ooooo

The eastern sky had just begun to turn gray when Jason noticed that the *Dead Valencia* was rocking. Rim-Hadad got up to look around. Suddenly a dark figure leapt aboard, not from the dock but from the river itself. Water splashed across the deck as the slender form of a woman flew at Rim-Hadad. Before the barbarian could even raise his club, she was on him. Jason couldn't twist around fast enough to see, but a moment later he heard a cry and a heavy splash and realized he was alone.

Hooves clattered along the dock. Jason peered into the pre-dawn shadows and saw what he took to be a horse and rider, followed at a distance by several runners. Then he blinked. The rider sat where the horse's head should have been, and his bare torso merged into the horse's chest. The creature was half man and half horse: a centaur.

"River nymph, I am here!" cried the centaur in a heroic baritone as he clattered to a stop. "Toss!"

A weighted rope shot out of the water, and the centaur lunged and grabbed it. Then he backed up on mighty equine legs, heaving at the rope. Suddenly, Rim-Hadad burst out of the water. The centaur pulled him up onto the dock, where he lay sputtering and gasping, his arms secured to his sides.

Then people surrounded Jason, and the *Dead Valencia* pitched from their hustling footsteps.

"Are you the harpy's shaman?" someone asked. "Are you the Academy's enemy?"

Jason nodded frantically and soon found himself cut loose and un-gagged. He saw that he owed his freedom to eight or ten people, humans and lumins.

"We can't linger," said a rich tenor. The speaker was a lumin: a short man with two hairy goat legs ending in cloven hooves. "We'll take you to safety, young shaman. Can you sail this boat?"

"Yes," Jason exclaimed. "It's my boat. What about him?" He pointed at Rim-Hadad.

"Don't worry about him," said a grim-faced, bearded man with a white scar covering what should have been his right eye. "He'll make a fine, strong galley slave for some lucky whip-master."

"No," said Jason. "Can't we ..." His rescuers looked confused. "Can't we just leave him here?"

"We can't," the one-eyed man snapped. "He'll tell the Academy too much."

"Your charity does you credit," said a female voice. Jason found a tall, pretty girl about his own age beside him, dripping water from her naked body. She had green hair and gleaming eyes, and her hands and feet were webbed. "I'll see to your barbarian—and see that he's released where he can do no more harm, if that's your wish."

The one-eyed man seemed about to argue, but torchlight flared on the shore, and someone yelled in the distance.

"They're coming," the goat-legged lumin. "Come, we must get clear of the city—now!"

ooooo

"But why doesn't the Aristotle Academy like shamans and lumins?" Jason asked, trying to ignore the creepy surroundings.

"They say shaman power handicaps mankind, and so do we lumins who provide it," said Semiramis, the snake-woman. "They say man can achieve great things without shaman power." She frowned, and Jason found it hard not to stare. Semiramis had the upper body of a woman, with dark skin and Babylonian features. But below the waist, she was a giant snake. And instead of arms, she had eagle's wings—currently folded modestly over her human torso.

"It's really half true," she continued. "All over the Greek and Macedonian lands, men have achieved wonders in architecture,

medicine, mathematics, astronomy—and largely without shaman power."*

"Oh, you're always saying that," complained Nomios, the
goat-legged lumin. "You've been duped by Aristotelian propaganda. They've turned you from the true path."

Nomios was a satyr. He reminded Jason of graduate students who sat in cafés back home, using big words and trying
to impress girls with talk about oppression and "the will of the
people." But unlike most of those students, Nomios had pointed
ears, a goat tail, and two small horns growing out of his curly
hair. Jason stared at the horns whenever Nomios spoke. He wondered if they itched. And staring at the horns helped him avoid
the awkwardness of looking down. Nomios wore no clothes and
proudly displayed the nakedness between his hairy goat legs.

Semiramis bristled at Nomios' accusation. "You know, I'm
not some ignorant immigrant from the left bank, star-struck
by Greek philosophy. I'm just giving credit where it's due.
They make some good arguments."

"Not that good," growled Zenon, the one-eyed man. Zenon
was a citizen of Athenopolis, and he seemed to be a priest,
merchant, and soldier all at once. "We'd live poor lives without
shaman power and lumins." He touched the angry white scar
over his forever-shut eyelid. "I didn't fight the Persians for ten
years to build an empire with no priests or oracles."

The camp's location disturbed Jason almost as much as the
lumins' strange bodies. An Academy ship had pursued them all
day, according to Semiramis' airborne reports, so finally Nomios
had suggested a hiding place. On an island near the right bank,

---

* The Hellenistic scholars were worthy heirs to Plato and Aristotle. Archimedes
calculated pi, while Eratosthenes worked out the Earth's circumference—and got it
almost right—and Euclid developed geometry imposed on high-school students to
this day. Aristarchus argued that the Earth revolves around the sun, but the idea
didn't catch on for another seventeen centuries. And Hero of Alexandria built the
first steam engine, though he couldn't apply it to anything practical. Egypt's capital,
Alexandria, was the intellectual hub of the Mediterranean world, graced especially
by the ancient world's largest and most famous library, as well as the great temple
to the muses: the *mouseion*, giving us the word "museum."

~ William Gallo, *Saints & Satyrs*, 62-63.

they'd found a chilling landmark: a colossal skeleton, stretched out alongside the river. An immense crown of metal spikes lay near the skull, as if the Statue of Liberty had fallen and rotted where she lay. "It was once a giant lumin, of course," Nomios had explained. "A bit unnerving at first, but that's good because pretty much everyone avoids this place." They'd concealed the *Dead Valencia* nearby, behind a deserted temple. Then Jason and his new companions had hidden beneath the dome of the giant skull.

Nomios stoked the campfire, which sent a steady stream of smoke into upper reaches of the huge cranium. "In any case," he continued, "the struggle is mainly political. Commando operations like this morning's rescue ... well, they're very rare. And of course, we lumins avoid real combat with humans."

"More's the pity," Zenon muttered.

"Usually," continued the satyr, "both sides work through the Assembly and the courts."

His voice drifted off. Semiramis was preening her wings with the tip of her snake tail, so the giant feathers no longer covered her bare human torso. Nomios stared, stroking his goatee beard, his mouth half open.

"Nomios!" Zenon barked.

"Oh!" he cried. "Sorry." He tore his attention from the snake-woman, who rolled her eyes. "As I was saying, both sides usually work through political channels. The Academy tries to push shamans and lumins out of public life, and we resist in the name of truth and spirit." He glanced again at Semiramis.

"But what about Crocker?" Jason asked. "What's he got to do with all of this?"

"We were hoping you could tell *us*," said Zenon.

"Crocker arrived several years ago," Nomios explained. "He lives with the Academy leaders, but he doesn't involve himself in their deception of the masses. He disappears every so often for weeks or months at a time. Whatever his business, he conducts it quietly."

"And what about his boss, the Rector?" Jason asked. "Do you know anything about him?"

The three shook their heads, and Jason sighed. Now that

he'd escaped—at least for the night—he wondered if he'd been wrong to flee Crocker. The man might've told him something about his father, and about the Rector. But Crocker had hired barbarians to kidnap him. He couldn't imagine trusting such a person. And then there was the Diokles factor. Falling into that man's hands was not an option.

"There is something more about Crocker," said Semiramis. "He's supposed to come from far downriver, and that makes me wonder. There's a prophecy about the lands downstream. The oracle of Apollo spoke it long ago." The snake-woman looked eagerly at her companions.

"Well, come on," Zenon growled. "Let's hear it."

Semiramis' gleaming eyes took on a faraway look. Her snake tail swayed like a charmed cobra as she chanted:

> In downstream lands, far, far away,
>   near the river's very mouth,
> *Daimones* hide and magic fades,
>   and shamans live in doubt.
> But those who know wait on the day
>   when help will come by boat.
> Hekate sees her people's tears;
>   the goddess sends them hope.
> From upstream lands a savior comes:
>   a shaman strong and brave.
> While scholars quake, the true will hail
>   a dawning bold new age.

Semiramis' verses hung on the cold air as fire shadows danced across the giant skull's interior. "What has that got to do with Crocker?" Zenon finally asked.

"Well, the prophecy tells us someone's committed a terrible wrong far downriver," she said. "And it says the wrongdoers are scholars—or at least scholars will quake when the wrong is undone. And it even suggests this wrong has to do with *daimones*—lumins—and with shamans." Semiramis looked back and forth at her listeners. "This Crocker comes from far downriver, doesn't he? And he's a friend of scholars: the

Aristotle Academy. He may be a scholar himself, and he's certainly made enemies of shamans and lumins. Maybe he's involved in this terrible evil the oracle mentioned."

Zenon grunted and ran callused fingers through his silver-tipped beard. "I think the temple of your theory rests on a foundation of 'maybes.'"

Nomios crossed his goat legs and turned to Jason. "What do you think, Honorable Jason?"

"I dunno. I guess I don't have much experience with prophecies." He felt a little better about shaman power, now that he'd entered the reaching trance on his own terms—without an amulet or a lot of superstition. But he wasn't sure anyone could tell the future, much less tell it in rhymes.

Something else troubled him. Now that he understood the Aristotle philosophers better, he found it hard to hate them. They were just trying to do away with superstition: with priests, fortune-tellers, boogeymen, and all the rest. Jason looked up at the stars, glimmering through the eyeholes of the colossal Statue of Liberty skull.[†] Was he on the wrong side?

ooooo

Semiramis flew several miles up and down the river the next morning and reported no sign of the pursuing ship. So they broke cover, crossed to the left bank, and returned upstream. Using the reaching trance, Jason and Zidu eventually arranged to meet at the edge of a tiny woodland: an unlikely spot for

---

† The Statue of Liberty was modeled on the Colossus of Rhodes, a Hellenistic statue of the god Helios. That's why Lady Liberty wears a spiky crown. Helios was the Greek god of the sun, so his statue wore a crown of solar rays. The Rhodians built the Colossus in the early 200s. It stood over a hundred feet tall: about the same as the Statue of Liberty. It had a bronze skin around an iron and stone frame. Unfortunately, less than fifty years after the Colossus was finished, an earthquake knocked it over. An oracle warned the Rhodians not to rebuild, so the Colossus lay on its side for almost 900 years, until the Arabs finally sold it off for scrap.

~ William Gallo, *Saints & Satyrs*, 53.

Academy scouts. Semiramis had spotted the meeting place from the air, and she flew ahead to guide Jason's friends there.

Zidu and Tia arrived the day after the *Dead Valencia*, on foot, dirty and hungry. Jason's bear hug almost crushed Zidu. But he found himself tongue-tied with Tia. She looked prettier than ever, even bedraggled and separated from the makeup kit she'd left on the *Dead Valencia*. Finally, they hugged briefly.

"I'm glad you're safe," she said. "After all, I promised the high chantress I'd see you to that Roman priestess."

Semiramis flew off, but Zenon and Nomios stayed with the companions. According to Zenon, they were less than two weeks' journey from Tarraco-Hispania. Jason was eager to move on. He didn't want to give the Academy time to find him. And he kept thinking of Yakov's warning: his concern that Jason might wake up before he found his father. Tia and Zidu, however, were exhausted. So the travelers rested two days by the edge of the woods. Nomios propositioned Tia at least a dozen times during those two days, but she only laughed.[‡]

ooooo

Late one morning several days later, Jason sat by the bow, trailing his bare feet in the cool water. The wind had fallen, so the *Dead Valencia* drifted on the current as Zidu manned the tiller. They were always wary of pursuit, but at the moment, no other ships sailed nearby. Sunlight slanted across the deck and the wide ribbon of blue water.

"Jason," said Tia, coming up behind him. "When you called Zidu with the reaching trance, while you were away, what amulet did you use?"

He looked up. "I didn't have an amulet."

She sat down next to him and dipped her feet in the water. "Then how?"

---

‡ It's kind of weird that satyrs have become so popular in children's stories. They were the sexual predators and rapists of Greek mythology.
~ William Gallo, Lectures, History 78.

"You don't need an amulet. That's just—"

He'd been about to say *superstition*. But he and Tia hadn't talked much lately, and he didn't want to ruin it.

"It's just not necessary," he continued. "The trance is something you do with your mind. You don't need anything else."

"But how do you call the god? How do you get divine help?"

"I'm sure divine help's really ... helpful. But you can do it your own way if you have to, without a god or goddess."

"I don't believe *that*," she snapped, crossing her arms.

"You know, it's hard to explain anything to someone who gets mad every time you open your mouth."

"Well, maybe you should open it less often."

Jason started to formulate a snappy retort, but then he burst out laughing. After a moment, Tia smiled, and she, too, started laughing. "Will you show me?" she finally asked, regaining her composure.

They spent the next two hours practicing. The golden sun, the quiet, and the windless current were perfect for the trance. Jason slipped in and out easily, but Tia couldn't let go of her supposed need for divine help. She kept reaching for her blue beetle amulet, so Jason gently removed it, shivering as his fingers brushed her neck. Tia sat silent a long time, her chest slowly rising and falling, as Jason thought how pretty she looked—like an Egyptian princess, like Cleopatra.§

---

§ The famous Cleopatra wasn't really Egyptian. She was Macedonian and Greek. She may not have been the raven-haired beauty we imagine, either. There's a fair chance she was a redhead, and not particularly pretty, though she must have been attractive anyway, and smart.

Cleopatra VII was queen of Egypt from 51 to 30 BC. Like a good Ptolemy girl, she married one little brother and then the other, but she ruled without them. She was an effective queen, but she faced a crippling problem: military dependence on Rome, the new superpower. Romantic relationships with two Roman strongmen helped. But Julius Caesar got himself assassinated, and Marc Antony lost a civil war, which cost both him and Cleopatra their lives. After her death, Cleopatra's Roman enemies painted her as this manipulative *femme fatale*—which actually kind of backfired, turning her into a romantic icon for later centuries. Anyway, Cleopatra was the last Hellenistic ruler and the last monarch of ancient Egypt, so her death marks the end of two eras.

~ William Gallo, Lectures, History 78.

Then Tia's eyelids fluttered open. "I did it," she whispered. "I was there, by the starlit pool, in the reaching trance. I did it without an amulet!"

After that, the awkwardness between them melted away, and they could talk again.

ooooo

On another afternoon a week later, the travelers walked along a bustling road outside the high stone walls of Tarraco-Hispania's provincial capital. Here, in the Roman Empire, ended the journey they'd begun in Egypt. Senusret had said: "Go to Tarraco-Hispania and find the high priestess of Isis in the capital. She will know you." Butterflies fluttered in Jason's stomach. This priestess was his only link to his father.

Several legionnaires stood before the great gate. They wore iron breastplates and helmets and carried javelins, as well as red, rectangular shields. Jason asked one where to find the high priestess of Isis.

"That's the proconsul's mother," said the man. "You've better have important business if you bother someone like that." But he gave them directions.

The city's buildings were square and sturdy, built of hard, burnt brick, as well as concrete, stone, and wood. Red tile covered most roofs. And dotting the city were the domes and arches of coliseums, temples, aqueducts, and half-moon amphitheaters. After several wrong turns, they found what they thought must be the right street. It was lined with two-story houses, fronted in some cases by shops. At the far end, two more legionnaires stood before the door to a large, plaster-covered house.

"The one with the guards—that must be it," Jason whispered, adjusting his backpack and biting his lip.

The guards ignored Jason as he stepped forward, so he passed between them and knocked on the plain wooden door.

A balding, blond man opened it, wiping crumbs from his lips. "Yes?" he asked, his mouth still full. He wore a belted

tunic hanging to his thighs and leather sandals, like most of
the men they'd seen in the streets. "Who knocks at the door
of Quintus Flaccus Pomponius?"

"Um, I'm Jason Oliver Gallo. I've come to see the high
priestess of Isis ... the proconsul's mother, I guess. Is this the
right house?"

The man stared. "Did you say 'Gallo'?" Jason nodded. Then
the man straightened his tunic. "Please wait here."

He shut the door, but after a minute it opened again. This
time, a silver-haired man in a green tunic stood alongside the
doorkeeper. "Are you the one called 'Gallo'?" he asked. Jason
nodded. "Honorable sir, you have long been expected in the
house of Quintus Flaccus Pomponius! Please enter—you and
your companions are most welcome."

They left the dusty street and found themselves in another
world. The man in green led them through marble-floored
atriums open to the sky, as well as elegant rooms. The house
was decorated with gold and silver ornaments, handsome furniture, and finely sculpted busts. Servants, probably slaves,
worked or stood at attention, all clean and dressed in colorful
tunics. The place looked like an art museum.

Near the back of the house was a tiny paradise: a courtyard
where a portico of white pillars surrounded a garden and bird-
bath. They passed through and into a richly furnished room.
There the man in green asked them to wait.

The three sat on backless, wooden couches, cushioned in
blue cloth. After they'd waited ten or fifteen minutes, Jason
got up to pace. Soon he fell to examining the paintings on
the stucco walls. One was a lovely pastoral scene, where satyrs
like Nomios danced by a fountain. But the painting behind
Jason's couch interested him more. Two regal women stood in
the foreground, and a third sat on a couch, staring off to one
side. They had beautiful, strong faces, and they looked like
sisters. One of the standing women had turned away from the
viewer, but she was looking back over her shoulder. Her eyes
were green.

"Oh, my God," said Jason. "I know this woman!"

"Of course you know me," said a voice from the entrance. They turned to find three figures in the doorway: an eight-foot snake with gleaming lumin eyes, a brawny man, and a very old woman, draped in a sky-blue dress. The woman had white hair tied in a bun and a thousand wrinkles, but she stood straight and steady. Her eyes were as green as the snake's scales, and Jason knew he'd seen those eyes before. But she'd been younger then. He opened his mouth, but no sound came.

"Have I aged so much since we last met?" she asked as she glided into the room.

Tia and Zidu rose and bowed, but Jason stood still. Finally he found his voice: "Doctor Valencia."

"Yes." She smiled and held out her arms. "I offer you a belated welcome to my world, Jason Oliver Gallo."

10

Confessions
of a Noble Roman

OVER THE COURSE OF two hundred and fifty years, the empire sucked in Latins, Greeks, Carthaginians, Numidians, Celts, Egyptians, the whole Fertile Crescent, Asia Minor—all the Hellenistic kingdoms—Spain, Gaul, North Africa. The list goes on and on. By 31 BC, the Mediterranean was a Roman lake. How did they pull this off? And why Rome and not Naples or Carthage or Athens or Sparta or one of the Hellenistic kingdoms? Historians debate the reasons, but I'll tell you one factor I think was crucial. The Romans had hard heads. They flat-out refused to lose a war, no matter what the cost ...

Rome gave the Mediterranean more than two centuries of prosperity and relative peace: the Pax Romana. The empire was a massive free trade zone, with consistent coinage, pirate-free seas, low taxes, sophisticated laws, and great road, river, and postal systems. Greek-born Classical culture dominated, eventually leavened with Jewish-born Christianity. Urban life featured paved streets, good plumbing, and impressive public buildings, along with dingy multi-story apartment houses. So Roman society looked a lot like the modern West, right down to the quality consumer goods and professional sports: gladiatorial games, chariot races, etcetera. During the 100s AD, the empire's people were richer and more comfortable than any society before or since, until the twentieth century.

~ William Gallo, Recorded Lectures, History 78.

ooooo

"Won't you embrace me, Jason?" asked the old woman.
"Are you out of your freakin' mind?" He struggled to say more—to yell and scream—but he couldn't find the words. "Who are you?" he finally sputtered.

"Well, if you won't embrace me, I'll sit." She settled herself on one of the blue couches. The big man—apparently a servant—stood behind her, his thick arms crossed over his chest. And the snake lumin curled up at her feet and regarded the travelers from under hooded eyelids. "You may sit also," the old woman said.

With an uncertain glance at Jason, Tia sat on one of the couches. But Jason remained standing, and Zidu sat on the rug by his feet.

Their hostess sighed. "Very well, then." She rested her hands on the wide armrests, like a queen on her throne. "In answer to your question, Jason, my name is Aurelia Valentia Pomponi, daughter of Titus Aurelius Valentio, widow of Gaius Flaccus Pomponius, mother of the proconsul Quintus Flaccus Pomponius, and high priestess of the temple of Isis." Her green eyes held Jason without wavering, but her tone softened. "As for the other name you know, I never used 'Doctor Valencia' before we met, though as a priestess and a shaman of long experience, I think I have the right to call myself 'doctor.' In any case, you may call me Lady Aurelia."

Jason's face felt hot. "What gives you the right to send me here?" He stepped forward, fists clenched and teeth bared. "What—"

The brawny servant scrambled around the couch and headed for Jason—who froze, though he did not retreat.

"It's all right, Jugurtha," Lady Aurelia called. "Jason is obviously angry, but I don't think he means me any harm. Come back over here."

With a dark-eyed glare at Jason, the big servant retreated behind the couch and waited, clearly ready for another leap into action.

"I am sorry I angered you, Jason," said Lady Aurelia. "But I stand by my choices. What I did, I did for your father. I spoke the truth about his plight here in the world of Fore. He is very dear to me, so I brought his son here to rescue him."

"But ... who *are* you? And what do you care about my father?"

"Before you were born, Jason, before your parents even met, your father was my lover." She smiled. "They called me 'Secunda' then, because I was the second of three daughters. And that's what your father called me, and still does."

Jason stared. He'd heard the word *secunda*, in his father's sleep-talk at the hospital.

"I fled an unwanted marriage to travel with your father when I was a girl," continued Lady Aurelia. "He was a dream voyager discovering the Jericho River then, much as you are now." Her smile softened. "He was a beautiful youth, too. I have watched you your whole life, through his eyes and through the ether, and you remind me of him more every year."

Her lover? First, Candi, now this. What did these women want with his history-obsessed father? "I don't understand. You're an old ... If you were a girl then, how—"

"How is it I'm a wrinkled old fig now, while he's not past middle years?" She smiled. "You could more easily imagine Doctor Valencia with your father, couldn't you? I told you long ago, time in Fore flows faster than time in your world. At least, it usually does. You've spent months in Fore while your real body has lain asleep in the other world, most likely for only a few hours. Well, time flowed faster for me than for your father. He was two years older once, but now I could be his grandmother." She sighed and glanced at Tia. "It is this difference that dooms love between worlds."

"Yeah, but what the—" He couldn't master his anger enough to ask the right questions. "But you were younger before, when you were Doctor Valencia."

"That was only my shadow, projected into your mind. Your society has such prejudices against the very old, I thought it better to appear at what you might call 'a professional age.' So I molded my shadow to fit my form from long ago."

The sun had set, so the silver oil lamps provided most of the room's light. Their glow softened Lady Aurelia's wrinkled features, and Jason found it easier to see Doctor Valencia in her face. He stared, trying to take it all in.

"Lady," said Tia, "does this mean you can visit Jason's world?"

"No, child. None of us can. Our people are dreams to his. The most we ever can do is visit their minds." She turned to Jason. "I appeared in your mind's eye, Jason, almost as soon as I realized your father's danger. You saw me standing outside your house, or so it seemed, but I could come no closer, or speak to you."

"You mean you weren't really there that day, outside my window? I was just hallucinating?"

"In a sense. It was my first attempt. But soon I realized your sleeping mind would hear me better, and I would have to visit you in a dream. I tried to reach you the very next night, but your medical men foiled me, by taking your father away to that hospital. His sleeping mind was my anchor in your world, my touchstone, so when they removed him from your house, I could no longer find you. You may thank your sister for my success. Thank her for insisting that you spend the night in the hospital. I only succeeded when you fell asleep a few feet from your father, and began to dream."

"Thank her?" Jason barked. "Why, so I could get kidnapped in my sleep?" He was yelling now. "Who do you think you are? You didn't give me a choice about coming here! You just pushed me through the door!"

"If I could have asked you, I would, Jason. But I could only reach you in dreams, and no one thinks clearly then. Your consent would have meant little or nothing. Besides, *would* you have consented? I'm not so sure. You are selfish, like so many boys your age, and you harbor this unnatural hostility to your father."

"It's not so unnatural," said the snake lumin, her calm voice cutting through the tension. "Look at Jovis Pater.* He overthrew

---

* The prehistoric Indo-Europeans worshipped a supreme god called Sky-Father, or something like Dyeus Pater. To their Latin descendants, Dyeus Pater evolved into Jovis Pater, or Jupiter. To their Greek descendants, Dyeus Pater became Zeus Pater, or just Zeus. That's why Jupiter and Zeus look so much alike. It's not that the Romans copied Jupiter from Zeus. In a way, the two really are the same god. (The Aryans of India worshipped a sky god from the same source, called Dyaus Pitar.)
~ William Gallo, *Historical Factoids*, 55.

his father and stole the old god's kingdom."

Lady Aurelia's tone softened. "I'm sorry. Perhaps it's not so unnatural. In any case, Jason, would you have come, had I given you the choice—had it been in my power?"

"Hell, no."

"Well, then, I did the right thing—for you *and* your father. You're glad to be here, aren't you?"

"I … you …"

"Of course you are. I can see it in your face, your body. You've grown into a strong, brave young man. You've led an expedition through unfamiliar lands, relying on your wits and little else. You'll keep all that growth of spirit when you return to your own world, assuming you survive. You'll be stronger, more confident—after a single night of dreaming. That's a precious gift. What's more, you're doing *right*, Jason, in the eyes of all the gods. A son *should* rescue his father."

"Can you send me home?"

"No. Only someone in your world could do that, by waking you back in the hospital room."

"You can't go home now," said Tia in a meek voice. "The Great Senusret sent you here, to Tarraco-Hispania. He said your trip serves a greater purpose."

"The Great Senusret can kiss my puckering ass," Jason snapped.

Tia's eyes widened and her mouth dropped open.

"And so can you," he hissed at Lady Aurelia. "I'm leaving."

"Leaving!" she cried. "Where are you going?"

"Back to our boat."

Jason thought he saw Lady Aurelia's hand shake as she brushed a strand of silver hair out of her face. "I thought you'd stay here, in my house. I was hoping you'd be my guest, so we could talk and I could help you."

"Do you know where my father is?"

"No." She shook her head. "No, but I've learned where he was shortly before he disappeared. And I know what danger stalked him. I know a great deal that you need to know."

"Great. Feel free to send me a note." He headed for the

door, with Zidu at his heels. Then he turned. Tia had risen to her feet, but she wasn't following them.

"Well?" he demanded. "Let's go."

"My job was to make sure you got here," said Tia, her tone icy. "That's all Nebetit said I had to do."

Jason's stomach clenched. "Fine."

"Jason," called Lady Aurelia, "please don't go." But he and Zidu were already in the garden, headed for the front door. The Roman lady's voice followed him. "Go then, but please come back. I want to help you. My house is open to you, whenever you wish. Please come soon—for your father's sake!"

Neither Jason nor Zidu spoke as they made their way through the dark streets, out the gate, and back to the docks. Jason knew the *Dead Valencia*'s deck would seem a hard bed after the luxury of the house of Quintus Flaccus Pomponius. But he was glad to see the ship. "Thanks for coming with me," he said to Zidu as he sat down in the dark, trembling.

"Of course," said the lion-man. He lay down, cat-like, on the deck.

They sat in silence, staring up at the watery stars. Some of the day's heat still hung on the air, and the river was quiet. "Do you think I was wrong to yell and all that?" Jason finally asked.

"No," Zidu answered. "But I do think we should return. We will need Lady Aurelia's help finding your father."

"We?"

"I am with you, to the end."

Jason nodded, unable to speak. Tears flooded his eyes. Zidu moved over and rested a paw on his leg. And there they sat for a long time, as the moon rose over the aqueduct and the city walls.

ooooo

Jason and Zidu returned to the house of Quintus Flaccus Pomponius the next morning.

"I'd like your help finding my father," he told Lady Aurelia.

"But I'm not staying in your house. And I'm not your son or your grandson, just because you used to ... be with my dad. I'm not going to forget what you did."

"I understand, Jason," she said. "You're proud, like your father." Her expression was solemn, though Jason thought he saw tears in her eyes. "I will help you—both of you."

Lady Aurelia's duties demanded her attention most of that day. Her son the proconsul was away, and she governed Tarraco-Hispania in his place. So they agreed to talk in the evening.

That night, Jason and Zidu dined with Lady Aurelia and her snake lumin. Jason didn't want the meal, preferring that they stick to business. But their hostess insisted, and after so long on the river, he found it hard to turn down a large cooked meal. They reclined on couches in a room decorated in red and black and lit by lanterns on brass stands. They ate cow's udder stuffed with liver, eels, flamingo tongues, and many other dishes Jason skipped, along with some good bread, pork, and baked fruit. Courteous, quiet slaves brought the food and whisked away the empty dishes and trays, only to replace them with more.

Tia didn't join them, and the servants hadn't let Jason see her that day. "The Lady Tia declines to meet with you at this time," a slave had informed Jason. Apparently, though, the Egyptian girl had spent some time with Lady Aurelia the previous night, telling her about the companions' journey. So at dinner, Jason merely filled in the details.

"Have you learned the nature of your father's research here in Fore?" Lady Aurelia asked when he'd finished.

"No. I was hoping you knew." His tone was neutral—never friendly. "All we know is it had to do with lumins, especially this one we met." He told her about the Minotaur.

Lady Aurelia sighed as a slave cleared away her tray. "His research is a mystery to me. Your father became very secretive during his last few visits." She smoothed her yellow dress with knobby hands. "In fact, he has not truly shared his mind since your mother's accident." She shook her head. "There are black threads in the Fates' tapestry, and your mother's passing was one of the blackest. Afterward, your father became very silent. I know he took less joy in his trips to Fore after she was gone. His only happiness came from his work and his children."

Mainly from his work, Jason thought.

"He came here for knowledge then, not for adventure. He was studying your world's past, and he studied lumins, too. I don't know why, but I suspect there is one here in Fore who does."

"The Rector?" Jason asked.

Her face was grim. "Yes, him. I do not know his name, but I have learned that 'Rector' is a title. It's some sort of republican office, I think, like 'consul' or 'prefect.'† The Rector's full title is 'Rector for Enforcement,' and his job is to *hunt*. I don't know what he hunts or why, except that he once hunted your father, Jason, and now he hunts you." The room seemed to turn cold.

"The Rector leads no city or empire," Lady Aurelia continued. "His people are called the International Empirical Society: a league of what your people call 'scientists.'" Jason's eyebrows rose. "They operate in the lands far downriver, and they wield tremendous power, though I don't know how, since they seem to have no armies." She sighed. "I know little more. The Society's lands lie beyond my reach. All I know is that, like the Aristotle Academy, they oppose shaman power. They seek to replace priests and priestesses with people like themselves, with scientists."

Zidu shook his head, and Jason stared at Lady Aurelia, troubled that he'd apparently teamed up with a witch—literally—in a struggle against scientists. "This might explain something we heard upriver," he said. "There's a prophecy."

---

† The Romans called their state "the public thing": the *res publica*—giving us the word "republic." Even after the first emperors took over, Rome stayed more or less republican. Augustus Caesar was essentially Rome's first president, though he looked more like a banana republic military dictator than George Washington. His title was respectably republican. *Imperator* meant something like "commander," and it wasn't until much later that it evolved into a royal rank, giving us the word "emperor."

~ William Gallo, Lectures, History 78.

"In downstream lands, far, far away, near the river's very mouth …" the snake lumin hissed, "… *daimones* hide, and magic fades, and shamans live in doubt."

Lady Aurelia nodded. "We know this prophecy. It tells of a great evil, probably the Empirical Society."

"And it may tell of your father," said the snake lumin. "We have wondered if he might be the promised savior—'the shaman strong and brave' sent by the goddess Hekate. That may be why the Society fears him."

Lady Aurelia looked lost in thought, so Jason spoke: "We learned something upstream that might explain what's keeping my father here." He'd told her about their meeting with Yakov, the dream voyager, in Hebrew Judah. "Yakov said sleep works like a portal between my world and Fore. A dream voyager has to fall asleep here if he wants to go back home. If he's not asleep, he won't hear an alarm clock or notice when someone's shaking him, back in my world. Yakov thought maybe something's keeping my father awake, all the time. Does that make sense?"

She pursed her lips. "I've never heard that sleep is the portal in both directions, but it does make sense. And as a dream voyager, this Yakov may know better than I. But what could keep your father awake so long? Even if men sat by his side shaking him whenever he nodded off, he would eventually sleep."

They pondered in silence.

"Let's cut to the chase," Jason finally said. "You said you could help me find my father."

"When I brought you to Fore, I did not know where he was. You gave me my best clue: your father had mentioned Nagiru, from First Lagash, in his sleep talk. So I brought you to Fore, to a thin place near that city." She looked distressed. "But Jason, I never dreamed the Rector's reach extended so far upriver as Sumer. If I'd known barbarians lay in wait for you, I would have brought you here, to my own thin place in the temple of Isis, despite the distance from Nagiru. I am so sorry."

"Whatever."

She sighed. "At that time, I hoped your father had gone upriver, to Sumer, far from the Society's territory. But shortly after you arrived, I heard word of him. In my constant searching through the ether, I touched the mind of a lumin who'd seen him." She rolled a silver wine cup between her hands, her face troubled. "It was odd. This lumin's mind was strangely turbulent, and closed to me. I did not understand and still don't. But at least I learned that your father visited this lumin, not long before he disappeared. His name is Quennel, and he lives in a town called Laurac, in the kingdom of Capetian France. It's a little more than a month downstream on the right bank." She smiled ruefully. "I'm afraid you face another long journey. I only hope you have enough time left here in Fore."

ooooo

That night, Jason lay on the *Dead Valencia*'s deck, looking at the stars and thinking of the coming journey. Once again, he'd travel down the Jericho River. He wondered about the lands downstream. If he traveled far enough, would he find a country like a dream of home: a land of refrigerators, cars, and computer games?

He wondered what sort of lumins might live in Fore's version of his own time. What shape would they take? He doubted that they'd look like centaurs, sphinxes, or talking snakes. Those were myths from the past. What then? Would they be superheroes? He imagined Batman and Wolverine with gleaming eyes, lending their power to modern-day shamans. Or maybe he'd find Godzilla downriver, or Uncle Sam, or the Loch Ness monster. Maybe he'd find angels in blue jeans, or Mickey Mouse, or even a computer-generated hero from one of his games.

No, he thought. None of those sounded likely. Jason couldn't picture modern lumins. He wondered if he'd ever meet one.

ooooo

Tia refused to see Jason, so two days after his dinner with Lady Aurelia, he more or less snuck up on her. The slaves had told him she'd be singing a blessing that afternoon at Lady Aurelia's temple, the temple of Isis. So he attended the service and walked back with her—or rather, slightly behind her. She hardly spoke to him.

She did, however, grudgingly agree to sit with him in Lady Aurelia's garden. "It was a beautiful service," she said without smiling, once the slaves had deposited fresh fruit and cups of wine and left them alone. "They have some strange rituals here, but it was still beautiful. There's nothing more important than the gods' blessings." She glared at him—almost the first time she'd looked his way.

"Uh … yeah." Jason didn't know what do say. His family included a mix of religious backgrounds, as well as national ones, but he'd grown up with no formal religion. "It was really nice. It was a pretty ceremony."

"It was beautiful," Tia corrected. "Lady Aurelia knows how to move people. She's the best, strongest shaman I've ever met."

"Yeah, I'm pretty crazy about her myself."

Tia smirked, and they sat in awkward silence. Finally, Jason got to the point. "Look, I'm really sorry about what I said, about the Great Senusret." He scanned her face, which wore no expression at all. "I didn't mean it. At all."

"That was the most vulgar, disrespectful, ugly, unholy thing I've ever heard in my entire life."

"Well, I don't like to do anything halfway."

Her cheek twitched, and Jason thought she'd suppressed a smile. "You should pray to Osiris for forgiveness," she said primly, "and sacrifice in the temple. You insulted his spiritual son, and the gods take vengeance when you least expect it."

"Okay, I'll pray for forgiveness."

"No, you won't." She shook her head. "I just hope you'll learn better sense on our journey."

"*Our* journey?" he exclaimed. "You're coming?" Jason struggled to keep a huge, dopey grin from taking over his face.

"Yes, now that you've apologized—if I'm still welcome."

He nodded vigorously.

"I want to study with Lady Aurelia, but I can do that after: when I get back. For now, I think I should go with you. I think Blessed Mother Isis wants me to help find your father and defeat that evil Rector. Lady Aurelia says your father's one of us—he's god-fearing—even if his narrow-minded, vulgar, disrespect- ful *son* isn't." She looked away. Lanterns cast dappled shadows among the leaves and flowers. "I think Isis‡ has a plan for me, and it starts with your quest. Besides, I know what it's like to be an orphan. I don't want you to become one—you or your sis- ter. And you're so ignorant. Lady Aurelia thinks I can help you."

Jason just kept his mouth shut.

ooooo

Lady Aurelia accompanied them to the dock. She hugged Tia and even Zidu tenderly, but Jason stood with arms crossed, and she did not touch him.

"You are your father's son," she said. Tears ran down her face. "You resemble him more than you know, and I'm proud of you. Give him my love when you see him."

She stood waving from the bank, surrounded by her atten- dants, as the travelers floated down the river. Then she was gone. A lump rose in Jason's throat.

Tarraco-Hispania fell into the distance behind them as the *Dead Valencia* sped along the right bank. Sunlight danced on the miles-wide ribbon of blue water and warmed the green and gold lands along the shore. The ship floated past pros- perous cities and towns, abounding with bathhouses, temples,

---

‡ This latter-day Isis cult was more Greek than anything else, despite its Egyptian origin. Isis worship was probably the empire's strongest eastern-born cult until the rise of Christianity. The two had a lot in common. The Isis cult featured a chance at personal salvation, holy communion, the death and resurrection of a god—Isis' husband Osiris/Serapis—and a divine trinity: Isis, Serapis, and their son Horus. Also, Roman art pictured Isis holding baby Horus, in a pose a lot like Christian images of the Virgin Mary and Baby Jesus.
~ William Gallo, *Saints & Satyrs*, 89.

and amphitheaters, and set among orchards and lush fields of grain.

But as the days wore into weeks, the cities fell away behind them. They sailed along a quieter shore, home to grand estates, dark forests, and only a few towns. At the same time, the weather turned. Late summer rain-showers drenched the companions repeatedly. Then, one afternoon, came the storm.

A barrage of thunderclaps caught them off-guard and far from shore. Lightning ripped across angry skies as the wind rose and raindrops filled the air. "Someone grab the tiller!" Jason shouted as he seized the main line and fought the wind for control of the sail. "We've got to get to shore *now!*"

Zidu and Tia both scrambled aft. But a wave crashed over the deck, drenching them both and sending them sprawling. Tia grabbed the gunwale, but Zidu's lion claws could find no grip. He disappeared into the waves.

"Zidu!" Jason shrieked. He heaved on the main line, trying to turn the ship around. But as the prow veered across the wind, another rain-laden gust struck the ship. Jason felt the deck fall out from under his feet. The last thing he saw before water surged over him was the trapdoor to the tiny hold snapping open as the ship turned on its side. He heard wood cracking as the Jericho River's cold fury buffeted him. Then the torrent pulled him under.

PART TWO

THE RIGHT BANK

11

Dark Shore

THE EASTERN HALF OF the empire—known eventually as the Byzantine Empire—continued long after the 400s. But the western half was gone by the end of the century. That's where we turn our attention now; specifically, to Western Europe.

The Western Roman Empire didn't really fall. Rather, it outsourced itself into oblivion. As the Germans and other barbarians invaded, desperate emperors recruited them as soldiers, and their kings and warlords as governors. Eventually, these barbarian kings simply stopped obeying orders from the emperor.

The Franks and the other barbarians might have done better if they'd invaded further east. Western Europe had started slipping long before the 400s. Over the next few centuries, the population fell, lifespans dropped, the economy crumbled, and Classical literature and science faded away. Cities and towns disappeared, along with law and order, leaving a simple farming society, plagued by crime and war.

Religion was everything during the Dark Ages. The Roman Church was the imperial government's last surviving franchise. During the early 500s, bishops—many of them former Roman senators—converted the country folk, as well as the barbarian warriors. As the centuries rolled by, the Church took the conversion campaign beyond the old Roman frontiers, bringing new barbarians into "Christendom"—the culture we call Western Civilization.

~ William Gallo, *Saints & Satyrs*, 110-112.

ooooo

"Rector!" Shaw gasped. "Finally a message from Crocker!" The Rector for Enforcement looked up from his papers and held out a hand. The young man passed the letter, extending his arm to avoid coming too close. The Rector smiled. He guessed Seiki was leering at Shaw from his shoulder.

He broke the apple and moon seal and scanned Crocker's efficient hand-written report. "Damn!" he barked, startling Shaw. Seiki was unperturbed. "They haven't got him." He shook his head. "They did, but then they lost him."

"Where?" Shaw inquired. "If you don't mind my asking, sir."

"Athenopolis." The Rector kept reading. "Crocker thinks he's headed downstream."

"To Tarraco-Hispania?"

"Yes, there's no stopping that now. But where will he turn next?" The Rector rubbed his chin, his eyes narrow. "Crocker's sending agents to Arabian Carthage, Lombardia, Laurac … all our suspected venues."

"Is there anything we should do on our end, Rector?"

The Rector stared up at the vaulted ceiling and at the grim portraits of his predecessors on the walls. "Maybe not," he finally said. "In a way, young Mr. Gallo's been doing Crocker's job for him—for us." He looked at Shaw. "Crocker says Jason started in Sumer, escaped our agents there, and was ultimately caught in the Persian Empire. That's a long way he'd traveled downriver, on his own initiative. It's reasonable to guess he'll continue in the same direction. He'll pass along the dark shore next: barbarian lands, Arthur's Britain,* the Carolingian Empire … closer all the time."

The Rector chuckled as Seiki rested a skeletal hand on his

---

* Historians have suggested King Arthur was a Roman-Celtic warlord named Ambrosius Aurelianus, who lived around 500 AD. He may have fought Britain's barbarian invaders: the Angles, Saxons, and Jutes. But some historians consider Arthur pure myth. In fact, one theory says he was a Celtic bear god who evolved into a human king through centuries of retelling. One thing is certain: if there was a King Arthur, he didn't eat his lamb and leek stew with the Knights of the Round Table. Knighthood wouldn't appear for another several centuries.

~ William Gallo, *Historical Factoids*, 66.

ear. "I doubt Jason has any idea of our power downstream—how easily we can take him once he's reached our own territory. He's sailing into our hands."

ooooo

Sneezing and coughing, Jason trudged up the rocky beach. His head ached, and he was shivering. His jeans were still damp, and he'd given his sweatshirt to Tia, who had only the dress she was wearing.

He looked up the slope at their benefactor. Abdallah's royal blue jacket and turban stood out against the gray sky.

"Ah, my friends," he said, turning to face them, "I told you this was a poor country and home to a rough people. Soon you will see how true I spoke. But have no fear. My customers are my friends, even when they're heathens. The German barbarians will welcome you and offer you a roof and a hot meal, though neither may please you much when you see them."

Abdallah was an Arab trader from the left bank. His boat had been crossing the river when the waves and wind overcame the *Dead Valencia*. He'd rushed to the rescue, and he and his servant had pulled the three travelers from the angry waters. But the boat itself could not be saved. The *Dead Valencia* lay broken at the bottom of the river.

"I don't care if they live in holes in the ground, so long as it's dry," said Tia. Her black hair hung in damp strings under a head-cloth Abdallah had lent her, and streaks of makeup crept down her cheeks, like spider's legs. Zidu followed on quiet feline feet, scanning the countryside.

The quest to rescue William Gallo had stalled weeks from its destination: the town of Laurac in Capetian France, where they hoped to find the lumin Quennel. Jason had no idea how they'd reach Laurac now. The trip would take months by land, and time was not on their side. Jason feared he might wake up at any moment back home, his quest a failure.

The Arab led the companions through fields of crops and pastures where undersized cattle grazed,[†] and then past a few stone structures that looked like the ruins of a Roman town. Soon the party reached a square, brick tower, apparently the remnant of a defensive wall. A lodge had been built against the tower's side. Abdallah's rings sparkled in the last light of day as he pounded on the lodge's thick door. Jason gulped. The Arab wore a handsome, curved scimitar by his side, but otherwise the party was unarmed. He missed Rim-Hadad.

The door creaked open and a man with a blond beard appeared, snarling and grasping a heavy axe. But then the guardian's face broke into a slow grin. "I remember you," he said, taking in Abdallah's colorful outfit. "You're the Mussulman." He opened the door and ushered the party inside, out of the cool evening air. There they found a noisy, torch-lit hall filled with people and heavy wooden tables and benches.

"Ugh," Jason muttered. "Smells like a pigs' locker-room."

The boisterous men and women guzzling ale around the tables stank, and the hot, nearly windowless hall trapped the stench, leaving it nowhere to go but a small hole in the high ceiling. That hole served as chimney for a fire pit in the middle of the hall. The smell of burning logs improved the ambience, but the rancid odor of the evening meal did not. Haunches of pork and mutton sat steaming on great trays, adding their meaty aroma to the more human smell on the air. Straw covered the floor, where dogs fought over discarded bones.

"You'll get used to the smell," Abdallah whispered as they strode through the hall. "Please be respectful." He directed this last remark to Tia, who'd put a hand over her nose and mouth.

Abdallah presented them to the barbarian lord, called the chieftain: a heavy-set man with blond hair spilling onto a

---

† The term "Dark Ages" will trigger a snit from many historians. They prefer "Late Antiquity," and some say the post-Roman period wasn't a dark age at all, just a time of transformation. This is one of the more inane arguments stalking the halls of the world's history departments. I mean, for God's sake, the livestock even shrunk. They'd forgotten how to breed cows and pigs.

~ William Gallo, Recorded Lectures, History 113: Comparative Decline (Spring Semester 2002).

fur-lined tunic. He sat on a wooden throne at the far end, and like most of his men, he wore a heavy sword.

"Well met and welcome!" the chieftain cried heartily.

The chieftain's companions pushed ale-horns into Jason and Abdallah's hands. The Arab politely declined, reminding their hosts that his religion forbade alcohol. But Jason soon found he could neither refuse the insistent Germans nor put the ale horn aside. It curved at the bottom, so he couldn't set it down without spilling, until it was empty. And when he dropped his guard after downing a pint of strong, sweet liquor, a grinning woman with apple cheeks filled the horn again. Soon his head rang and the hall vibrated with a half-pleasant, half-nauseating buzz.

Eventually, Tia, Zidu, and a slightly dizzy Jason found their way to a long bench before an even longer table. As the night wore on, they ate and listened to their hosts' talk.

"This is all fine for now," Tia finally whispered, "but what are we going to do tomorrow?"

"I dunno," Jason replied. "I don't get the feeling these people are really rich or anything." He looked around at the roughly clad German barbarians. "I don't think any of them's just gonna hand over a boat or supplies."

"And we have little or nothing to trade," Zidu whispered. They'd lost all their supplies with the *Dead Valencia*, except for Jason's backpack and one other bag. "Let us hope this chieftain is a generous man and will not throw us out into the wild when the morning comes."

They continued to eat, listen, and look around the hall. Zidu was not the only lumin there. A strange gleaming-eyed creature ate near the chieftain. He had a human body, but he stood little more than four feet tall. His head was too big, and his limbs were knobby and gnarled. Jason stared at him.

"That is the chieftain's dwarf," said a man who'd just sat down across the table. "He's a pagan creature, like your lumin, I guess."

Jason looked at the speaker: a lean, beardless man with a bizarre haircut. The front half of his scalp had been shaved, while greasy locks hung down from the back half. Instead of the felt tunic and trousers on most of the men, he wore an off-white robe.

"You're not a Christian, are you, lad?" the man inquired.

"Well, sort of. Who are you?"

"I am Brother Gabrial, monk of the Columbine order." The monk bowed from his seat. "My lumin and I have come from the Irish lands to rescue pagan souls from the Devil's fire." [‡]

"Your lumin?" Tia asked.

"The blessed saint who guides and inspires me." The monk turned to point behind him. On a bench near the wall sat another lumin. She looked perfectly human: a thin, pale woman, middle-aged and wearing a plain dress. But her eyes gleamed, and a halo of pale golden light hung over her head, which was slightly bowed and covered in a tight hood.

During their last week sailing through the Roman Empire, they'd seen saints in most major towns, as well as angels: human-looking lumins with eagles' wings. But they'd seen none of these new lumins up close.

"She's almost human," Tia whispered.

"She is human," said Brother Gabrial, "and was no different from you or me before she died, except freer of sin."

Tia's eyes widened. "She died and became a lumin, just like the Great Senusret."

"I bet she smells better," Jason muttered.

Brother Gabrial favored Tia with a fatherly smile. "Do you wish to be saved, daughter? You can, you know. Mary Magdalene, of blessed memory, was a harlot once, and now she sings with angels in the bosom of the Lord."

"Saved from what?" Tia asked.

"From damnation and hellfire and everlasting perdition," the monk explained.

[‡] When Christianity spread across Ireland, monks stepped into the leather boots of the druids: the local pagan clergymen. It's a good thing the monks were celibate, because they also apparently adopted the druids' traditional haircuts, which may be the most offensive in recorded history.

~ William Gallo, Recorded Lectures, History 109: Art and Literature of the Middle Ages (Spring Semester 1994).

"Gabrial!" cried a mighty voice as a hand clamped onto the monk's shoulder. It was the German chieftain himself, standing behind the monk with a greasy mutton chop in one hand. "Are you trying to save this wench or saddle her?" He laughed, and the sweat on his forehead glistened in the firelight.

"My Lord!" the monk exclaimed, twisting around to face the chieftain. "I am a man of the cloth. This young woman's soul faces the same peril as yours."

"My soul?" said the chieftain. "My soul belongs to mighty Wotan, who may tear it in two if it does not please him. Can you save me from that, monk?"

"Only the Lord Jesus Christ can save you," the half-bald monk replied, "but I can show you the way."

A few of their tablemates chuckled, but the chieftain's eyes narrowed. "Then come with me," he suddenly cried, hauling the monk to his feet. He dragged Brother Gabrial toward the end of the hall.

"Abdallah!" the chieftain bellowed, as they approached the wooden throne. "Abdallah ibn Mahmud, come up here!" The Arab trader appeared from some corner and strode across the open central aisle, where the fire burned in its pit. To Jason, Abdallah looked like a prince among these barbarians. His neatly trimmed beard, his baggy trousers, his silky blue turban and jacket, and his pointed shoes stood in marked contrast to the Germans' rough grooming, not to mention their stench.[§]

The chieftain rested a hand on the fur cloak hanging over his chair as he regarded the Arab trader and the Irish monk. "My people!" he announced. Noise in the hall fell to a low murmur. "My people, before us this night stand two honorable men, a Christian and a Muslim." He spread his arms, taking in the colorful Arab and the rangy monk. "Each of them swears

---

§ It was the Dark Ages for Europe, not for the Arabs. They forged a mighty empire during the postclassical period. And it wasn't a dark age for the rest of Asia or Africa either. In fact, just as Europe was turning inward and focusing on local events and local barbarism, the Arabs and Asians were sharing knowledge and goods across the Silk Road: the world's greatest trade network.
~ William Gallo, Lectures, History 113.

his faith to a single god." He grinned. "And each thinks our gods are mere phantoms or demons." A low growl rose from the tables. The Arab and the monk shuffled their feet.

"Well, maybe they're right!" shouted the chieftain. A few of the diners gasped. "These Christians surround us, with their constant praying and their charity. Even our own *kin* worship the bleeding god nailed to his cross, and have done for generations. And on the other side of the river, where men dress in silk and eat off plates of gold, everyone's turned Muslim. They all pray to Allah, and their armies fight with Heaven's fury." His glaring blue eyes took in the now silent hall. "One man can't stem the tide of a rushing river, can he? Nor can one tribe. I say we join these men of one god, tonight!"

Many Germans gasped this time. None looked more horrified than the knobby dwarf lumin sitting near the chieftain.

"But which one?" an old woman finally asked. "Which one will we join?"

"Yes, which?" cried the chieftain. "Will we be Muslims or Christians?" He stared at his people, then rose and clapped a hand on Abdallah's shoulder and another on Brother Gabrial's. "These men will help us choose!" he bellowed, shaking them hard. "They will debate for us and teach us the merits of their gods. Then, when they've entertained us enough, I will choose whichever argues better. And we'll have our new god!"

Roars of approval met his declaration, along with a few shouts of protest, including from the dwarf lumin.

"But my Lord, I am no scholar," Abdallah entreated over the cheering. "You cannot put such a weight on my shoulders."

"I can and I have!" the chieftain roared, baring yellow teeth at Abdallah and then turning to snarl at Brother Gabrial. "I want you to argue, so you will argue!" Several men laid hands on swords as the reluctant advocates faced each other in consternation.

"Are these people crazy?" Tia whispered. "How can they have only one god?"

All eyes fell on Brother Gabrial and Abdallah. The monk recovered his composure first. "The religion of Jesus Christ is the one true faith!" he cried as the chieftain sat down, still glaring at him and the Arab.

Silence fell, until Abdallah, in a wooden voice, responded: "No! The religion of the Prophet Muhammad is the one true faith."

Silence fell again. "That's not good enough!" the chieftain finally roared, pounding the arm of his great chair. "Convince me!"

This time, Abdallah spoke first. "Well," he said uneasily, "we all know … we all know the Christians admit there is only one God … but they really worship *three*." His voice grew stronger. "They have their father god, their son god, and their ghost god, don't they? Three gods! It makes no sense." The assembly murmured, the chieftain nodded, and Jason guessed that Abdallah had scored a point. Abdallah finished with, "We Muslims truly worship one God, almighty Allah."

Brother Gabrial's face turned purple. "Blasphemous ignorance!" he cried. "There is only one God, and the Holy Trinity is the essence of true faith." He launched into a complicated explanation of the Trinity. Jason listened as Brother Gabrial discussed the Father, the Son, and the Holy Ghost. The explanation confused him, but he guessed it didn't really matter if anyone understood. He was sure the monk would win. These people were Germans, and Jason didn't remember any German Muslims from the history his father had taught him. He did remember that German barbarians had conquered half of Europe and become Christian. If Fore worked anything like the real world—like real history—Brother Gabrial had to win.

A hushed conversation drew his attention from the two advocates. Across the table and near the wall, several men huddled together. Jason could barely hear their conversation, but he heard enough to guess they were *betting* on the debate's outcome.

"Wait a second," he whispered. He jumped to his feet and rushed around the table, startling his companions. The ale put a slight sway in his walk. "What are you guys betting?" he demanded as he approached the circle gathered under a torch bracket.

The men looked at him with interest and made room in their circle. "The question is, foreign lord, what are *you* betting?" answered one. He had a prominent nose, sea gray eyes, and dark blond braids hanging over his shoulders.

"I want to bet on the monk, and I need a boat," Jason said confidently. "I need a good sailboat to get me and two others downstream. If any of you's got a boat, I'll bet something for that." It was a stroke of genius. Whatever Jason bet, he couldn't lose. The odds on Brother Gabrial were perfect—a hundred to zero.

The men looked at each other and murmured. "You can buy a boat if anyone has one," the gray-eyed man said. "Or you can have one built. Either way, you need something to trade, preferably money, since no one knows you. Do you have any money?"

"No," said Jason, thinking fast, "but I have these clothes." He fingered his T-shirt and jeans. Everywhere he'd gone in Fore, his clothes had been a source of fascination. In most lands, they'd marked Jason as a great man—a prince or a lord. "I've got more in my bag."

The gamblers rubbed their beards and peered at his outfit, particularly his jeans. But the gray-eyed man shook his head. "You'll need at least fifteen pounds for a good boat—"

"Twenty," interrupted another man, short and broad in the chest.

"All right then, twenty. Those clothes are very fine, but even a whole bag wouldn't be worth twenty pounds. I wouldn't risk more than three for them."

"Maybe four," said the short man.

Jason sighed. Now what?

"You do have something worth a lot more," said the gray-eyed German. His bushy eyebrows drew together as he sized Jason up. "What are you willing to risk?"

Jason's head swam. "Whatever it takes."

Gray Eyes stared across the crowded, smoky hall. His gaze fell on Tia. "That girl isn't your wife, is she?"

"No."

"But she is yours?"

A murmur of appreciation rose among the other gamblers. They liked Tia. Their eyes held Jason, and their faces wore expressions of respect.

"Yeah, she's mine," he said. "Of course."

"Lucky man," the short gambler exclaimed, smacking Jason on the shoulder. Jason flushed.

"Good," said Gray Eyes, "because that girl's worth ten pounds, maybe fifteen. I'll bet you fifteen: good coins, too, some of 'em Greek. If you win, you'll be well on your way to a new boat." The gamblers nodded enthusiastically.

Jason looked across the room. At that moment, Tia turned from the debate and caught his eye. She smiled, curious. He shot an artificial grin back.

His face tingled. It wasn't like he'd be risking anything. He knew he'd win, so there was no chance of Tia finding herself enslaved. Brother Gabrial had to win the debate. This was obviously a European country, with German rulers, and that meant Christianity.

Tia would probably be proud of him when he won a new boat. She might even hug him.

A tiny voice at the back of his mind argued that this was a bad, bad idea. But he raised his chin to face Gray Eyes and wobbled a bit on his feet. The short German put a hand on his back to steady him.

"Fifteen's too low," said Jason. "I'll bet on the monk, and I'll put the girl up against twenty-five pounds."

"Twenty-two," said Gray Eyes, grinning, "and you've got a bet." He spat on his right palm and held it out to Jason.

Jason stared at the puddle of spit. "Twenty-two then," he said softly. He spat on his own palm, and they shared a tight, squishy handshake.

"Witnessed!" the others cried.

"I am Dagobert, son of Walafrid," said Gray Eyes. "May Wotan¶ favor the better man."

"Jason, son of William. Go, Wotan!"

Jason felt buoyant again as he made his way back along the table, wiping the spit off of his hand. He'd soon have a new

---

¶ Wotan was the German high god, known as Wodin to the Anglo-Saxons and Odin to the Scandinavians. He gives us Wodin's day, or *Wodnesdaeg* in Old English; which, in modern English, is Wednesday.
~ William Gallo, *Historical Factoids*, 70.

boat. He stopped short to avoid tripping over the saint lumin, who still sat with her back to the wall. She looked up at him, her face calm, her eyes and halo glowing. Was that a look of motherly disapproval on the saint's pale face?

"'Scuse me," he said softly, and he walked around her.

He ambled back to his place on the bench between Tia and Zidu. For some reason his bet—his sure thing—suddenly filled him with anxiety. And the buzzing in his head was no longer pleasant.

But he couldn't lose. He knew Brother Gabrial would win. Still, his heart pounded against his ribcage like a hammer on an anvil. He kept looking back at the saint lumin. Had she done something to him?

Brother Gabrial was arguing that Islam had no leader with the pope's spiritual dignity, since the Muslim caliph was an earthly king, not just a man of God. Both advocates had thrown aside their hesitation and now waged verbal warfare with gusto. But the assembled barbarians grumbled, looking bored. The chieftain sat on his wooden throne tapping his fingers and glaring.

"Enough!" he suddenly bellowed, interrupting a startled Gabrial. "Enough of this tripe!" He rose from his chair. "How can a man choose on such nonsense, such manure?" Murmurs of agreement rose from the assembly. "There's only one true way to choose: the way of strength, the way of the warrior.

"You two!" he roared, pointing at the advocates. "You will wrestle. He who first pins his man, his faith will be our faith."

Jason gasped and the Germans cheered. Abdallah was taller than Brother Gabrial, and he was easily fifteen years younger.

"My Lord," Brother Gabrial cried, "I am a man of peace, a man of God. I do not wrestle."

Yes, thought Jason. *He's a man of peace. He doesn't wrestle.*

The chieftain spat on the floor. "I know you monks. You do what you have to, including shed blood. Well, tonight you'll wrestle for me, or you'll see your god quicker than you think. *Now!*"

"Oh my God, what have I done?" Jason moaned as the combatants reluctantly took off their outer clothes.

"What do you mean?" Zidu asked. "What is wrong?"

Zidu's and Tia's eyes bore into Jason. He looked at Abdallah's thick chest and Gabrial's stringy body as the two circled, arms outstretched. "I, I made a bet on the debate, with one of those guys behind us. I bet the monk would win—that they'd all become Christians. I was sure because ... because I have a way to know, from my own world ... because these people turned Christian in my history." He looked at his friends. "But I didn't think they'd end up wrestling!"

Tia's dark eyebrows crinkled. "What did you bet?"

He gulped. All the pleasant effects of the ale were gone. He felt nauseous. "I bet *you*. I bet you against the price of a new boat."

Tia's mouth opened slowly.

"Jason!" Zidu gasped. "How could you do that? Tia is not yours to bet."

"I was sure we'd win," Jason said humbly. "I knew ... My dad was always telling me all this history. There wasn't even a chance ..."

"But why did you not ask Tia?" Zidu exclaimed. "Risk or no risk, it was her choice to make."

A shout interrupted them. Abdallah had tackled Brother Gabrial. The two rolled across the floor as the cheering Germans yanked snarling dogs out of the way. But the monk squirmed aside and scrambled to his feet.

Jason turned to find Tia still staring at him, tears quivering in her eyes. Over her shoulder and across the table, Jason's betting mate leaned against the wall. Dagobert met Jason's gaze and crossed his arms. Then he nodded at the combatants: at the aging monk and the hardy Arab merchant in the prime of his life.

And then a grin spread across his face.**

** Not too many Europeans converted to Islam, except in Spain and Sicily. But Christianity did have a rival at home. As we've seen, the Jews had immigrated during Roman times. Unlike most modern Hebrews, these Dark Age Jews actually proselytized, converting a lot of their neighbors and servants.

The most dramatic Jewish conversion happened outside Europe, in Central Asia. According to legend, in 861 the king of the pagan Khazars invited Jewish, Muslim, and Christian scholars to debate. The Jews won, so the Khazar court adopted Judaism. The debate part probably isn't true, but the Khazar king and many nobles did adopt the Jewish faith.

~ William Gallo, Lectures, History 113.

12

Medieval Spirits

THE WORD "MEDIEVAL" COMES from the Latin for "middle ages." Traditionally, it referred to the thousand years from the late 400s to the late 1400s. But today, I think most of us associate "medieval" with the second half of that thousand years. I'm talking about the age of knights and castles, Gothic cathedrals, Crusades, and troubadour songs of courtly love. For historians, it's also the time of manor farms, craftsmen's guilds, feudalism, and bubonic plague.

During the late 900s, Western Europe's economy grew, finally pulling the region out of the awful Dark Ages. Peasants cut down forests, drained swamps, and cultivated new lands. Trade grew, too. Don't get me wrong. The West was still backward and hardscrabble poor compared to the Byzantine Empire, not to mention the great Islamic countries. But the new wealth gave it a vigor it hadn't known for centuries.

Medieval society developed three uniquely Western features. First, a really dynamic and independent merchant class—a bunch of creative traders who planted the seeds for capitalism. Second, the parliamentary tradition, which mostly grew out of the feudal king's obligation to consult with his barons. And third, the separation of church and state, punctuated by nasty battles between popes and kings.

~ William Gallo, Lectures, History 78.

ooooo

Abdallah stepped back toward the fire pit and stumbled, and Brother Gabrial leapt on him. But the Arab had lost balance for only a moment. He pivoted and grabbed the rushing monk's arm. In an instant, Gabrial was on his belly with Abdallah on top of him. And in another instant, Abdallah had flipped the monk onto his back and held his lean shoulders to the straw-covered floor.

Cheers shook the hall, and Jason's heart sank. He was dizzy and nauseous. "I won't do it—the bet," he whispered to Tia, who would not look at him. "I'll fight if I have to. I won't let anything happen to you, Tia. I'm sorry!"

Suddenly, the hall fell silent. Abdallah looked up from his pinned adversary. A dagger skittered across the floor. "Pick it up," said a grim voice. The chieftain had risen from his throne. "Pick it up and finish him. Send him to your infidel's Hell. Then we'll all be Muslims together."

A dog whined, but otherwise silence reigned as Abdallah picked up the knife and then stared at the chieftain. "But ... but," he began.

"Do it," the chieftain growled. "I mean to see blood tonight, and if it's not his, it will be yours."

"My soul is prepared," said a quiet voice. Abdallah looked down at the pinned monk. Brother Gabrial's breathing had slowed, and he looked calm. "Do what you must, my friend," he continued, staring into the Arab's eyes. "Maybe God means for these people to see how a Christian dies. If I can bring them to Him this way, so be it." He closed his eyes and began to sing softly, in Latin, Jason guessed.

Abdallah stared down at Gabrial. Then he rose to his feet, releasing the monk, who stopped singing but did not rise. The Arab faced the chieftain across the fire-lit hall, wearing only his baggy, red trousers. "I will not," he said evenly, tossing the dagger aside. "I will not kill an innocent man, a man of God, for your entertainment. Do as you please, but I will not."

The chieftain threw back his head—and roared! The cry reverberated among the thick wooden rafters as he spread his arms like a bear. But then his open mouth bent into a grin,

and the roar turned to laughter. "HA-HA, HA-HA!" he bellowed. "I *thought* you wouldn't! Well then you *lose!*" He strode
over to the combatants and hauled Brother Gabrial to his feet.
"Ready to die so soon?" he shouted at the Irishman, who'd
begun trembling but otherwise maintained his composure.
"Well, not just yet. Don't you know you've won, you fool of a
monk? You've won! Wave your magic cross or do whatever it
is you do. We'll join your church."

A gasp passed through the hall. Some Germans smiled,
others shook their heads, and a few spat. The dwarf lumin
turned away.

Jason reached for Tia's arm, smiling from ear to ear. "We've
won!" he exclaimed. "We've—"

A blow to the belly sent the air rushing from his lungs. He
doubled over. Tia had punched him!

"Don't touch me!" she hissed. "Don't even come near me!"
She rose and stormed off as the Germans nearby giggled.

"I had better go with her," said Zidu, jumping off the bench.
"I cannot believe what you did, Jason."

Jason found himself alone, rubbing his belly and watching
the saint lumin glide across the hall to join Brother Gabrial
and their new convert, the chieftain.

He sat on the bench for over an hour as the talking and
feasting swirled around him. He'd won his bet. They'd have
money for a boat, if they could find one, and maybe some extra
for supplies. But what had he done? What had come over him?

"Jason, son of William," said a stern voice. He looked up to
find his betting mate, Dagobert, silhouetted against the fading
firelight. The German had pinned a cloak over his shoulder
with a bronze brooch, and he stood tall and solid. Jason looked
at the sword by his side and the leather armbands on his thick
wrists, and shivered. He would have fought Dagobert for Tia,
and he certainly would've lost.

"Your monk showed some courage at the end, didn't he?"
the German growled. "Who could have guessed?" He shook
his head, then held up a jingling leather bag. "Your winnings.
That's twenty-two pounds. You can count them."

Jason looked at the pouch, but suddenly it was snatched away. Tia stood beside them, her eyes blazing. "I think those are mine," she said. She glared at Dagobert, then at Jason. Then she stalked off.

Bushy brows rose over Dagobert's gray eyes. "Looks like you've got some problems managing your girl," he said, smirking. "Enjoy your winnings—if you can get them back."

Much of the company slept on the floor of the great hall that night. The three travelers slept there, too, though Tia lay among the women and would not even look at Jason.

"I don't think you should speak to her," Zidu whispered as he stretched out next to Jason's borrowed blanket. "She knows you thought you could not lose, but you have deeply offended her."

"Will she leave?" Jason whispered. "Will she go back to Tarraco-Hispania?"

"No," the lion-man replied. "She has no way back, and she believes in our quest. She thinks Lady Aurelia and Senusret and Nebetit would want her to see it through. But our journey is less a joy for her now."

Snores soon filled the room, but Jason lay awake. He felt desolate—a feeling he knew, as if he'd experienced it before, or seen it.

He *had* seen it—the night before the coma, when he yelled at his father, "You're probably glad she's dead!" For just an instant, as his father turned back to his computer, his face looked desolate.

What had come over him that night—or this one? Jason lay in the dark of the Germans' lodge, and his eyes filled with tears.

ooooo

Jason woke early the next morning and left the lodge. Outside, brick and stone ruins, like the dried bones of extinct dragons, cast long shadows over the crops and grasses. The German barbarians lived at the edge of a Roman ghost town. Jason saw the remains of an aqueduct and what looked like an amphitheater.

He found an unlikely twosome on the meadow in front of the lodge. Brother Gabrial was kneeling there, with Abdallah in a similar position nearby. The monk was motionless in prayer, his palms pressed together before his face and his eyes closed. The Arab, on the other hand, rose and fell like a reed in the wind as he touched his forehead to a prayer mat. But despite the differences in practice, the two seemed united. Their faces wore expressions of reverence and peace. Jason felt an odd pang of jealousy.*

He made his way across the fields and down to the river, hoping to do some thinking in private. He soon found a quiet cove lined with trees. But he wasn't alone. A boy of ten or less sat by the water, patching a piece of sailcloth. Jason gasped as he saw the treasure the boy guarded. "A boat!" he whispered.

A handsome ship, built of dark wood, bobbed in the quiet cove. Its single mast rose to meet its crossbeam, forming a **T**, and Jason guessed the sail would be square. The prow and stern curved high above the water.

"Is it yours?" he asked the boy.

The youngster laughed. He wore little more than rags— probably a peasant or slave. "No, sir," the boy said. "This belongs to my master, the chieftain."

Later that morning, Jason and Zidu sat in the sunlight in front of the hall, discussing Jason's find. "I'm sure I can figure out how to sail it," Jason said. "But how do we get the chieftain to sell? And Tia has all the money."

"I think Tia will be reasonable," said Zidu. "After all, what else can she do with the money, if she does not plan to return upriver? I think we should try to buy this boat."

---

* Medieval Christendom and the Muslim world were hostile, but they did trade, and many ideas flowed into Europe from the more sophisticated Arab lands. For instance, Arabic numerals (originating in India) eventually replaced the cumbersome Roman system. And Arabs taught the West a great deal of science. They gave us English words such as "carat," "zenith," and "zero," as well as "alchemy," "alcohol," "algebra," and "alkali," based on Arabic terms starting with *al*, meaning "the."

~ William Gallo, "Middle Eastern Influence on the Spiritual Literature of the High Middle Ages," *The Springfield Journal of History*, 23. 332, 340 (1997).

"To tell you the truth, I'm not crazy about just walking up to the chieftain and asking if he's got any used boats to sell." Jason thought of the bellowing bear of a man who'd made Abdallah and the monk wrestle. "Maybe you could ask his lumin to help. You know, that dwarf-thing from last night. You could ask lumin to lumin—maybe find out if it's even worth talking to the chieftain."

"Let us try."

They found the dwarf lumin in the nearly empty hall, sitting by the cold embers of the previous night's fire, muttering. "What do *you* two want?" he snapped as they approached.

"I am very sorry to interrupt your thoughts," said the lion-man. "I am Zidu, lumin of Sumer, and this is Jason Gallo, my shaman. I had hoped to ask if you might help a fellow lumin. We have a business proposal for the chieftain, but we do not know how to ask."

The dwarf grasped the thick belt over his tunic and glared up at them with beady, gleaming eyes. This was Jason's first chance for a close look at the strange lumin. The creature had very large hands and feet. His head was ugly, with an enormous nose, pointed ears, and craggy features. "What kind of business?" he demanded.

"We travel down the river, to distant lands," said Zidu, "but our boat is lost. Jason has noticed that your master owns a fine boat. We would like to buy it."

Bushy brows rose over the dwarf's eyes, and he stared into space for some time. Finally, just as Jason was becoming uncomfortable, he nodded and hopped off his bench. "We haven't been introduced," he said, still glaring. "I am Mime, and I've been both rune master and jewel smith to these people." He abruptly held up a gnarled hand, and Jason shook it while Zidu bowed.

"Yah, you're right," Mime continued. "My master's got a boat. Or I should say my *ex*-master. My faithful service ended when the craven coward chose the baptism, just because the prince commanded it. Christians have no use for lumins like me."

"*What?*" Jason exclaimed. "The prince?"

Mime spat. "You didn't think that little show last night was real, did you? The major domo told me this morning: a messenger arrived three days ago. The prince is a Christian, and he wants all his lords to take the baptism. The chieftain just wanted some fun with that Arab and the monk before he knuckled under. He'd never have let the Muslim win." Mime bared his crooked teeth. "So now they'll all be Christians, and some pale-faced saint or angel will take my place, and never a word of thanks, I'll wager."

"They could not send you away," Zidu exclaimed.

"Couldn't they? In six months, that monk and his henchmen will be talking about 'bad pagan influences.' Then I'll be out. It always happens that way. It happened to my cousin Alviss less than a century ago."

"So, back to the point," said Jason, "what about the boat?"

"You're going away, you say—somewhere far from here?" They nodded. "And you must be pagans of some sort, like me." Mime inclined his head pointedly at Zidu. "Well, I want to come with you. Take me, and I'll convince the chieftain to sell you the boat, for a good price."

"Sure," Jason said. "Uh, we'd love to have you. But … are you sure the chieftain will sell?"

Mime spat again. "He'll be happy to, if *I* leave with the boat. If I stay around, it'll be awkward, especially when the Christians push me out. He knows it's coming, and he knows some of his men won't like it."

"Oh," said Jason. "Okay … well, yeah."

"This seems a good bargain," said Zidu, nodding at Jason. He turned to Mime. "Your story has a familiar ring, my friend. I know your pain. We lumins live to be needed. I hope you will find people who need you once again."

Mime's ugly face softened. "I hope so, too."

ooooo

The Germans often called dwarves "black elves," so the companions gave the new boat that name, to thank Mime.

The *Black Elf* was faster and sturdier than the *Dead Valencia*. It was built of hard, lightweight oak, held together by iron rivets and bolts. The deck was narrow, so the four were cramped when they slept aboard, but no one minded.

Despite their enthusiasm for the new ship, the travelers made for a quiet crew. Mime rarely spoke and often cursed or complained when he did. And Tia never spoke to Jason, though he apologized again and again. He didn't blame her. In the bright light of day, his lack of chivalry[†] amazed him.

They sailed along the right bank for nearly two weeks. Eventually, the forests dominating the shore gave way to more substantial farms and villages, as well as a few walled towns and stone castles. On a field before one of these castles, they saw men covered in silvery armor, charging each other on horseback and wielding long sticks.

"They're knights practicing jousting!" Jason exclaimed.

"Idiots," Mime muttered.

A stop at a small town revealed good news: they'd arrived at Capetian France. They reached their destination soon after. The town of Laurac was a cluster of one- and two-story houses, grouped around a tall church and enclosed by a wooden wall. A castle on a nearby hill dominated the surrounding countryside.

They moored the *Black Elf* and left Mime to keep an eye on it. Butterflies rose in Jason's stomach as he, Tia, and Zidu made their way among the thatched-roof houses and cottages. The townsfolk wore simple clothes: tunics and close-fitting trousers on the men and long skirts and gowns on the women. Not sure whom to ask, Jason finally approached a passerby.

---

† Chivalry grew out of two propaganda campaigns and a fascination with adultery. The early knights were basically thugs: robbing, raping, ransoming hostages, and so on. To transform them into what would eventually be called "gentlemen," the Church spread two new ideas during the 900s and 1000s. The Peace of God discouraged attacks on women, peasants, and the Church. And the Truce of God discouraged fighting on holy days. A less religious force helped tame the knights, too, by encouraging respect for women. Courtly love was romantic devotion to a woman, usually someone else's wife. Together, these three trends shaped the knights' code of conduct, called *chevalerie*, Old French for "horsemanship"—or chivalry.

~ William Gallo, Lectures, History 78.

"Excuse me, ma'am," he said to a chubby woman leading three children down a cottage-lined street. "We're looking for someone: a lumin named Quennel. Can you tell us where to find him?"

The woman looked startled. She gathered her children and hurried away, whispering, "Heathens and harlots!"

Jason blinked. What? He shook his head and tried again, with two clean-shaven young men coming from the other direction. "Excuse me," he said, "we're looking for ..."

One of the men spat, and the other crossed himself hastily. "What's going on here?" Jason asked his friends.

Someone laughed from across the street. A big man sat under the eaves of a wood-framed house, cooling himself with a leather fan. "Foreigners, aren't you?" he asked.

"Yes," said Jason humbly. "Are we doing something wrong?"

"Well, that depends who you ask. But in a word, yes." He beckoned them over. Their informer wore an embroidered knee-length robe and a boxy yellow hat. "I'll help if I can. When you're lost, ask a Jew, they say. My people know what it means to be strangers in a strange land."

He ran long fingers through his beard, which was thick and flecked with gray. "Well then, what have you done wrong? First off, no one wants to see a heathen lumin like your friend here. It's bad luck, and who knows what else? In fact, if you're not careful, you'll have the priests after you, wanting to exorcise your demon, God forbid." He shook his head. "Then, on top of that ..." He glanced at Tia. "Meaning no disrespect to the young lady, people here don't mind a prostitute much, but one should not ... How to say it? Well, one shouldn't flaunt her, if you see what I mean."

"A prostitute?" Tia demanded. "Just who here do you think is a prostitute?"

Uh-oh, Jason thought.

Their informer sat back. "Why, you, young lady. Have I misunderstood?"

Tia's fists clenched, and Jason scanned her quickly. Her outfit wasn't even remotely revealing. She wore one of the garments she'd bought with their gambling winnings: a shape-less, brown tunic-dress with long sleeves and a skirt falling nearly to her ankles.

"It's your hair, child," their informer continued. "It's uncov-ered. That's how a prostitute advertises. Didn't you know that? All these goyim think you're a prostitute, I guarantee it."

Jason stared open-mouthed at Tia's black hair, shining in the sun. Then he looked around. The other women on the street wore veils or hats over their hair. So had most of the women they'd seen for weeks, he realized.

"I don't care what a herd of ignorant foreigners think," Tia growled. "I'm not covering my hair for anyone."

Their informer looked quizzical. "How is it you don't know about prostitutes and demons? Where do you come from, anyway? Are you Mongol-men?"‡

"No," Jason answered. "Look, it's just ... We're from really far away, and they have different customs there. She's not a prostitute, and he's not a demon. We're just here looking for someone. Can you help us? We're looking for a lumin named Quennel."

"God in heaven!" croaked the big man. "What for?"

"Uh, we're trying to find someone, Professor William Gallo. Ever heard of him?"

Their informer shook his head.

"Well ... can you tell us where to find Quennel?"

The big man rose to his feet, picking up a canvas bag. "I sup-pose one should help, but ... well, I can't say much. I won't." He gulped. "If you want to find ... *him*, go into the woods behind the castle at night. Take the path from the northeast tower until

---

‡ The record for biggest land-empire ever goes to the British—but second place goes to a small band of barbarian horsemen whose leader started out as a poor outcast. I'm talking about the Mongols and Genghis Khan, in the 1200s. The Mongols con-quered China, Russia, Central Asia, and much of the Middle East, including Persia. They never did push far into Europe, but the West still benefited from the spread of knowledge through the empire—particularly of gunpowder—brought home by trad-ers and diplomats, and by globetrotters like Marco Polo, who apparently traveled all the way from Italy to the Mongol capital in China.
  ~ William Gallo, Lectures, History 78.

you reach the big clearing, the one with the mushrooms. Then just wait till the moon's up. If you don't see anything, go back every night of the moon until they come." His voice fell to little more than a whisper. "But whatever you do, don't make them angry. And don't mention my name." He pressed his hand to his forehead. "That's all I'll say, Lord protect me. Good luck to you." With that, he bowed and hurried away.

They headed back to the *Black Elf*, now very conscious of locals cringing in fear at "demon" Zidu.

"Why did you bring me here?" cried Mime when they returned. "They're all Christians, every one of 'em. It's worse than home. One fool waved his cross at me and yelled, 'Begone, foul spirit!' And a little urchin came right up and asked if I really eat children who don't mind their mothers. I told him I do, and I threatened to eat him right there." The dwarf lumin glared up at Jason. "And then there was this nosy giant. Walked right up and started asking me questions, like he was the major domo or something."

"Questions?" asked Jason.

"Yah," said Mime. "He wanted to know who my shipmates were, and where we were headed, and why. Just came right up and asked."

"What did he look like?" Jason demanded.

"He was dark, with a dark beard," said the dwarf, "and a big, beaky nose. He looked like a Moor, only he wasn't dressed like one. Some kind of barbarian, I'll bet. And he was huge. A head taller than you, Jason, probably more. And muscles to match. A warrior for sure."

"Oh, God!" said Jason, "You didn't tell him anything, did you?"

"Yah, well, not much." Mime looked confused. "I said I work for a lord called Jason, and then I told him to bugger off. Why?"

Silence fell over the company.

"We should move the boat," Zidu finally said, "to some-place secluded."

ooooo

They hid the *Black Elf* upstream, in the woods. Then, once darkness had fallen, they returned to the town on foot. They quickly found the narrow path leading into the woods behind the castle's northeast tower. They wound through the forest until they stumbled into a clearing. Tia carried a candle she'd bought from the German barbarians, and though it cast only a weak light, it revealed a circle of mushrooms near the center of the clearing.

"This must be the place," Zidu whispered. So they sat on damp grass and waited.

After more than an hour, a crescent moon rose over the black trees, joining Fore's watery stars.

Jason could never remember afterward which came first, the music or the lights. Some time during that night, an eerie melody whispered through the trees. The song was sorrowful, and Jason found himself thinking of his mother. As the music swelled, he realized he held Tia's hand.

The lights looked like dancing stars. At first, they floated lazily among the trees. But then they picked up speed, just as the music did, and swirled into the glade to revolve within the circle of mushrooms.

"Eyes," Mime whispered. "They're lumin eyes."

Jason strained his own eyes and saw that the dwarf was right. The travelers had been watching the glowing eyes of lumins: night spirits dancing ever faster in the ring of mushrooms. Now that he could see the bodies, Jason realized these lumins were tiny. Hardly any stood more than a foot tall, and many were half that size. Some came in animal shapes: birds, squirrels, and foxes. But most looked human, though with butterfly wings or sharp pixie faces or stretched, misshapen limbs. Jason saw devil horns, pointed ears, rodent snouts, blue skin, antlers, and other features too strange to describe. They danced in a starlit whirlwind, some running and leaping through the grass, others flying under their own power or on the backs of birds or bats.

At the center danced the musicians themselves. An eight-inch green boy with long, pointed ears played a double pipe. And a bone-thin woman, even smaller and with the head of a bluebird, sawed frantically on a tiny fiddle.

"They must be fairies," Jason said in a hushed voice.

"When fairies dance, the world's a dream," whispered a high, cruel voice by his ear, "but feral spirits make you scream!" The voice laughed, and the laughter swelled into a hideous screech that tore at his eardrum. Jason batted at his ear, but suddenly little hands grasped his clothes, pulling him toward the circle. He tried to resist, and Tia's hand tightened on his. But soon he found himself inside the ring of mushrooms, dancing and swirling like a madman. He cried out and tried to flee the ring, but the music surged through his blood, commanding his body to run and twirl and leap.

The tempo increasing to an impossible, frenzied rush, and Jason's heart raced. Soon he wasn't the only full-sized dancer. Tia whirled among the tiny beings, and so did Mime.

Finally the music grew so frenzied that Jason thought his head and heart would burst. He cried out as he tumbled through air, music, and shimmering stars, and then light and sound disappeared.

ooooo

Jason awoke, as though from the most pleasant sleep of his life. He found himself lying face-up in the moonlight, his T-shirt and jeans damp from the grass. He tried to rise, but he could move only his head. He looked along his body and saw silver threads stretched across his torso and his arms and legs. Tia lay next to him, also tied down and also awake, and Mime sat nearby, unbound.

"I understand that, Great King," said Zidu's voice, "but these two are different. They are both shamans, and the young woman is a priestess and the disciple of an ancient cult, one that respects all lumins." Jason strained and saw the Sumerian lion-man sitting nearby, his back to the two humans. "And the boy is learning to use his—"

"Listen not, king of mine!" called a piping voice. "Let's drain their blood to spice our wine!"

Jason saw leering fairies seated just inside the ring of mushrooms. Their eyes glowed like captive stars. Another tiny voice cried: "Let's roast their brains and stew their eyes, and bake 'em in a shaman pie!" Piping laughter came from all directions.

"As I was *saying*," Zidu continued, "the boy is learning, becoming a shaman. And he is the son of the very human you said was your friend. He is Jason Gallo, son of Professor William Gallo. He is here to ask your help finding his father. Like his father, he is a friend."

"Friend of mine or friend of yours; feed them both to wolves and boars!" This came from a fairy with bat wings, a nine-inch man's body, and a boar's head. The other fairies screeched with laughter and the speaker grinned, displaying needle-sharp tusks.

"William Gallo *was* our friend," said a voice, "though we threw him in the bog when he first came here."

"'Twas fun for us but not for him," another fairy piped, "though who could mind a moonlit swim?" More vicious laughter.

"But it is the son who lies before us now, not our friend, the father," continued the newer voice. It was lower than the others. "I do not like the look of this young man. He watched our revels with a cold eye that knows no love of spirit. If this boy truly is William Gallo's son, I think him an unworthy heir, and I see no reason why he should live."

Jason shivered.

"Perhaps we should test the boy," said another voice, softer and higher, "before we judge him unworthy of his father." A brief silence followed.

Then the lower voice said, "Stand aside, Sumerian, and let us look again, now that they're awake."

Zidu moved. Behind him, a male and a female fairy sat on a throne-like rock at the foot of a mossy oak. These two were larger than the rest, especially the male, who Jason guessed must stand close to a foot and a half. They wore silver circlets on their brows, and they had noble, feral faces, with high, slanting cheekbones. The male—the king, Jason was quite sure—had snow-white skin and silver hair. He wore silver armor from neck to toe, so clear it reflected like a mirror. But while the king's beauty lay in winter white, his queen shone with color. Golden hair flowed down to her knees, and her skin was the deepest peach, covered by an almost transparent gown. But her true color lay in her wings. Wide butterfly wings sprouted from her back, framed in black but alive with swirls of rainbow pigment.

The king stepped delicately off his throne and walked across the grass to stand between Jason and Tia. He stared at Tia a long time. "This girl is no enemy of mine," he said. "Let her up, but guard her well, in case she resists when we slaughter the boy."

Squealing fairies rushed to cut Tia loose, but they did not let her leave the ring of mushrooms. A fairy with the body of a scarlet lizard sat on her shoulder, holding a tiny sword, like a scalpel, against her throat. Tia's eyes were wide, and she sat perfectly still.

The fairy king stood near Jason's face, glaring at him. Jason shook from the strain of holding his head up and from fear of the apparently insane lumins.

"Very well," said the king, "we will test this boy and see if he is worthy of his father. He has not William Gallo's love of spirit, but perhaps he has his wit. If so, we will consider him our friend. If not, we will fill our bellies with his blood."

The assembled fairies cackled.

"But King Quennel—" Zidu began. The fairies' angry screeches cut him short. Jason looked at the lion-man with a start. This was Quennel?

"Silence, Sumerian," said the king. "Try my patience again and you'll find yourself imprisoned in crystal for a century."

King Quennel regarded Jason again, and Jason fought to control his shaking. Finally, the fairy spoke in a singsong tone.

> Little man of spirit cold,
> Answer quick; be brave and bold.

Your father's wit you must now prove;
Speak true or else your life you lose.
Gathered here are spirits fierce
Whose shrieks the moonlit silence pierce.
How came we to this woodland glade?
How were we into fairies made?
What *are* we few, so light and airy?
What does it mean to name us "fairy"?
Tell me if the truth you see.
Answer quick, or ghost you'll be!

Jason blinked. "Wha-what are you? You want me to guess
… what you are?"

The tiny king did not answer, and no fairy moved or spoke.
Jason looked desperately at his friends, at Tia sitting nearby with
a tiny blade at her throat and at Mime next to her. They looked
confused, and tears shone in Tia's eyes. He turned to Zidu.
Jason guessed he knew the answer. But Zidu could not help.
Jason stared around the silent glade, at the lovely little queen,
smiling indulgently from her throne, at the strange forms of
the slavering fairies, and at the silvery king. *What does it mean
to name us "fairy"?* Did it mean they were all tiny serial killers?

He let his head fall the ground and he looked up at the
swimming stars. *Fairy, fairy, fairy* … what did it mean? One
who is gay? No. One who is fair? Too simple and stupid. What
were these creatures? Obviously, they were lumins. But these
lumins were different. They were wild, vicious—not the least
bit hesitant to kill a human being. And they lived alone out
here, without humans. Most lumins wanted only to serve
human beings. He'd never seen any without humans.

Yes, he had! Jason thought of the Minotaur: a lumin alone,
without human companionship. And the Minotaur had been
half insane, and violent, too, just like the fairies. Jason's fists
tightened by his sides, pulling cool shoots of grass from the
earth. He screwed his eyes shut. What was the connection?

"He cannot guess," said King Quennel, his voice low and
deadly. "Let his blood flow!"

"Wait!" Jason cried over Tia and Zidu's shouts. "You're *abandoned* lumins! You're abandoned by human beings!" He raised his head, staining against the silvery threads, and his glance fell on Mime. "You're abandoned *pagan* lumins, and they've given your places to saints and angels! They kicked you out!" His voice shook. "They all became Christian, so they kicked you out. You were their lumins when they were pagans, and then they threw you out! So you came here, and lived together, and you all became fairies! You're abandoned lumins!"

The fairies stood frozen, expressions of surprise and grief on their tiny faces. Only the queen moved. She rose to stand before her stone throne. "He has his father's wisdom," she said. "He has guessed our sad story and told it, and not without feeling."

All eyes fell on the king, who stared at Jason without expression. "Very well," he said, "we will not drink your blood, Jason son of William, Gallo of the other world. You have spoken well. We will consider you a friend, like your father."

"A friend! A friend!" the assembled fairies shrieked. "Whose flesh we will not rend!" They swirled around Jason, cutting his silver threads. Jason swayed from relief and from the rush of blood from his head as he sat up.

But before his pulse had slowed, the fairy queen rose with a flutter of rainbow wings. "Now humans must fall silent," she said. "We have dealt with two of the three who danced with us. Our business with the third is of the most serious kind."

King Quennel crossed the mushroom ring to stand in front of Mime. "Brother," he said, looking up at the dwarf lumin, "I know your plight. You search for home, but the home you seek can never be yours again."

"A better home awaits you," the queen crooned.

"I don't understand," Mime mumbled, staring at the tiny monarchs. "I'm not one of you. I don't understand what Jason said."

"We have all passed through the change," said the king. "Now your time has come."

The eerie music began again.

"But how …?" Mime's voice shook, but his ugly, misshapen face softened.

The music grew louder, and the fairies began to keen and sway. The melody was softer than before, and lonelier. As the air filled with sound, the queen hovered above Mime's head on butterfly wings.

"You know how," she sang. "You have already forsaken humankind in your heart. Join your brethren, and you will no longer be alone. This is why you came here, though perhaps you did not know it."

Mime put his hands over his mouth, his eyes wide. Next to Jason, Tia held her blue beetle amulet to her lips and watched with tear-flooded eyes.

"Move!" she suddenly whispered. "Get out of the way!"

She pushed a confused Jason across the grass to sit with Zidu outside the ring of mushrooms, as the fairy troop swirled around Mime. The music swelled. Mime raised his arms and the lumin glow of his eyes spread over his whole body. His rough, low voice joined the fairies' high-pitched keening.

Jason's heart caught in his throat. Soon all the lumins but Zidu glowed with spiritual fire. Jason could no longer see Mime in the swirl, but he could hear the dwarf's low voice calling over the higher fairy singing. The music rose and fell again and again for what seemed ages. Then Mime's voice faded away.

The music and the fairies' glow faded soon after, and the tiny lumins returned to their places. Jason looked frantically for the dwarf as the smiling king and queen mounted their stone throne. A fairy knelt in front of the king. The monarch took the kneeler's hands in his own as the two spoke in low voices. Then the little fairy repeated the same ceremony at the queen's feet. Jason peered at the kneeling creature. It was a six-inch man with pointed ears and a nose too large for his face. And from his shoulders sprouted two furry moth wings, gray but marked with black patterns, like ancient runes.

"Is that Mime?" Jason gasped as the king and queen gently touched the fairy's head.

"That is he," said Zidu, his face long, "though I never would have guessed it could be done."

King Quennel looked up from his new vassal and smiled. "Now, my friends, we eat and drink and make merry while the moon rides high!"[§]

ooooo

The fairy fest went on for hours. The little people ate from leaves and drank from acorns. They begged the travelers to take their fill, but the three diplomatically chose not to over-tax their hosts' generosity and settled with tiny portions. Jason enjoyed the night and the company of his strange new friends, despite his anxieties. He especially enjoyed seeing taciturn, bitter Mime so happy. The former dwarf laughed and danced with his new tiny brethren, and he even sat on Jason's shoulder.

"My debt to you, I'd gladly pay," he exclaimed in a piping voice. "You turned my doom to joy and play."

"Doom still awaits," Zidu whispered, once Mime had gone. "They have put it off, but they have also ensured its coming."

Finally, as the revel began to wind down and the moon sank, Jason approached the king and queen and asked about his father.

"Ah, William Gallo," slurred the drunken, silvery king. "An unusual and wise man. We enjoyed his company and his researches."

"His researches? What was he studying?"

"*Us*," said the queen, shifting her tiny, shapely body across

---

§ In other words, Christianity did not erase pagan gods and mythical beings. Some became saints, while others went underground into fairytales. In Germanic mythol-ogy, the white-skinned goddess Freya meets a troop of dwarves who have crafted a beautiful and powerful necklace. In exchange for the treasure, Freya sleeps with each of the misshapen creatures. Some scholars believe this myth evolved into a fairytale, *Snow White and the Seven Dwarfs*. To take another example, the Tuatha De Danaan were a race of elves or mini-gods from Irish pagan mythology. They lived under Ireland's many *sidhes*, its hills and mounds. Christianity eventually replaced pagan beliefs, but the Irish still respected and feared the Tuatha De Danaan as the spirits of the hollow hills—as fairies.

~ William Gallo, *Saints & Satyrs*, 197.

the rocky throne. "He watched our revels and joined in, when-ever we let him. But most of all, he asked questions." She smiled and brushed a waist-length strand of golden hair out of her face. "He asked me about times long past, times I hadn't considered for centuries."

"He asked most of all about our lives after we lost our places among humans," said the king, "and about the change."

"It took him months to guess our true nature," the queen continued. "Yet his son unmasked us in a single night. You are wise beyond your years, Jason Gallo."

No one had ever said Jason was smarter than his father. "Your Highnesses," he said, "there's something strange going on with my father. I said I couldn't find him. He's trapped here in Fore, and I think—at least there's a theory—he may be trapped because he can't go to sleep. If he can't fall asleep here, he may not be able to come back to my world." He sighed. "It's kind of complicated."

Jason thought of Yakov and his theory—that sleep served as the portal between worlds—that a dream voyager must fall asleep in Fore to wake up at home.

"Do you have any idea? Do you know of anything that might be keeping my father awake, all the time?" He bit his lip. Maybe the fairies had done something, some mischief that robbed his father of sleep.

The two monarchs looked at each other. "No," said King Quennel. "I could not imagine such a thing."

"Well, do you know … do you have any idea where he went after he left here?"

"No," said the queen thoughtfully as the king shook his head. "He did not say where."

Despair washed over Jason. King Quennel had been his last clue. If he couldn't even *find* his father, there would be no rescue, no miraculous recovery, no overjoyed reunion with Athena in the hospital room.

The companions sat at the edge of the mushroom ring, watching the fairies. "What do we do now?" Tia asked softly.

Jason turned to face her and Zidu. "We're not beaten yet,"

he said. "There's still someone here in Laurac who must know something about my father."

ooooo

Two days later, Jason walked alone through dappled sunlight and shadows, along a woodland path upstream from Laurac. Birds sang, and squirrels scrambled through the leafy canopy above. Jason's heart jumped at every noise, but he kept his step light, almost casual. After a while, he began to whistle.

Then he heard rustling as something far larger than a squirrel headed his way. A dark giant leapt out of the trees on to the path in front of him. It was Rim-Hadad. The barbarian held a long, steel sword in his right hand. He raised the tip to hover an inch from Jason's throat. "It was kind of you to walk past my camp," said Rim-Hadad. "Now don't move, my friend. You're my prisoner."

Jason did not move. Somehow he managed to keep his voice calm as he said: "No, Rim-Hadad. You are *my* prisoner."

A sardonic smile crossed the barbarian's bearded face, but it turned to shock as silver lassoes fell from the trees. They snapped taut around him, pulling his arms to his sides. The sword clattered to the ground as more shining threads wrapped the captive. Shrieking, laughing fairies sprang from the trees.

"Spiders we who sting with glee!" they sang. "We'll hang our prey from old elm tree!"

In moments, the roaring barbarian hung upside down from a high branch, dangling by his ankles.

Jason approached the squirming, yelling prisoner. He grabbed a handful of silvery thread and halted the barbarian's rocking. Rim-Hadad fell silent.

"Now, *friend*," said Jason, "I want to know everything you know about my father."

13

Renaissance and Reformation

DURING THE LATE 1300S and 1400s, Italian scholars collected all this knowledge from the Arabs, Chinese, and Byzantines, and from the Classical past, and then built on it. Soon, new ideas spread across Western Europe, powered by the printing press, adapted from China in the mid-1400s. This rebirth brought along capitalism, royal bureaucracies, bigger cities, three-masted galleons, globe-trotting explorers, tights and codpieces for men, and inventions like the telescope—not to mention guns, also adapted from the Chinese. Some pretty amazing art and architecture blossomed at the same time, including da Vinci's paintings, the Sistine Chapel, Michelangelo's David, and eventually Shakespeare's plays.

Renaissance technology led to bigger ships and new navigation tools. The result? The Age of Discovery. In 1492, Columbus sailed the ocean blue and stumbled across the Americas. And Portuguese ships reached India in 1498 and China in 1513. For the first time ever, a single trade network connected the entire planet, with Western Europe—that primitive backwater—as its hub.

But trouble was brewing on the religious front. In 1517, a German professor-monk denounced certain practices of the Catholic Church. Martin Luther's criticism touched off a revolution: the Protestant Reformation. Westerners left the Catholic Church and formed new sects, like the Lutherans and Calvinists. Naturally, the traditional powers tried to stamp out these new faiths, while the Protestants tried to force their views on unwilling Catholics. The result was more than a century of bloodshed over Jesus' gentle, peace-loving religion.

~ William Gallo, Recorded Lectures, History 22: Modern Europe and the West (date not recorded).

ooooo

"Wat are you going to do if I won't tell you anything,"
Rim-Hadad sneered, "Kill me? Ha!" Somehow he
managed to look haughty, despite hanging upside down,
trussed up like a spider's prey.

"Yes, kill him, kill him," the fairies chimed from the surrounding branches, "and when—"

"No more rhymes!" Jason barked. He looked around at their
hurt faces and remembered that these were half-mad lumins.
"Please." He was glad King Quennel and his queen weren't there.

"I learned a lot from you, Rim-Hadad," Jason said, turning back to the smirking barbarian. "I learned that a brave
man sometimes has to dirty his hands with a little blood, for
his friends. Wasn't that what you said when you killed that
Babylonian priest, to save Tia and me? Well, it's even truer
when you're saving your own father. Plus, if you don't help
me, you're useless, and I can't have you following me." He
shrugged. "Besides, I wouldn't have to kill you myself. All I'm
going to do is leave you here, with my little friends."

The fairies snarled, and Rim-Hadad glanced around
uneasily. A green-skinned female with flower petal wings sat
on a branch not far from his head, methodically sharpening a
tiny, razor-like sword.

"Cut me down," Rim-Hadad said, "and I'll tell you what I
know."

Jason shivered with relief as the fairies cut the barbarian
down. They sat him up against a tree, still tied. Mime fluttered
over to land on Jason's shoulder as Rim-Hadad spoke up again.

"*He* has your father. The Rector has him."

"*Where?* And what's he doing to him?"

"I don't know what they're doing with him. You can have
your little murderers cut my throat, but that's a fact. But as for
where, he's at their headquarters. The Rector's the chief of this
group, you see—"

"The International Empirical Society."

Rim-Hadad nodded. "You've learned a little, by Amurru. Yes, that's what they call themselves. They're in a town called Oxbridge, and that's where they've got your father. It's down the river another two weeks, maybe more."

Jason's heart leapt. "How do you know?"

"Crocker said so. He saw your father the last time he went there. And that's where they said I should bring you if I caught you much downriver from Athenopolis. I'm to bring you to the Rector, in Oxbridge."

Jason sat back and stared up at the blue sky. Finally, after all these months, he was really learning something.

"You'll never get in to see your father," Rim-Hadad added. "It's a great place, Crocker said, and he said your father's better-guarded than anyone in Fore." He shook his head. "These people know their business. What are you going to do, steal him out from under their noses?"

"Shut up. I'm asking the questions." Jason bit his lip, trying to think what else he needed to know. "What do these people want with me?"

"They didn't tell me." Rim-Hadad shifted in his silvery bonds. "But they aren't going to kill you. Crocker said: 'We didn't kill the father, and we won't kill the son.' By Amurru, I swear those were his words."

Jason rolled his eyes. That gave little comfort, even if it was true. The Society might plan a fate worse than death, such as trapping him in Fore by keeping him awake forever.

"There's more, Jason," Rim-Hadad continued. "Crocker said you've been listening to all the wrong kind of people. He said he knows about you, and he knows what matters to you. He said you'd *like* the Society if you learned more about them."

"Yeah, I'll be sure and donate to their next charity drive. So why try to catch me if that's true? Why didn't they just talk to me?"

"I don't know. But I know they don't like taking chances, especially not about this business with you and your father. Whatever it is, it's very important to them."

"How did you find me here? How did you know I'd come?"

"I didn't know for certain." Rim-Hadad was sweating. "But Crocker thought you'd come. He knew your father spent a lot of time here."

"Well, what about Tarraco-Hispania? You knew I was going there. Why didn't you try and get me there?"

"Don't you know? Those Greek lumins of yours put me on a ship back to the left bank. I was a prisoner for days. By the time I got back to Athenopolis, we guessed we were too far behind. Besides, Crocker didn't want anyone hunting in Tarraco-Hispania. They're afraid of that high priestess of yours. This Society isn't strong upriver. They like to stay hidden and avoid attention from upstream rulers."

Jason's eyes narrowed. "I'm going to be asking you more questions later—a lot more—but I have one more for now. Why are you still following me? What's the Society to you?"

"They haven't *paid* me!" the barbarian exclaimed. "I never delivered you, so I didn't get my gold." He seemed to struggle with himself. "The son of a great man like Nablanum shouldn't tend another man's herds."

Jason snorted. "You've told me a lot about your father, and it sounds like he was a great man." Rim-Hadad's dark eyebrows rose. "I wonder how he'd feel about a son who lies and tricks his friends, for gold."

The barbarian did not answer.

ooooo

"You've got two choices," said Jason. "I can leave you here with these fairies, and they'll keep you prisoner—for a long time this time … if they ever let you go." He shrugged. "You'll be out of my hands." The fairies grinned and snarled, sharpening tiny weapons and licking tiny lips. "Or you can help me and even get a chance at earning your gold, the honest way."

They'd cut Rim-Hadad's feet loose and marched him to the campsite. He'd wisely made no attempt to escape. But that hadn't saved him from some rough treatment at the fairies' hands. One little man with a rat snout had torn a fistful from Rim-Hadad's beard. The fairy said he needed it for shirt laces. Others had pricked him with tiny swords and daggers. But for the most part, Jason had protected the prisoner. Now Rim-Hadad sat against a tree, waiting to learn his fate. He looked scared. He looked surprised, too.

"Help you?" he asked.

"I want you to come to this Oxbridge place with me. They're expecting you, so you can get into the Society's headquarters. You'll tell the Rector you can't find me, but you think I'm upriver, and you need more supplies. And you'll find out where they've got my father and what they're doing with him. Then you'll come back and tell me, and you'll help me with whatever I decide to do. If I decide to just walk into Society headquarters, I'll go with you, so you can deliver me and get your gold. But if I don't, you won't get any gold. You have to agree to that, because you've really lost the gold already, unless I decide to help you get it."

Rim-Hadad smiled. "By Amurru, you're a crafty one, and a brave one, too. You honor me to offer your trust again."

Behind Jason, Tia snorted and Zidu sighed.

"I'm not trusting you that much," said Jason. "From now on, you won't carry any weapons. And you'll have a guardian keeping an eye on you all the time." He touched his shoulder, where Mime perched. The former dwarf rubbed his hands and glared at Rim-Hadad. "Even when you go into Society headquarters, Mime will be with you. If you double-cross me, he'll fly back and tell me right away. You'll never see me again."

"But there's one other condition," he continued. "If you want to make this deal, you're going to have to swear—on your father's soul. You'll ask demons to tear apart the soul of Nablanum and eat it if you break your promise."

Rim-Hadad recoiled as if he'd been slapped. Jason remembered the campfire horror story the barbarian had told the night they met. The hero had broken an oath sworn on his father's name, and demons had devoured the innocent father's soul. Rim-Hadad and his nephew had shivered with fright, and they'd believed the story. And for Rim-Hadad, his father's honor was everything.

The barbarian's face was lined and pale. That was good. If he agreed too easily, it'd be suspicious.

"You are right," Rim-Hadad finally said, speaking slowly. "I have already lost my gold and my freedom, and maybe my life to these mad lumins. If you give me back my freedom and even a chance at my gold, I'll be in your debt. This bargain is better than I deserve. I *will* swear on my father's soul." His face softened. "You honor me, Jason. I never would have thought it, after what I've done. Oath or no oath, if you trust the son of Nablanum again, you will not be sorry. I'm in your debt already, just for offering this to me."

ooooo

So to everyone's surprise, the crew of the *Dead Valencia* was reborn and reformed. The reunion, however, wasn't a warm one. Jason didn't trust Rim-Hadad and didn't plan to take any unnecessary risks. Mime would help them in Oxbridge before flying back upstream to his new people. But even that didn't satisfy Jason. He had an inkling of another plan to keep the barbarian off balance.

As they sailed down the Jericho River, Rim-Hadad took on extra chores and apologized the moment he so much as stepped on anyone's foot. "Never again will you regret trusting the son of Nablanum," he told Jason. "Like a pup to a hunter, I'll be to you."

Despite the barbarian's efforts, the *Black Elf*'s crew was tense. Zidu spoke very little to Rim-Hadad, and Tia would not speak to him at all.

One evening, they pulled ashore near a field of wheat beneath cool, cloudy skies. As they set up camp, they watched a three-masted galleon float down the river. The ship was a towering fortress of wood beneath wing-like sails of all sizes. Over the past two weeks, river traffic had grown more impressive.

The settlements along the right bank had changed, too. The heavy stone castles had fallen away, replaced by villas of brick and wood, presiding over orderly estates. And the towns had expanded, spilling out of their walls. Along their streets, substantial houses crowded together, home to men and women in complicated, colorful outfits, as well as uniformed foot soldiers armed with pikes and muskets.*

As the galleon faded into the sunset, Tia stood up. "I'm going for a walk," she said. Jason watched her disappear down a path through the wheat. Lately, whenever he caught Tia's eye, he found himself tongue-tied—and she would only smile and look away. He didn't know if she was still angry over his bet with the Germans. She spoke very little, and they were never alone. So after she'd been gone a few minutes, he followed, leaving Zidu relaxing and Mime guarding the barbarian.

The wheat waved and whispered in the breeze as he hurried after Tia. Soon he saw her up ahead and called out. She turned and stood still, framed by wheat, and Jason's pulse quickened.

"Tia," he said, relieved to see her smiling. "Tia, um, I wanted to ..."

He stopped and just smiled back. Then suddenly they were hugging. It was such a relief after the tensions of the past weeks. Jason's head spun, and he lost whatever he'd planned to say as he breathed in the scent of her hair.

And then they were kissing. They smiled and hugged and kissed each other's faces and necks and lips. They tried to sit without letting go, and they fell, and they laughed as they rolled in the wheat. Tia smelled so good. Her lips and skin felt so much softer than he'd expected. He'd never had the chance to find out—not really—not with Tia or any girl. He kissed her again and again and couldn't believe she kept kissing back.

---

* The gun didn't really come into its own until the 1620s, when the king of Sweden figured out how to exploit it. Gustavus Adolphus turned most of his infantry men into musketeers and trained them to fire together. The result: massive volleys that devastated Sweden's Catholic enemies during the Wars of the Reformation. Soon, all the Western powers fought with these rows of highly drilled musketeers.

~ William Gallo, Recorded Lectures, History 22.

After a long time, they lay together, hidden by the wheat, as the early stars twinkled in the violet sky.

"I'm sorry about that bet with the Germans," Jason breathed into her ear. "I'm really sorry—"

"I *know*," she exclaimed. "You said so a thousand times."

He leaned back enough to look at her face.

She was still smiling, but she shook her head as if he were an idiot child. "Enough is enough."

They lay daydreaming a while, then Tia said, "The worst thing was it didn't seem *like* you. All those strange beliefs you have about slavery, and the way you treat me ... I couldn't believe it." She put a hand over his mouth as he opened it to speak. "Don't start apologizing again. I'm just saying it was a surprise."

"It's just that—" Jason started, talking around Tia's hand. She removed it. "It's just ... I guess when those Germans asked if you were mine ... they were really impressed. I didn't want to disappoint them, so I said yes. Then things got out of hand." He watched her face. She nodded.

"Anyway," Jason continued, "I'll never do anything like that again. I won't use anyone, I swear. And men aren't supposed to own women where I come from, or act like they're in charge all the time."

"What do you mean? Men always lead. The gods made men to rule."

"Uh, yeah." Jason hoped to avoid a debate. "But it's different where I come from."

"How?" she demanded. So he told her about the modern world. He tried to explain feminism and civil rights and even dating. Then he told her much more. He even found his way to movies and music and high school. It was a strange conversation, and Tia clearly thought his people were crazy. But she listened, and she asked many questions.

ooooo

"Have no fear, you'll face no strife," piped Mime a week later. "Fairy scout will guard your life."

"Good luck to both of you," said Jason, catching Rim-Hadad's eye. "We'll see you tonight, or tomorrow if necessary."

"That you will," said the barbarian heartily. "And by Amurru, you'll be glad you trusted the son of Nablanum."

With that, Rim-Hadad left, hiking through the woods on his way to the pastureland and the town beyond, with Mime fluttering above his head.

The *Black Elf* had reached Oxbridge the night before, in a country called the Two Britains.[†] The travelers had set up camp in a woodland upstream. From there, Rim-Hadad and Mime would make their way to the headquarters of the International Empirical Society, at the center of Oxbridge. Rim-Hadad, if he honored their bargain, would tell the Rector he was still hunting Jason and needed supplies and money. He would also try to find out where the Rector was keeping Jason's father, and why. Then he'd return to report. But he'd find a surprise when he got back to the camp.

"The plan leaves much to be desired," said Zidu, once Rim-Hadad was out of earshot, "but I can see no better way. And at least it gives our side the advantage of surprise." One rear leg came up to gently scratch his bearded cheek, like a cat. "I am eager to play my part, and I still believe I am the best choice for the job."

Jason sighed as he and Tia cleaned up the campsite. "I still don't like using you as the messenger. It feels like ..." he glanced at Tia "... like something I promised I'd never do again." Jason

---

† In 1603, Queen Elizabeth I of England died with no children and few close relatives. Her first cousin twice removed inherited her throne and became King James I. James, however, was also king of Scotland. So England and Scotland had the same ruler, though they remained separate nations. This "personal union" continued through the 1600s and occasionally put the king in an odd position. In 1640, for instance, the Scottish parliament sent an army to invade England. As king of both countries, Charles I (James's son) had to pay the defending English army *and* the invading Scots. It wasn't until 1707 that the two countries agreed to a formal union, creating the Kingdom of Great Britain.

~ William Gallo, History 22, Third Handout.

had thought of hiring a local to wait for Rim-Hadad. This messenger wouldn't know where to find the secret campsite. He'd only know a prearranged time and place—a very public place—to meet the companions. But Zidu had simplified things by volunteering. He'd pointed out that he and Jason could communicate over distances with the reaching trance, so they could avoid a lot of dangerous moving around. "It feels like what I did betting on Tia," Jason continued.

"This is not similar," said Zidu. "You used Tia without her knowledge or consent. In this case, I am fully informed, and I have volunteered—happily. I am the best to go for so many reasons. For one, they can learn nothing from me that could be used against you. No one questions an unwilling lumin. Truly, Jason, your feelings are noble, but you have no cause for concern. This is the right choice."

"Okay," said Jason, "but if it looks like they've sent a lot of people, I think you should just run or hide. There's no reason to deal with them."

Zidu smiled. "I will my friend. But it is you and Tia who should take care. I am not very vulnerable to human weapons. If the barbarian turns against us, and these Society men find you've left this campsite, they will likely scour the countryside."

"We'd better go," said Tia, who'd finished loading blankets and supplies back onto the *Black Elf.*

Jason looked at Zidu. The Sumerian lumin appeared relaxed as he sat in the dappled sunlight at the center of the clearing. "You know," said Jason, "we haven't separated on purpose for months—since I met you. It's sort of weird."

Smile lines creased Zidu's dark face. "I will miss you, too, Lord Jessun-gallu." Jason smiled, too. "But we will be reunited. In any case, I leave you in good hands."

Jason blushed. He wasn't sure what Zidu knew about him and Tia, but the lion-man generally missed very little.

"Take care," Jason said, hugging Zidu quickly. Tia did the same, and they left.

They caught a good wind and made their way up the Jericho River, against the current. Startling green countryside blanketed the right bank, on their left now that they were traveling upstream. They passed a few small woods, but the Two Britains was mostly a land of farms and pastures. "There must be more sheep in this country than people," said Tia as they passed yet another pasture dotted with fleecy, white grazers.

They reached the secret campsite in under an hour. Jason had spotted it on the way to Oxbridge the day before. An abandoned watermill perched next to the river, surrounded by trees and tomato vines[‡] that clearly hadn't been tended in months. Jason and Tia dragged the ship ashore and leaned it against the mill's stone wall, which hid it from anyone coming upstream. Then they covered it with branches and vines, hiding it well enough from anyone coming downstream. The camouflage would likely fool inland travelers, too, though Jason saw nothing but brilliant green pastures for miles.

After that, they waited inside the mill for most of the day. The internal walls were gone, leaving the stone building empty except for a few fallen beams and the massive wheels that must once have turned with the river's current. The roof had fallen in, too, so the view above was a square of moving gray sky, colored here and there with patches of blue. It made for the perfect hiding place—and very cozy. This day with Tia was one of the plan's fringe benefits. They'd had so little private time. They spent the afternoon kissing and caressing.

Finally, the sky began to darken.

"No news is good news, right?" said Jason.

Mime hadn't arrived to report treason from Rim-Hadad. The shadowy mill grew cold and damp. Tia leaned against

---

‡ The new world trade network gave Africa and Eurasia a suite of American crops that boosted their populations. Some of the key imports in this "Columbian Exchange" include tomatoes, potatoes, bell peppers, pumpkins, and peanuts. The Americas also pumped silver and gold into the Eurasian economy—most of which ended up in Chinese and Indian hands, since they had the industrial goods Europeans wanted. For its part, the Americas received chickens, horses, cattle, sheep, bananas, rice, wheat, and a long list of other crops and animals. Unfortunately, the Americas also received Eurasian diseases such as smallpox, measles, and the flu, which together killed on an apocalyptic scale.

~ William Gallo, *Historical Factoids*, III.

Jason, and the two kept each other warm and talked quietly as they waited for nightfall. Soon the first stars began to twinkle in the square of sky above them.

"I'd better meditate and listen for Zidu," said Jason. So Tia moved aside, and he sat up straight, breathing slowly and listening for the lion-man.

After close to an hour, worry broke Jason out of his meditation. "Where can he be?" he asked, opening his eyes.

He was surprised to find Tia meditating, too. She sat in the darkness nearby, wrapped in a blanket, breathing slowly, and holding her blue amulet. "What are you doing? You won't hear Zidu, will you?"

Her eyes fluttered open. "Yes, silly, I will. How long do you think it takes to form the shaman bond, when you spend day and night with a lumin? Zidu's my lumin now, too, and I'm his shaman."

Jason blinked. He had a special bond with Zidu and a special bond with Tia. He'd never guessed the two shared their own bond. "Anyway," he changed the subject, "he was supposed to call by now. What do you think's going on?"

"I don't know. I haven't heard anything. We'll just have to keep trying."

They listened for hours, and several times they moved beyond meditation into the reaching trance. They saw the starlit pool in their minds and called for Zidu across the waters. But they got no response. Eventually, they took turns, switching off between listening and sleeping. But their growing dread made sleep difficult, and as the night wore on, they still sensed nothing.

After what seemed an endless span of hours, the square of sky above their heads turned morning gray. "This isn't like Zidu," Jason whispered. "He's the most reliable person I've ever met. He couldn't have just forgotten, could he?"

"No," said Tia, "but what could happen to him? No one hurts a lumin."

"I shouldn't have left him doing a job I was afraid to do. It's me they want."

"Don't be stupid. He was the perfect one to go, and he insisted. There's only one solution. I'll go back and see what happened."

"No way! I'm not sending you, too."

"Well, *you* can't go," she said. "Like you said, you're the one they want. If Rim-Hadad did turn traitor again, they'll be waiting for you."

"I don't care. I'm going. You're …"

"… a woman," she finished for him.

Darkness still cloaked the abandoned mill, but Jason could see her smirking.

"That's what you were going to say, isn't it? So all that nonsense about men and women in your world really *was* nonsense. What did you called it—*femism*? Did you make that up?"

"Yeah, right, that's how I get my kicks—making up social revolutions. *Feminism* has nothing to do with this. You're not going."

"I am going."

They sat shivering in the morning cold, glaring at each other. Finally, Jason sighed. "All right. We'll both go. Let's give it another hour or two. He was supposed to call in the morning, too. If he doesn't, we'll go together."

ooooo

The little woodland was peaceful in the morning sun. They heard nothing but birdsong. To their relief and disappointment, the previous night's campsite was empty, home only to shadows and leaves. They saw no sign of Zidu, nor of Rim-Hadad.

"Oh no!" Tia cried as they poked around the clearing.

Jason whipped around and saw Tia kneeling beside an elm tree, cradling a bundle in her hands. At first, Jason thought she'd found a stunned bird. But then his blood froze.

"Mime!" he gasped. The fairy lay curled up and still, except for the twitching of his gray and black wings. "God, what happened to him?"

Tia looked up, her eyes full of tears. "He's barely breathing. I think he's dying."

Jason fell to his knees. Mime's chest rose and fell in ragged pants, and his face was gray. "We've got to help him! What do you do for hurt lumins?"

"They almost never get hurt," Tia cried. "I don't know. We don't even know what's wrong with him." She shook her head. "When a lumin's badly hurt, like from a fight with another lumin, you need shaman power. You need a healing ritual."

"Okay. You're a trained shaman, and I can help. What do we do?"

"No!" She shook her head. "We need *lumins*, for the power. And they should come from Mime's own land. When they're really close to darkness, they need a familiar voice to call them back. They need lumins who speak the same language of spirit."

"You mean we need German barbarian lumins? Or fairies?"

She nodded and held Mime against her chest. "We might. Foreign lumins might not be able to do enough."

"I don't think Mime has time for *any* lumins," Jason whispered.

The fairy's wings twitched again, and then he lay still. Jason moaned as Tia placed a finger against Mime's chest and then in front of his mouth. Then she delicately lifted one of his tiny eyelids. Mime's blue eye stared back at her. The lumin glimmer was gone.

"Zidu," Jason whispered. "If they can do this to Mime, what have they done to Zidu? What have *I* done?" He covered his mouth. "I sent him—I sent both of them—to face *my* enemies."

They buried Mime beside the tree where they'd found him. Tia hiked out to the pasture nearby and picked a double handful of wildflowers, which they sprinkled over the spot.

"Maybe he just died," said Jason as they stood staring at the tiny grave. "Zidu said the fairies had all reached the last part of their lives, like the Minotaur. He said they'd fade away, now that they've given up on humans."

"Mime didn't fade away," said Tia, wiping her eyes. "Lumins know when the end is coming, like the Minotaur did. And

Mime had just become a fairy. He expected to live with the others for a long time."

Jason sighed. "Yeah, but he didn't have any wounds or anything. How could—"

A stick snapped nearby, and they froze. "Someone's coming!" Tia hissed. They darted behind Mime's elm.

Footsteps sounded as a very large figure pushed through the undergrowth. It was Rim-Hadad.

Jason looked at Tia. She nodded slowly, and he nodded back. Rim-Hadad had come alone. Maybe he'd been good to his word. And he'd find them anyway. Slowly they emerged.

"There you are!" the barbarian's deep voice boomed. "Oh my friends, do you know what's happened? A terrible thing: I never would have dreamed such a thing in my worst nightmare!"

"Zidu," Jason demanded. "Where's Zidu?"

"The Rector has him, by Amurru! And his men shot poor little Mime with some magic tool. I never saw any weapon work so against lumins. Is Mime with you? Did he live?"

Tia pointed at the flower-strewn grave near their feet. Rim-Hadad closed his eyes and shook his head. "These people are mad. It is an offense against the gods. I would not have thought it could be done. I must sit down. Such a day and night I have had."

They all sat on the ground, and Jason gave Rim-Hadad some water. Then the barbarian told his story.

"I went straight to the town and to the place where the Society has its headquarters. I walked in and told the men there who I was, and I said I'd come to see the Rector for Enforcement, just as Crocker said I should.

"The men were surprised. But it wasn't the son of Nablanum that surprised them, it was Mime. He was flying around the little room, a guardhouse they call 'the porters' lodge.' And these guards there, these porters, they could not believe their eyes, as if a gazelle had walked into their tent and laid down for the taking. One of them fetched a weapon. It looked like nothing I've ever seen. I did not think it could ever deal out death, or even that it *was* a weapon.

"And neither did Mime. The man aimed it at him, and a bolt of lightning shot out one end and hit the little creature. *Lighting*, by all the gods! Mime screamed, and he flew away. But I could tell he was hurt, for he flew like a dove with broken feathers. And two of the men followed, carrying this tube—a weapon."

"This weapon," Jason demanded, "was it a gun? Did it make a loud bang?"

"*Gun.*" said the barbarian. "I do not know that word. But this hardly made a sound."

"What could it be?" Tia whispered. "What could hurt a lumin so? And who'd want to?"

"By Amurru, these men are mad," Rim-Hadad growled.

"Go on," said Jason. "Tell us the rest. Tell us about Zidu."

"They made me wait a long time. Then they brought me in to see the great man, this Rector for Enforcement. I did not know what to do, now that Mime had gone. So I kept to my path, like a lion stalking its prey. I honored our bargain, Jason. I told the great man just what we'd agreed—that I still hunted you and thought you could be found upriver. He asked many questions, and I answered always the way you wanted. I revealed nothing.

"But while I was there, these madmen, these porters, came back. They told the Rector they'd caught what they called an 'Oriental lumin.' And they brought him in, lying on a plank. It was Zidu—out cold!" Now Rim-Hadad's voice cracked. "A noble lumin of Sumer, and they'd struck him down like a beast. I never thought such a thing could be done."

"What next?" Jason insisted. "What did they do?"

"By Amurru, I wish you'd let me keep my sword. I'd have shown them some respect for gods and spirits. But I could do nothing. They took Zidu away, and the great man, the Rector, he asked many more questions about you. Then two more men came, covered in layers of foolish cloth like the Rector, and all three asked questions. They asked about you and why you came to Fore. For hours, they surrounded me, jabbering like hyenas. I told them nothing they could use to find you, Jason. I honored our bargain."

"What about my father? Did you find out where he is?"

"He is there," said Rim-Hadad. "In that very place, the Society's place. They told me."

Jason's heart leapt. So close!

"Finally, they gave me a room," the barbarian continued. "I couldn't get away to come see you, so I slept the night in the great house. Then this morning, the Rector called for me again.

"He asked where you were. And when I insisted I did not know, he left the room. But soon he came back, and he gave me a message on paper for you. He insisted I take you this message. He did not believe me."

Rim-Hadad reached into his tunic and handed Jason a thick piece of folded paper. A red wax seal held it closed, stamped with a circular emblem: a full moon next to an apple. Around the borders, the seal read, "INTERNATIONAL EMPIRICAL SOCIETY."

Jason broke the wax. The handwriting looked familiar. He glanced at Tia and then read aloud, his hands shaking: "'Dear Jason, Congratulations on coming so far. Please go right away to see the Rector for Enforcement at the headquarters of the International Empirical Society, in Oxbridge. You will understand soon.'"

"Oh my God," Jason whispered as he looked up at his friends.

"What?" Tia exclaimed, grasping his shoulder. "What's wrong?"

Jason's hand shook. "It's signed by my father."

14

Enlightenment

BY THE LATE 1600S, Europe stood at the center of the world trade network. The result was increasing wealth, though not yet on the level of China or India. The more telling result was increasing *knowledge*, thanks to all those ships pulling into European ports loaded down with ideas and techniques and discoveries from around the world. And Europeans were hungry for scientific knowledge—for the fruits of reason—since religious fanaticism had left such a bad taste their mouths, thanks to the Wars of the Reformation. What you get, then, is an age of Enlightenment.

The Enlightenment gave us social critics like Voltaire, who loved making beef cutlets out of the West's sacred cows. But I think Enlightenment thinking reached its peak in the sciences. In 1687, Sir Isaac Newton proposed the three laws of motion and the theory of gravity. Revolutionary stuff. They were just a bunch of simple equations, but they seemed to govern everything—from the moon to a flying cannonball to a resting boulder to an apple falling from a tree and bonking Newton on the head. You also get a long list of inventions that set the stage for bigger things. Those include the steam engine, the vacuum pump, the thermometer—invented by Gabriel Fahrenheit—the spinning frame, and the marine chronometer.

The new thinking also produced enlightened despots. Absolute monarchs such as France's Louis XIV and Prussia's Frederick the Great led rationally organized bureaucracies—with no interference from less, uh, scientific forces, like the church. But the same set of enlightened ideas produced an itch for rational government, in other words, freedom and democracy. Not a happy combination!

~ William Gallo, Lectures, History 22.

ooooo

Oxbridge was a dense cluster of rectangular wood and brick houses. Many were handsome, with decorated gables and moldings beneath slanting roofs. Wooden signs hung above narrow doors on some of the houses, with captions such as "Coffeehouse,"* "Solicitor," and "Doctor of Medicine: Teeth Pulled, Blood Leeched, & Humours Purified."

The buildings fronted lively avenues full of wagons, horse-drawn carriages, and pedestrians. Many of the townsfolk stared at the three travelers. Jason guessed that once again their clothing stood out. He wore jeans and a T-shirt, while Rim-Hadad wore a belted sheepskin tunic, and Tia had pulled on Jason's sweatshirt over a simple skirt. The locals, on the other hand, dressed in intricate and colorful outfits. The women wore long dresses and bonnets over their hair. And the better-dressed men wore three-cornered caps over long hair, as well as swallow-tailed coats and stockings. They reminded Jason of George Washington and Benjamin Franklin.

The town seemed to be missing something, though at first he couldn't put his finger on it.

"Jason," Tia whispered as they followed Rim-Hadad around a corner. "Have you seen any lumins?"

He looked around. People, horses, and a few stray dogs shared the streets, but he saw no lumins, not even the saints and angels they'd seen everywhere else in recent weeks. "No. That's weird. It's like where I come from."

---

* The Turks introduced coffee to Europe in the late 1400s. A lot of Westerners thought it was the devil's brew, but according to legend, Pope Clement VIII found he liked coffee in 1600 and literally baptized it. Coffeehouses grew popular during the 1600s, particularly in England. They actually helped liberalize English society, because the different classes mingled there. It's even been suggested that coffeehouses helped bring down royal power. Ale had kept the British happy and stupid, the argument goes, while coffee filled them with vim and argument, which spurred political griping. Maybe that's far-fetched, but King Charles II did try to ban coffeehouses in 1675. He failed, so it's at least possible the leaders of the Glorious Revolution hatched their plot over coffee.

~ William Gallo, *Historical Factoids*, 120.

Tia shivered. "I don't like this."

A row of large brick buildings ran along a broad avenue.
Rim-Hadad approached a door in one of these. A stone disk
hung above it: a copy of the apple and moon seal they'd seen
on Jason's father's letter. Jason and Tia followed the barbarian
through the door and found themselves in a plain room with
a single window looking out on the street.

"I have returned," said Rim-Hadad to two men in brown
waistcoats, sitting behind a high desk. "Tell the Rector for
Enforcement that Rim-Hadad is back, and he's brought Jason
Gallo."

"Welcome back, Mr. Hadad," said the elder of the two porters. He nodded to his fellow, who rose and left.

Jason clenched his teeth and tried to stay calm.

"That is the weapon," Rim-Hadad whispered as they
waited, "the thing they used against Mime." He nodded at
a yard-long tube leaning against the wall behind the porters'
desk. It looked a bit like a rifle, but not much. It had a long
steel barrel with some brass fittings and a bulky wooden box
attached to one end. Jason had never seen anything like it.

"It's evil," Tia said quietly.

The strange instrument was not the only weapon in the
room. Two muskets rested against the wall near the mysterious tube. And the remaining porter wore a saber by his side.

Soon the younger porter returned with a pale young man,
dressed like the porters but with more ruffles and lace. "You
are Mr. Gallo?" he asked.

Jason nodded, too nervous to speak.

"I am Mr. Shaw," he continued, his expression unreadable.
"Please come with me—all of you."

He led them through the lodge to a wide, enclosed courtyard,
like a country garden stuck in the middle of the bustling town.
For all his fear, Jason couldn't help admiring the place. Flagstone
paths divided a perfect lawn into four rectangles. The surrounding buildings resembled country manor houses, with ivy hanging
from wooden eaves beneath tiled roofs. Lead-paned windows
looked out on narrow flowerbeds surrounding the grass.

Mr. Shaw's wooden-heeled shoes clattered against the flag-stones as he led them to a door at one end of a brick arcade. The halls beyond were dark and cool, furnished with polished wood and rich carpets. They climbed to the second floor and stopped before another door.

"One thing I forgot to mention," Rim-Hadad whispered as Shaw knocked. "The Rector has a strange beast in there with him, some kind of sickly monkey that sits on his shoulder." Jason and Tia stared at him. "I didn't want it to surprise you too much."

Jason gulped as a muffled voice called, "Please show them in, Mr. Shaw."

"The Rector will see you now," said the young man. He opened the door and stood aside. Inside was a vaulted chamber, its walls covered with stern portraits, bookshelves, and polished cabinets. Behind the desk stood the Rector for Enforcement.

As he looked into the Rector's pale face, Jason's mouth dropped open.

"Mr. Shaw," said the Rector, straightening his rust-colored vest, "would you have Mrs. Wood send up some tea for our guests and for me?"

"Yes, Rector," said the young man. He bowed and closed the door.

The Rector now turned to Jason. He extended a hand, ringed by a lace cuff. Jason shrank back, confused. On the Rector's right shoulder sat what looked like a small monkey. It was hairless and covered with pale, wrinkled skin, as if it were a hundred years old. Tiny black eyes with no whites peered at the travelers, and one little hand rested on the Rector's head.

But it was not this bizarre being that confused and shocked Jason. He knew the Rector's face, though he'd never seen it look so gray.

"Dad?" he whispered.

ooooo

"Are you just going to stare, Jason?" asked his father. "Won't you shake my hand?"

They shook hands. But then Jason could do little more than gape at his father, with his ponytail and old-fashioned outfit and the bizarre, withered monkey-beast perched on his shoulder. His eyes were sunken, and they looked glazed with manic energy. Stranger still, he offered Jason no warmth. Could this be about Jason's outburst during their last fight, that awful comment about his mother's death?

"I'm sorry to be rude," said Jason's father, turning to Tia. "I am William Gallo. And you are Miss …?"

"Tia," she said in a guarded voice.

"Miss Tia, welcome," Jason's father bowed from the waist. He turned to Rim-Hadad and extended a hand. "And I'm glad to see you again, Rim-Hadad." He favored the barbarian with a sardonic half-smile, an expression Jason knew well. "I guess your information on my son's whereabouts was inaccurate."

"If you'd told me he was your son, my memory might have served me better."

"Touché. Why don't you all have a seat?"

The three sat in stuffed chairs facing the polished wooden desk. As his father took a seat across from them, Jason found his tongue: "Dad, what are you doing here?" His voice broke. "And what's wrong with you?"

"I'm fine, Jason, thank you. As for why I'm here, I'm a fellow of the International Empirical Society. In fact, I'm one of the Society's senior officers. The board of governors has appointed me Rector for Enforcement. Aren't you proud to hear that?"

"But the Rector's been hunting me," Jason exclaimed. "He sent this Crocker guy to catch me. That was you?" His hands shook.

"I'm sorry," said his father. "The Society operates very carefully upriver and maintains strict secrecy, since we don't have much power there. I would have liked to send you a simple message, inviting you to meet me here in Oxbridge, but first we had to determine whose side you were on. The woman who brought you to Fore is something of a fanatic and a dangerous enemy of everything the Society stands for. I was afraid she'd influenced you and you might not listen to reason. And I didn't want to let anyone upriver know where I was. Lady Aurelia is a powerful witch, and she can read minds, even from some distance. Since the moment I reached Society Headquarters, we've been afraid she might try some idiotic rescue."

"But Lady Aurelia said this Society was hunting *you!*" Jason exclaimed. "We thought they were the enemy." Could he have been working with the wrong people?

"No, Jason. The Society isn't my enemy, or yours. I did disagree with the membership for a long time, but my beliefs and values matured some time ago." One eyebrow rose. "You should be glad. I've come around to your point of view. Yet you stare at me as if I'd taken away your television privileges."

"My point of view?"

At that moment, the office door opened, and a woman glided in, carrying a silver tea service and a basket of biscuits. She poured hot tea for each of them.[†] As his father turned to thank her, Jason noticed that the hairless monkey-thing on his shoulder had no tail. Jason also noticed strange growths on its back. Knobby, wrinkled lumps grew from its shoulders, as if the beast had a double-hunchback.

"Yes, your point of view, Jason," his father continued when the woman had gone. "You've never thought much of myth and magic and my former studies—at least, not since you were a little boy. Did you think I didn't know? Well, you should like the Society. We oppose anyone who peddles myth or magic. We advocate for reason and logic." He sipped his tea. "You share the Society's core values, Jason, though you may not be fully conscious of them."

"How?" Tia asked. "How does this Society oppose myth and magic? What does that mean?"

Jason's father gave her an owlish look. "I suppose there's no harm in explaining the Society's mission right off. It's certainly

---

† Dutch and Portuguese traders brought tea to Europe from the Far East early in the 1600s. In England, coffeehouses helped popularize the watery brew, but apparently Charles II's queen made it chic. Catherine of Portugal was a big tea-drinker.
~ William Gallo, *Historical Factoids*, 121.

no secret to anyone downriver. And you especially will have to understand, Jason." He straightened his lace collar. "I hear you ran into the Aristotle Academy upriver. Well, the Society's taken the Academy's philosophy to its logical conclusion, completing a greater revolution than the Academy can imagine. We've taken power from priests, witches, and other shamans. Here and in the lands downstream, scientists shape humanity's thinking, just as shamans do upstream. Scientists are the priests of the modern lands. We've accomplished this amazing enlightenment by removing the source of the shamans' supernatural powers: the lumins."

"You mean by killing them?" Tia demanded. "By killing lumins?"

"Yes, termination is the usual solution. The result is that there are almost no lumins here in United Britain and the surrounding right bank countries. A few angels and saints lurk in churches, and a few fairies still hide in the woods, but that's all. And the fairies disappear altogether downriver, and even saints and angels are very rare. In countries like our home, Jason, lumins are virtually extinct. *That* is the Society's gift."

"Gift!" Tia spat, gripping the arms of her chair. "This Society is a curse. It's an insult to all the gods!" Next to her, Rim-Hadad shifted uneasily.

Jason's father half smiled. "You remind me of someone I used to know, Tia—another passionate woman from upstream." Jason thought he saw a hint of warmth in his father's eyes. "However, this calls for reason, not emotion. The Society's gift is the modern world, something you couldn't possibly understand."

"Lumins," said Jason, trying not to tremble. "What about my friend? You caught my friend, Zidu. He's a lumin, and he's my best friend. What—" His throat constricted. "What are you going to do with him?" He no longer cared who was right, Lady Aurelia or the Society.

"Do you mean the Mesopotamian sphinx our porters caught yesterday?"

"Yes. Will you let him go?"

His father sighed. "I can't do that, Jason. The board of governors has strict rules on captured lumins. But your friend is safe for now, here in Empirical Hall."

"Can I see him?" Jason demanded. "I need to see him."

"Eventually you will, but not now. I didn't ask you here to commune with Eastern spirits."

"Then why *am* I here?" he cried, rising from his chair. "What's *with* you? This is how you say hello after all this time? And why are you with this awful Society? I don't believe you'd ever kill lumins. And ..." Jason's voice had grown very loud, and he felt his face flush. "And what the hell is that *thing* on your shoulder?" He jabbed an accusing finger at the naked, wrinkled creature perched near his father's ear.

The monkey-thing responded with a wide, leering grin, but Jason's father was not amused. "Calm down, Jason!" he ordered, rising from his own chair. "Sit down and get a hold of yourself!"

Jason sat, breathing hard. He held his fists by his side, suppressing an urge to smash one into his father's face.

Jason's father shook his head. "Maybe if you'd listen more carefully, Jason, you wouldn't be so upset. I told you why I'm with these people. I've joined the Society. As for this 'thing,' as you call her, she's my helper. This is Seiki, and she's a cultivar, a being created by science. She helps me with my work, and she helps me stay here in Fore. It's hard to explain, and we have more important subjects to discuss."

"Does she keep you awake?" Jason demanded. He shivered as the skeletal creature leered at him again through black-in-black eyes. "Does she keep you from falling asleep? Is that how she *helps* you?"

His father sat back down, his eyebrows arching. "Yes, that's more or less what she does. How did you know that?"

"Is that why you won't wake up?" he cried. "Is it because sleep is the portal between worlds, and you can't wake up back home unless you fall asleep here?" Jason spoke quickly, to keep from sobbing. "Is that why she keeps you awake, so you won't hear the alarm clock back home or feel me shaking you, or anything? Is it so you can stay here in Fore forever?"

"Get a hold of yourself, Jason. You've got it right, but there's no reason for hysterics. I'm fine." He turned to stare at the rows of books on his walls, shaking his head. Then he drew a deep breath and faced Jason again. "If it weren't for this silly yelling, I'd be feeling very proud of you right now. Few people understand the connection between Fore and our world. You've done some excellent detective work."

"Dad, I've been searching for you for months. I've tracked you all the way down the river from Sumer. I've been trying to rescue you so I can bring you back home. Don't you want to come home?"

"No, Jason. This is where I belong."

"So you're abandoning me? You're abandoning Athena?" His father looked stung. "Athena's alone at home, Dad. If you don't come back, she won't have any parents. It'll be like when Mom died, but worse."

Jason's father drew a long breath, his face pale. "The world can be hard, and men of conscience must make many sacrifices. Athena will survive, and she'll recover after a time."

Jason gaped. After another deep breath, his father leaned across the desk, his eyes glittering.

"As for you, Jason, far from abandoning you, I'm inviting you to stay with me. I want you to join the Society. You have all the skills and values to be a great man among these people. I'm inviting you to embrace a new life."

After a long silence, Jason said, "Don't hold your breath."

His father stood and turned to face the barred window behind his desk, twisting his hands behind his coattails. The leather, the polished wood, and the thick carpets muffled any sound. Dim sunlight glinted off the teacups on the desk. Tia shot Jason a fierce, encouraging smile. Rim-Hadad just pulled at his beard.

"You've changed, Jason," said his father without turning. "I think this trip has done you more harm than good. The Jason I knew would've been proud to advance logic and science over myth and magic."

"You've got my friend locked up," said Jason. "Can I see him now?"

"I can't let you see him, at least not yet." He turned around. "But I will. That's the best I can offer you now. Why don't you stay here in Empirical Hall, as the Society's guest? We'll talk more. You don't understand our role, the service we provide. It's my fault. I haven't taken the time to explain, to introduce new ideas gradually. But I'll make up for it. In fact, I'd like you to join me and some of my colleagues for supper tomorrow night. You can bring Tia if you'd like. We'll talk more then."

Jason looked at Tia. He guessed she wouldn't want to stay with these enemies of lumins, but they had to help Zidu. He was relieved to see her quick nod. "All I care about is my friend," said Jason, rising to face his father. He managed to keep his voice steady. "I'll do whatever I have to for Zidu."

ooooo

Mr. Shaw showed Jason to a second-floor suite in a building called Bachelor House. The rooms had wood paneling, a fireplace, a view of the courtyard garden, and comfortable furnishings. Jason soon learned, though, that the closest thing to a toilet was a chamber pot his manservant took away after use.

After settling themselves in their rooms, Jason and Tia met in the courtyard outside Tia's building, which was called Lady Alice House. They didn't ask Rim-Hadad to join them, still not sure where his loyalties lay. Two men sat on a bench at one end of the garden, debating the flow of bile through the human body. The travelers chose a bench at the other end. Tia had put on an ankle-length dress, apparently a loaner and not a very good fit. She also wore a very small bonnet over her hair. Jason stared.

"I thought you were ignoring *stupid, ignorant* local customs about clothes," he said.

"The servants said I had to, or I couldn't even walk around. They called my clothes 'indecent.' Anyway," she shrugged, "I'll do whatever I have to for Zidu."

Jason nodded, glad the staff seemed to consider his jeans and T-shirt decent.

"Look," he said, "I just want you to know ... that's not what my dad's usually like. Or at least ... he's not ..."

Tia squeezed his hand. "I know," she said. "That's not the man Lady Aurelia described at all. They must have driven him mad. These awful people have driven him mad."

Jason shivered. "Did you ... did you understand what he said about that monkey thing—that *cultivar*? Did you understand what it was?"

"No," said Tia. "I've never seen anything like it. He said it was created by the power of science. I was hoping you knew what that meant."

Jason shook his head. Could Seiki be a clone or some kind of test-tube baby gone wrong? He doubted it. Oxbridge didn't seem advanced enough for that kind of technology.

He sighed. "I don't know what to do about my dad. I don't know what to do." He clenched his teeth. "I think we should just focus on Zidu for now. Let's walk around, see as much as we can. Maybe we can figure out where they're keeping him."

Empirical Hall was made up of six courtyards, each as peaceful and pretty as the first—like gardens surrounded by country houses. For the most part, both the courtyards and the buildings stood open for exploration. The chapel, the library, the great meeting halls and study rooms, and even the offices and laboratories were beautiful. Stone towers, vaulted passageways, and brick and ivy facades greeted them everywhere. They found scholars and scientists working and debating, and they learned that the Society's work included research and teaching, as well as lumin-hunting. But nowhere did they see a sign reading "lumin detention center" or any hint of Zidu's whereabouts.

"Have you seen any doors leading to the outside?" Jason asked late that afternoon.

Tia thought about it. "No. They all lead into the court-yards, not outside." She scratched her head. "Could we get out a window if we had to?"

"I don't think so. The courtyard windows are normal, but I haven't seen any to the outside without bars. Even my dad's window had bars."

Aside from the porters' lodge, with its armed men, they could think of only one way out. A canal ran through the complex, separating the front courtyard from the other five. "I want to know if we're prisoners here," said Jason, so they made their way back to the canal.

A graceful, wooden footbridge crossed the water. It was a work of engineering genius, according to a plaque posted on one end: made of interlocking beams without a single nail or bolt. Several punts—like long, flat canoes—lay on a narrow dock below the bridge. But another armed porter sat next to the bridge.

"Can we use one of those boats?" Jason asked the porter.

"Oh, certainly, sir," he said, "with permission from the Rector for Enforcement." When Jason asked about swimming in the stream, he replied, "Oh, sir, you wouldn't want to do that. All manner of refuse gets thrown in the river. I couldn't allow it."

Jason and Tia exchanged narrow-eyed glances as they crossed the bridge and returned through the first courtyard to the porters' lodge. Jason made straight for the door at the other end of the little office, and the twilit street beyond.

"Just a moment, there, young sir!" cried the chief porter, scrambling out from behind his desk to block the way. "Where's the fire?"

"No fire," said Jason casually. "We just wanted to walk on the street. Is that a problem?"

The chief porter was a big man with a barrel chest. "Well, sir," he said, looking at his companion, "if you need anything from the town, I can send my man here to fetch it."

"No, thank you. We'd just like a walk in the fresh air."

"Sir, the air's much fresher in the courtyards, you know, without all that city filth."

"Well, thanks for the weather report. Are you going to let us out or not?"

The porter took off his tri-cornered hat and fingered it. "I'm very sorry, sir. You're not to leave. You and your lady-friend here."

"What are you, cops? Where do you get off telling us what to do?"

The porter looked at his colleague and then at the floor. "We don't make the rules here, sir. We're just honest wage-earners,[‡] doing like we're told. It's the Rector for Enforcement, sir: his orders. You can't go until he says so. Begging your pardon, sir."

As they left the porters' lodge, Tia said, "I've never met such polite jailors."

ooooo

"We have very few slaves here," said Mr. Van Ginkel, struggling to speak around a mouthful of half-chewed beef. "Mostly they go to the American plantations. But I can assure you, the slave trade does no disservice to these Negroes. They're like children. We bring them productive labor and the guidance of a firm hand, not to mention the comforts of Christianity."[§]

"Yeah," said Jason, glancing at Tia, "I'm surprised the Africans don't line up and beg to be slaves." He sighed and picked at an overcooked Brussels sprout with a silver fork.

"Our young Mr. Gallo sounds just like his father," said Lord Grey, smiling and twirling a crystal wine glass. He turned his blue eyes toward Jason. "Your father has complained about the slave trade since the moment he got here. *Hypocrisy*, he calls it, and *evil*. Strong words, but he's convinced a good many of us,

---

‡ By around 1700, wage-earners outnumbered peasant farmers in Britain. In other words, most Britons earned salaries and used them to buy whatever they needed, instead of producing their own food and goods on their farms. This quiet revolution soon spread to other nations.... The wage revolution marked the end of the 10,000 year age of agricultural dominance—and the rise of commerce as the world's number-one economic activity.

~ William Gallo, *Historical Factoids*, 185.

§ The West's latter-day slave trade justified itself through racism—through a bizarre theory that Africans and Amerindians were less than human—unlike ancient slavery, which was an equal-opportunity employer.

~ William Gallo, Lectures, History 22.

including myself."

Jason looked at his father. He hadn't realized any of the man's old values remained. "A lot of the fellows already hated slavery before I got here," said Jason's father, looking up from his meat. "In fact, the chapters downriver don't let their members own slaves." One eyebrow rose as he looked at Jason across the candlelit table. "The Society also fights racism and sexism downriver. Does that surprise you, Jason? Did you assume we were a force for injustice?" Jason blinked. He'd assumed exactly that.

"Injustice indeed!" Mr. Van Ginkel exclaimed. "In my opinion, our brothers downriver—and *sisters*, if you can believe it—are quite mad, whatever their achievements." He wiped his forehead. Mr. Van Ginkel appeared to sweat a lot. Jason wondered if his black vest and coat were too tight.

He was struck again by the strange change that had come over his father less than an hour before. As the five had sat down around the elegant table, Seiki had left her usual perch on his shoulder. The wrinkled, tailless monkey-thing had scrambled onto a chair against the wall, apparently not welcome at the dinner table. At that moment, Jason's father had sighed, as if relieved. The lines of his face had softened, and he'd even smiled. Jason kept glancing at him, trying to understand.

He kept looking at Tia, too. She wore a burgundy dress with yellow trim: a much better fit than her borrowed outfit from the day before. The long skirt hung very wide, and Jason could tell it annoyed her. But the dress revealed Tia's shoulders, and she'd brushed her long, black hair. She looked lovely.

Tia seemed less impressed with Jason's appearance. She'd laughed when he walked into the drawing room where the diners had gathered before the meal. The serving staff had told Jason he'd have to wear borrowed clothes for what they called "formal hall." He'd put on the wooden-heeled shoes, the stockings, the knee-length breeches, the lacy white shirt, the patterned waistcoat with its brass buttons, the deep blue, swallow-tailed topcoat, and even the cravat. But he'd flat out refused the curly-haired wig.¶ Even without it, though, he knew he looked foolish, and he kept fidgeting under the stiff fabrics.

"Your father has many enlightened views, Mr. Gallo," said Lord Grey, who wore a similar outfit but looked dashing. "Some may be better suited to our colleagues downstream, though we're honored to have him here in the senior chapter." Lord Grey seemed bright and thoughtful, and he was handsome and relatively young. "Actually," he continued, "we disagree among ourselves and between chapters on many issues. Only our love for science and truth unites us."

"No one who loves truth would kill lumins," said Tia, a bit too loud.

Silence fell over the table. Then Mr. Van Ginkel spoke: "You agree with Miss Tia, don't you, young Mr. Gallo?"

"Yes."

The three Society fellows exchanged glances. "He's not the least bit grateful," said Mr. Van Ginkel.

"He doesn't understand," Lord Grey added.

"And that's why I asked you gentlemen here," said Jason's father. "Jason, Lord Grey and Mr. Van Ginkel are the Society's foremost experts on our world and its relationship to Fore. They're among the few people in Fore who really understand our world, much less know it exists. That's why I wanted you to talk with them."

"Mr. Gallo," said Lord Grey, "you grew up in a land of modern wonders. You understand the advantages of modern farming and plumbing and medicine and all the other sciences, correct?"

"I guess so."

"In fact, in your country, those conveniences far outshine anything you'll see here in Oxbridge. Just like the people at the

---

¶ Louis XIII of France went bald during the 1620s, and his son Louis XIV followed suit fifty years later. Their solution: long-haired wigs. Not too surprising, but here's the weird part: their courtiers imitated them, even the ones who had hair. Pretty soon, the wig fashion spread across Europe. Basically, the wig was the Enlightenment version of the tie.

~ William Gallo, Lectures, History 22.

very end of the Jericho River, your people enjoy conveniences and comforts and security unknown to any other people in history, isn't that right?"

"I guess."

"Well, doesn't it strike you as odd that all those modern wonders appeared so suddenly in your history? I mean, your world has more than five thousand years of written history. Scientific advancement crept forward slowly for most of that time—and sometimes crept backward. Then, in the last three centuries, science abruptly raced ahead, producing all these miracles. Didn't you ever wonder why knowledge moved forward so suddenly?"

"Well, I guess I never thought about it that way."

Mr. Van Ginkel leaned over his nearly empty plate, his rosy jowls jiggling. "You may thank *us* for that," he said.

"This is very complicated," continued Lord Grey. "But to put it the simplest way, the Society's work here in Fore made the sudden advance of science possible in your world. As you know, we have removed lumins from the modern lands, the lands at this end of the Jericho River—especially the right bank lands. By doing so, we removed magic from the dreams of modern people in your world—starting with Europeans. We opened their minds to scientific thinking."

Jason shook his head. "What?"

"Fore and our world are linked," said his father, his sunken eyes intense. "Each influences the other. Our dreams have shaped the world of Fore, but Fore also shapes our dreams. People in our world see Fore when they sleep. In other words, events here in Fore show up in our dreams. Do you understand that?"

"I guess so," said Jason, "but how does that—"

"Ask yourself," his father interrupted, "how often have you woken up with a new idea or a new way of looking at things? Probably more than you realize. Dreams influence the way you think, so *Fore* influences the way you think.

"In our world, people of past times dreamed of magical spirits, so superstition and magic crowded their minds. The Society removed the source of magic from Fore and from our dreams. They removed the lumins. That freed our minds to think clearly. By removing the mental pollution and confusion caused by magical dreams, the Society made possible the revolution in rational thinking, in our world. The Society gave us the Enlightenment."

"You mean ... lumins here in Fore used to show up in our people's dreams," Jason asked, "and kept them ... from thinking like scientists?"

Lord Grey nodded vigorously. "More or less. Lumins used to put the magic in your people's dreams. But now, thanks to the Society's work, almost no lumins haunt the modern right bank. Western people in your world tend to dream of those same lands along the right bank: the modern lands, downstream. So now they're dreaming of lands without lumins: without magic. Magic has left their dreams. That's allowed your people to apply their minds to science and reason."

"In other words," said Mr. Van Ginkel, "you and your people—in your world—owe everything you have to the Society, here in Fore."

Jason snorted. "I'm glad to see you've all got healthy egos."

"It's true," his father insisted. "Even before I joined the Society, even when I disagreed on so many points, I accepted this truth."

"Fine," said Jason. "Whatever. I don't care about any of this crap. You guys want me to stay here and join your little club or whatever. Well I can't, because I've got a little sister at home who needs me, and unlike her *dad*," he shot an acid glance at his father, "I care about her. But I'll do anything *else* you want."

Tia stiffened.

"Okay? Anything—on one condition. You've got to let my friend Zidu go. If you do, I'll do whatever you want."

The three fellows kept silent. Lord Grey looked sad, and Mr. Van Ginkel shook his head.

"At least can I see him?" Jason exclaimed.

"You'll see him," said his father. "I ... The three of us will have to discuss it. We need to pick the right time. If you can be patient, I'll at least tell you *when* very soon."

"Doesn't sound like I have much choice," said Jason, "especially since we're your prisoners as much as Zidu."

ooooo

After dinner, the three fellows—and Seiki—walked Jason and Tia downstairs. They'd eaten in a building called the Governors' Lodge. Maroon carpet covered most of the entry hall. Antique suits of armor decorated the wood-paneled walls there, along with hunting trophies, documents in calligraphy, and portraits. Lord Grey pointed out one of these portraits, a large painting of a man with a long nose and a serious face.

"That is Sir Isaac Newton, the Society's greatest inspiration," he said. "When he was a young man in your world, the story goes, an apple fell on his head. Newton realized that the same force that brought the apple to ground also pulls the moon and keeps it in orbit. He showed us that God is not some magical foreman directing teams of angels and spirits and ordering random miracles. Rather, He is a mathematician working through universal natural laws—laws that operate in the same way on an apple as on the moon."

Near the Newton portrait, beneath a bronze apple and moon seal, hung one of the strange weapons they'd seen in the porters' lodge. Jason peered at the rounded box of polished wood attached to the steel barrel. Unlike a rifle, it had no trigger, though a small brass lever perched on the box.

"Ah, the exorpult," said Mr. Van Ginkel, coming up behind Jason. "Have you ever seen one before, Mr. Gallo?"

"Not up close. I guess this is your big invention."

"Yes," said Lord Grey. "I'll show it to you if you're interested." He reached up and gently removed the exorpult from the wall. "Tom," he asked, turning to one of the servants standing nearby, "would you run to the armory and bring us a hot crystal?"

The servant returned quickly, carrying something small in a black handkerchief. Lord Grey unwrapped it and held it out for Jason and Tia to see. It was an oblong crystal, about the length of a finger, and it glowed red.

"Don't touch it, Jason," said Tia. "It's evil."

"I'm sorry you feel that way, Miss Tia," Lord Grey replied, "but truly there's no evil in a hot crystal. In fact, it's not even hot, despite the name. The crystal is charged with an unusual kind of dream energy, called 'narcopheric radiation.' It's similar to the energy that circulates through lumin bodies." He smiled at Jason. "It's quite harmless to humans. Would you like to hold it?"

Jason shook his head, though he did want to hold the red crystal.

Lord Grey opened a small door in the rounded box on the exorpult. Inside, Jason saw lenses, metal fittings, and more crystals, though none red or glowing. Lord Grey slid the hot crystal between two metallic clips and shut the gearbox door. Then he raised the weapon and grinned at Mr. Van Ginkel. "Casper," he said, "would you do me the honor of serving as my target?"

"I would be happy to, my good fellow." Mr. Van Ginkel walked to the other end of the entry hall. Jason guessed his fat body would make an easy target for Lord Grey.

"The hot crystal is good for three or four shots before it has to be recharged," Lord Grey said. "Once you've got it in the chamber, you aim the exorpult just like a musket." He raised the weapon to his shoulder and aimed the barrel at Mr. Van Ginkel, across the candlelit hall. "Then you simply press the triggering lever to make the connection."

Lord Grey pressed the two-inch lever on top of the gearbox. Jason thought he heard a tiny crack, like a static shock. At that instant, a jagged bolt of brilliant red lightning leapt from the barrel to Mr. Van Ginkel's chest and into the wall behind him.

"Don't look so startled!" cried Mr. Van Ginkel. "I'm none the worse for wear. The energy passes harmlessly through many materials, and even through men and women."

So I guess it passes pretty easily through lard, thought Jason, though part of him was shaken.

"It does not, however, pass so easily through lumins."

"What does it do to lumins?" Jason asked.

"It disrupts the passage of dream energy through their bodies," said his father from the doorway behind them. "A bolt like that would stun most lumins. Several over a short period, or a higher intensity bolt, would be terminal. There's no use sugarcoating it. This is what we do here."

"I'm going back to my room," Tia hissed, "so I can pray for demons to devour all your souls." She stormed out, and Jason followed.

ooooo

Jason and Tia met Rim-Hadad for an early dinner the next day. The barbarian growled as they ate in the small buttery near the kitchens.

"These sons of scorpions still haven't paid me," he complained. He tore into a chicken leg with his bare hands, refusing the tableware. "They say I lied. But I brought you here, and that's all Crocker said I had to do. If I knew where they kept the gold, by Amurru, I'd just take it. I haven't seen a warrior here who could stop me."

Finally, after the meal, Jason turned to Tia. "I can't wait any longer to see Zidu," he said. "Why don't you go wait in your room? I want to talk with my father alone."

The servants had said no one could see the Rector without an appointment, but he raised his hand to knock on the office door anyway. Then, instead, he simply opened the door and walked in.

"Jason, what do you think you're doing?" his father snapped, looking up.

Jason twitched as he noticed the papers scattered across the desk. Sketches and maps decorated his father's notes, just like at home.

"Jason," his father repeated. "I'm busy here."

"I don't care. I want to talk to you. Now."

"Jason, you don't just barge into the office of the Rector for Enforcement. Nor do I have the time—"

"I don't CARE!" Jason bellowed. He leapt forward and, in a

single motion, swept every paper, every quill pen—everything—off of his father's desk. "I don't care about your goddamned WORK!" he screamed as teacups and inkwells shattered against the floor.

Jason's father rose and took a step back, gaping. Seiki grasped his collar for balance.

"Listen to me! Listen! Listen! LISTEN!" Now Jason was pounding his fists on the bare desk, his voice so loud it tore at his throat. "All you ever do is work! All you ever care about is work! All day, you're always working—and you never listen to me! Now, LISTEN! I want my friend back! I want ZIDU! Do you hear me? Now! Now! NOW!"

Father stared at son as Jason's chest heaved and his breath hissed through bared teeth. Then his father snarled and opened his mouth to speak. But at that moment, the door burst open and a porter tumbled into the room, followed by Mr. Shaw.

"Rector!" cried the porter. "Are you hurt?"

"No, Archibald," said Jason's father. "I'm fine."

Jason turned to glare at the two intruders, shaking.

"I'm sorry for the disruption, Archibald, Mr. Shaw, but this is between father and son. You may leave us."

The two men looked at the papers and broken cutlery. Black ink and brown tea had splattered everywhere.

"Yes, Rector," said Mr. Shaw, his face even paler than usual. "But ... but I'll be just down the hall. And Archibald will stay nearby." These remarks were directed more to Jason than his father.

"Who do you think you are?" Jason's father snarled once the porter had closed the door. They glared at each other across the bare desk. "No one behaves that way in Empirical Hall. And no one tells me what to do. My work is important to me. I'm sorry if you don't like it, but that's how it has to be. Is that clear?" His eyes blazed, and Seiki's skeletal face stretched into a grin.

Jason suddenly felt very cold. "You know, Lady Aurelia forced me to come here. I wouldn't have done it for you. The only reason I kept looking is so you can wake up back home and wake me up, and get me out of here quicker. And I did it for

Athena, too, because she loves you for some reason." His voice was flat, dead. "Personally, I couldn't care less if you die or stay here forever or whatever. Since Mom died, you've never done a thing for me. Nothing. And I wouldn't lift a finger for you."

Jason's father stared at him. Then, for just a moment, his face turned ... desolate.

"All right," he said. "We'll go—now. We'll go see your lumin."

He threw a dark cloak over his coat, grabbed a three-cornered cap, and led a stunned Jason past the porter in the hall and out of the building. They crossed the arching bridge over the stream without speaking. Jason's father hurried through the next court-yard to an ornate building, which Jason vaguely remembered housed laboratories. But instead of entering the main wing, his father withdrew a key from his waistcoat and unlocked a heavy door on the ground floor hallway. A staircase led down to the building's underbelly. There he picked up a lantern. He led Jason to another locked door and opened it with another key.

They entered a long, dim stone room. Its wooden tables were littered with equipment: glass tubes and beakers, brass scales, magnifying glasses, pumps, calipers, and primitive microscopes. Three exorpults, like the one Jason had seen the night before, rested in a stand by the far wall.

A leather-bound tube took up the chamber's far end. It looked like a giant exorpult. But unlike the handheld versions, it had no gearbox. The metal fittings and lenses and crystals were exposed, including a giant glowing red crystal at the center of it all.

At one end of the tube, in an iron cage, was Zidu.

"Zidu!" cried Jason, rushing to his friend.

The Sumerian lumin had been lying on the cage floor like an old dog, but he raised his bald head at Jason's cry. Jason knelt and stretched his fingers through the bars to touch his lion flank.

Zidu smiled. "It is good to see you, my friend." His voice was hoarse.

"What have they done to you?" Jason moaned.

Zidu's face was drawn. He hardly moved, not even his tail swished. And worst of all, the light in his eyes was almost gone.

"They have not killed me," said Zidu wearily, "and that is something." He lowered his bearded chin to rest on lion paws. "But I cannot guess what they plan."

"I can," Jason whispered, turning to face his father. "You've got to let Zidu go," he pleaded. "I'll do whatever you want."

"I'm sorry, Jason." His father looked weary. He'd put the lantern down on a table, and it cast shadows across his face.

"What's that?" Jason demanded, jabbing a finger at the long tube facing Zidu.

"It's a modified exorpult," said his father. "It's very powerful but set to a low charge, so it doesn't kill."

"I know what you're doing with it," Jason said in a hushed voice, his hands shaking as he edged toward the wall behind the long tube. "I know what this is all about."

"I'm not surprised," said his father, his black cloak swishing around his ankles as he approached Jason. "You're very intelligent. Now if you'd only—" He stopped.

Jason had snatched one of the hand-held exorpults from the rack nearby.

"What are you doing?" his father demanded.

Jason popped open the door in the gearbox. The red glow within told him all he needed to know. He raised the exorpult to his shoulder and pointed it at his father.

"No—Jason! NO!"

Jason wasn't listening. He pressed the lever on top of the gearbox and heard the static crack as the circuit closed. Blinding red lightning streaked across the dim room.

But he hadn't aimed at his father. The bolt struck Seiki and sent her tumbling from her shoulder perch.

His father gasped and stumbled as Jason took aim again.

15

Revolutionary Weapons

THE FRENCH REVOLUTION WAS a lot more radical than the American Revolution, and a lot less successful. In the end, Napoleon crowned himself emperor and pretty much ended France's first experiment with democracy—if you can call the Terror "democratic." Still, in a lot of ways Napoleon governed like a true son of the Revolution. He modernized the administration, established equality before the law, and protected individual rights. And his troops spread Revolutionary ideas across Europe, including democracy and nationalism. So when the other powers finally dragged the emperor down in 1815, they found they couldn't put the genie back in the bottle. France's example—and America's, too—sparked new revolutions across Europe and Latin America....

A different kind of revolution struck the U.K. Capitalists began building factories, taking advantage of steam-powered machines and other inventions. Great Britain, which really isn't very big, outstripped even China and became the most productive nation in the world—and in all history up to that point. But soon the U.K. had rivals. During the 1800s, the Industrial Revolution rolled across Europe and North America. It was the ultimate coup for the nations of the north Atlantic. They completed their four-hundred-year leap from the edge of the civilized world to the very heart of the world economy.

~ William Gallo, Lectures, History 22.

ooooo

"Jason, no!" his father cried again. He scrambled across the floor and threw himself over Seiki's twitching body.

Jason fired anyway. The brilliant red bolt passed right through his father and struck Seiki, sending her into convulsions.

"Please, Jason … stop," his father moaned, scooping up the sickly creature and holding her to his chest. "Please don't!" His voice shook, and he was crying. "She's my lumin. Seiki's my lumin, and I'm her shaman!"

Blood roared in Jason's ears as he edged forward. His father huddled on the stone floor, holding Seiki. Shuddering sobs wracked his body. Jason lowered the exorpult. He'd never seen his father sob. Had he made a terrible mistake?

But then his father rose, and he was smiling through the tears. Jason knew that open smile. His father held Seiki in one arm and grabbed Jason with the other, pulling him in for a rough hug. "I'm sorry, Jason," he cried. "You've saved me. You've saved your father. I've missed you so much!"

Jason's own eyes filled with tears as he hugged back. Abruptly his father grabbed his shoulder and held him at arm's length. "You did the right thing. I'm so proud of you. But you can't fire at Seiki again. You nearly killed her. She's my lumin, just as Zidu is yours.

"You guessed right. We would have made Zidu a cultivar, just like Seiki. There are some things only lumins can do, so the Society uses some, but not until we've changed them, warped them. Zidu's eyes would've faded, and his body would've shrunk and deformed. He would've held you here in Fore, awake for the rest of your life, just as Seiki holds me. But it's not Seiki's fault any more than it would've been Zidu's. She's suffering more than any of us."

"But what *happened* to you?" Jason exclaimed. "Why were you so …?"

"It was Seiki." He tightened his grip on Jason's shoulder. "She's the Society's creature now. What they did, it broke her will. And thanks to the joining, she's doing the same to me." He looked down at the withered, hunchbacked monkey-beast, and Jason shook his head. The joining? "She keeps me awake with lumin power," his father continued. "Day and night, I can't sleep because Seiki's joined to me. And she's in my mind, weakening my will. It opens me up to suggestion. It's like brainwashing. But you've knocked Seiki out and woken me up."

"What'll happen when she wakes up?"

"I'm not sure." He shook his head. "It'll start again. But if they want to brainwash me, they'll have to start all over. I'm free for now. And we have to get you free, and your lumin, and your girlfriend."

"But, Dad, you'll come with us now. We have to get you out, too."

"No, Jason. I can't leave. I'm joined to Seiki, and she obeys the Society." His words were clipped, urgent. "She won't let me leave any more than she'll let me sleep."

A knock sounded on the door, and they both jumped.

"Hello?" said an unsteady voice. "Is someone in there?"

"Yes, Betsy, it's me, William Gallo."

"Rector! I didn't expect you at this hour. I heard yelling. Is everything all right?"

"Yes, Betsy. We're just working with a difficult lumin in here. There's nothing to worry about. Thank you."

"All right, Rector. I'll leave you be."

"We may not have long," Jason's father whispered, producing a key from his waistcoat. "Explanations can wait. Can you carry Zidu?"

The key opened Zidu's cage. The lion-man proved as limp as a rag doll. He was very heavy, but Jason was sure he could carry him a short distance.

"Good," said his father. He unlocked a small door in a dark corner. "These tunnels lead all over Empirical Hall." He turned and rustled in a cabinet next to one of the long tables. Soon he withdrew a large towel and threw it to Jason. "I want you to wrap Zidu up and carry him down that passage." He nodded to the darkness beyond the open door. "Open the third door on your right, that leads to the Bachelor House basement. Once you're there, go up to your rooms and wait for me."

"Where are you going?"

"I'll go out the front door and fetch some supplies, and Tia, too. Is she in her room?"

"She should be."

"I only hope no one notices Seiki gone from my shoulder." He looked at the sickly being, curled up in the crook of his arm, still convulsing slightly.

"I'm sorry, Dad," said Jason.

"No. You did the right thing. You've brought me back. And you've given your lumin a chance. Now go."

ooooo

Safe in his suite, Jason eased Zidu onto the couch and covered him with a blanket. Zidu smiled weakly. "I knew you would come," he rasped.

"Just rest. We're not out of this yet." Jason packed his back-pack and then waited, wringing his hands.

Soon a knock came at the door. "Jason, it's Dad."

Tia was there, too, smiling for the first time in days. "I could tell your father was different the moment I saw him," she said. "Thank the gods, we're leaving." Then she ran to the couch and threw her arms around Zidu. But her smile turned to a gasp when she saw his drawn face and the weak light in his eyes.

Jason wondered about the other injured lumin—about Seiki—with a pang of guilt. His father had a bulge on his right shoulder, underneath his black cloak. "No, this is just a trick," said the older man, following Jason's gaze. "It's a bunch of balled-up handkerchiefs. Seiki's here." He withdrew the cloak, and Jason saw a fabric sling hanging under his father's arm, with a bundle inside. "It's not ideal, but she'll be all right."

He'd also brought a wooden chest. "This is going to be uncomfortable, but I think it'll just fit Zidu. We've got to put him inside and close the lid when we go. Can we do that?"

Zidu raised his bald head and nodded weakly.

"Good. We don't have much time. Where's your boat?"

Jason explained as best he could, and his father nodded.

"Okay, you'll manage. Here." He handed over a jingling leather bag. "It's British sterling. They'll take it pretty much anywhere throughout the zone, thanks to British industry, so you won't have any trouble. And I've got something else for you, which I hope you won't need as much as the money." He reached into his waistcoat and withdrew an old-fashioned pistol with a double steel barrel.

"A gun?"

"I could only get one, and I imagine you're more familiar with guns than Tia, thanks to all that computer gaming. This is a flintlock, like the guns they used in the American Revolution. Do you know how to use one?"

"Just point and shoot?"

"No. You have to load it and cock it." Jason's father touched the two ornate steel hammers hanging over the gun's curved, wooden handle. "Then you point and shoot. You've got two shots before you have to reload. Here's ball and powder." He handed Jason two more bags, then hastily explained how to load the weapon. "I've already loaded both barrels. I wish I could spend more time explaining this, but I'm relying on your ingenuity and caution. Just remember: these things aren't reliable like modern guns, they can go off half-cocked—literally. So don't *ever* point it at yourself." *

Now he perched on Jason's windowsill. "I'm going to tell you everything I can—everything you'll need to know. But we can't talk long, and I'll have to keep a lookout." He glanced out at the courtyard below. Shadows stretched across the lawn as darkness crept into the sky above. But they didn't light a candle, preferring to talk in the gloom.

---

* The flintlock gun appeared during the early 1600s. It played a central role in the American Revolution, the French Revolution, and countless other struggles around the globe. The flintlock probably gave rise to three modern English expressions. First, the guns often fired early, "going off half-cocked." Second, flintlocks often misfired, producing a spark in the firing pan but no bullet: "a flash in the pan." Third, flintlock muskets were often delivered in three parts: "lock, stock, and barrel."

~ William Gallo, *Historical Factoids*, 188.

"I came to Fore looking for *our* lumins, Jason—for the spirits of Western Civilization in the twenty-first century." He spoke quickly and in a low voice. "I was looking for the very creatures the Society *says* it's wiped out. In each of Fore's countries, lumins represent everything magical and mystical to the people. It's easy enough to know what ancient Greeks and Egyptians found magical. I wanted to know what's magic to our people: to modern Americans and Europeans and Australians—to all Westerners. Once I knew that, I was going to tell people in my book: the new one I was writing."

Jason thought of Candi and how she'd gushed about his father's work, particularly about the new book.

"I wanted to make a difference in our world. We citizens of modern nations are the most spiritually starved people in history. In the age of science, we analyze, rationalize, define, and calculate the odds, but we feel little awe. We don't believe in magic, so we've lost the wonder that inspired our ancestors. My book would've told people how to regain that awe, that wonder. With that magic back, our people could enjoy richer, happier lives. And it's not just our people. Our industrial, rational viewpoint has spread across the world. My book was supposed to offer the whole world a dose of modern magic."

He glanced out the window. "The Society couldn't let me publish that book. If modern people saw magic all around them, in their daily lives, they'd dream of magic at night. Then shamans and lumins would grow stronger in Fore's modern lands—here on the right bank and all across downstream Fore. In the long run, it'd spell the end for the Society. That's why they captured me and brainwashed me, and that's why they won't let me go."

"I don't understand," Jason exclaimed. "Are you saying there's magic in our world? Real magic?"

"It depends what you mean by magic. Our world has no sorcerers or spells of power. We have no lumins, at least not in the literal, physical sense. But that doesn't mean there's no magic. People in past times saw magic all around. They believed mystical forces lurked in every tree, every stalk of wheat, every person. Our ancestors lived in a world of wonder, and that inspired them. That's the real, spiritual magic of our world, and that's what we've lost."

"But ... but what do you mean we've lost it? What about religion? There's tons of religious people back home."

"I'm not really talking about religion. Lots of us believe in the same God as our ancestors, the same temples and churches, but we don't witness the same daily magic. Few of us thank a local saint or spirit when we get a promotion or recover from a cold, and few see magic in our garden or the eyes of our dog. We can explain almost everything through science and coincidence, even if we believe in God, so we don't recognize daily magic. That's what we've lost: that sense of wonder. Well, I want to put it back in our lives."

"And modern lumins will help you do that?" Jason asked, glancing at Tia. She looked confused, too.

"Lumins give me my guidepost." He leaned forward, his eyes glittering. "In every land, lumins represent the things that mystify mankind. In ancient Egypt, they're sphinxes and talking baboons. In Greece, they're satyrs and nymphs. In Medieval Europe, they're fairies and saints. Those creatures take their shape from myths and legends, from the magic that inspired their people.

"Our lumins represent *our* magic, Jason. What's magical to modern Americans and Europeans—and all the people we influence and who influence us? To find out, I needed to *see* modern, right bank lumins. Industrial-world lumins. I needed to know what shape they take. Maybe they're spirits of nature. If so, we should commune with redwoods and dolphins, and the environment itself. Or maybe they're spirits of good health, and we should look to the rhythms of our bodies for inspiration, and to yoga and exercise and vitamin supplements. They could be the spirits of communal events, the things we share in groups: movies, concerts, football games, elections. They could even be spirits of commerce. If so, I'll tell people to put their faith in our amazing economy, and revere the bull and bear of the stock market. Whatever they are, these modern lumins will guide me to the thing that most inspires our people."

"Then you'll explain it in your book," Jason said slowly. He remembered the unfinished manuscript on his father's desk, back in the other world, entitled *Modern Magic*. "You'll tell people to pay attention to that part of their lives, because that's magical."

"That's right. Our people need something to fill them with wonder, something to take them out of their day-to-day concerns, the way myths and legends transported our ancestors. And I don't know anyone who needs that magic more than my own son." His eyes held Jason's. "You analyze and criticize and calculate the odds as much as any modern man, Jason. I love your intelligence and your critical reasoning, but I want more for you. That's part of why I started that book. It's as much for you as for anyone."

Tia snorted, then looked uncomfortable. "So all your time here in Fore," she said in quiet voice, "you were ... looking for your people's lumins?"

"Yeah," said Jason. "Why did you stay with the Minotaur and the fairies in Laurac? We met them, but they're not—"

"You met the Minotaur and the fairies?" His father looked alarmed. "I wish I could hear more about your trip, but there's no time." He glanced again at the twilit courtyard beyond the window, then turned back to Jason and Tia. "I was studying *abandoned* lumins. I wanted to learn what they do when they're in trouble and when they lose human companionship. I've studied lots of others besides the fairies and the Minotaur, some who coped much better.

"I wanted to figure out how modern Western lumins might live and where they might hide, so I could find them. I don't think the Society's come close to wiping out our lumins. I think our spirit friends still hide downstream, in large numbers, even on the right bank."

"And did you find them?" Tia demanded.

"That's the cruelest irony. I did find one, but she knew almost nothing. In the right bank lands all the way down the Jericho River, I found Seiki." He touched the sling beneath his dark cloak. "In fact, I helped her escape from the Society. But they'd already gone to work on her, and she was warped and half-crazy. She didn't even know her real name or what she used to look like, and she had no idea where to find more of her kind. Anyway, the two of us searched—for quite a while.

"Eventually the Society got too close, and we had to run. We tried to get upstream, but to make a long story short, we didn't make it. They caught us in Bernadotte Sweden,[†] not far from here." His voice fell. "Then they finished what they'd started with Seiki."

Now he spoke even more quickly. "You've got to understand the Society. The things you learned at dinner last night were true. The Society *has* played a role in making modern science possible, in our world. But what my colleagues didn't say is that it works both ways. Our world and Fore *are* linked, but we influence Fore just as much as it influences us—at least, we influence *downstream* Fore. Just as events in Fore shape our people's dreams, our dreams shape Fore.

"So if my work succeeds, if people in the waking world start seeing magic in their lives again, they'll dream of magic much more. Shamans and lumins will grow stronger here in Fore. I think we'll see a magical revolution downstream, in the river's modern, industrial countries. It'll crush the Society."

"You must be the savior," said Tia. "You're the savior promised in the prophecy, sent by the goddess Hekate."

"In downstream lands, far, far away, near the river's very mouth," Jason's father intoned, "*daimones* hide and magic fades, and shamans live in doubt." He glanced out the window. "I don't know, Tia. But I do know the Society fears just that. They're afraid I am the promised savior. And they fear you, too, Jason. They're afraid you may help me or rescue me—or that *you're* the savior. That's why they've hunted you—why *I've* hunted you."

---

† The French Revolution created unheard-of opportunities for regular guys. Napoleon exploited these better than anyone, but second place goes to Jean-Baptiste Bernadotte, who rose from private in the French army to king of Sweden. An illustrious career brought Bernadotte ever-higher rank in the revolutionary army, until he finally became a marshal under Napoleon. Then, in 1810, the Swedes offered to make him heir to their ailing king. This regular guy's family still sits on the Swedish throne, and his other descendants include the monarchs of Norway, Denmark, Belgium, and Luxembourg.
~ William Gallo, Lectures, History 22.

He reached out to grasp his son's shoulder. "Jason, I've explained this so you'll understand me—so that you'll understand what I've tried to do. When you get home, I want you to write down everything you've experienced here, everything you've seen, everything I've told you. I want you find all my notes and the manuscript for my book. Preserve them. Preserve everything I've done. Share it all with Athena when she's old enough.

"And I want you to find someone who can help—some historian, maybe Candi, or maybe one of my friends. Somewhere, there's someone who can finish my work, who'll find modern lumins and let the world know that magic isn't dead, that we can lead richer lives." He drew a shuddering breath, and Jason thought he saw tears waiting at the corners of his eyes. "Or maybe when you're older, you'll take an interest yourself ... and you can finish my work. That would make me very proud."

"But what about you?" Jason asked, his hands shaking.

"I'll be gone by then." His father's voice was very low. "But I'll live on in you."

"No!" Jason yelled, rising to his feet. "I'm not leaving you!"

"You have to!" his father exclaimed. "My fate's tied to Seiki's now. The Society's locked us together, as part of the joining. Seiki's power keeps me here, and her mind's retreated into darkness. We have no way to heal her, and so long as she serves the Society, I stay captive and awake."

Jason looked desperately at Tia, whose eyes had filled with tears. Heal Seiki? There must be a way.

"Wait!" he cried. "What about other lumins—her own kind?" He wheeled on Tia and grabbed her hands. "When Mime got hurt, you said his own kind could heal him. You said other fairies could help—or barbarian German lumins—if they speak the same language—"

"Language of spirit!" Tia exclaimed. "Yes! If they're from the same people, lumins can always help each other."

"I already thought of that," Jason's father rasped, grabbing his son's shoulder again and turning him. "I couldn't find Seiki's kind, Jason. They'd have to be Western lumins, from the lands of the twenty-first century. I was there, on the right bank, by the sea, and

I couldn't find them. And that's the heart of Society territory."
His eyes were wide, his voice urgent. "You've got to leave Fore.
You've got to get safe, Jason. Our lumins are too well hidden."

"*You* found one," Jason asserted. "I'm not leaving you here.
I'm not losing you, too! I'm going downstream, to look."

His father's eyes squeezed shut, and he grasped his forehead.
"You can't," he said. But then he glanced at the window—and
gasped. "Oh, God. There's Edwards, headed for the labs. He'll
check on Zidu soon. Come on, get him in the box. We can't argue
now. We've got to go. Soon the whole place will be up in arms."

They scrambled to cram poor Zidu into the chest as Jason's
father hastily explained his plan. They'd leave by punt, on the
stream. The way was longer, but they could move the chest
faster by boat.

"What about Rim-Hadad?" Tia inquired.

Jason had forgotten the barbarian. "Do you think we can
trust him?"

"I wouldn't," said his father. "Helping you won't earn him
any gold. Besides, we've got no time to find him."

Early evening stars shimmered as they approached the
footbridge and the stream.

"Good evening, Bert," Jason's father called to the porter. To
Jason, his forced cheer sounded ragged, unconvincing. "We'll
be needing a punt, if you don't mind."

"A punt, Rector?" asked the burly man, hurrying out of his
booth to help with the chest.

"Oh, don't worry about this," said Jason's father. "My son
and I can manage it. I'm sending these two off to King's
College for the evening. Could you please ready a punt?"

Jason glanced nervously at the saber and pistol on the porter's belt as the man nodded. "Just these two, Rector? Should I
send someone to, er, help them?"

"No, thank you, Bert. We've reached an understanding, my
son and I. I don't think we'll have any trouble tonight. Isn't
that right, Jason?"

Jason nodded vigorously, expecting alarm bells any second.
With a quick "Yes, sir," the porter scrambled down the stone

steps to the narrow dock at the foot of the embankment. The water flowed dark and quiet under the bridge nearby. Two punts had been stacked on the dock. The porter slid one into the water and held it still as Jason and his father eased the chest aboard. Then Jason held the boat as Tia got in.

"Thank you, Bert," said his father, grasping a long wooden pole and handing it to Jason. "I expect they'll be back in three or four hours. Would you make sure the dock lantern's out?"

"Oh, of course, Rector. It's always there, and I'll be here myself, till I'm relieved at midnight." He rubbed his pug nose. "Rector, are you sure you don't want me to send someone with them?"

"No, thank you, they'll be fine. Could you give us a minute, though, Bert?" The porter looked confused, but then he nodded and climbed back up the stone stairs.

The two Gallos faced each other on the dock. Jason's father spoke just above a whisper. "Jason, it's a million-to-one odds, and it's too dangerous."

Jason raised his chin and met his father's eyes. "I'm going."

His father face contorted, and he took Jason's arm. "I have to tell you something. I'm sorry. When your mom died … it was hard. I just buried myself in work because it kept me from thinking about other things. And Athena … she seemed so vulnerable. It took all I had to support her. I let myself think you didn't need that much. Between Athena and my work—my escape—I didn't leave room to be your father. I'm sorry." Tears glimmered again in his eyes. "And I robbed myself, too. Seeing the young man you were becoming … it could have helped me recover. I want you to know you're still my first-born, even if I haven't been a good father. You're still the baby boy I brought home from the hospital that day—and you always will be."

"Dad, I'm sorry, too," Jason answered, desperate for more time. "I'm sorry about what I said—how I got forced to come here, and how I'm just rescuing you for Athena. I'm glad I came. And not just for Athena anymore. And I'm sorry about Candi. It's none of my business—it's fine. You should be happy." He had so much to say. "And I'm sorry about what I said that night at home, too, about you being glad Mom died. I didn't mean it."

"I know." He squeezed Jason's shoulder and glanced up at the porter. "I knew you didn't mean it. I'm proud you want to save me. But promise you'll never blame yourself if you can't, or if you come to your senses and turn back." He gulped. "I love you, and I'm very proud to be your father. Now you've got to go."

Jason stepped into the punt and found his balance standing at the back, as he'd been told. His father gave the punt a gentle nudge into the current. Jason looked back only once, afraid of tipping over. His father stood next to the porter, two black figures on the dark embankment.

"Bye," Jason whispered.

Once the punt had drifted under the graceful footbridge, Jason slid the heavy pole into the water and let it drop until he felt the end thump against the streambed. He held his breath and pushed down on the pole, sending the punt surging forward, slightly off course. He'd seen young men punting on the stream several times over the past two days. They used poles to propel the boats, like Venetian gondolas.

The companions listened for alarm bells or shouts behind them but heard nothing. Tia cracked open Zidu's box a few times, to give him air. Her expression grew more grave every time she looked at him. None of the companions spoke as they drifted past courtyards and large houses twinkling with candles and lanterns. Jason slid the cold, dripping pole into the water and pushed off again and again. After a little trial and error, he learned to steer well enough.

Some time later, a narrow dock loomed to their left. Beyond it stood a massive, Gothic-style building, like a medieval castle tamed and retrained to serve as a townhouse.[‡]

---

‡ Neo-Gothic architecture comes from the Romantic movement, which also led to literature like Grimm's Fairy Tales and Goethe's novels and plays, as well as music like Beethoven's. Romanticism embraced passion, imagination, mysticism, and nationalism. This was really a rebellion against the Enlightenment's dominant style, Neoclassicism, which called for harmony, clarity, and simplicity. Neoclassicism gave us composers such as Mozart and buildings with straight lines and slender white columns, like the U.S. White House and the Petit Trianon palace at Versailles.

~ William Gallo, Lectures, History 22.

"I think this is the spot where your father said to get off," Tia said.

After climbing ashore, they crept past the great house and trudged along the quiet, nearly deserted streets, lugging Zidu's heavy box between them. They jumped at every noise and shadow.

"Haven't these people ever heard of street lights?" Jason grumbled as they braved another dark alley.

But soon the streets gave way to open meadows, and the two saw the darkness of the great river in the distance.

ooooo

By the time they reached the *Black Elf,* Jason could think of little but the pain in his arms and back, due to the weight of Zidu's box. The ship lay just where they'd left it, hidden by a thin screen of leaves and branches. A pile of dead flowers marked Mime's grave at the foot of an elm nearby. They put the box down as soon as they arrived, gasping with relief.

As they approached the ship, a tall shadow stepped out of the woods. The sound of metal scraping against metal broke the night's quiet as Jason and Tia whipped around.

"Rim-Hadad!" Tia gasped.

"Just you, Jason," said the barbarian. "They can catch another lumin. I won't be part of that. I just want you."

What light there was glinted off the long, curved saber in the barbarian's right hand. He raised it to point at Jason.

Jason reached under his shirt and withdrew the pistol. "Don't do this, Rim-Hadad," he warned. He pulled back one hammer and pointed the weapon at the barbarian. His heart raced, and he hoped the darkness would hide his shaking.

The barbarian stepped forward, and the sword point hovered a foot from the gun's double barrel. "I'm sorry, Jason. I don't want to do this, but the vipers didn't pay me. They say they will if I bring you in now." A tear rolled down his cheek and into his beard. "The son of Nablanum shouldn't—"

"Yes, he should!" cried Jason, sliding his finger along the cocked trigger. "You're better off herding someone else's goats than turning traitor on your friends!"

"I kept my word!" the barbarian roared. "By all the gods, I honored my father's name, *and* our bargain. I swore I'd deliver you only if you agreed, and you did agree. Now our bargain is fulfilled, and you will come with me!"

"Back off!" Jason shouted, "Or I'll blow your head off."

Rim-Hadad glanced left, at the nearby woods, and Jason's eyes followed. Suddenly, a massive hand clamped onto his wrist and twisted his arm up. Jason yelped at the pain, and the gun fired with a clap of thunder. But the barrel now pointed at the watery stars, not at the barbarian.

"None of these little magic weapons for you!" Rim-Hadad growled. "Now come along."

Jason leaned back and brought his right foot up in a side kick, striking with all his might. He caught Rim-Hadad in the belly, and the barbarian doubled over. Jason tried to twist his wrist free but succeeded only in dropping the gun. He managed to grab Rim-Hadad's sword wrist with his other hand, though, and before the barbarian could straighten, Jason brought his knee up into the bigger man's face.

Rim-Hadad roared but let go of Jason's wrist. Jason turned and dove for the gun but careened into Tia, who had leapt after the weapon, too.

"You don't know how!" he screamed at the girl, as he finally closed his fingers over the gun.

He turned, pulling the second hammer back, to find Rim-Hadad almost on top of him, bloody-faced but looking solid as a mule, his teeth bared and his saber raised.

A crack and a flash tore through the night.

16

Colonial Safari

BY 1900, AFTER A four-century expansion, Western nations ruled eighty-five percent of the land on God's green earth.

Western conquest was absolutely devastating for people who'd never met Eurasians before: Native Americans, Australian Aborigines, Polynesians. But for most Asians and a lot of Africans, Western imperialism brought pretty minimal change—at first. Conquerors had come and gone before. But during the 1800s, imperialism got a lot more disruptive, for everyone. The Industrial Revolution was spreading across Europe and North America, and Western nations needed markets for their goods and massive supplies of raw materials. So they reorganized native economies to serve as colonial feeders for industry. This industrial-type colonialism bankrupted traditional craftsmen, commandeered natural resources, and left everyone dependent on Western trade.

~ William Gallo, Recorded Lectures, Special Program for the Audio Education Foundation: "Reverse Imperialism: The Spread of Third World Religious Beliefs in Europe and North America" (San Diego, October 28, 2010).

ooooo

R im-Hadad fell to his knees, his mouth open. The saber dropped, and he stared up at Jason. Then he looked down at the blood escaping between the fingers he'd pressed to his chest.

"You throw thunder," he murmured, "like a god ..."

Shivers raced up Jason's spine. He and Tia leapt forward and caught the falling barbarian. They kicked aside the saber and eased Rim-Hadad onto his back.

"Oh, God," Jason moaned, "what did I do?"

Rim-Hadad coughed, and blood trickled out of the corner of his mouth. "No," came a gurgling whisper. Then he went limp, and Jason thought he'd already gone. But his whisper returned: "I am sorry. You deserved better from the son of Nablanum."

Tia gripped one of his big hands. "You'll meet your father soon," she said. "Tell him you always honored him. Tell him even your enemies respected the name of Nablanum."

Rim-Hadad nodded and coughed up more blood. Jason threw aside the smoking gun and grasped the barbarian's other hand. "I'm sorry, too," he moaned. "I'm sorry, Rim-Hadad."

"By Amurru," the barbarian whispered. He shuddered again, and his eyes rolled up. Tia gently closed them. Jason could only stare—at the pistol, at the blood, at his friend's body.

Tia wanted to bury Rim-Hadad.

"They're *chasing* us," Jason argued. "Someone's heard the gunshots. They'll be here soon, and we'd better be gone. Whoever comes, they'll bury him."

So while Jason tore the screen of branches off the *Black Elf* and prepared to get underway, Tia dragged Rim-Hadad to lie next to Mime's grave. She took the saber and laid it on his body and rested his hands on it. And she poured soil onto his chest, along with half of Mime's wilted flowers. Then she said a prayer to Osiris, god of the dead, while a guilt-ridden Jason stood by in impatient silence.[*]

---

[*] Obviously, we can blame the gun for an endless list of tragedies. But guns have actually done us all some good. They ended the threat from barbarians. Nomad herders couldn't build rifles or cannons, so their military advantages faded to zilch. Think about how rare we are in history. We don't have to worry about barbarian invasion. For the past few centuries, the more industrial society—usually a colonial power—has won almost every war, thanks to the gun.

~ William Gallo, e-mail message to Candace Fleming, "RE: Tutoring Topics" (March 16, 2011).

ooooo

They sailed downriver all night and through the next day, afraid of pursuit from behind. Zidu looked awful, and Jason was afraid their hasty journey might kill him. And from everything they'd heard, the threat to lumins grew worse downriver. But Jason's path lay that way, and Zidu and Tia insisted on coming with him.

As the sun set on their second night, they decided to risk a brief stop so Zidu could sleep on solid ground. They pulled ashore at the edge of a dark woodland, and Jason jumped onto the bank, rope in hand. "Oh!" he cried as a small figure rose out of the bushes nearby.

It was a little boy in ragged clothes. Startling blue eyes held Jason's. Then the boy slowly held out his hand. He was very thin.

"Ciaran!" a shrill voice called.

Jason looked up to see a woman rushing out from under the nearby trees, holding her long skirt in both hands. She stopped short as she took in Jason and the *Black Elf.* "A boat!" she cried.

"A boat! Someone's come!" a voice called from further up the bank. Night was falling, so Jason couldn't see clearly. But he saw movement under the trees—lots of movement.

"Please take us with you, sir!" cried the woman, rushing forward to grab the silent boy's wrist. "We're starving! In God's name, please!" Her eyes were wide—the same brilliant blue as the boy's.

"Jason!" cried Tia, before he could do more than open his mouth. "Get back in the boat! Get in right now!"

He looked back. Tia's eyes were wide, too.

"Get in!" she yelled, leaning over the side. She pointed at the bank behind him. "They'll swamp the boat! We've got to go! Now!"

He turned, confused. Dark figures moved beneath the trees.

"A boat!" someone cried. "Please, take my children!"

People were running, heading for Jason and the woman and the boy.

"It's mine!" cried a man, emerging from the trees. "I saw it first!"

"You idiot, Jason!" Tia screamed. "They'll swamp us! They'll swamp Zidu!"

Jason turned and splashed into the river, then hurled himself up onto the *Black Elf*, setting the boat rocking.

"Oars!" he cried, and then he and Tia were rowing furiously.

He looked back as they labored against the oars. Dozens of people had rushed from the woods, and several had thrown themselves into the water. One swimmer came within feet, but now the current caught them, and the *Black Elf* slid out of reach.

"What was wrong with them?" cried Jason as he struggled to raise the sail, despite the darkening sky.

"Famine," said Tia. Her face was hard, but her voice quivered. "They would've taken our food and our boat—and thrown Zidu in the water. Starving people will do anything."

Jason gulped. "What do we do now? It'll be full dark soon."

"We can't stop if there's a famine on the right bank," said Tia. "I think we should cross to the left bank." She drew a shuddering breath, but then her voice grew steadier. "We can rest there. Maybe we'll get past the famine, downriver, before we come back. Besides, the Society's from the right bank. We'll be safer on the left."

"Maybe," said Jason. "But the Society could be on the left bank, too."

Tia did not answer. As the *Black Elf* turned across the wind, Jason thought of the little boy's blue eyes and his outstretched hand.[†]

---

† In many ways, Ireland was just another British colony, with little influence. So the imperial government didn't exactly bend over backwards to halt the great potato famine—and the Irish will never forget it. The famine redrew the demographic map of the British Isles, and America, too. Ireland lost half its population, and it still hasn't climbed back to the old numbers. Britain and the U.S., on the other hand, got large Irish populations, as millions fled starvation and disease. Finally, Ireland became an English-speaking country, since the famine nearly wiped out the Gaelic-speaking counties.

~ William Gallo, Lectures, History 22.

ooooo

Mud-brick houses dotted the left bank, though more substantial buildings rose over the towns. The greatest structures
had slender towers topped with minarets and thick walls of
stone covered in ornaments. A few had high domes, too, or rows
of pointed arches. The buildings reminded Jason of *Aladdin* and
Lawrence of Arabia. Farmland surrounded most towns, bisected
by irrigation canals, like the ones Jason had seen in Sumer. But
salt flats lay all around, too, and the land seemed harsh and dry,
with little of the lush greenery he'd seen upstream.[‡]

"Look at that!" Tia gasped during their third day sailing
along the left bank.

Jason looked across the water at a vessel with no sails, a
steamship. A smokestack rose over the decks, and enormous
side paddlewheels churned the river.

He nodded. "That's not really modern, but it's not that far
off. The end of the river can't be much further."

As if to prove him right, a more surprising vessel chugged
past them later that day. It was a Victorian battleship, a floating fortress of iron, bristling with enormous guns, its tall
smokestacks belching black clouds into the sky.

Zidu was improving but needed more rest on dry land. So
late the next morning, they pulled ashore near a range of low
hills and hid in a palm grove. The area looked deserted, so they
doubted they'd run into any Society agents. Zidu slept all that
day and then snored on past sunset. Jason managed to relax, too,
putting aside guilt about Rim-Hadad and the awful memory of
the famine and the blue-eyed boy, and fear for his quest.

As the crescent moon rose into the clear sky, he and Tia
crept to the edge of the grove. Jason smiled as he pulled her

---

‡ The name "Fertile Crescent" isn't a cruel joke. Forests, swamps, and rich grass-
lands once dominated the region. But countries such as Iraq, Lebanon, and
Israel-Palestine have paid a heavy price for five thousand years of civilization.
Over-farming, over-grazing, and over-clearing have salted the soil, stripped the
countryside, and spread the desert.
 ~ William Gallo, *Historical Factoids*, 19.

close, breathing in the scent of her hair. They hadn't been alone and safe for well over a week. Tia smiled, too, and closed her eyes as he kissed her lips.

ooooo

Jason awoke with the sun the next morning. He smiled as he felt the warm girl curled up next to him and remembered the night before.

Voices interrupted his reminiscence. He looked around the shadowy grove. He could just see Zidu, sleeping a few dozen yards away, half hidden by palm trees. The lion-man hadn't spoken.

"Little urchin swore he saw some kind of genie," said a voice. It came from the beach.

Jason turned that way and peered out from the trees. Four men strolled along the sand. The one in the rear wore a robe and a cloth over his head: the kind of Arab costume they'd seen on many locals. But the other three wore Victorian clothing: off-white jackets, high leather boots, and most bizarre of all, narrow, brown business ties. They had pale skin, like the lighter people of the right bank.

"I hope the little Mussulman was right," said one of the men. "Terrible hunting this trip. Almost not worth coming."

Two of the white-clad hunters wore exorpults slung over their backs. These were sleeker than the ones he'd seen in Oxbridge, but there was no mistaking them. They must have been hunting lumins. They stopped on the beach and looked around, and Jason noticed pistols on the hips of the two men with exorpults. The third hunter in white carried a rifle.

"Well, I don't see any sign here," said one of the hunters. "Shall we head inland?"

Swearing silently, Jason retreated into the grove. He scrambled back to Tia and shook her awake. "Quiet," he whispered as she blinked up at him, annoyed. "There are men on the beach with exorpults. We've got to get Zidu out of here."

Tia scrambled to her feet and followed Jason to Zidu's bed of leaves and grass among the trees. It pained Jason to wake the lion-man, but he had no choice. "Zidu," he whispered as he shook the tawny, lion shoulder. "Zidu, wake up. We've got to get out of here!"

Jason rummaged in his backpack for the pistol, drew it out, and loaded it quickly, shivering. It looked pathetic compared with the guns the hunters carried.

They hurried out of the grove and headed into a sandy ravine, hoping the scraggly bushes and trees would hide them. They followed the path through the hills for several minutes until it dead-ended in a tiny valley, strewn with rocks and floored with dry, sandy soil.

"Great," Jason whispered. "Now what? If we go back, we'll be headed right for them, and if we climb up, we'll be visible for miles."

Tia was staring over Jason's shoulder. He whirled, raising the pistol. But instead of lumin-hunters, he found an old man in worn robes and a red fez-type hat.

"Jinni safari?" the man asked softly.

"What?" Jason replied. "You mean the hunters? Yes."

"Come with me." The old man turned and darted up the hillside, his sandals slapping the rocky soil. Then he disappeared into a dim cave mouth half hidden by bushes.

Come, he motioned, reappearing to squat at the edge of the cave. They scrambled into the cool, rocky chamber. "You, that way," said the old man, pointing at Zidu and then at the back of the cave. Another passage opened up in the rock there. It was narrow and black, unlike the outer cave, which caught some of the morning sunlight. "In there I keep my blankets and baskets. Crawl in and lie still."

Zidu obeyed. The old man faced the other two travelers and raised a finger to his lips. "The French don't know I'm here," he whispered, "so make no sound."

Jason and Tia sat on a floor mat. Their host sat on a rickety wooden bed. As they waited in nervous silence, Jason's eyes wandered over the old man and his lair. Their host was very lean, and his beard was gray and bristly. A black tassel hung over one side of his dark red fez. His cave was surprisingly comfortable. Mats covered much of the floor, and wooden boxes lined the uneven walls. Odds and ends crowded the tops of these makeshift shelves, especially bottles, dishes, fish-hooks, cooking utensils, and oil lamps.

After they'd waited for a quarter hour, they heard voices outside. "Maybe over the hillside, up there, or back south." "Why don't we try …?" For a moment, Jason smelled cigarette smoke.§ When the odor and the voices faded, they all breathed a sigh of relief.

ooooo

"Thank you," said Jason as Zidu crept out of the crevice at the rear of the cave. The old man looked at Zidu with obvious interest.

"Are you a jinni?" he asked.

"I have never heard that word," said Zidu solemnly. "I am Zidu, lumin of Sumer."

Their host looked confused. "He's from far upriver," said Jason. "Very far. Do those hunters come here often?"

"No. Mostly the safaris leave us alone, but once in a while they pass through." The old man stood up suddenly. "But I've been rude." He touched his chest and bowed. "I have been alone so

---

§ Tobacco comes from the Americas, where some tribes smoked, snorted, chewed, and drank various concoctions; and yes, they even took tobacco enemas. Around 1500, Western sailors brought tobacco back to Europe. According to legend, one of the sailors smoked in public, and the Spanish Inquisition locked him up, afraid he'd been possessed by the Devil. But despite a rough start, European tobacco use spread pretty quickly. At first, pipes, snuff, and cigars dominated the industry. But during the 1600s, the poor in Spain collected cigar butts and wrapped them in little shreds of paper. They'd invented the "little cigar," eventually called—you guessed it—the cigarette. During the early centuries, doubts about tobacco's health impact competed with claims that it could cure any disease, including cancer. Today, there's no doubt. Scientists estimate tobacco-related diseases killed a hundred million people during the twentieth century.

~ William Gallo, Lectures, History 22.

long, I've forgotten my manners. The blessings of Allah be upon you. You are very welcome in my humble home. I am Ramazan, son of Hamza. The Arabs of this country call me Ramazan the Turk." He smiled. "I was once a soldier in the Sultan's army."

Jason and Tia rose and bowed, too, and introduced themselves.

"Are you Muslims?" Ramazan asked.

"No," Jason answered. "I … I guess you'd call these two heathens. They've got lots of gods."

Ramazan nodded slowly, looking uncomfortable. "And what about you, my friend?" he asked Jason. "You do not seem a heathen. Are you a good Muslim, or a Christian, or a Jew?"

"Well, I guess I'm not really that much of anything. I didn't grow up with a lot of religion."

"Oh." Ramazan looked confused for a moment, but then he offered the travelers water and dried fish. They sat in the cave, eating and drinking, as Ramazan told them the surrounding country was called Al-jiria and had once been a proud land—part of a great Ottoman Turkish empire, at least in name. "The Sultan—may Allah bless his footsteps—ruled all the lands of the left bank, for miles along the shore. I was a sergeant in a proud Ottoman regiment in those days. But then the French came and took Al-jiria for themselves, and killed so many people, the streets ran with blood." He sighed. "They say these Europeans go conquering everywhere, even to the other great rivers, even the China River and the Indian River and the others far away. They thirst to own the whole world. And Allah gives them victories, for reasons only He knows, even in the lands of His true servants." Ramazan shook his head.

"And do they bring the Society with them?" Tia asked. "The International Empirical Society?"

"I know that name," Ramazan exclaimed. "This International Society, they are the ones who sell these terrible lightning weapons. The French gentlemen buy them for the jinni safaris."

"Exorpults," said Jason. "That would make sense." He sipped water from a small wooden cup. "On the right bank, the Society's pretty much in charge, at least when it comes to lumins. They've hunted most of them down. Is it the same here?"

"Oh, no. Many lumins live in this land. The French do have their safaris now and then. And sometimes even a few Arabs hunt with those lightning weapons—always rich young men who went to school on the right bank and forget the old truths.

"I've heard that down the river, even more sons of the left bank stalk lumins, but here in Al-jiria the poachers are few. But they do hunt, usually jinn but sometimes even angels— whatever they can find. They don't catch too many, though. The jinn of these lands know how to hide, and, of course, most of the local people help them."

"How to hide?" Jason asked, glancing at Zidu. He sensed Ramazan meant something more than just sneaking into a back room or cave. "How do they do it?"

"Oh, here and there," said Ramazan. "The jinn are very crafty."

"Will the hunters come back?" asked Zidu. His face was long and gray.

"They usually stay a few days," said Ramazan, "but I doubt they'll come back into the hills if you stay out of sight another day or two. You are welcome to hide here, lumin Zidu. You are a heathen spirit, but hospitality is a blessing we offer to all."

ooooo

"With another two days of rest, I will have recovered," said Zidu.

So they stayed in Al-jiria. Jason seethed with impatience. He could wake up in his own world at any moment, ending his quest. But he owed Zidu a break.

Several times, Jason asked Ramazan how the local jinn managed to hide. "Oh, a clever jinni can hide away safe and sound," he'd answer. Or, "These French, they don't know where to look. The hiding's the easy part."

Ramazan's mysterious answers only increased Jason's certainty that the old man knew something, something Zidu might find useful. But Tia put an end to his inquiries.

"Don't you have any manners?" she demanded. "He's our host. We can't push him if he doesn't want to tell. Just leave it for now."

Their second night, they shared a meal of flatbread and fish with Ramazan. The light of an oil lamp cast dancing shadows on the irregular stone walls as the travelers told the old man about their adventures. Ramazan replied in kind, telling them about the exploits of his youth. He smiled and laughed as he described battles against Greeks, Serbs, and Arabs. And he beamed as he told them that he'd once seen the Sultan in person. "I saluted him in proper fashion, soldier to commander." He sighed. "I cut quite a fine figure back then, as handsome as any man in the regiment." He stood abruptly. "Here, stay right there, and I'll show you." He dove into one of his boxes and withdrew a bundle. Then he scurried out of the cave, grinning.

Soon he reappeared. He still wore the red fez, but he'd replaced his robe with a worn military uniform. The jacket was navy blue, with embroidered insignia on the high collar and sleeves. A handsome saber hung from the white belt, and he'd stuffed baggy, light blue trousers into the tops of red leather boots.

"Wonderful!" cried Tia. "You look so handsome!"

Ramazan's chest rose, and he stood at attention. "This was the uniform of an infantry sergeant in my day," he said. "The Sultan's enemies would quake with fear when they saw these colors."

"Wonderful," said Tia again.

Jason wondered why she was gushing over Ramazan. To him, the old man looked silly. He must have lost weight since his younger days. The uniform hung from his shoulders like a hand-me-down from a big brother.

Ramazan sat down on the floor mats, beaming at Tia. "Ah, you are good people, and courteous guests. You make this old Turk happy. I would like to help you. There is a secret that will aid your journey. A way to hide heathen Zidu. You can even travel in broad daylight, and no enemy of lumins will know he's there." His face turned serious. "I will tell it if you will promise to keep it secret. You are not Muslims, but I will trust your oath if you swear on whatever you hold holy."

Tia and Zidu quickly swore by the gods of Egypt and Sumer. Then the old man turned to Jason. "You must promise, too. On what can you swear, Jason Gallo?"

Jason looked at Ramazan and then at his own hands, folded in his lap. "I guess a few months ago, there wasn't really anything I could swear on, not if I really meant it." He scanned the cave, searching for words. "But I had a friend … who wasn't very honest. One time, though, I made him swear on the name of his father, Nablanum. And he kept his word, even though he had a lot of reasons not to."

Jason's throat grew thick. For some reason, he thought of the blue-eyed boy, starving on the right bank. But then his mind returned to Rim-Hadad.

"Things didn't end up very well between him and me. He still wasn't very loyal to his friends. But he never broke his word when he swore on his father's name. That was holy for him. So I'll swear on my friend's father's name, Nablanum." He gulped. "And I swear on the name of my own father, Professor William Peter Gallo." He looked up at Ramazan, blinking back tears.

"That oath is sincere," the old man said, his tone gentle, "so I will accept it." He rose, picking up the oil lamp and taking a second lamp from a shelf. "Let us go outside, my friends. We need more room than my poor cave can offer."

They followed him to the moonlit valley, exchanging mystified glances. Jason thought Ramazan would light the second lamp, but he didn't. Instead, he held it up for them to see. It was large and very handsome, made of dark metal and finely engraved. Ramazan began to rub it with a cloth, as if polishing the metal.

"Come out into the night, my friend," he murmured. "Ramazan the Turk has guests who need your help."

Black smoke puffed out of the lamp's spout, like steam from a kettle. But the smoke did not thin or blow away.

"Oh!" cried Jason. "I know what's going to happen!"

The smoke rose into the sky, dimming the stars. Then the column grew thicker. Soon the gaseous pillar blocked the stars completely. Then it took shape. Thick tendrils coalesced into arms and legs, then a head and torso. The column became an enormous man with dusky skin and a black beard, and glowing lumin eyes. He towered over them, bare feet now firmly planted, dressed in puffy trousers of blood red and a matching turban above gold hoop earrings. Flames licked his skin, as if he were smoldering.

"Behold, the secret of the lamp!" cried Ramazan, waving his hand with a flourish at the jinni.[¶]

ooooo

Jason and Tia bought supplies in the nearby village the next day, while Zidu practiced with the jinni. Entering and leaving a jinni lamp was apparently no easy task.

"The lumin must become attuned to the lamp, or the bottle," Ramazan explained when Jason and Tia returned. "He must project himself into the tiny world within."

"Could Zidu use any lamp or bottle?" Jason asked.

"Oh, no. The power lies in the container itself. Arab magicians from far upriver created these little homes for jinn, and built great power into them. Most are shaped as lamps or bottles. I have an extra, a bottle that once housed a female jinni. The safari caught her in the open." He looked downcast. "I will give that bottle to your Zidu."

Finally, toward the end of the day, Zidu announced that he'd mastered the trick. "Come and see, my friends," he said. "It is a thing to behold." He led them out into the sandy, dry valley beyond the cave. The smoldering jinni stood nearby, his arms crossed over his chest, as Ramazan placed the bottle on the ground. The old Turk's gift was a handsome bottle, made

---

¶ The jinn (or djinn) are spirits of fire. Muslims believe they have free will, unlike angels, so they can choose good or evil. Certain powerful humans can command jinn, for example, King Solomon, who had jinn servants. Some Muslims believe that Iblis, the Devil, is a mighty jinni. The most common English name for jinni is "genie," but that word doesn't come from Arabic. Génie means "spirit" in French. When scholars translated The Arabian Nights' Entertainment into French during the 1700s and 1800s, they used génie because it sounds like jinni.
~ William Gallo, Historical Factoids, 80.

of ceramic, engraved and painted. Zidu faced it with his eyes closed, his forehead wrinkled. Then suddenly his body dissolved into black smoke. Jason and Tia cheered as the thick cloud streamed into the bottle-top. Zidu was gone.

Jason picked up the bottle.

"I can see you!" came Zidu's tiny voice from the mouth. "Oh, Jason, I wish I could show it to you. It is like a king's chamber in here, with soft couches and a crystal ball to show the world outside. And if you leave the top uncorked, I can speak to you. I will travel like a prince of spirits."

Jason laughed. "You *are* a prince of spirits, Zidu. It's about time we treated you that way."

But as they shared their last meal with Ramazan that night, a feeling of gloom descended on Jason. "Look," he finally said, "I don't see how we can possibly find these modern, Western lumins on the right bank."

Zidu and Tia faced him.

"I mean, we saw Mime turn into a tiny fairy, right? Now we've found out lumins can hide in special lamps and bottles. No wonder my dad never found any." He shook his head. "What are we supposed to do, go to the end of the river and look in every bottle?"

"Then what are we doing?" asked Tia, her voice small.

Jason was silent a long time. "I think we've just gotta go," he finally said, "and hope they'll come when we call them."

"You mean the reaching trance," said Zidu.

Jason nodded.

"Don't you think your father tried that?" Tia asked.

"He must have," said Zidu. "He has the shaman gift, like all the dream voyagers."

"I'm sure he did," said Jason. "But they didn't come ... didn't choose him. I'm sure he didn't give up after that, knowing him, but I bet it was a waste of time."

"I think you must be right," said Zidu, his face long. "We must pray that my brethren downstream choose us."

"If they didn't choose Jason's father," said Tia, "then he's not the savior."

That night, as he lay in his blankets, Jason wondered about the lumins downstream. Would they come when he called? And he wondered even more what they'd look like, what they would *be*. What was magical to his own people, to the people of the modern West?

17

Modern Magic

THE HISTORY OF THE world wars, the rise of American power, the Cold War—the whole industrial age—takes up less than three percent of civilization's timeline. Think about that. It's less than two hundred years, out of more than five thousand since civilization sprouted up in ancient Sumer. It *feels* like more than three percent, though, because the pace of change is much faster than ever before.

Humanity's numbers have skyrocketed, thanks to modern innovations. Yet supplies of food and goods have grown even faster. That's never happened before. Some places do suffer awful, distinctly modern poverty. But humans overall live safer, cleaner, more comfortable lives, and enjoy more *stuff*, than ever before—even though there are more of us.

We've achieved this productivity by controlling an unprecedented share of environmental resources. Our species has always had a huge impact on the biosphere, even back in caveman days. But modern industry has vastly accelerated that impact. What we get is a long list of major environmental impacts, particularly climate change. For better or worse, human beings will play the dominant role in defining the biosphere of the future.

Modern societies only work when we're growing more prosperous—when we're just plain growing. That raises a serious question: Is modern life sustainable? That's not just an environmental question. It's social and political and historical. How long can any society keep growing?

The modern age marks the end of our course on Western Civilization. Some might argue that it also marks the end of the history of Western Civilization itself—that our society and its neighbors have merged into a global civilization.

~ William Gallo, Lectures, History 22.

ooooo

To Tia and Zidu, the right bank grew stranger every day. To Jason, it grew more familiar. Trains ran along the shore, connecting tall cities aglow with electric lights. And motor-powered ships soon outnumbered sailboats on the river. The largest looked like floating towns behind metal walls. Then came the airplanes. Zidu gasped the first time they heard a propeller's buzz and looked up to see a biplane.

"I begin to understand the Society," he said. "Truly, this science of yours breeds wonders shaman power never could."

Yet wonder blended with terror as they cruised the modern lands. Twice the *Black Elf* sailed past furious battles on the shore. Even Jason, who'd seen countless war movies, shivered at the artillery's thunder.

But the travelers passed through the war zones unharmed. Jason grinned with anticipation as the noise of cars filled city streets along the shore, and skyscrapers stretched up forty stories and more.

"Who lights all the lanterns?" Tia asked as she stared at the glow of a city skyline.

Jason smiled and explained about light switches and electricity. He'd been explaining everything.

Soon jets and helicopters replaced most of the propeller planes in the sky. Suspension bridges, freeways, sports arenas, and nuclear power plants bloomed along the shore. Each prompted awed questions from Zidu and Tia and lengthy explanations from Jason.

"I guess Egypt may not be the heart of the world," said Tia quietly. "This land is magnificent."

On the fourth morning after their return to the right bank, they saw something that turned Jason's blood cold. A passenger jet crossed the river from the left bank. Before their eyes, it crashed into a gargantuan skyscraper at the heart of a great city. Jason stood on the *Black Elf*'s deck, trembling, as the building collapsed in a cloud of smoke and fire.

"Was that meant to happen?" Zidu asked. "Was it an accident?"

"It wasn't an accident," said Jason, gritting his teeth. The plane had flown straight into its target. "That was done on purpose." Then he whispered: "We're almost there. We've almost reached the end."

ooooo

Jason and Tia stood on the beach, breathing ocean air and staring at the endless waves. Zidu's bottle hung from its strap, slung over Jason's shoulder. Tia watched the people playing and relaxing on the pale sands. "I love the way the women dress," she said. "No one tells them to cover their hair."

"You're from upriver, aren't you?" said a voice.

They turned to find a barefoot, youngish woman in jeans. A pair of flat-heeled leather shoes dangled from her fingers.

"What makes you think so?" Jason asked, wondering if she wanted to sell them something.

"The young lady's dress," she said, nodding at Tia, who was wearing one of the simple tunic dresses she'd bought from Mime's Germans. "And you, too," she continued, smiling at Jason. "You look sort of untamed, like you come from a wild country." She sighed and looked out at the water. "I bet you two have never seen the ocean before."

"I haven't," said Tia.

"It's a sight, isn't it?" The woman brushed wind-blown hair out of her eyes. "It gets me every time." She watched the waves a while, then wished them a good day and continued down the beach.

"Jason," Tia said, "is it normal here for strangers to talk to each other, without any introduction?"

She sounded nervous, but Jason just shrugged. "It's not unusual. I guess it happens a lot more here than upriver."

They changed half the silver coins from Jason's father into paper money. Then they went shopping. Jason smiled as Tia walked out of a dressing room wearing jeans, a white linen blouse, and white tennis shoes. She'd pulled her hair back in a ponytail secured with a plastic clip.

"You look like you could've sat next to me in high school alge-bra," he said. "Except if you had, I would've learned even less."

Tia blushed. She'd replenished her lost Egyptian makeup with modern eyeliner, but she still wore her turquoise bee-tle amulet, now on a stainless steel chain stamped "Made in China" in tiny letters.* To Jason, she was modern and ancient—and beautiful.

For caution's sake, they bought a baseball cap for Jason and a pair of sunglasses for each of them. "First it's dark, then it's light," Tia kept saying as she slid the glasses up and down her nose. They delighted her, as did the modern shops and streets and people.

That night, Jason and Tia shared a pizza at a beachside res-taurant and saved the leftovers for Zidu. Then they splurged and checked into a motel. The room smelled of cleaning fluid and had a shower and bath—and Jason remembered again how it feels to be clean and comfortable. But the color TV made him feel more at home than anything else, even though he didn't know any of Fore's sitcoms.

"How do they enter this box?" Zidu demanded, staring at the characters on the screen. "And how do they leave?"

Jason did his best to explain, but by the time they went to bed, Tia still wondered if the "TV people" had souls. And Zidu mused: "If they can disappear when you turn a knob, perhaps this 'TV' would make a good hiding place for lumins."

ooooo

"I'm getting nothing here," Jason said with a sigh the next afternoon. He and Tia had spent the day walking through busy commercial centers, as well as ugly warehouse districts,

---

* "Made in China" may be the big catchphrase for the later industrial age. China was once the world's great factory, before the rise of Western powers, and nowa-days it seems the Chinese are reclaiming their industrial clout. Whether they also become a world power remains to be seen.
~ William Gallo, Lectures, History 22.

tree-lined residential neighborhoods, and beachside tour-
ist areas. They'd seen no lumins since the jinni, except Zidu,
and they planned to try the reaching trance soon. But some
local exploration still seemed the logical first step. The search
had ended at a public library, where Tia goggled at the quantity of books, and Jason searched Fore's Internet for word of
lumins.[†]

"I thought you found something," said Tia, fingering the
neck of Zidu's bottle.

"Yeah, there's a few websites about lumins, and some pro-
lumin articles. They all complain about the Society and how
terrible it is that lumins are extinct around here. But none
of 'em says anything about what modern lumins might look
like, or where they might hide. I think a lot of these people
are crackpots anyway." *Kind of like my dad*—or so he'd once
thought. "The more, uh, scientific articles say things like
lumins are 'associated with shamans and witchcraft,' and
they're dangerous because they've got 'unpredictable psychic
energies.' That doesn't help us."

Jason shook his head and glanced up at Tia. "You know, the
weird thing is how little I've found about lumins at all. Except
for a few crackpots, and I guess the Society, no one here seems
to care about them."

Eventually, they gave up on the library and headed for
the riverside dock where they'd moored the *Black Elf.* They'd
checked out of the motel, planning to preserve cash by sleeping

---

† In 1969, the U.S. Department of Defense took the first step toward a worldwide
computer network when it launched ARPANET: the Advanced Research Projects
Agency Network. ARPANET helped university researchers and government agen-
cies share computing resources. It was an uber-network that originally connected
four computer networks at U.S. universities. It rapidly added new networks and
users, and soon it featured e-mail and other communications applications. The
Internet launched during the late 1970s as an even broader network—highly
decentralized—using ARPANET technology to connect several networks, including
ARPANET itself. The Internet served as a government and academic tool at first,
like its predecessor. But during the 1990s, Internet use spread through the general
population, thanks to commerce: the same force that had once spread Sumerian
cuneiform and Canaanite alphabets.
~ William Gallo, *Historical Factoids,* 254.

on the boat. But their way back took them past the motel parking lot. As they walked by, Tia grabbed Jason's arm. "Isn't that the Society's symbol?"

Two black SUVs were parked in the lot, along with a police car. The SUVs' front doors bore a bronze-colored emblem: the moon and apple seal of the International Empirical Society. Jason gulped. "Just keep walking," he instructed. "Act casual."

They walked on, hoping sunglasses, Jason's cap, and Tia's new clothes would hide them. They kept their eyes on the passing cars, the trees planted along the sidewalk, the stoplight at the corner ... anything but the motel. As they passed the lobby, a boy of ten or eleven walked out, bouncing a tennis ball. Jason had seen him and his parents the night before—a black family, dressed like tourists. The boy walked behind Jason and Tia until they reached a street corner two blocks away. Then Jason turned.

"Hey," he said, flashing a casual smile, "what's going on back there in the motel?"

"Oh, you mean the cop and the Society guys?" The boy shrugged. "I guess it's a boogeyman hunt." He sighed wistfully. "I bet it's a false alarm. They never find anything."

Jason nodded wisely. "Yeah, they never find anything."

Once they'd put half a mile between themselves and the motel, Jason and Tia ducked into a public park. They sat on a bench under a tree.

"What do we do now?" Tia said quietly.

"I don't think we should go back to the *Black Elf*," said Jason. "If they found the motel, maybe they found the boat."

"Maybe they weren't even looking for us. Maybe it was just a coincidence."

"That's some coincidence."

"My friends." Zidu's came voice from the bottle in Tia's lap. "I think we have made poor use of our time, as it seems we may have very little left before we have to flee. Our best plan is to call these modern, Western lumins through the reaching trance. Let us do so as soon as possible—tonight. If we find them and they will come, I suspect they can help us hide. If not ..." His voice trailed off. They had no backup plan.

ooooo

Fore's stars glimmered and rippled in the black sky. There was no moon, so Jason and Tia could see very little. They sat under a tree, huddled close, waiting. Soon it would be late enough.

They'd hidden in a woodland behind a school playground. The place was quiet and empty. Perfect.

"I think it's late enough," Jason whispered into Tia's hair. "No one's coming this way." She nodded, and they drew Zidu's bottle out of the backpack.

"Okay, Zidu," said Jason. "Let's do it."

In the darkness, they could hardly see the black smoke streaming out of the bottle's mouth. Then Zidu was with them, his lumin eyes glowing. "I am ready, my friends."

They sat on the leaf-strewn ground at the center of a tiny clearing, facing each other in a triangle. They breathed slowly, searching for the reaching trance. Jason had trouble at first. He needed a while to breathe through his fright over the Society SUVs. But finally he saw the endless pool of still, black water in his mind's eye, and the stars twinkling on its surface. He felt Zidu's presence there, and through Zidu he felt Tia.

Now is the time, Zidu thought across the ether. *Call them, and we will add our voices to yours.*

As he had done in Dur-Babylon, and again in the Greek lands, Jason called across the ether. He called for lumins and for help. His mind cried out that a friend of lumins needed aid, that he sought healing power for an injured lumin from this very land. He called for those who could reach Seiki's damaged mind and bring her back from darkness—and save her shaman, his father. Zidu and Tia's minds echoed his call, adding strength to his voice.

He could not tell how long he called. Hours, perhaps. He only knew that for a long time, the ether did not answer. Then he felt them. Many minds hovered on the edge of the ether or the edge of the clearing, or both.

He called again, with all of his strength, and the hovering minds answered, *What do you offer in return?*

Jason sat back, stunned. Could that be the lumins? The voice in his mind had been so cold. "What do you mean?" he asked. "What do you want?"

You ask us to risk death, replied the chorus of hidden minds. They chanted in unison, like children reciting the pledge of allegiance. *Yet you offer nothing, so we give nothing.*

What could he possibly offer them? Despair rose through Jason's body, and he opened his eyes—and gasped at what he saw. Gleaming eyes had appeared in the darkness. Figures began to step out of the trees—ten, fifteen, twenty of them, even more. Still caught up in the mental nimbus of the reaching trance, Jason could feel their minds. And he could *see* the lumins of the modern West. He saw too many images to grasp at once, too many amazing shapes and colors. But he saw enough. Even in his despair at his quest's failure, he understood.

As he rose to his feet, dizzy, Jason saw a trembling gray phantom, somehow horrible to look at, but compelling at the same time. He felt its rages and loves and creativity, and he knew it was a lumin of psychology, a spirit of the subconscious. He saw a black specter surrounded by a corona of golden-white light—a walking black hole, a lumin of cosmology. He saw a sphere of luminous fluid, full of colored organelles and twisting chains of amino acids—a cell, a lumin of biology. He saw many more, and he touched their minds and understood. He saw a sleek white robot on rubber treads and a swirl of quarks like colored balls. He saw a greenish alien with huge eyes and spindly fingers, and a chimp with the mind of a poet.

"You're spirits of *science!*" he whispered.

A lumin stepped forward. It was a woman with glowing eyes and transparent skin. Her body was full of colorful organs and tissues, rushing blood and fluids, and ivory bones. She was beautiful, and Jason knew she was a lumin of medicine, of hope for the sick.

"In the Age of Reason," she said in a lovely, deep voice, "it is science that mystifies us and fills us with wonder. But science gives no gifts for love or charity, and nor will we. We will serve only the one who serves us. We will serve the savior who comes to redeem us, who will live for us and for our land, who will lead our revolution. We will serve no one else."

Tears flooded Jason's eyes. He couldn't live for them. He'd come to rescue his father. After that, he'd leave Fore. He'd return to his own world if he could, and to his sister and his father, he hoped—even though leaving Tia and Zidu would break his heart. He couldn't lead their revolution.

Jason looked frantically at his friends, who had risen to stand beside him. Zidu's eyes glowed bright in the darkness as he faced Jason.

"Have faith," the lion-man whispered. "Your father never saw these lumins, yet here they stand before us. They have come for some reason."

Then Jason faced Tia, but she did not see him. The Egyptian priestess's dark eyes held only the lumins as she said, in a small voice, "I will serve you, if you will let me. I will live for your cause. I will dedicate my life to you."

On the face of the lumin spokeswoman, transparent lips rose into a soft smile. "Then lead us, savior," she said. But the noise of the other lumins nearly drowned her out. Jason heard hurricane winds, synthetic bells, animal howls, bursts of static, whale songs, and dozens of other sounds, beyond recognition, as the lumins broadcast their welcome to Tia.

"It is Tia," Zidu said. "*She* is the savior."

Joy radiated from Tia's face as she stepped forward. "Follow me now," she said, "as we strike a blow for truth and spirit."

The lumins joined hands—and tendrils and claws and limbs of light. The glow of their eyes spread over their bodies, filling the glade with silver. Jason could feel shaman power surge, like electricity in the air. The lumins focused a tidal wave of light and energy on Tia. Power surged into her, and she, too, began to glow. He felt and saw the ring of humans and lumins reach out across the miles. He swayed and almost fell. In his mind's eye, cities, forests, and farms raced by beneath them, as if the lumin chorus flew across the world of Fore, though Jason knew they had not moved.

Then he gasped and saw a stone chamber with a barred window. His father sat at a desk, wrapped in blankets, writing by candlelight with a feather pen. Seiki perched on his shoulder, her warped, hunchbacked monkey's body as sickly and wrinkled as ever. Jason's father looked up, as if he'd heard something. But the swarm of lumin minds ignored him. They swept in on Seiki, and Jason heard their call. Across the miles and across the ether, they sang to her. Her own kind called her back from darkness and madness ... and after resisting for seconds, or minutes, Seiki came.

With a high-pitched squeal, the shriveled creature leapt off Jason's father's shoulder. As she rose into the air, her body expanded. Her double hunchback ballooned into mighty wings. Her skin stretched and faded to blackness. Jason's throat caught as he saw Seiki in his mind's eye. She was beautiful—the black silhouette of a winged woman, rimmed with golden fire and filled with stars. A modern-day angel, a lumin of space and time, she hurled her night-black body against the bars of the window. They burst in a flash of light, and Seiki was gone, melting into the sky.

Jason's father stood open-mouthed. But then his eyes fluttered. He swayed and fell to the floor in a heap, smiling. William Gallo was asleep.

A moment later, he simply vanished. The cloud of lumin minds swirled again, and the scene faded. But before it did, Jason saw his father's door fly open. Two Society porters rushed in to stare dumbfounded at the broken, empty chamber.

ooooo

As the sun set the next evening, Jason stared out the storm window at the windswept beach. A fire crackled in the fireplace, filling the living room with the scent of woodsmoke.

"All that time in Oxbridge," he mused, "the Society hardly noticed Tia. All they cared about was me and my dad, when the real savior was right under their noses."

"They were wrong about Tia," said Zidu, "but they were right to fear you and your father." He lay on a rug near the fireplace, basking in the heat. "You and he do represent a threat. He will finish his book now, thanks to your rescue and the things you have learned. His ideas could change the way your people think about science and magic. Perhaps your world needs a savior, too."

"Your efforts will fuel ours," said Panfauna. "And ours will fuel yours. The two worlds are linked." Panfauna was a lumin of evolution, his body always changing. When they'd met the night before, he'd been a lycaenops: a late Paleozoic reptile and an ancestor of the mammals. He'd had a scaly body, big fangs, and a wolf-like face. But since then he'd slowly evolved into a cynognathus: still a fanged predatory reptile, but much more like a mammal. He now had rodent ears and light hair covering most of his body, even his reptilian tail. Only the gleam of his eyes remained the same.

Jason shook his head, finding it hard to take his eyes off Panfauna. He was delighted to realize the Society had it wrong. Dreams of these scientific lumins could never block rational thinking. His father's magical revolution would spring from science itself.

"I still can't believe the role you've asked me to play," said Tia. She loosened the blanket around her shoulders and sipped from a mug of hot cider. "It's flattering to be called savior, but it's frightening. And it's … it's hard to believe that prophecy was about me. All I did was offer to help."

"The lumins felt your sincerity," Claire replied from an easy chair. "And they saw in you the power and the training in ancient shaman ways—something no one from our land can offer."

Claire owned the safe house, and though she wasn't a shaman, she was one of the few humans the lumin chorus trusted. She was a chemist—somewhere in her fifties, Jason guessed—and she'd volunteered to take charge of Tia's education. She was also a member of the Society; a dissident, apparently one of many.

"As for the prophecy and the future," Claire continued, shaking her head, "call it fate or some kind of quantum feedback loop[‡] or whatever you like, but the lumins know the future when they see it."

"Sometimes we can smell destiny," said Panfauna brightly, his rodent nose twitching. Then his voice softened. "But that never tells us enough about the future. It could still be a hard fight, and long, with many losses. The real work lies ahead of us."

"Yes," Tia breathed. "I know it does."

Claire stood up. "Well, that's enough destiny for one night. I think I'll get started on dinner. Then I'd guess you travelers will want to sleep."

They hadn't slept the previous night. Jason had been afraid to close his eyes. He still was.

"C'mon Panfauna," said Claire. "Why don't we see if those reptilian paws are any use in the kitchen?"

Claire and Panfauna left, and Tia reached across the couch for Jason's hand. "I think you're partly to blame for all this," she said. "All those things you taught me, about science and feminism and slavery, and about the way people live here at the end of the river. And you taught me to enter the trance without an amulet. I think you were training me to be modern … to be a modern shaman."

"Maybe," said Jason, "but I think you would've been a great choice even if I hadn't done anything." He grinned at the fiery, ferocious girl he'd met in Egypt's Middle Kingdom. "You'll make a fantastic revolutionary."

They sat in silence a while. They'd been fighting a creeping sadness all day, but now Jason couldn't resist the gloom. Finally, he turned to Zidu. "What will you do now?" he asked.

---

‡ Quantum physics is about as magical as modern science gets. That's why physicists coined the term "quantum weirdness." For example, some physicists think that by observing a subatomic particle, an experimenter can help shape its nature *in the past*. In other words, events today can determine events long ago. It's like time is a river: the water flows in one direction, but the wind can blow any which way.
~ William Gallo, Lectures, History 78.

"I'll stay here," said the lion-man, looking up at Tia. "Tia is my shaman, just as you are. She will need my help. This magical revolution is a noble quest. To protect my fellow lumins and change the way these people think." He shook his bald head. "I will be honored to play a part."

Jason smiled sadly. "Good. I'm glad you'll be together."

They sat in silence again, staring at the dark beach beyond the windows. After a while, Tia slid across the couch to lean against Jason. "I'm afraid to go to sleep," he said. "I don't want to leave you two."

"We'll always be with you," Tia whispered, "in your dreams."

Epilogue

Into the Future

TO MOST ANCIENT PEOPLE, time was cyclical. Anything that changed would eventually change back. The seasons turned and returned, droughts and floods traded off with years of plenty, farmers sowed and reaped, kings rose and fell, and the stars drifted back and forth across the sky—all in endless repetition. I think the ancient view has a lot going for it. You know, "history repeats itself." But ultimately, I don't buy it. Yes, it's true that historical patterns repeat here and there. But just as often the story takes off in a new direction. I think the early Hebrews had a better view. It's the vision you get in the Bible, which is a story of movement into an ever-changing future. We inherited that vision from the Hebrews, and it's how most Westerners imagine history. To us, history's not a circle, it's a line. We move forward into an uncertain future.
~ William Gallo, Lectures, History 113.

○○○○○

Jason dreamed of Lady Aurelia. A serpent curled around her outstretched arm, and she smiled from a boat floating on a lake of rippling blackness and reflected starlight. But then someone shook his shoulder. Was that Zidu? Was it Tia complaining about his snoring? Was it Rim-Hadad, ready to face another day's adventure?

He blinked and took a deep breath. A scent of fabrics, antiseptics.

"Jason?"

Whoever it was shook his shoulder again. He was comfortable, lying on a soft bed. But he had a backpack strapped to his chest, and he was fully dressed.

"Jason?"

He opened his eyes. Fluorescent lights above, morning sunlight streaming in through the window. White stucco, curtains … the hospital room. He blinked and his vision cleared, enough to see two familiar faces. Athena leaned over the bed, her eyes dancing, her smile wide. And next to her was Jason's father. He was dressed in his hospital pajamas, his face was puffy from too much sleep, and his cheeks still sported unshaven, scraggly stubble, but he was awake.

"Jason," he said, grinning. He grabbed his son in a bear hug and pulled his daughter in with the other arm. "You did it!"

Jason laughed, overjoyed and half unbelieving.

"You're home!" his father cried. "And so am I."

MAPS

You can find larger copies of the following maps,
for use in classrooms and other educational settings,
at http://DavidTollen.com/resources-for-teachers/.
(The website offers additional teaching and learning resources too.)

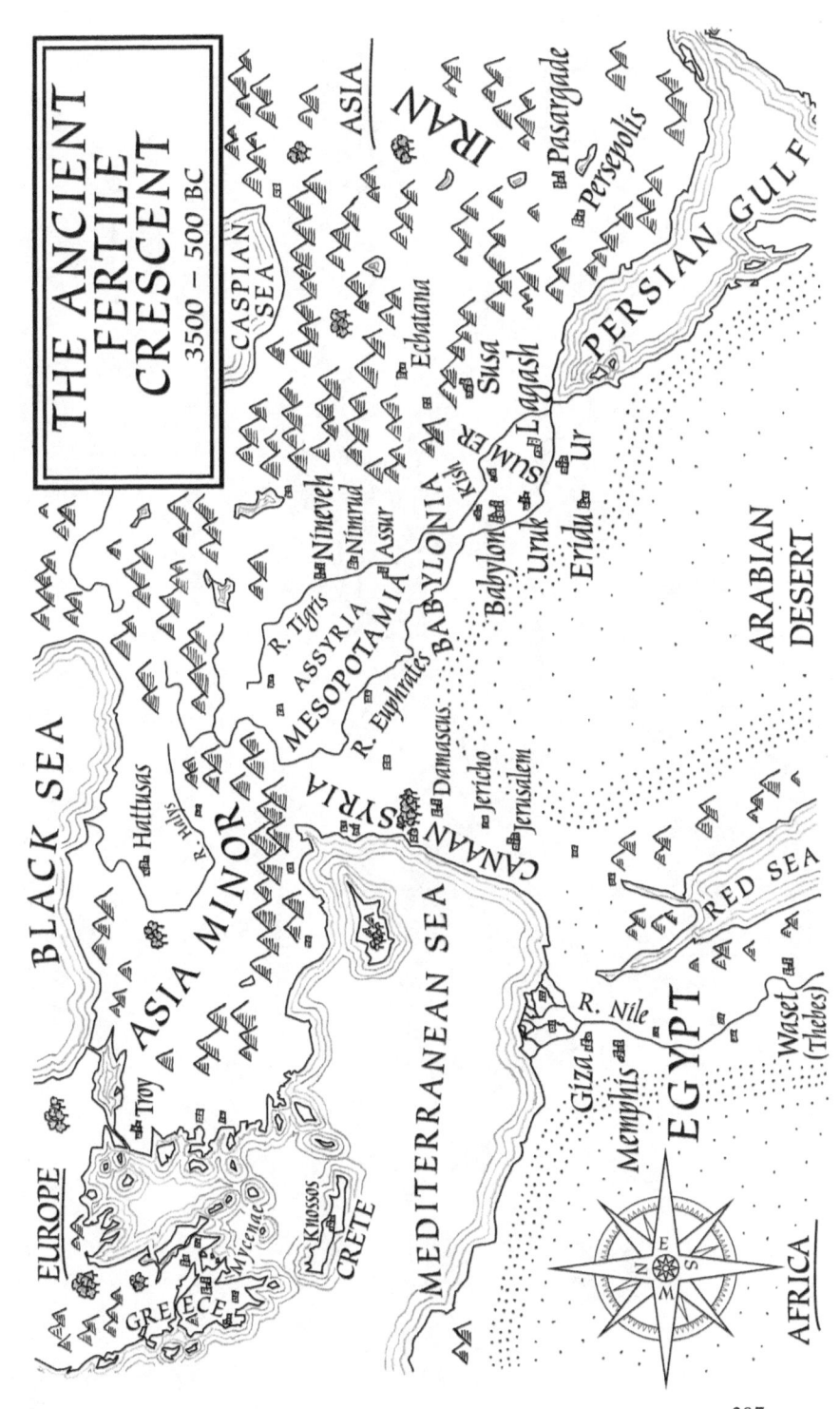

THE ANCIENT FERTILE CRESCENT
3500 – 500 BC

EUROPE

BLACK SEA

ASIA

CASPIAN SEA

IRAN

Pasaryade

Perseyolis

PERSIAN GULF

Ecbatana

Susa

Lagash

SUMER

Ur

Eridu

Uruk

Babylon

Kish

BABYLONIA

Nineveh

Nimrud

Assur

R. Tigris

ASSYRIA

MESOPOTAMIA

R. Euphrates

Damascus

Jericho

Jerusalem

CANAAN

SYRIA

Hattusas

R. Halys

ASIA MINOR

Troy

Knossos

Mycenae

GREECE

CRETE

MEDITERRANEAN SEA

ARABIAN DESERT

RED SEA

Giza

Memphis

EGYPT

R. Nile

Waset
(Thebes)

AFRICA

297

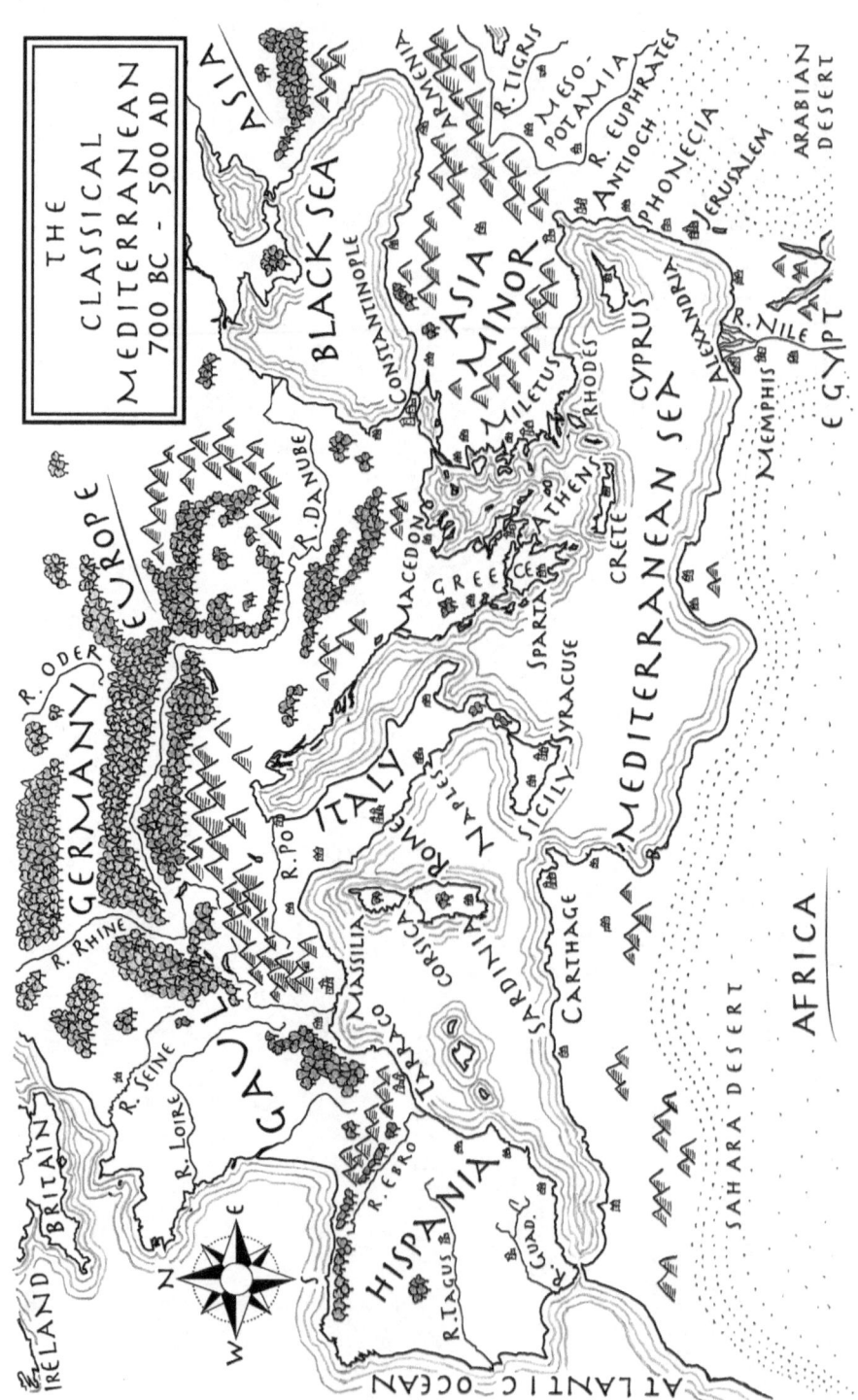

THE CLASSICAL MEDITERRANEAN 700 BC - 500 AD

ASIA

EUROPE

ASIA MINOR

ARMENIA

R. TIGRIS

MESO-POTAMIA

R. EUPHRATES

ANTIOCH

PHONECIA

JERUSALEM

ARABIAN DESERT

BLACK SEA

R. DANUBE

CONSTANTINOPLE

MILETUS

RHODES

CYPRUS

ALEXANDRIA

R. NILE

MEMPHIS

EGYPT

GERMANY

R. ODER

R. RHINE

MACEDON

GREECE

SPARTA

ATHENS

CRETE

MEDITERRANEAN SEA

GAUL

R. SEINE

R. LOIRE

R. PO

ITALY

ROME

NAPLES

CORSICA

SARDINIA

SICILY

SYRACUSE

CARTHAGE

BRITAIN

IRELAND

MASSILIA

TARRACO

R. EBRO

HISPANIA

R. TAGUS

R. GUAD.

SAHARA DESERT

AFRICA

ATLANTIC OCEAN

N E S W

298

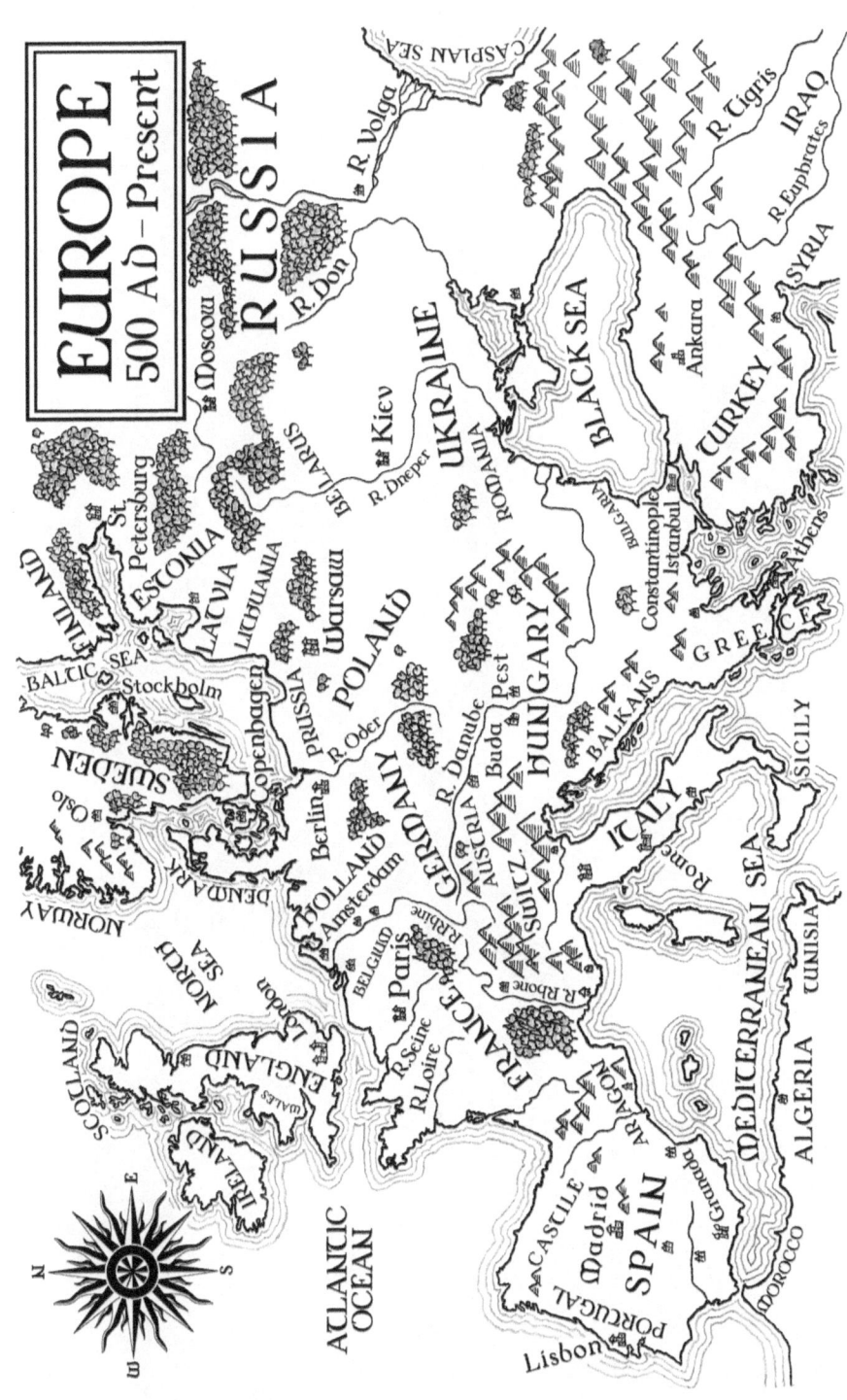

TIMELINE

The Ancient Middle East
and Western Civilization

You can find an electronic copy of this timeline,
for use in classrooms and other educational settings,
at http://DavidTollen.com/resources-for-teachers/.
(The website offers additional teaching and learning resources too.)

YEARS BC

c. 9600	Start of full-time farming in the Fertile Crescent; first farming settlement at Jericho
6500–3500	Start of the Bronze Age in the Middle East
c. 5000	Start of irrigation in Mesopotamia
c. 3500+	Rise of cities/civilization in Sumer (Southern Mesopotamia/Southern Iraq); start of writing in Sumer/start of history
c. 3300	Rise of cities in Egypt
c. 3150	Unification of Egypt
2700+/-	Sumerian civilization spreads north in Mesopotamia
c. 2600	Start of Old Kingdom period in Egypt; pyramid building begins
c. 2350	Sargon of Akkad conquers Sumer and establishes Mesopotamia's first empire
c. 2160	End of Egypt's Old Kingdom period; start of First Intermediate Period
c. 2040	Start of Egypt's Middle Kingdom period
2000+/-	Spread of civilization beyond Mesopotamian and Egyptian river valleys, including to Canaan, Asia Minor, and Minoan Crete
c. 2000+	Invention of the chariot; Greek barbarians reach Greece; conquest of Sumer by Amorites
c. 1790-1750	Hammurabi establishes Mesopotamian empire based in Babylon
1600s	Rise of Hittite power in Asia Minor
1633	Hyksos conquer Egypt; end of Middle Kingdom period; start of Second Intermediate Period
c. 1620	Volcanic eruption destroys Minoan Thera (possibly source of Atlantis myth)
c. 1600	Rise of Mycenaean civilization in Greece
1600+	Kassites conquer Babylonia

1570	Start of Egyptian New Kingdom period
c. 1500	Earliest records of cat breeding, Egypt
c. 1450	Mycenaean Greek conquest of Crete
c. 1400	Phoenicians develop widely used alphabet
c. 1250	Fall of Troy
1250+	Start of several waves of barbarian invasion into the Middle East and southeastern Europe
c. 1200	Start of Iron Age in the Middle East and southeastern Europe
1100s	Fall of Mycenaean civilization in Greece; start of Greek dark age
1100+	Israelites begin conquering Canaan
1085	End of New Kingdom period in Egypt
c. 1000	Time of Israelite kings Saul and David in Canaan
c. 800	Time of the poet Homer
700s	Rise of the polis in Greece; end of Greek dark age
700s	Spread of Assyrian empire; start of barbarian cavalry raids on the Fertile Crescent
721	Assyrians destroy kingdom of Israel and exile Israelites' ten northern tribes ("Ten Lost Tribes")
671	Assyrian conquest of Egypt
612	Babylonians and allies conquer Assyria
589	Babylonians (King Nebuchadnezzar) destroy Jerusalem and exile leading families/Babylonian captivity; exiles begin to develop Jewish monotheism
539	Persian Shah Cyrus of Iran conquers Babylon; rise of Persian Empire
538	Shah Cyrus lets exiled Jews return to Judah
c. 509	Roman nobles replace their king with elected consuls, establishing the Roman Republic
500+	Rise of Classical society in the Greek city-states
490	Greeks fend off Persian invasion

480–479   Greeks fend off second Persian invasion

431–404   Peloponnesian War between Athens and Sparta
           and their allies, leading to Athens' defeat

c. 430–322 Greek/Athenian philosophers Socrates, then Plato,
           then Aristotle

338   King Phillip II of Macedon conquers Greece

334–323   Alexander the Great of Macedon conquers the
           Persian Empire and beyond; start of the Hellenistic
           period

275   Rome achieves mastery of Italy

264-201   Punic Wars/Rome defeats Carthage

206–30   Roman Empire expands throughout the
           Mediterranean, including Hellenistic kingdoms

44   Assassination of Julius Caesar

30   Death of Cleopatra VII, queen of Egypt; end of
           Hellenistic period and of the ancient kingdom of
           Egypt

27   Caesar Octavian becomes Augustus, Rome's first
           emperor

YEARS AD

c. 30   Ministry of Jesus Christ

44+   Roman conquest of Britain

117   Roman Empire at its largest

250+/-   Near fall of the Roman Empire due to Persian and
           barbarian invasion, civil war, and other factors

293   Roman Empire begins to divide into eastern and
           western regimes, connected to Diocletian's reforms

392   Christianity becomes state religion of Roman Empire

312   Roman Emperor Constantine begins process of
           recognizing and supporting Christianity

400s   Rise of Germanic kingdoms on Roman territory

410	Visigoths sack Rome
476	Deposition of last Roman emperor in the West/"end" of the Roman Empire
c. 500	Start of European Dark Ages; time of King Arthur
634-733	Spread of Arab empire and Islam through Persian Empire, the Levant, North Africa, and Spain
700s	Frankish kingdom spreads across much of Western Europe
800	Frankish king Charlemagne crowned emperor
843	Treaty of Verdun partitions Charlemagne's empire
830-955	Primary raids of the Vikings, Magyars, and Saracens on Western Europe
900s	Medieval economic recovery begins in Western Europe; rise of feudal system
1000	Vikings discover America
1054	Final separation of Greek and Roman Christian churches
1066	Norman Conquest of England
1073	Start of long-term conflict between papacy and great Western kings, particularly Holy Roman Emperor
1096+	Crusades
1200s+	Evolution of nation-states in Western Europe; decline of feudalism
1206-1368	Mongol empires in Asia
1300s	Europeans start manufacturing guns
1348	The Black Death strikes Europe
1378-1417	The Great Schism/division of the papacy and battle over control of the Roman Catholic Church
c. 1450	Start of the Modern period: Renaissance begins in Italy; European Age of Discovery begins; invention of the mechanical printing press

1453	Ottoman Turks conquer Constantinople (Istanbul), ending Byzantine (East Roman) Empire
1492	Arabs (and Jews) expelled from Spain; Columbus discovers America
1500s	Rise of European colonialism
1500–1650	Spanish and Portuguese conquest of Latin America; possible 90% drop in native population
1517	Martin Luther launches protest that will become the Protestant Reformation
1510	Launch of modern slave trade/African slaves sent to the Americas
1545–1648	Wars of the Reformation
1559	Tobacco introduced to Europe
1581	Russian conquest of Siberia begins
1600s	English, Dutch, and French begin to colonize North America
1600s	Spread of coffee and tea across Western Europe
1620s	King Gustavus Adolphus of Sweden develops musketeer warfare
1632	Galileo publishes theory that the Earth orbits the sun
1638	Russian Empire reaches the Pacific Ocean
1648	Peace of Westphalia ends the Wars of the Reformation and codifies the nation-state system
1648–1789	Age of Enlightenment (as described by Immanuel Kant)
1687	Newton proposes three laws of motion and theory of gravity
1688	Glorious Revolution/British parliament seizes power from the monarch, establishing constitutional monarchy
1698	Peter the Great of Russia launches modernization campaign
c. 1750	Rise of Neoclassicism in European culture

1756-1763	Seven Years' War (French and Indian War) between Britain and France and their allies/first world war
1776	Adam Smith publishes *The Wealth of Nations*, laying the foundations for economics
1776-1781	American Revolution/America gains independence from Great Britain; dawn of Age of Revolutions
1789	Start of French Revolution
1800+/-	Start of Industrial Revolution in Britain
1800+/-	Rise of Romanticism in European culture
1800-1850	Americans and British colonize most of North America; rise of industrial colonialism worldwide
1804	Napoleon crowns himself Emperor of the French
1803-1815	Napoleonic Wars in Europe
1808-1871	Revolution, national unification, and/or national independence in Latin America, Belgium, Greece, Italy, Germany, and elsewhere
1818	British become primary power in India
1845-1849	Irish Potato Famine
1859	Darwin publishes *On the Origin of Species*/theory of evolution by natural selection
1861-1865	U.S. Civil War; end of American slavery
1868-1912	Meiji restoration in Japan
1880-1900	Partition of Africa among European powers
1895-1939	Freud popularizes psychology
1895	New Zealand grants women the right to vote, the first in a long list of democracies to authorize women's suffrage
1900	European capture of Beijing, China
1900+	Planck's quantum hypothesis advances study of quantum physics
1905-1916	Einstein advances theories of general and special relativity

1914–1919	World War I between Germany/Austria and Britain/France/Russia/America and their allies
1917	Russian Revolution (communist)/birth of the Soviet Union
1939–1945	World War II between Germany/Japan/Italy and Britain/America/Soviet Union and their allies; Nazi German Holocaust
1945	U.S. nuclear attacks on Japan/start of Atomic Age; establishment of the United Nations
1948	Establishment of the state of Israel
1945–1975	De-colonialism/most European colonies become independent
1945–1989	Cold War between the United States and the Soviet Union and their allies
1949	Communist revolution in China/establishment of the People's Republic of China
mid-1900's	Development of the personal computer
1957	Establishment of the European Economic Community, eventually leading to the European Union
1957	Soviets launch Sputnik I, the first manmade satellite, launching the space age
1969	American Apollo II mission lands first humans on the Moon
1970s	Development and launch of the Internet in the United States
1991	Fall of the Soviet Union
2000+	Awareness spreads of climate change and modern industry's other impacts on the environment

CITATIONS

Below are the works quoted by Professor Gallo in the text above.

- All biblical quotations come from the King James Bible.

- Footnote on p. 23: The drawing of Sumerian cuneiform and the translation come from Langdon, *Tablets from the Archives of Drehem, with a Complete Account of the Origin of the Sumerian Calendar, Translation, Commentary, and 23 Plates*, Librarie Paul Geuthner (Paris 1911).

- Footnote on p. 50: The quoted text comes from *The Electronic Text Corpus of Sumerian Literature*, Oriental Institute, University of Oxford: The Marriage of Martu, t. 1.7.1, 126-141 (updated 11/21/2005). Note that *The Marriage of Martu* refers to the Amorite patron god, rather than an individual Amorite or the Amorite nation.

- Footnote on p. 61: The hieroglyphs translation comes from A. Gardiner, private letter to H. Carter (discoverer of Tutankhamun's tomb), August 25, 1923.

- Quote from Professor Gallo on p. 175: Roger Collins deserves some credit for the first sentence of the quoted passage. He wrote that "the western Empire delegated itself out of existence." Collins, *Early Medieval Europe 300-1000*, Second Edition, Palgrave (1999), 95.

QUESTIONS
FOR DISCUSSION

These questions offer a guide for deeper conversation about *The Jericho River* and the histories of the ancient Middle East and Western Civilization. Each set of questions lists a topic, like "Babylonia." Each set also lists one or more of the following learning objectives:

- "text comprehension," or understanding of the novel and its notes about history;

- "critical thinking" about the history explored by the text; and

- "extension" of the discussion to history not covered by the text.

The most difficult questions are grouped at the end of each section and labelled "challenge questions."

Few of the questions have right or wrong answers, but suggestions for addressing them appear online at http://DavidTollen.com/Resources-for-Teachers/. The website also offers several additional resources for teachers, including more discussion questions.

Part I: Ancient Passage

The Fertile Crescent and the Mediterranean World
Prehistory and Ancient History,
including Bronze Age, Iron Age, and Classical Antiquity

1. *Prehistory:* **extension**
Jason's adventure begins in Sumer, which Professor Gallo calls "the world's first civilization" in the introduction to Chapter 1. What came before? Jason sails downstream from Sumer, into later societies; what would he see if he sailed *up*stream instead, into *earlier* societies? What kinds of cultures, economies, and technologies would he find? What kind of lumins?

2. *Fertile Crescent:* **text comprehension**
What is the Fertile Crescent? Can you trace the actual crescent on this book's map entitled *The Ancient Fertile Crescent, 3500 – 500 BC*, on page 297? What ancient lands are included? What is the significance of the Fertile Crescent in the history of Western Civilization? What does Professor Gallo say about the Fertile Crescent in Chapter 16? How has the Crescent changed since ancient times, and why?

3. *Nomad Pastoralists:* **text comprehension, critical thinking**
In Chapter 2, how do Rim-Hadad and his people feed themselves? How is their way of life different from those of other ancient peoples in the story, like the Sumerians and Egyptians? Why does almost everyone in the novel call Rim-Hadad's people "barbarians"? In the introduction to Chapter 2, Professor Gallo compares nomads like Rim-Hadad with the people of "civilized lands." What does he mean by "civilized," and why don't the nomads qualify? Is that fair? Why or why not?

4. *Ancient Egypt:* text comprehension, critical thinking
Why is Chapter 3 called *Death in Egypt?* What role does
death play in Jason's adventure in Egypt, and how does
that story reflect ancient Egyptians' beliefs about death?
How do you think the Egyptians' view of death shaped
their lives? Is it likely they feared death less than we do,
or more? Why?

5. *Slavery:* critical thinking
In Chapter 5, Tia and Tidal—both slaves—say there's
nothing wrong with slavery. What arguments do they
offer? Do *any* of the story's ancient characters (people
Jason meets in Part I) object to slavery? Is it possible that,
in ancient times, kind, decent people believed in slavery?
If so, how would their underlying beliefs about freedom,
equality, and human nature have to differ from modern
ones?

6. *Babylonia, Hebrews, and Sumerian Influence:*
text comprehension
In Chapters 5 and 6, what similarities do you see between
Babylonian and Sumerian architecture, religion, and
lumins? What role does the Sumerian language play in
Babylonia? Then, how does Sumerian influence appear
again during Jason's adventure in Hebrew Judah in
Chapter 6? Why do the Hebrew tales resemble Sumerian
myths? And why *did* the long-lost Sumerian culture exercise such influence over Babylonian and Hebrew history?

7. *Hebrews:* text comprehension, critical thinking
During his visit to Judah in Chapter 6, Jason stumbles
across ancient ideas and culture that seem familiar to
him. What are they, and why would someone from 21st
Century Western Civilization find these ancient concepts
familiar? What else did the ancient Hebrews contribute
to the modern West? Do the ancient Hebrews in the story
seem rich or powerful? If they weren't, what explains their
influence over modern Western Civilization?

8. *Ancient/Classical Greece and the Hellenistic World:* **text comprehension, extension**

   In Chapters 8 and 9, why do the Greek philosophers struggle against lumins? What does that struggle represent in the history of ancient Greek philosophy? Philosophy offered new ways of thinking: what were they, and how did they differ from the spiritual beliefs represented by satyrs, centaurs, nymphs, and other lumins?

9. *Persian and Roman Empires:* **text comprehension, critical thinking**

   In Chapters 7 and 10, about the Persian and Roman Empires, Jason doesn't visit Persia or Rome. Does it make sense to explore these empires without visiting the lands they're named for? What does Jason gain or miss by *not* going to Persia or Rome? What are the advantages of looking at an empire from the point of view of its provinces: the people who don't rule the empire or even live near the central government?

10. *Ancient Societies Left Out of the Story, Geography:* **extension – challenge questions**

    In this book's two ancient history maps, on pages 297 and 298, identify each country Jason visits in Part I, *Ancient Passage.** Which important societies of the ancient Mediterranean world does Jason's story *leave out*? What kind of people and lumins might Jason have met in those societies?

---

* Cities in the world of Fore have names similar to those of historical cities, but they are not identical. Jason visits First Lagash in Sumer, for instance, while our world's Sumer had a city simply named Lagash. The cities in this book's maps match actual history. Also, the maps do not identify empires, like the Persian Empire, but they do list countries and cities found within those empires.

Part II: The Right Bank

Western Europe and its Colonies
Late Antiquity, Dark Ages, Middle Ages (Medieval Period),
Renaissance, Enlightenment, Age of Revolutions,
Industrial Revolution, Colonialism

11. *The Dark Ages (Late Antiquity):* **critical thinking**
What traces of the Roman Empire does Jason find
when he visits the Germanic chieftain and his people in
Chapters 11 and 12? What do you think it was like for
Western Europeans of the Dark Ages (from about 500
to 1000 AD), living in the shadow of a more sophisticated culture? Today, we assume the passage of time
brings progress—that the future will be better. But during
Western Europe's Dark Ages, knowledge and technology
declined, populations fell, and life got shorter and more
dangerous. How would Dark Ages Europeans' worldview
likely differ from ours as a result? Do modern fears of
climate change and other environmental problems give us
a Dark Ages perspective on the future? Why or why not?

12. *Medieval Europe:* **text comprehension**
In Chapter 12, why is Mime upset with his own people (his
humans)? Why are the fairies upset with *their* humans?
What has changed in the lives of these lumins—and
what religious development does this change represent,
between the Roman Empire and the Middle Ages? How
did this development alter Western Europeans' lives during the early Middle Ages?

13. *Enlightenment:* **text comprehension, extension**
Why is the Rector's (Professor Gallo's) organization called
the International *Empirical* Society? What is *empirical
reasoning*, and what role did it play in the history of the
Enlightenment? What is the connection between empirical reasoning and science? How did the Enlightenment
resemble the rise of Greek philosophy (during the 500's
BC), which Jason encounters in Chapters 8 and 9?

14. *Rise of Europe, Colonialism:* text comprehension
    What do Chapters 11 and 12 (the start of Part II) tell us
    about Western Europe's power and sophistication during
    the Middle Ages? How has the balance of power between
    the West and the rest of the world changed by Chapter 16
    (toward the end of Part II)? What explains the change?
    What clues can you find in Professor Gallo's chapter intro-
    ductions and notes, from Chapters 13 through 16? What
    else in Western Europe's history, not covered by the book,
    explains the change in Western power? What social prac-
    tices, government institutions, technical developments, and
    other factors lie behind the change?

15. *European Geography, Eastern Europe:*
    extension – challenge questions
    On the map on page 299, *Europe, 500 AD - Present*, can
    you identify each country Jason visits in Part II, *The Right
    Bank*? Which European countries does the story leave
    out? Which empires?[†] What kind of people and lumins
    might Jason have met in those lands? Among the lands
    left out are the entire Byzantine Empire and the rest
    of Eastern Europe—countries like Russia, Poland, and
    Bulgaria. Is Eastern Europe part of Western Civilization?
    Why or why not?

16. *Latin America:* extension – challenge questions
    Jason never visits lands representing Latin America.
    Are countries like Mexico, Brazil, and Nicaragua part
    of Western Civilization? Why or why not? What kind
    of people and lumins might Jason have met in Latin
    America?

---

† Again, this book's maps do not identify empires—just the countries found within
them.

The Jericho River in General

17. *Ancient vs. Modern Beliefs and Values:*
    text comprehension
    Do Tia's values or her character change during the jour-
    ney? If so, how? What does she learn and from whom?
    At the end of Chapter 17, is she qualified to serve as the
    savior of the modern lumins? Why or why not?

18. *Middle Eastern and Western Civilizations:*
    critical thinking, extension – challenge questions
    The Jericho River flows alongside both European and
    Middle Eastern lands. Does it make sense for a single river
    of culture and history to connect both Middle Eastern
    and Western Civilization? Should each have its own river
    instead? Why or why not? Were the two actually the same
    civilization at some point? If so, when in history did they
    divide, and how?

19. *Slavery:* **critical thinking,**
    extension – challenge questions
    Slavery plays a regular role in Part I, *Ancient Passage,* par-
    ticularly in Chapter 5. Is the morality of slavery different
    when the characters discuss "Negro" slavery in Chapter
    14? If so, why? How did ancient slavery differ from recent
    European and American slavery, particularly the enslave-
    ment of Africans and Amerindians?

20. *Ancient vs. Modern Spirituality:* **critical thinking,**
    extension – challenge questions
    In Chapters 14 through 17, what does the apparent absence
    of lumins suggest about modern, Western spirituality and its
    differences from past people's view of the world? Were past
    people more spiritual or more apt to see magic in their daily
    lives, as Professor Gallo argues? Were past people more *reli-*
    gious—and what's the difference? Would you give the same
    answers for modern Americans as for modern Europeans?
    How about Australians, New Zealanders, Canadians, etc.?

21. *Ancient vs. Modern Spirituality and Views of Science:*
critical thinking, extension – challenge questions
In Chapter 17, Jason discovers "lumins of science" in the
Jericho River's downstream, modern lands. What does
that suggest about modern, Western spiritual beliefs? Do
modern people view science the same way past people
viewed spiritual forces? How so—or why not?

SAMPLE LESSON PLAN

Following is a lesson plan for working with *The Jericho River* in class. An editable copy of this plan is available at http://DavidTollen.com/Resources-for-Teachers/. The website also offers additional resources for teachers, including more lesson plans.

Thank you to Rudy Edwards of Goshen High School in Goshen, Ohio. She developed many of the ideas for the lesson plan below and used them in her own class.

THE JERICHO RIVER
AND HISTORY

Learning Exercises and Journal-as-You-Go

High School Version

This lesson plan uses *The Jericho River* to teach history. It calls on students to journal as they read the novel and then to complete four writing and visual arts exercises related to the novel.

This plan is most appropriate for classes covering broad periods and several societies, such as World History or Western Civilization. It is intended for high school but can be adapted for middle school or college classes. The plan addresses societies from Western and ancient Middle Eastern Civilizations, including those addressed in the social studies state standards for many grades and states.*

The plan incorporates multiple learning objectives, particularly writing, visual arts, and textual analysis. It also includes options for partner and small-group work and supports multiple learning styles so that all students can access the material. And it addresses at least one Common Core standard: Practice Close Reading skills (CCSS- Literacy.RI.8).

The *Student Instructions Handout* below provides guidance for the students.

Learning Outcomes

- Familiarity with the key historic societies of Western Civilization and ancient Middle Eastern Civilization.

- Writing skills.

---

* *The Jericho River* features the following societies: Sumer, nomad pastoralists (particularly Amorites), ancient Egypt (Middle Kingdom), Minoan Crete and Mycenaean Greece, Babylonia (Kassite period), Hebrew Judea, Persian Empire, Classical Greece, Hellenistic Greece, Roman Empire, Dark Ages Western Europe (early Medieval), High Medieval France, Renaissance Western Europe, Enlightenment England, Napoleonic/revolutionary Western Europe, and European colonial empires.

- Analytical and creative skills, particularly analysis of historical information.
- Visual arts practice.
- Love of history, by connecting fantasy and myth with the past.

General Description

While reading *The Jericho River*, students will journal, recording quotes from the text and writing their own questions and observations related to those quotes. Once finished with the novel, students will choose four projects from a list that includes both short writing exercises and visual arts exercises. The list is in Step 3 of the *Student Instructions Handout* below. Finally, as an extension or option for differentiation, you (the teacher) may assign an oral presentation on one of those projects.

This plan involves at least two 45-minute lessons, as well as additional lessons for optional oral presentations. But lesson duration is flexible, depending on your preferences. You may add still more lessons if you want to work with students while they are reading and working on their projects. This plan also involves homework or independent classwork.

Materials

Each student will need:

- *The Jericho River*, by David W. Tollen (3d. Ed.; Winifred Press 2018);
- *Student Instructions Handout*, below;
- Writing facilities; and
- For some projects, art supplies: paper, colored pens or pencils, paint.

Pre-Activities and Choices

Before starting, decide whether the students will complete their creative projects in groups (learning communities) or as individuals. Reading and journaling about the novel, however, should be individual tasks.

Also decide whether to include oral presentations at the end. Any student doing an oral presentation should choose one of the visual arts projects and give the class a five-minute presentation on his/her project and related work. (The visual arts projects are bullets "i" and "j" in Step 3 of the *Student Instructions Handout*. Lessons 2, 3, and 4 below lay out the projects and options for oral presentations.)

Activities

Below is an activities outline. Timeframes are just recommendations. You might also add lessons or class-time between Lessons 2 and 3 if you want to work with students on their journals or reading.

This activities outline works hand-in-hand with the *Student Instructions Handout*, below.

- **LESSON 1 – Launch and Assign Journal-as-You-Go**
  45 minutes
  Pass out *The Jericho River* and the *Student Instructions Handout*, and explain the lesson. Explain that: (a) the novel uses a fantasy story with a teenage hero to trace the histories of ancient Middle Eastern and Western Civilizations; (b) as they read, students will visit key societies that laid the foundations for and/or made up these civilizations; and (c) students will learn additional facts from the book's chapter introductions, footnotes, maps, and timeline. Assign the journal-as-you-go exercise: students will record quotes from the book and their own questions, thoughts, observations, and revelations. See Step 2 of the *Student Instructions Handout* for details of the journaling task.

- **Homework – Read and Journal**
  4 weeks
  Students read *The Jericho River* and journal about it.
  Consider requiring that students turn in journals periodi-
  cally, to confirm progress and to correct misunderstandings.

- **Final Journal Collection**

- **LESSON 2 – Creative Project Selection**
  45 minutes
  Discuss the list of creative projects in Step 3 of the *Student
  Instructions Handout.* Consider having students brainstorm
  and add projects to the list. Then, have students choose
  four projects, either as individuals or in groups. Consider
  an extension, too: require that students choose at least one
  visual arts project ("i" or "j" from the list in the *Student
  Instructions Handout),* and assign an oral presentation about
  that project. Or, as an option for differentiation, let students
  decide whether to do an oral presentation, and have them
  include a visual arts project if so.

- **Homework – Four Creative Projects**
  2 weeks
  Students prepare their four creative projects.

- **Creative Projects Collection**
  Consider staggering due-dates for the four assignments, to
  gauge and ensure progress.

- **[Optional Extension/Differentiation]
  Lesson 3 – Explanation of Oral Presentations**
  10 minutes
  For any student doing an oral presentation, explain what
  you expect to hear and see. See Steps 5 and 6 of the *Student
  Instructions Handout.*

- **[Optional Extension/Differentiation]
  Lesson 4 – Oral Presentations**
  Variable duration.

Student Instructions Handout

The handout below guides students through the lessons. Text for optional extension and differentiation appears in brackets. So *before printing the handout, remove the brackets and the text within them if you don't choose the option in question—and also remove this introduction.*

THE JERICHO RIVER ASSIGNMENT

Read *The Jericho River*, journal your impressions, and complete four related projects chosen from a list of writing and visual arts exercises. [Deliver a five-minute oral presentation to the class, describing one of your assignments].

1. **Launch,** *in Class*
   We'll discuss this lesson and *The Jericho River*, as well as your journaling assignment.

2. **Reading and Journal-as-You-Go,** *Homework*
   Read *The Jericho River*. As you read, keep a two-column journal. In the left column, record quotes from the novel that interest you, along with the page number or e-book location, as well as identification of the society the story visits at the point of your quote (e.g., "Sumer," "Roman Empire," "Renaissance Europe"). On the right side, record your observations, questions, and ideas related to the quote. Make at least twenty journal entries, one each for the title, the prologue, the seventeen chapters, and the epilogue. (Additional entries are welcome!)

3. **Creative Project Review and Selection,** *In Class*
   We'll go over the list of possible projects, below. [We'll also brainstorm about additional, similar projects to add to the list.] Then, you'll choose four projects. [If you're doing an oral presentation, you'll need to choose at least one of the visual arts projects: "i" or "j" from the list below.] The possible projects are:

   a. Write a top-10 list of interesting historical facts you learned from the novel, with page number or e-book location citations.

b. Write a glossary of twenty history-related terms or concepts from the novel, including their definitions/explanations. Choose only words we don't use in typical conversation (unless we're discussing history).

c. Compare *The Jericho River* to our textbook, _____: one page.

d. Describe your favorite *historical secondary character* from the novel: one page. (Characters are "historical" if they come from Jason's adventures along the Jericho River, Chapters 1 through 16. So you wouldn't choose Jason's sister, his father, Candi, etc. And in this project, "secondary" refers to any character other than Zidu, Tia, Rim-Hadad, and Jason.) What do you like about the character? What don't you like? What challenges does the character face as a result of his or her society's culture, laws, politics, or environment?

e. Discuss the historical relevance of the novel's title, *The Jericho River:* one page. Why would "Jericho River" make sense for a timeline river winding through the history of Western Civilization and Middle Eastern Civilization?

f. Write a news story about an event from the novel, as if you were a reporter: one page. If it's a historical event from Professor Gallo's notes, discuss its historical significance. If it's a fictional event from Jason's adventure, discuss what it suggests about the underlying history.

g. Write a blog post about the history you learned through the novel and your impressions of that history and the way it's presented in the novel: one page. (Don't hesitate to express your own views, even if they differ from the book's interpretation or from standard descriptions of history.)

h. Write a newspaper editorial based on a controversial history-related issue in the novel: one page. The controversy could surround how the novel or its characters interpret or misunderstand history. It could also cover choices made by the characters, so long as you involve history by addressing how past values or the story's historic settings shape those choices. You could also discuss a controversy about choices made by real historical figures or societies discussed in Professor Gallo's notes.

i. Create/draw a color postcard featuring events in Jason's adventure or historical people, places, or events discussed in Professor Gallo's notes. You can go online to find images, but don't trace or print them; this should be your own work. On the back of the postcard, describe the illustration as if you witnessed it on your own trip down the Jericho River. Address the card to a friend or family member.

j. Create your own lumin: a mythical creature who might help you in modern life. Draw the lumin in color on 8.5"x11" paper, or larger, or create it out of other materials, such as clay or cardboard. Write a description of the lumin, explaining what values (e.g., charity) or institutions (e.g., democracy) it represents.

4. **Four Projects,** *Homework*
Work on and complete all four of the projects you've chosen.

5. **[Oral Presentation,** *Homework*
If you've prepared a visual arts project – "i" or "j" above – prepare a five-minute oral presentation, describing it to the class. Explain your work and elaborate.]

6. **[Oral Presentations,** *In Class*
You'll give your oral presentations and listen to those of your classmates.]

Due Dates:

- Finish *The Jericho River* and journal: _____
- Turn in your four assignments: _____
- [Oral Presentation]: _____

About the Author

DAVID W. TOLLEN earned his B.A. in history from U.C. Berkeley and went on to earn law degrees from Cambridge University and Harvard Law School. He is passionate about history and enjoys speaking and teaching about the past—and writing imaginative stories that spread knowledge of both history and science. *The Jericho River* is his first novel. His second, *Secrets of Hominea*, is a fantasy adventure shaped by history and science.

David also writes and speaks about the law. He is the founder of Tech Contracts Academy™, which provides training on software licensing, and also of Sycamore Legal®, a San Francisco law firm. And he is the author of the American Bar Association's bestselling manual on technology contracts, *The Tech Contracts Handbook*.

David lives in Northern California with his wife, a teacher, and their two sons.

For more information and resources—including future books, blog posts, speaking engagements, and tools for educators—please visit www.DavidTollen.com.

There's another world out there ... a land of satyr scientists, giant priestesses, troll explorers, and dwarf spies—a home for Homo sapiens' closest cousins.

SECRETS of HOMINEA

David W. Tollen

Coming soon ...

Please visit www.DavidTollen.com to learn more.